Stony Kill

Stony Kill

Marie White Small

SelectBooks, Inc.
New York

This edition published by SelectBooks, Inc.
For information address SelectBooks, Inc., New York, New York.

First Edition

ISBN 978-1-59079-311-4

Library of Congress Cataloging-in-Publication Data
Small, Marie White.
Stony Kill / Marie White Small. -- First edition.
    pages cm
  Summary: "Following her mother's sudden death, a Brooklyn baker abandons her sometimes violent father and a long-suffering partner to stay on the family farm of her childhood along the Stony Kill river--a place of both joy and great sorrow holding the truth of mysterious past events of murder and gun violence that must be understood and resolved"-- Provided by publisher.
  ISBN 978-1-59079-311-4 (pbk. : alk. paper) 1. Violent deaths--Fiction. 2. Family secrets--Fiction. 3. New York (State)--Fiction. I. Title.
  PS3623.H57866S76 2015
  813'.6--dc23
                                        2015010807

8748

Book design by Janice Benight

Manufactured in the United States of America
10 9 8 7 6 5 4 3 2 1

To my husband, Frank Ernest Small
And to my daughters,
Erin Elizabeth Wentworth and Dara Kristin Wentworth
And in memory of the child our family lost.

Acknowledgments

My heartfelt thanks to Stefano Donati for walking the miles with me. Thanks also to Kerin Sulock, Brandon Ayre, John Goodrich, Cam Steinke, Paul Rousseau, Shawn MacKenzie, Eric Devine, and all the members of North Gotham Fiction Writers who graced our doors over the years.

Love and deep thanks to Anne and Dave Bone for your help and guidance.

With profound gratitude to Steve Eisner, Jon Reisfeld, Eberly Sharier, and the staff at WWCR.

My deep appreciation to Rachel Ekstrom for always being there and to Nancy Sugihara for your expert guidance and kind support. My deepest thanks to Kenzi Sugihara for believing in my story and to Kenichi Sugihara for your kindness and going the extra mile on my behalf. And special thanks to Meryl Moss for being an early advocate and cheerleader.

My grateful thanks to Lara Asher, Janice Benight, and Brad Briggs who's input expertly shaped a manuscript into a beautiful book.

With love and gratitude to my mother, Regina White, and my late father, William White, who arrived in Heaven with my manuscript on a memory stick tucked into his breast pocket. Thanks for putting up with me. To Cathy, Dan, and Patty: thank you for the years of love and laughter.

1

Not long before my mother died, she told me a story I'd never heard before. It was 1965, the year before she married my father. Spring had come to the Northeast nearly a season ahead of itself. By May, the fields rippled with thigh deep, green-gold grasses: sweet timothy, alfalfa, birdsfoot trefoil, clovers, reed canarygrass, ryegrass, and tall fescue. All the kids along Sweet Milk Road knew the species names; they were weaned on the sweat of haying, and my mother and her brother Morgan were no different.

It was a clear, bright Sunday morning—a perfect day for the first cut of the season. The fields around the farm were filled with the buzz and clang of sicklebar mowers and balers while my mother Lydah and Morgan stood toe-to-toe in a field blanketed with egg-yolk colored mustard blooms. They scrapped with one another on the strip of land between their farm and the Deitman property where no one could hear them.

At first my mother laughed at her brother's suggestion, like a latecomer for Sunday dinner who asks for the platter of fried chicken to be passed, only to find the plate is empty, and the laughter trickles into awkward silence. She pleaded with Morgan, but he was of no mind to hear her. His decision, he claimed, was best for the family: She would marry Michael Deitman on her eighteenth birthday, and their families and land would be united, an isthmus to wealth and stability.

All of that was changed when a bullet ripped through the leaves, shearing the air. Before either of them heard the sound of the report, it shattered Morgan's breastbone and sprayed bright red blood onto my mother Lydah's face and hair. Morgan looked at her, his eyes filled with terror as he fell dead into the yellow mustard blossoms.

"Who did this?" I asked.

"Well," she stammered, "of course it was an accident. You have to know that, Joss. Someone was in the high birch grove shooting at the birds. . . ."

I didn't challenge her, but I wondered how she came to believe this. And who could have fired from nearly a quarter of a mile and struck down Morgan with such precision?

During those first three days before anyone else knew what had happened, my adrenaline-driven mother dragged Morgan's body to the cottage in back of the farmhouse and hid him in a macabre game of hide and seek—first in the closet, then under the stairwell to the cottage, and finally behind the old woodstove—all their favorite childhood hiding places. While the crows sat in the trees above and watched. On the third day, she carried him to the river and washed him in the cool running water, then laid him in the tall grass.

Even when the coroner came to take him later that afternoon, she still refused to believe he was dead. She sat on the back porch all that summer rocking, worrying the floorboards for days that lingered into weeks. She did not cry or speak for months and only bathed in the river.

I think about this story as an April wind blows my red Mini Cooper along I-84 West, and soon north along the Taconic Parkway. I try to distract myself, turning up the radio, flipping through the FM stations, but still I hear her voice.

"I had no one," my mother told me. "My brother was the only one left, and then he was gone, too. I convinced myself that he was sitting on Heaven's back porch. That if I waited on our rear balcony, he'd be back. I don't know why, but I washed and ironed all of his pajamas and packed them in a suitcase. You do crazy things when you lose someone. I think that suitcase is still in one of the upstairs closets."

She said she'd look for it but never did. I wonder if it's still there. I try to push away these thoughts by doing what I always do: measure the day by road signs or how many times I pass the same truck. An attachment from girlhood and those hopscotch counting rhymes from my school days—*one-ery, two-ery, zigger-zoll, zan. . . .* But on this morning I gauge my time, tapping out the minutes by heartbeat, dropped lanes, or the whirl of the car's cozy heater and classic rock tunes buzzing in my heart like a lullaby.

It's what my dad always did back when we all lived in the city— crank up the radio while he drove. He'd holler, "Hey, Paulie-girl! Get in the van." With my mother scolding, "Paul! Her name is Joss Ellen—not 'Paulie-girl!' Not 'Boy-o' either!" But that name, "Paulie-girl," was lassoed around everything I knew myself to be. As a six-year-old, I was always ready for an adventure with my father, Big Paul.

We'd fly in that rattletrap van with the tunes blaring. He'd bring me to his tailor shop on East Forty-Second between Lexington and Third. I'd jump out before the vehicle stopped and run through the jangling back door, hollering, "Liam! Where are you?"

Liam Michaels was my father's apprentice and an occasional guest at the farm. He'd drive upstate to play with my father's jazz group that met there on Friday nights. I'd steal into the millhouse where they played to hear Liam's melancholy Irish tunes flow across his fiddle strings. I used to beg him to bring his violin to the tailor shop, but he never would. He always said it wouldn't be proper in a gent's shop. I'd nod though I didn't understand why, or what a "gents' shop" was.

"Liam!" I'd holler again.

"Is that you, Jossy?" he'd ask.

I could never answer fast enough. He'd scoop me up and lift me onto his shoulders, and then stand in front of the tall mirrors. I'd laugh and screech, terrified of being up so high, and hang onto his hair or squeeze my arms around his neck.

He'd cough and choke. "Tell the truth, girl! Are ya trying to kill me, or do you just like me that much?" He'd pull my hands away and grab me around my waist. "Oh my God!" he'd say. "Look at that two-headed thing in the mirror!"

"It's me, Liam," I giggled, all the while reeling in woozy panic. My dark red curls, just like my mother's, bounced in the mirror image, and my startled expression stared back at me with my father's same grey eyes.

"There you are!" he'd point, with a goofy smile plastered across his face and a shock of black hair falling into his eyes. "How's my girl? What are ya—on a ladder? Come down from there. I got a little bit of ribbon in my pocket I saved for ya."

My father would barrel through the back door, yelling, "What's going on in here? Paulie-girl, don't bother the help!" He'd wink at me and disappear into his office.

He'd check his stock and special order sheets, and then we'd pile back into the van and charge off to the garment district. There my looming father, nearly six feet tall and wide in the shoulders, would haggle with some witless slob over the best gabardine. Daddy would reiterate his secret every time: *Look them in the eye and smile, but walk away before you back down. Just be soft with every step.* Once he'd get his price, he'd buy remnants of cerise or saffron taffeta to make my sister and me something for school. For Naomi, it would be a blouse with pearl buttons or a crinoline skirt, but for me, he'd always fashion something man-tailored: a vest or jacket spit in my father's image.

"Stand still," he'd say while he'd mark the fabric with chalk and pins that scratched my skin. Back then I never winced.

I'd turn slowly while my father stood, scrutinizing his work, commanding me to stop, or turn, or walk across the room as he'd watch the garment move in the swing of my arms. What emerged would be flawless: pale gray herringbone with pockets piped in apricot, a vivid lining at the pleat. In the mirror, I only saw my father's eyes, his smile.

Back then, I thought I was special.

On Friday nights, we'd go to the Floridian on Flatbush Avenue for sweet fried smelts with lemony rémoulade sauce. The same diner he used to go to with his own Pops. "Here he comes," some waitress named Dolores or Ronnie would shout above the din: "The dapper tailor dressed to the nines with his little one." We'd sashay down the aisle between the tables, he in his striped shirt and red braces, a vest or jacket, shoe-shined and natty. Me in a replica—never a skirt or a bit of lace. Big Paul, square-jawed, with smoke-grey eyes that could darken instantly, would smile at the other diners as if they were his guests, always with the witty comments, tipping his fedora or porkpie, or whatever was perched on his head that evening.

We'd slip into a booth and order drinks: cherry soda for me and Cutty Sark straight up for Big Paul. Before the first sip, we'd clink our glasses while I stared in awe at the myth that was my father. And when our hot plates came out, we'd slather on that tart sauce and slide those sugary fish down our throats, barking like penguins for more. We were hungry. We were the boys out for all we could get.

The best times were in early April—the annual trip from our Bronx apartment off Fordham Road, heading north to go upstate to Red Mills Farm in Canaan, my mother's childhood home. Big Paul and I went each year for spring cleanup. We'd race up the Taconic Parkway, the windows rolled down, the radio blaring hard rock more reckless than the wind. The smell of new green would fill the van, and we were greedy for all of it. We'd suck in that air clear through our heads; we'd plug our ears with stomp and thrum. We'd kick the floorboards in that tinny van, careening toward Canaan. And yell because we could. And because we had abandoned all sensibilities.

From the Parkway, we'd follow 295 into Canaan, winding onto Old Queechy Road and then Sweet Milk Road. Another quarter mile up a steep hill loomed Red Mills Farm with its house, cottage, and gristmill on the river named Stony Kill. Once we'd unpacked buckets and rags, Big Paul would build a campfire out back to grill hamburgers. After supper, we'd walk down through the cornfield and climb over barbed wire fencing that led to the former gristmill and the wide dam along the Stony Kill.

We'd work nonstop for three days: painting, putting up new curtains, scrubbing tile and linoleum. We'd clear every crevice, buff all the mirrors, the faucets and china plates, too. Every glass sparkled. And he'd always say, "You and me, Boy-o, we have to make this place shine for your mother and Naomi, just right for my girls. Everything perfect. Otherwise, they won't come here with us guys. Right, Paulie-girl?"

"Right," I'd whisper. "But Daddy, I want to be one of your girls, too."

He would put his arm around me and hug me close. "Joss, don't you know you're more than that? You're my Paulie-girl, my Boy-o!"

I'm still his Paulie-girl, and as dreadful as it is, that name still vibrates in my heart with its rhythm and cadence.

The ring of my cell phone startles me, bringing me back to the flying traffic and the road that spools onward. It's my father again. "Hey, Dad," I say.

"Joss, where are you?" His voice is shaky.

"I'm almost in Canaan. I can't talk now, Dad. I'm driving. I'll call you when I get there. Okay?"

"What the hell are you going out there for?" The voltage is back in his voice.

I tell myself just to breathe, and keep it light. But his words topple me. I am fallen, trampled in his steamroller words.

"Hello! Hello! You still there?" My father's rasp crackles through the car.

"I'm here, Dad."

He drones on. "Leaving Wyatt, too. Christ what's wrong with you? He's a good guy—"

"That's none of your business." I don't wait for his argument, his sarcastic retort. I press the phone. He's gone. The wide sloping road calls me back. I watch the treetops keel like dizzy drunkards in the rising wind. Ahead the sky has darkened. A storm is rolling in. I push the gas a little harder, hoping to get to Canaan before it hits. The airwaves fill with static as I fiddle with the radio knob, but my father's words creep in, an interloper, a juggler tossing pieces of my soul into the air.

I drive on, imagining what my mother would have thought about all of this. She'd be glad that I was coming to live in her house—now my house—even if it was only part-time. The farm has been in her family for generations.

She had told me years before, "You need to promise me you'll keep the farm in the family."

I nodded, standing next to her in the bakery, learning knife skills at eight years old. She had been showing me how to chop apples, walnuts, and sage leaves for apple-sage cakes when she asked for my promise. I didn't understand what she meant—keeping the farm in the family—but I gave my word.

"You remember this," she said. "It's your promise."

"I will," I said, bobbing my spring-loaded head.

It was unusual for her to say anything like this to me. Mostly she kept to herself at the bakery, always listening to the others prattle on about landlords, lovers, where they would be going after work. Other than a nod, a subtle shake of her head, or a laugh, she never had much to add to the conversations that swirled around the kitchen. I took her confidence in me as a sign, an opening for answers.

"Mommy, why does Daddy—"

She stopped me, her finger to her lips, "Shhhh," she commanded. She pulled me off the stool and into the dry goods pantry where no one would hear her. "We don't talk about your father, Paulie-girl."

The way she said that name, the look that came over her face like swiftly moving air currents, confused me.

She bent down, her face close to mine. I could smell the coffee on her breath as the words rushed over her lips, her saliva spraying across my face.

"You made your choice. He's who you want to talk to, not me. Understand?"

I nodded back then, not realizing what I understand now. My family had always been split into two camps. Each of my parents chose a child to be theirs. I was my father's girl; Naomi was my mother's. Though there were land grabs along the way—inheriting Red Mills Farm was just another, this time from beyond the grave.

I push through a torrent of rain and wind that sluices across the lane. Ten miles north I am on the back side of the squall, where the road is dry, and a flock of starlings slices the sky into black speckled ribbons. I scan the treetops for raptors, red-tailed and Cooper's hawks ready to pick off the stragglers. By mid-morning, I turn onto Sweet Milk Road, watching the dark sky in the distance and a show of lightning strikes. The faded gristmill emerges on the horizon with crows lined on the gable end. A deluge of memories catches me: the smell of overripe tomatoes, the rocking treehouse in the winter wind, sparks streaking from tiny, hand-sewn birch bark canoes racing on the rolling river, and Haley. Haley, my nephew, his bowl-cut dark hair and endless brown eyes—he and the farm are my claim—land that has been in my family for generations, family land and the history it bears.

The door of my clockwork car squeals open as the smell of the copper-fired air and that oh-so-wanted-green of April rushes through me, the fragrance of it drifting in scraps against the last of the persistent snow. The hills are swathed in a painterly wash of chartreuse. I breathe it in, the pot liquor of spring, past my mother's front gardens, now a sea of yellow daffodils nodding their happy faces at the sun. Soon enough, there will be Verbascum and red poppies, lupine, and columbine. I can see the pinky-red geraniums with their lime-green leaves sitting in the living room windows. They are descendants, too. Started from a geranium slip by some great-great grandmother of this house too many generations back to know. I kick along the stone driveway and head toward the house. The noise scatters the crows perched in the high elms. They caw and call, watching me pitch against the still-charged atmosphere.

I listen for the shrill of raccoons after the thunderstorm, or for the first peep frogs of spring. The voices of screech owls and coy dogs in the near-morning hours still ring in my memory. But most of all it is the carrion river that has pulled me back, the Stony Kill, with its wild brown trout hidden in murky pools.

When I climb to the porch, I peek through the floor-length windows into the sunny living room of my childhood. I remember my mother the last time I saw her there. She had moved back into the big house and was sitting on her graceful settee, yards of white sateen billowing onto the clean paper-covered floor as she hemmed a bridal gown.

I'd had tea with her that day, while she pulled a threaded needle in her delicate fingers, tipped with gaudy purple-pink nail polish, through that shiny fabric in a swift clean arc. I never understood why a woman with such a refined sense of color and style loved those horrid nail colors. We'd talked about small pleasantries—the weather, how lovely the gown in her lap was, and new recipes I was trying at the bakery. Get-togethers like this weren't common; we had lost our way more than ten years ago.

On a November morning when I was twenty, my mother, Lydah Van Vliet Ryckman, handed me the keys, the combination of the safe, and a stack of papers to sign, and all at once the responsibilities of running the bakery fell onto my shoulders. She left Brooklyn and the bakery that she had run for years and never looked back. She returned to Canaan, to the farm and land owned for generations by the Van Vliet family, known as Red Mills, and took up dress design.

"Where did you learn to sew like this?" I asked on that last day I visited. "It's so beautiful."

"Where do you think?" she laughed. "I learned from your father. I wasn't always a baker, you know. We started his business together. He and I were a team."

As she spoke, I watched her face light up. It was a rare look at who she had been with my father in their early years—young, happy, and in love.

"So why did you leave?"

"Your Aunt Marie was having health problems, and your father wanted me to help out his sister at the bakery. He promised it would only be temporary."

She set down her needle and looked up at me, her eyes steely. "But what happened was that I had become a better seamstress than your father and a better designer. He would have none of that. So off I went."

I sat frozen to the armchair, my thoughts whirling as the pieces of my family lined up and cascaded like tumbling dominoes. I didn't know what to say as I watched her return to her needlework, carefully attaching the last of the folded hem to the body of the gown. The sun caught her bowed head and red hair, silvered along her temples, pink half-glasses perched on her nose. I saw her more clearly than I ever had. When she finished, she stood with the faint dove-gray satin gown held high, sparkling in the afternoon light. It had diminutive, satin covered buttons, lace edged tulle peeking out from below the hem, and a bronze colored ribbon at the bodice.

"The bride's a redhead like me. These colors will work for her."

They surely would. The dress was at once dazzling and understated.

"I should make you a dress like this—just in case."

"I don't think so." The words fell out of my mouth.

She looked up at me, her grey-blue eyes unwavering, and asked, "What will you do with the farm when I am gone?" She had that kind of prescience.

I stared at her, flummoxed, speechless.

"Well? I'm waiting," she said.

"Aren't you leaving the farm to Naomi?"

"Why would I do that, Joss? Your sister's life is in Pennsylvania. You know she doesn't want anything to do with the farm. And you—you have always done what I have wanted."

It was harsh, what she said back then. But true. My sister has gone on while I have wallowed in the past. What would Naomi do with the farm, but sell it? I knew my mother would never want that. I turn away from the porch windows, still broken, reeling, and not knowing any other way other than to run. I am not yet ready to unlock the tall double doors. Instead, I hike past the stone-walled gardens my father used to use for his tomato patch. In between the tomato plants were hillocks of cucumbers, squashes, and fat striped melons. Beyond the stone walls were the bean fields, low plants bordered by pole beans. But his most prized crops were the rows and rows of sweet corn: Early Sunglow, Golden Bantam, and Silver Queen, all of it tended more by local high school kids than my father.

I slog on past the dam and the deep river water it holds back, trudging through the still-wet fields, across the broken down fence, through that section of land where my mother and her brother stood arguing all those years ago. I look beyond to the birch grove and imagine a sniper sniffing the breeze like a wild animal for the taste of it, its warmth and wetness. Finding the air currents, holding back, waiting for just the right moment to squeeze the trigger. Who and why race through my mind as the crows fly above, following me in a canopy of budding limbs. Their rusty-hinged calls shiver through my bones. I watch them pursue me. A crow will trace a fox, a wild dog, any predator. It's what scavengers do to feed.

Am I, too, a predator, scavenging for bones of the past?

Maybe so. It has taken me a long time to understand what she had meant by choosing my father over her. Only she had it backward. They chose. We were the Maginot Line of my parent's uneasy truce.

On through the soggy cornfield, the light streaks through the early morning cloud cover. In the distance I see the tree house suspended from its perch over the deepest part of the riverbend, its tin roof shining beneath bent limbs. I haven't been out to look at it in years.

A shiver runs through me. This is where my story begins: Ghosts in the pools and eddies still fly under these icy waters. They are angels of the river. Though I have tried, I have never out-run them or this roiling water. My feet slide deeper into the wet ground, rooting me to the land. I lift my foot to the sucking sound of the mud filching my shoe, my foot covered in sludge as I pull myself free. *Goddamnit,* I curse under my breath.

I struggle through the thick briars to get a closer look at the tree house. It is no longer steady. A large supporting branch has broken, though the cabin itself still looks sturdy. Muddy water seeps through my shoes, chilling me to my core. I head back toward the farmhouse with childhood memories of tree house nights filling my head.

In the distance, faint a cappella voices drift through the air. On the other side of the road, mothers and girls in the high fields sing and sway in their brightly printed tops like giddy tulips. They bend with baskets and colanders and dig into that woman-scented earth: searching for fiddleheads to be steamed like asparagus, or cowslip stems boiled long for their sweetness, and the first shoots of dan-delion greens, that are tender and insistent, but bitter like endive.

It is the bitter I remember best.

2

The double front doors of my mother's 1805 Italianate scuff across the floorboards as I push them open. Once inside, I slide out of my muddy shoes and socks, the house key in one hand and a couple of religious flyers from under the door in the other. Sunlight streams through the tall windows, the faint smell of lemon oil lingers—the way it did when I was a child.

Cleaning was one of my Saturday morning jobs when I was a kid. My mother would leave the rags, dust mop, and lemon oil, along with a note with my name scrawled at the top of the page. The instructions were always the same: "Make sure you get all the bookshelves, the top edges of the mopboards, the staircase. . . ." She was particular about dusting.

I'd dust and polish all the antique furniture with that sunshiny oil, pretending to wipe away every fingerprint from great-grand-mothers and double great-great grandfathers, whose portraits with their ghostly white hands lined the upstairs hallway. I looked for fragments of their lives along the glossy hardwood floors and mop-boards—an edge of a footprint trapped in varnish, the smudge from a milk-painted finger along the mantle—but I never found stains or scratches from the old souls of the house.

When my mother would arrive home in the late afternoon, she'd inspect my work as she stood in the fading light with her arms crossed. There was always something not quite right. "You missed the register on the other side of the fireplace" or, "How many times have I asked you to soldier the books on their shelves after you dust?" I'd scurry around remedying my mistakes, trying to please her.

"You always get so distracted, Joss. Why is that?"

I'd shuffle my feet back and forth, knowing I didn't have an answer that would appease her.

"Never mind," she'd say.

When all was righted, she'd squeeze my hand or drape her arm over my shoulder and sigh. "I guess eventually, you'll learn."

She was right, however. I was an easily sidetracked child—a daydreamer, a woolgatherer. I hated cleaning and would get lost in the art books that lined the shelves—ones with illustrations of pink and purple skies, or snowflakes that looked like they were spinning in the painted air. Sometimes I took out paper and crayons and tried to copy the magical bookplates, but mostly I dawdled the time away and would then rush through my chores before she returned.

My mother was right about housework, too. Eventually, I learned. Careful housekeeping has become ingrained in me. I run my fingers along the edge of the hall table before I add the mail to the stack that is already there. Hanging from the front hall closet door is a pink chiffon dress, not yet hemmed. A spool of pink silk thread and a packet of fine needles sit by her teacup on a smaller table, as if she has run out to pick up the dry cleaning and will be back in just a minute.

But she won't.

I wander from room to room. The wide plank floors squeak in all the same places, I run my hand across the tables, the upholstery, the embroidered pillows she made with witty sayings:

Dare to Dream! Heal with Prayer & a Dose of Gin, Perfection is the Child of Time.

In the kitchen another of her architectural renderings sits on the table: an exact replica of the White House, the South Portico with its bowed façade, the North Portico, the East and West Wing Colonnades, the bays of windows—all of it made from sugar cubes, serrated like blocks of limestone, mortared in egg whites. Crumbling now, poached for cups and cups of tea. Or cheeked in my mother's mouth, daring tooth decay to take her, rather than the stroke that stole her nearly a month ago. The terraces originally above the galleries have slid off, the stairs deteriorated. Ants have begun to swarm and invade the structure, carrying off the American presidential palace, crystal by crystal.

My phone rings. It's my father again. "Dad," I answer. "What's up?" I wait to hear a reprimand about hanging up on him earlier.

"Whaddaya mean? I'm lousy. When are you coming home?"

"I'll be back in the city early Saturday morning."

"Christ, what's today—Tuesday? That's too long."

"You've got caretakers there, Dad. No different than if I were at the bakery."

"And they're lousy. Every damn one of 'em. Especially today's bargain—that Miss Ortiz!"

"Now what?" I run my hand through my hair, wishing the constant hassles with him would mysteriously end.

"She's a dictator. That's what. I was having a little fun—shooting paper airplanes out the window—not hurting anyone. People on the street were waving and laughing. But oh no, the dictator can't have that! I might fall out the window, or upset someone."

"Let me see what I can do. I'll talk with her—"

"What are you doing out there at the farm? You can't live there and run the bakery, too. Your mother tried that. It was no good."

"Dad—" I hear the exasperation in my voice. "I've got a great part-time manager." I shake my head, wondering why I'm telling him any of this.

"Listen to me! That never works—putting someone in charge of *your* business—you'll see."

I barely hear him as he rants. I am too busy rummaging through the pantry looking for an empty box.

"Are you listening to me, Joss?"

"Yeah, Dad," I reply, but I put my phone on speaker and search the lower cabinets. No box there either, at least nothing large enough to hold the crumbling sugar-cube White House.

He shouts through the airways. "Moving to Canaan when you were a kid for that year was the worst decision we ever made. I had no say in the matter. Your mother just up and left. Wrote me a goddamn note! Like a fool, I chased after her. But she was more of a drifter—full of wanderlust."

"I know, Dad, you've told me this before."

"Yeah, well, you need to hear it again. Don't be like her—always on to the next thing." I hear the anger in his voice. "You're doing just what she always did—running like a fool."

"Can you please stop!" I yell, surprised at my anger. "Don't you get it? She was my mother."

She's nothing but a wanderer. Useless. Got gypsy-blood in her. He'd turn his head in slow motion and spit on the ground. *She's bound to leave everything and everyone, including you. She was born to take the road, and that will never change.*

I stood in the dusky doorway, a ten-year-old, looking up at him, the slash of his deep red mouth pushing out words that became a gaping wound. I dissolved into the plank floor the way every motherless child does. Hadn't my father always been right?

I won't ever leave, Daddy.

Sure you will.

I promise I won't.

He smirked and left me standing in a puddle of confusion.

I assumed everyone's family was like mine. But at almost thirty-three, I'm still chasing my mother's wispy shadow, and am still my father's Paulie-girl when he needs me. The irony isn't lost on me.

I can hear him breathing at the other end of the line, but he doesn't say anything. Neither do I. Sunlight streams through the pantry back window—my mother's potted herbs nodding to the sun. I grab the half-filled watering can that sits on the ledge and give the plants an overdue drink.

"You still there, Joss?"

"Yeah, I'm here." I breathe in and let my shoulders relax. "But I have to get going. You keep making those paper planes, Dad. Make a whole big bagful, and we'll launch them together. Just like the old days."

"Yeah, like the old days." His voice drifts. "You never got the hang of that—the folding and cutting."

"Bet I could do it now."

"Bet you could," he laughs

"Gotta go," I say.

"Okay."

I hear the click on the line as I pull a piece of paper from the junk drawer, determined now to get it right. I begin creasing and folding, adding fold after fold, but it's useless. I don't remember all the turns and folds he showed me, but I recall my father standing at the open window of our fifth-floor apartment hurling paper airplanes down toward our heads.

I had been playing on the sidewalk with Carolina Hernandez from PS9 Ryer Avenue Elementary when my father raised the window, and those wild sailplanes drifted and flew in the air, raining down on us.

"Right here, Daddy," I shouted, stretching my arms into the air.

"Here you go, Paulie-girl! See if you can grab one," he laughed.

They flew in curlicues and smooth landings or rose and rose higher on the updrafts, like angels. We squealed and spun topsy-turvy, tracing them in the sky. We chased them down the sidewalks. And stopped traffic, darting between taxis and buses. Our screeching rang in the air. We reached for what we couldn't catch, while my father stood in the open window roaring with laughter.

He shouted to me, "I need you up here, Boy-o."

"But you're not a boy," Carolina said.

Her mocking voice and the sneer on her face embarrassed me. I was caught red-handed in the strangeness of my father and me. Back then, I wanted to be everything she was: quick to laugh and cotton candy cute. I tried to whitewash our oddness. "My dad always jokes with me that way," I said.

She stared at me, a smirk on her face. "You're weird," she said as she turned, twirling her flouncy skirt.

I laughed like it didn't matter, but I raced all the way up to our fifth-floor apartment so he wouldn't holler "Boy-o" to me again. He was waiting with paper and scissors, and an intricate lesson in cutting and folding. In an instant, he transformed a sheet of paper into a sailplane while I made a hodgepodge of crooked lines and clumsy folds. He showed me again and again, but I still couldn't manage.

"Now pay attention." His voice was brittle. "I'll show you one more time." His hands moved like dancers, and I was lost in all those turns.

"I don't want to do this," I said.

"Why not?"

"Because Carolina thinks it's weird that you call me Paulie-girl and Boy-o."

"That kid don't know nothing."

"You don't understand, Daddy!"

He never understood, and it's too late now. I find the broom and dustpan and sweep the sticky sugared kitchen floor, wondering why my father has always been so intractable. I put the broom away, but the floor is still tacky. In the back of the broom closet, I find a mop and bucket and scrub the floor until it's clean and shiny. I look up, almost expecting my mother to come through the door, pleased at my efforts. But I know she would have found something not quite right. That was her way with me. Just as I know my father won't ever understand the part he played in why our family fell apart.

What he did know, however, was my mother's restlessness. He said she was a person who craved change, and that she was always looking for a different doorway. Her headlong pursuit would alter my world irrevocably. It began the day my mother moved us to Canaan when I was eleven years old.

On a Friday afternoon, just after Christmas, I came home to my things packed in the back of my mother's car. She was standing on the sidewalk, shoving a few more boxes in the back of her car.

I put down my backpack and asked, "Where are we going?"

"To Canaan," she said. "You and I are moving to the farm."

"What? We're moving?" My mind raced. Was this a joke? Or maybe we were going to Canaan to prepare a surprise party. My father's birthday was on Sunday.

"Yes, we're moving." She sounded so happy.

I tried to think of reasons that would dissuade her. "But what about school? My friends? I don't want to move."

"Don't be contrary, Joss. You're coming with me. I've made arrangements for a new school. St. Marks. It's a Catholic school."

"With nuns?" I shrieked. "And what about Daddy?"

"He's staying here."

"But why?" At that moment, I felt smaller than I had ever been.

"Because someone has to take care of the farm. And because I'm the only one left from my family, so it's up to me."

"But Daddy and I get it ready every year," I pleaded. The wind picked up along the street, tossing a news page and a discarded paper cup along the sidewalk.

"I know you do, Joss." Her voice softened. "But it has to be different now."

I shivered in the cold as dusk marched across the sky. "Will Daddy come out to help?" I wanted reassurance that we would all be whole, that everything would be okay.

"You'll see your father, Joss. He'll come out to the farm to visit. Come on now, get in the car."

The word "visit" fell like the clank of metal hitting metal. There had to be something I could do. "Can't I go upstairs and leave him a note?" I asked.

"Just get in the car. You can call him later." That sharp edge had crept into her voice. I knew not to push any harder. I climbed in the front seat and slumped against the door.

"Put your seatbelt on."

I snapped the buckle and began fiddling with the radio.

"Not too loud, Joss Ellen. I know you and your father like to blast the music." She laughed.

I stared at her wide smile and wondered why she was calling me "Joss Ellen." It was her name for me when I had particularly pleased her.

"You'll see," she went on. "You and I are going to have such a special life together at the farm."

We drove on through the dark and the cold. She hummed softly to the radio. I curled into the seat dozing on and off, wishing there was a blanket in the car. We made one stop at a McDonalds for a "Happy Meal" and otherwise drove straight through to Canaan. It was after eight when we arrived, ushered in with big wet snowflakes that stuck to my eyelashes.

"Grab the suitcases," my mother ordered. "We'll get the rest in the morning."

I hauled in the bulky luggage, one piece at a time, then dragged it upstairs to our bedrooms. I would immediately have something of mine from home.

"Do you want some hot cocoa?" my mother called from the bottom of the stairs. "It will warm you up."

"No, thanks. I just want to call Daddy."

"Not tonight, Joss. We can call him in the morning. Okay?"

I nodded and headed for the bathroom.

"You're going to bed?" she asked.

"Yeah, I'm tired."

"Sleep well; we'll sort things out in the morning."

But instead of heading to the bathroom, I tiptoed into my mother's bedroom and picked up the phone on her nightstand, then dialed our home number. There was no answer. My father often worked late on Friday nights. I dialed the number for his shop workroom. Liam answered.

"Hey, kiddo! What's going on?"

"Can I talk to my Daddy?"

"He's with a customer right now. Can I have him call you back?"

"We're at the farm," I said. "Maybe he should wait until the morning." I knew if he called out here, I'd be in trouble with my mother.

"Oh, your Dad didn't mention anything about the farm. What are you doing there—getting ready for a big New Year's party?"

"No. Mom and I moved out here today, and I didn't get a chance to say goodbye to Daddy."

"Oh," Liam said.

I waited for more, but all I could hear was his breath. "Are you there, Liam?"

"I'm here, baby girl, I'm here. I didn't know about you moving. Your father didn't say anything—"

"I don't think he knows," I said.

There was another long exhale on the other end. "Listen, you call me whenever you like. I'll make sure your father gets your message."

"Okay. I better get off the phone now, before my mother hears me."

"Sleep sweet," he said. "I'll make sure your daddy calls you in the morning."

I stole out of my mother's room like a church mouse, scurrying along the edge of the wide hallway and into my room. The house was breathless and cold as I slipped in between the sheets, still in my clothes and jacket, and tucked my face into the covers, too. I drifted off immediately, the sleep of escape, dreamless and dry.

In the morning, I woke confused and sweaty, but happy, glad that I would hear from my Dad. I waited through breakfast and lunchtime, too. I finally called in the early afternoon.

"Sorry, Love, your father just stepped out. I'll remind him. . . ."

But he never called. Not that day or the next or the one after that.

At first I called the tailor shop every day and talked with Liam. He reassured me, saying over and over that my father would be out soon. When that didn't happen, I thought maybe my father was mad at me, that I shouldn't telephone so often. I wasn't supposed to call unless it was an emergency. I began calling three times a week and whittled that down as more and more time passed. Until mostly I stopped calling at all.

I didn't see or hear from my father for five months, and I asked again and again, "When is Daddy coming?"

"I think next weekend," my mother would say. Or, "He's very busy, Joss. You know that."

Her final answer came on a snow-dust covered day when the sun was hazy in the morning sky.

"Quit pestering me about your father. For all I know, he's never coming here again. Just as well." She slammed a red clay pitcher onto the counter that had always been in the house. It shattered, spilling water onto the floor. "Now look at what you made me do!"

I stopped asking.

My mother couldn't take care of the farm or me. We plunged into a jumbled world of chaos and confusion with so many pieces of my life gone or missing—my father, my old room, and even small comforts like my favorite books, games, and CDs.

"Mom, can you bring me back my things from my room?" I asked.

"Sure, sure," she said.

But she would forget, or not have time, or just get exasperated with me.

"We'll buy you new things here," she said.

That never happened, either. What I lost could never have been picked up at a department store.

She spent Thursdays through Sundays back in Brooklyn at the bakery, while I floundered with overnight babysitters and commuted on school days to St. Mark's with my new classmate Fletcher Goodwin from Edgefield Road. He and his mother would pick me up in their minivan, and as she drove, she would fix her hair or light cigarettes and drink coffee. And on weekends I was in the care of an older woman named Miss Euphrates from Churchtown, a dilapidated village on the outskirts of town.

The first time I met Miss Euphrates was on a Friday afternoon, a week after we had moved to Canaan. I had just come home from school. She was standing at the kitchen stove, stirring a pot of something that smelled delicious. Taller than my father, and long-legged with wide shoulders and a leopard print scarf tied around her wild hair, she turned and smiled at me. "Miss Joss? Is that you, girl?"

I looked around, wondering what other girl could be there. "Yup, it's me," I said.

"Well, it's good to see you."

She said it as if she had always known me, and as if I'd always known her and her deep, musical voice. Her eyes shone like black crystals. And I was mesmerized but intimidated, too.

"Hi," I said.

"People call me Miss Euphrates—like the river. That's because some of my people were from the part of the world where the Euphrates flows into the Persian Gulf and on into the Indian Ocean. That is how I come to have this name."

"I didn't know a person could be named after a river."

She laughed. "There's a snack for you in the refrigerator, and I'm making chicken fricassée for supper. You like chicken fricassée?"

"I don't know. I never had it. It smells good, though, Miss Eu . . . Euphra—"

"Miss 'U-fray-tees.' No worries, child. Soon you gonna know my name like candy on your tongue." She laughed again, with the peal of rich, deep bells.

"Why'd your mother give you that name?"

I watched her check the pot of chicken, stirring and sniffing deep into the pot. I wondered why she did that—smelling it like she did, but I didn't think I should ask.

"I guess we got time for some banton, a little storytelling," she said, and she pulled a plate of fruit and cheese from the refrigerator, then sat across from me at the kitchen table. "Long time ago there was a bwoy named Saleem, one of my mother's people. He lived on the edge of the Euphrates River with his madda and dada and many brothers and sisters. That bwoy, he fished that river every day. You got to know Saleem was a good bwoy, always helping his madda and dada. One Sunday morning he hooked an enormous mangar, nearly nine foot long. But as hard as he tried, he couldn't pull that fish into his little boat. And the mangar couldn't free his-self. So Saleem and the fish struggled for hours until night rolled in. Starlight scattering across that wide, wide river."

I sat across from her, my hands cupped around my face. "What happened?" I asked.

"That fish knew they was in dire straits, so he bargained for both their lives. He jumped up out of that water and spoke to Saleem."

"Real words? What did it say?"

Miss Euphrates voice was a whisper. "Be very still," she said. "Do you hear them? Those voices?"

I listened, holding my breath, but only heard the ticking of the clocks, the hum of the refrigerator. There were no voices. "I don't hear them, Miss Euphrates."

"Yes, you're a young one, still. It takes practice. All your life you must carefully listen. When you are old like me, you will hear the words from times past." She laughed again.

Her chortle was a powerful sound that vibrated through me, but I still wondered what that fish had said.

"You want to know, don't you?"

I nodded.

"Well, that's just it, Miss Joss—Saleem was so tired and confused, he didn't quite hear that huge fish. So he called and called to that fish, asked him to come back and tell the secret one more time. But that fish didn't hear, or just didn't want to speak again. It pains a fish to speak in words. So they struggled on into the night until they both fell asleep. That great fish rested and saved all his strength and under the light of the morning star, that fish, he rose up out of the water and repeated his plea to Saleem. 'If you let me go,' he said, 'your family will live on forever.'

"Saleem reached into the water, into that fish's mouth, and pulled out the hook. The finned monster swam away, leaving poor Saleem wana-gut—still hungry, and worried about how he would explain being gone all day and night, with no fish for the frying pan. When he told his madda and dada the story of the magic talking fish who promised children in every generation, his parents felt that Jah and Jiiizas had blessed them. They forgot all about their hunger and worries because they knew their family would live to the end of time.

"Many generations later my Madda and Dada married and wanted children of their own. But no baby came until nineteen years later when I was born. They couldn't name me Saleem because that's a bwoy's name, so they named me after the river where some great grandbaby of that talking mangar now lives under those waters." She smiled.

"Do you think that fish really talked?"

"It matters more what you think, Miss Joss. If you think it spoke, then it spoke. And sometimes it doesn't matter about the words. A thing that sounds foolish can be a gift. And sweet words can be a dagger."

"You mean if Saleem just made up that story, if it really was all a lie, it doesn't matter because it made his family feel good?"

"Exactly. You a bright one, Miss Joss. For the price of a lie, if it was a lie," she winked, "that bwoy gave his people hope."

I wondered if there was a way that I could give my parents hope.

"Now it's your turn, Miss Joss. What about your name?"

"I don't know any stories about my name. It's just Joss. Sometimes my father calls me Paulie-girl. That's because he's Big Paul. And sometimes he calls me Boy-o, too."

"See, you got a story about your name! You must be your dada's special one."

I searched her face, confused, wondering how she could tell what I was thinking, what only I knew. "How did you know?" I asked

"Just look in the mirror, Miss Joss. Anybody can see what your dada knows."

"Mom says he's coming out to see me. Maybe this month."

"I'm sure he's coming real soon."

I nodded. Surely this woman who understood the complexities of lies and truth was right. "Miss Euphrates, do you have some kids who could come over and play with me?"

She laughed, deep and brilliant, and looked into my eyes. "My babies are all grown and my husband been gone to Heaven. So it's just you and me, child."

"You must be sad."

"Like you are?"

I nodded.

She touched my cheek and said, "It's okay to be sad sometimes, but not all the time. Okay?"

"Okay."

"Maybe you can invite your schoolmate, Fletcher."

"But he's a boy!"

"When I was your age, my best friend was a bwoy."

"Why?"

"Because we watched out for each other. You know what I mean?"

I shrugged my shoulders. "Sort of."

She cackled, "You will, dawta-girl. In the meantime, we got fricassée to make. Do you know how to make a roux?"

I shook my head and weighed whether I could ask her a question or not.

"You got something on your mind?" Miss Euphrates asked.

"How did you know?"

"That's easy. I just look at your quizzical face. Go on—run on into the bathroom mirror and see for yourself."

She was right. My whole face was a question mark. I ran back to the kitchen and asked, "Why did you stick your head in the pot and sniff it?"

"Well then, come right over to the stove and pull up that step stool." She had me stand on the stool and breathe in the fragrant broth.

"Now you breathe that in and identify how it smells. Is it sour or sweet, salty, spicy?"

"It smells a little sweet and like chicken, too," I said.

"See now, we gonna transform this broth. You remember you said sweet. Okay?"

"Okay."

I was glad she was there, awed by her dark dewy skin, her rich laughter. I did what she asked—got the flour and olive oil from the pantry. She showed me how to blend the oil with butter in a hot stockpot, whisking and stirring and then adding flour until it was just the right consistency, an even ratio of flour to fat. While I whisked and whisked, she slowly added the hot broth that had been cooking on the back burner all afternoon. Magically the concoction thickened and became a luscious, shimmering sauce.

"It looks like gravy, Miss Euphrates."

"That's right, Miss Joss. You just made gravy."

"You taught me how to make gravy and I didn't even know it!"

She handed me a teaspoon and said, "Now taste and tell me what it needs."

I dipped my spoon into the bubbling sauce, blew to cool it, and then tasted it. "It's a little boring."

"Sweet, too, but flat—right?" she asked.

"Yeah, flat. How'd you know?"

"Something savory that smells sweet gonna taste flat. Taste and smell is first cousins. Jiizas don't give you senses for no reason. Most people, they forget to use them." She winked and added salt and pepper while we tasted until it was just right. "See," she said. "Just a little at a time. You can always add more salt, but you can't take it away. Fact is, once you put something out into the world—I mean anything at all—a lie, a good deed, a prayer, you can never take it back. You know what I mean?"

I nodded, even though she talked in circles that confused me. Back then, I didn't understand what she meant.

It's only now as an adult that I am beginning to appreciate all that she tried to impart to me. She was right; once something is out there, you cannot take it back. There is always a shadow.

Enough, I tell myself, crumbling the would-be paper airplane in my hand and tossing it into the garbage. There must be instructions on the Internet. I'll learn how to make these damn things just to prove I can. I finish washing the kitchen counters and sinks. Everything is tidy and clean except for the disintegrating sugar-cubed White House. I head upstairs to look for an empty box—something large enough.

I stand at the top of the stairs, peering down the long wide hallway lined with family portraits going generations back. They stare in frozen time, dressed in their dark clothing, framed in mahogany and gilt. I wonder fleetingly if I should remove them from their timeless perches, replace them with paintings that breathe air and light.

I peek into each room until I come to my mother's bedroom. Her nightgown hangs from a hook; her bed is unmade, waiting for her smooth, strong hands to right the folds. I stand just inside the doorway, reluctant to enter, held back by an old childhood caution: Our mother's room was private. Entrance was by invitation only, though I recall sneaking in regularly.

We had often come up from the city to celebrate Christmas on the farm. On a wintry day when I was five, I stole into her room, picking up her boxes of powder and lipsticks and pulled a small drawer open. I ran my fingers over the sleek camisoles and panties, and pulled out a peach-colored satin slip edged in Binche lace.

Over my head, I wiggled into that silky garment, hitching it around my waist and wearing my favorite red tie-up shoes. I stared at my reflection in Mommy's full-length mirror, thrilled with the image looking back at me. I was a movie star, a fashion model.

"Ahem. . . ."

I had heard my father's voice before I saw his reflection in the mirror.

"Better not get caught!" he had cautioned and laughed.

I could feel my cheeks burn.

"Let me help you with that, Boy-o. You don't need all these girly things," he'd scoffed. He pulled the chemise over my head, then folded it and placed it back in my mother's dresser. "There," he said. "She'll never know. Whaddaya say you and me go down to the beaver pond and do a little ice fishing?"

I stand in front of that same mirror now, holding her night-gown with touches of lace and ribbons to my frame. But there is little resemblance to my five-year-old self, and less to her, only her same wild curls. I lay the gown across her bed. It is not something I can wear. I am not her girl, though I wish I had been. I am still my father's Boy-o. His Paulie-girl. Not a real girl. I breathe into the soft cotton for traces of her. As if this could bring her back.

In this room, there is so much of her that defies her death—her closet with rows of shimmering scarves and blouses, all her dresses and suits, skillfully tailored in crystalline garment bags, and stacks of shoe boxes. On her dresser are the charming objects that fascinated me as a child: thimbles housed in Lucite cubes, lipsticks, and hand creams, the things I had longed to touch when I was a girl that now feel intrusive in my hands.

I quietly open the top dresser drawer, its contents neatly arranged with tatted hankies and undergarments, bundles of letters tucked below. Thumbing through them, I recognize my childish scrawl and find a photo of myself when I was five. In the picture I am standing in front of the house at Red Mills Farm, smiling in the sunlight. I must have cut my hair not long before the photo was taken. There is barely a nub over my forehead. I am holding onto a quilt that my mother made for me. I wanted it to be pink and pale green, but my father convinced her otherwise—she used squares of yellow, red, and green cotton. Much later, I had sewn buttons all over it slapdasheredly like scattered stars. It made me think of school buses and stoplights, and I called it my stoplight quilt.

My mother must have saved it for me, so it must be here someplace.

I dig through her drawers, carefully removing the contents, then lay them back just as I found them. I did the same with the cedar chest, but there is no quilt. I scour the boxes from the closet, search the wardrobe with no luck. She must have stored it in one of the other bedrooms.

I pull the heavy drapes back and open the windows in each bedroom to air them out and pore through the nearly empty closets and drawers. The hollow echoes of my rummaging disturb the quiet house, but my quilt is nowhere to be found. I try the hallway linen closets and the closet in the bathroom. Finally up into the attic, climbing the crooked stairs against reason and no railings. Goddamn, she promised she'd have her handyman put up railings. I worried about her trotting up and down these stairs.

At the top landing, I flip on the attic light. The long wide expanse is empty—cleared out and broom clean. Gone are my ice skates, the little rocking chair, Christmas decorations, boxes of letters and photographs. All of it gone, including my things I had stored here.

I slam the door at the bottom of the attic stairs and go in and sit on my mother's unmade bed. How could she have thrown away my things? My head pounds. Arguments with my father and confusion over Wyatt churn through my cluttered mind. I am skating on the edge of a razor blade, fearful that every move I make is the wrong one. I begin again going through my mother's room, jerking the heavy dresser away from the wall; I am furious and inconsolable. All I find behind the dresser is dust and an old blank Post-it note. But no quilt. Could she really have thrown it out? Why would she do that? Why did she leave me? And why this house to me?

I toss everything into the hallway, piling the empty drawers one into the other and dragging them into the hall. I pull those dour portraits off the walls, stacking them against the mopboards. There's been enough sorrow in this house. I don't want reminders. The wardrobe, her hope chest, now empty, a nightmare of nail polish, wristwatches, odd buttons, and costume jewelry strewn across the floor. Kicking the mess out of my way, I pull the bed all the way back. Tucked under the headboard is an old scuffed-up suitcase.

It must be the suitcase she talked about from years ago. I sit on the floor and stare at it, my heart still racing from my rage and adrenaline. I flip it around; it's not too heavy. I wipe the dust and grime off with my shirttail, lift it onto the bed, and snap open the latches. There's a layer of folded pink tissue on the top and underneath it are papery folded pajamas. These must be the pajamas she ironed and packed for her brother. Below the blue cotton sleepwear with its red piping, I see the edges of more pink tissue. I carefully sift through the case, and there, cradled at the bottom, protected by Rosemary sachets, is my stoplight quilt.

I lift it cautiously, pulling out the yards of bright patchwork. Worn in places and repaired by my mother's tiny stitches, her able hands, it is soft against my face. The dog-eared fabric smells soothing. I sit for a long time, my mind now quiet. The light in the room begins to fade. The weariness of the day creeps into my bones. I pull off my jeans and blouse and slide my mother's nightgown over my head. Lying back into the goose down pillows and curling into the sheets, I wrap myself in my yellow stoplight quilt. And I wonder, as I drift toward sleep, why I ever left my quilt behind.

Hours later I rouse, disoriented. The room is awash in late afternoon gold light, and I am still dreaming, swirling in gossamer through a dry striped empty parking lot. Looking for something or someone but hearing only hollow footsteps. Someone is knocking on the door, calling my name.

Wrapped in my quilt, I stumble over the clutter in the hallway, then race down the stairs and swing open the wide double doors. He stands in that glowing light, and for a brief second my breath escapes from me.

"What are you doing here?" I ask.

3

I should have known Wyatt would show up unannounced. He had a way of doing that right from the start. We met when he came into Madame Marie's Patisserie & Café, a black felt beret perched on his head and a book tucked under his arm, held together with rubber bands. It was early, almost dawn. He filled his mug with dark roast at the coffee bar. I noticed him while I loaded our hundred-year-old bakery case with the morning's first batch of croissants, bacon and egg hand-pies, raw, gluten-free breakfast tarts, and fruit-topped johnnycakes. He wasn't one of my usual early morning customers.

He turned and asked, "Are you Madame Marie?"

I laughed hard, tossing my head back, wiping my hands on the kitchen towel draped over my shoulder. He chuckled, too, looking like what I imagined a once-California boy would look like. No boy anymore, he had straight sandy hair spilling across his face, bright blue eyes, and beautiful hands—hands that seemed articulate and strong. I knew intuitively he was a guy unaware of his allure.

"Sorry," I said. "That would be my white-haired great-aunt. Her name was Marie. But yes, I am the owner, Joss Ryckman, the third generation of this bakery."

"Well," he smiled. "I am fond of wizened-haired gals, but you'll do, Ms. Ryckman."

I laughed and waited for him to introduce himself. When he didn't, I nodded for him to continue, recognizing the type. Some customers like to remain anonymous until they commit.

"I'm opening a new business," he said. "I'm here on Atlantic Avenue, just a few doors down. A bindery and print shop specializing in rare books and privately printed editions."

"Congratulations! I love it when new businesses open on our section of the avenue."

"Thanks." He grinned, rocking from foot to foot.

"I need a caterer for my grand opening. You do that—cater events?"

"Oh, sure. I'd love to, being neighbors and all." I handed him our catering menu and smiled into his blue, blue eyes. There was something about him—shyness maybe, a holding back that was palpable and appealing.

He chortled and sipped his coffee, spilling a little while he thumbed through the pages. I straightened the trays and wiped up the spatter before he noticed. I didn't want to embarrass him.

"May I keep this?"

"Absolutely," I said. "When you're ready, we can sit down and discuss options and so forth. Sound good?"

"Will do," he said with a quirky half-smile, barely glancing at me.

"How about something from the bakery case? On the house—a little welcome to the neighborhood."

"No, no. I can pay."

"No need. What would you like?"

"Are you sure? Everything looks so tantalizing. How about one of those bacon and egg hand-pies?"

"You got it. They're still warm. In a bag, or wrapped to eat?"

"I'll eat it now, thanks. Your baking is amazing." As soon as his words slipped out, he looked at me quickly then turned as if he were embarrassed.

"Amazing, eh?" I laughed. "So you've had something from us before?"

"Yeah, a friend sent me something from here." He half smiled and looked away, clearing his throat. "Another buddy and I were snacking on cookies by the side of the road—cookies from you. It was dusk; the moon was rising over the desert." He looked up at me and bobbed his head. "We were out in Arizona and these kids were running around. We gave them some cookies, too, and off they ran across the sand, screeching that the moon was following them."

"Nice," I said.

"Yeah, well, that was the intention."

I could hear the sorrow in his voice. There was more to the story, but I didn't pry. "I used to do that sort of thing," I said. "Always outside playing with my nephew and my best friend—I was kind of boisterous as a kid."

"I can see that about you—your wild curly hair."

I ran my hands through my hair, trying to damp it down. "Yeah, with the humidity in here, my hair goes crazy."

"Oh no, I like it. Very attractive." He nodded and smiled, and headed for the door. "Gotta run," he said.

"See you." I smiled and gave a little wave as he slid out the door. It was refreshing, his sweetness, even his awkwardness, a respite from my customers who were always in a rush, often brash and distracted.

He returned a week later with a book still tucked under his arm. I was waiting on other customers. He stood by the door until I finished, then stepped forward.

"Good morning!" I said. "Nice to see you again. How was that egg pie?"

"Delicious. Really good, thanks." He looked directly at me and grinned. "What I came by for is to ask you about a date. I mean, a date for my grand opening." His face colored slightly.

"I knew what you meant." I smiled, too, and felt my face get hot. "Let me look in my book," I said, thumbing through my calendar. "So what are you thinking?"

"A Friday afternoon into the evening, when people get out of work. April seventh."

"That works. Any idea how many guests?"

"Um . . . jeeze, I don't know. Didn't think about that."

"Well, you could start with friends and family."

"I don't know anyone here—not yet. And my family is in the Midwest."

"Oh, well maybe you should consider a soft opening at first. Get to know people, create a mailing list—that sort of thing. Then have your grand opening."

He looked puzzled.

"Sorry, I don't mean to be intrusive. I just like to see everyone in the neighborhood do well."

He nodded. "No, no, you're right. This is what you do."

I watched him run his hand through his beard. He needed a shave.

"I hadn't thought it out," he went on. "I'll have to get back to you." He stood in the doorway for a moment, looking at me, quicksilver in his eyes, a spark of the enigmatic in his gaze. As if he were holding back and wanted to say something more.

I smiled and said, "You remind me of someone."

"Who's that?"

"A man I used to write to, though we never met. He was a Ranger stationed in Iraq. I contacted one of those organizations that support the troops with letters and packages. They sent me a name, and I wrote for two years. Once in a while he'd write back—pages of questions about me, never much about himself. But I kept writing. Blathering on like an idiot. Kind of like I'm doing now."

He smiled. "You still write to him?"

"No. My soldier returned stateside, and I have no address for him."

He nodded, mumbled, "Your soldier," his cheeks coloring, then disappeared out the door.

I watched him brush past the door and turn headlong into the wind that blew across the avenue. He looked back at me, and I quickly turned to the bakery case, fiddling with the broken latch. I bet he could fix it. I looked up, but he was gone, and I laughed at myself for playing scenarios in my head. I'd always been good at that—falling for inept high school chemistry lab boys, beautiful study hall guys, timid bakery boys who struggled more than me with fifty-pound sacks of flour.

My latest was the soldier I wrote to, the soldier I fantasized about, the soldier who disappeared. Now it seemed my mysterious new customer could be my new folly. Still, I began waiting for him to stop by, surprised to be thinking of him every so often. I knew nothing about him, not even his name. It was clear he was a guarded soul. Days and weeks passed. He didn't come by, at least not when I was around. I looked for him less and less, telling myself it was better this way. Likely he would have become another man who leaves.

It was more than a month later when he stopped by on a Saturday evening, just after the café closed. He rapped on the window and waved his black beret in hand.

"Good evening," I said, as I unlocked the door. I could feel my face flush. "Come on in out of the cold."

He stepped inside, unwrapping the scarf from his neck. "That wind is biting tonight." He shivered and smiled at me. "I came by wondering if you'd like to grab a bite to eat—no big deal if you've got other plans."

"Um . . . no other plans," I said, wiping my hands on a dish-towel. "I was just finishing up in here. So yeah, dinner sounds fine, as long as you don't mind waiting a bit."

"No problem! But to pick a restaurant, I have to rely on your neighborhood savvy."

"Deal! Just one thing—I don't know your name."

"Yeah, I need to talk to you about that," he said, shoving his hand into the pockets of his jeans. I remember wondering why he was so mysterious, so self-conscious. I watched him shuffle his feet back and forth in the falling light like a kid caught in a prank, or worse—a lie.

He stands now in that same ungainly posture, rocking from one foot to the other, his hands tucked into his pockets, this time in the doorway of my mother's house.

"Look" he says, "I know I said I wouldn't follow you out here, Joss. But I'm worried about you. I have to make sure you're okay."

"Did I ask you to check on me, Wyatt?" I ask. My voice is flat.

He looks at me as if his opening has explained everything. Then again, he's not a guy who gives up easily. Two years earlier Wyatt's phone rang around 3:00 a.m. It was one of his buddies, Carl from Cicero, Indiana. Carl had struggled with the ghosts of war from his time in Iraq and often called Wyatt. I lay in the twi-light between sleep and wakefulness while Wyatt listened. He put the phone on mute and whispered, "Joss, I have to go. I'm going to keep him on the phone and drive to Indiana and get him some help. Otherwise, I think he's going to do it."

"Do what?" I asked, half asleep.

"He's never talked like this before. Something's changed. If I don't go, he's going to kill himself."

Hours later, Carl answered his front door, phone in hand, still talking to Wyatt, who was now standing in front of him.

But I'm not as aggrieved as Carl.

"I came to offer moral support," Wyatt said.

I shake my head, staring at him in that beautiful late afternoon light.

"What, Joss? What?" He smirks. "Aren't you going to invite me in?"

I hear the frustration in his voice.

"But we decided to end things," I say. "Remember?"

"You decided. There was no 'we' involved. I'm here nonetheless, Joss—"

"Because that's what you do."

He smiles that crooked half-sad grin. "Okay, but before I leave, can I use the bathroom? Oh, and I brought you some dinner—figured you wouldn't have anything in the house."

"Already you want something." I hear the sarcasm in my voice.

Wyatt hears it, too, and rolls his eyes and grimaces.

"All right, come on in." We walk through the living room to the kitchen, by the sugar-cubed White House, Wyatt's heavy bootsteps counterpoint to my bare feet.

He looks at me in the lighted room. "Nice quilt you're wearing."

"My mother made it for me when I was a kid."

"Sorry, I—"

"It's all right. How could you know? I'll change while you use the bathroom."

"How about some tea?" he hollers.

"Okay," I say, but part of me wishes I could tell him once he's finished using the bathroom and has had his tea, that it's time to leave. I know that's not how it will go. I owe him more, but I am numb, emptied out, with only the armor of my anger that screams, "Keep Out!" I plod up the stairs, navigating through the chaos of the hallway and change into jeans and a sweater.

When I get back to the kitchen, Wyatt has already turned on the kettle and set out teacups and saucers.

"So, what are your plans for the house?" he asks.

I stare at him, running my hands through my hair, not knowing how to answer. One month ago, before my mother died, Wyatt and I were together, and my father was doing okay enough. And now the three of us are alone, each rambling in a separate set of walls and windows.

He looks at me, the softness returns to his eyes, then turns away. "I'm sorry," he says. "I was just making conversation."

"I know, Wyatt." I have hurt him again and I feel bad about that. "Maybe less is more," I say.

"You're right, quiet works."

We sit in the dining room, watching the sunlight weep from pale gold to tangerine over the washed-out hills. The silence grows thick and unchecked, except for the ticking of all the clocks my mother collected over the years: mantle clocks, carriage clocks, and a grandfather in the living room. I used to count their soundings when I was a kid. There was a solace to those clicks and tocks, the gongs and whistles rolling through the house like a steady heartbeat, sixty beats per minute.

I watch Wyatt move through the motions of dunking the tea bag, squeezing it against the cup, then laying it on the saucer. His ink-stained fingers out of place in this delicate room. I don't know why, but I want to stretch my hand out to him, to coax those fair-haired tresses back, wash the smudges from his hands like I did so many nights early on. Back then he was dealing with grief dug in so deeply, it was palatable. It rose from his bones, his skin, the stench of some otherworldly place.

He'd wake from a sound sleep throughout our first spring and on into early winter babbling, screaming, crying. That sweat still stung his eyes. He couldn't see. The rot of sewage and corpses made him wretch, along with the acrid odor of ever-burning tires that saturated his clothing. He still smelled all of it every single day.

He was addicted to aftershave.

When he fully woke, he grinned at me in the low light of our bedroom and made bad jokes about another IED near-miss and a friend he now called Stumpy.

"We were all shot through with bullets and adrenaline—sometimes it didn't matter which. I stored rounds in my buttstock, rounds in my rucksack, and stored knives where I could get to them swiftly, and the enemy couldn't—in my boot, taped to my ribs, a bogey knife at my inside calf. I was a street fighter, an all-night reconnaissance assassin. Right? You know that, Joss?

"We were all so similar, reserved guys built like sleek arrows, quiet, invisible, self-possessed. Eventually most of them swore and cursed. They called everyone and everything a goddamn motherfucking asshole. I never did. I listened to Steve Perry in my head. Always heard his luminous voice. I can't hear it anymore. All I hear is the desert howl in my head. When will it stop, Joss. When?"

I don't think it ever completely stopped, but he deals with it and this is different; I don't know how or why, only that there's no room for him. Not now. I need to be alone.

He drinks his tea, pushing back his hair and gazing out the window.

I remember first noticing Wyatt's habit of brushing his hair from his eyes the night he came to the café to invite me out. And I remember thinking that something might not be quite right, regardless of how attracted I was to him. It seemed wiser to be on my turf. I didn't know him well.

When he came that evening I said, "We could eat here, if you like. You've seen my demure bar and café in the back, haven't you?" while thinking I should at least clean up a bit. "We could have something from the kitchen."

"Yeah, you told me about your café. I've been meaning to try it. I guess tonight's my chance, if you're sure?"

I didn't remember telling him, but I must have. "Yes, why not eat here!" I said. "Would you like something to drink? Wine, beer?" My guess was that he was a beer kind of guy.

"Either is fine," he said.

"Have a seat. I'll be right back."

"That's all right. I'll help. You must be tired."

I smiled and motioned for him to follow. In the bar, I grabbed glasses, a Rioja Gran Reserve, and a pitcher of lemon water. "How about bringing these to the table?"

"Sure," he said. He carefully lifted the tray, like new wait staff, unsure of the dynamics of weight and balance in real time.

"I'm going to run upstairs and change. My apartment is above the bakery. Help yourself to a glass of wine. There's bottled and draft beer in the bar if you're curious."

"Take your time," he laughed. "I grew up with a house full of sisters." His voice filled with happy mirth. I felt lighthearted as I ran up the stairs.

I jumped in the shower, then scavenged through my closet and the clean laundry piled in the corner. After a quick hot iron restored my grey, polished cotton blouse, I slipped into black silk slacks and added a copper-colored scarf. A touch of deep mauve lipstick, and I looked presentable.

Downstairs, I pulled together a baguette, blue cheese, and roasted pears. And for our entrée, warm spinach salad and butternut bisque with sage cream and spicy shrimp.

"There you are," he said. His voice was warm and gravelly. "You look nice. That rust color suits you. Brings out those touches of red and gold in your hair."

I blushed, surprised by his rush of words and articulate understanding of color.

"Being a bookbinder, it's all about materials and colors, so I always notice that sort of thing." He turned his earnest gaze on me.

"Right," I said. "The sensibilities of an artist." I set our salads on the table.

"Joss, you're no less an artist. Look at this salad. It's a feast for the eyes." He sipped his drink.

"That's the first hurdle," I said, amused by his pilsner glass. I'd been right. He was a beer drinker. "Food has to be visually appealing."

He stood and held out my chair for me. I could feel his warm breath on my cheek and smell the clean soap and water emanating from his skin. He pushed in my chair, and I watched him move to his seat, his gangly body and casual stance. I had let him in, not knowing if he was a good guy or not. I wanted to believe he was; I took the risk.

He sat facing me with clear, unwavering blue eyes. "I'm your soldier," he said.

"What? My what?" My throat went dry. I looked at him, and then quickly away, confused and unsure. My soldier? How could he be my soldier? Then I remembered the story about the desert and the kids chasing each other across the sand in the moonlight. Could those have been my cookies—cookies I had sent to him? And he just showed up now—dropped back into my life. I held back tears of relief, of validation, and of anger. I wanted to yell at him, to tell him how much it hurt me when he just walked away. I pulled myself together and looked back at him, more outraged than confused. "You mean you're Wyatt? My Wyatt? And all this time—"

"Yes, I'm your Wyatt," A slight smile played on his mouth.

"But why—?"

"I'm sorry, Joss. I just had to make sure you were who you said you were. But, yeah, I'm Wyatt Jacobs. I have this letter of yours . . . I keep it with me." He pulled an envelope from inside his jacket and laid it on the table. "I'm sorry; I should have told you the day I met you. I should have—"

It all fell into place—his cautiousness, his mystery.

"Those letters. I'm sorry. I just blathered on like you were a blank canvas."

"No! I looked forward to your letters. When I mentioned that I tried to sing "Waltzing Matilda" to a group of Iraqi kids but forgot the words, you sent them. Who does that? But in this one," he said, pointing to the envelope, "You asked me questions, like where was I born, how many siblings do I have? What is my middle name? Then you provided multiple choice answers. On the middle name question, my choices were: *a. None of your business; b. I'd rather not answer and continue to remain a mystery to you;* and 'c,' which was my favorite: *My middle name is Wyatt—that's right! Wyatt Wyatt Jacobs—what's it to you?* I laughed my head off. It was like you'd known me for years."

"But you never answered."

He looked away, staring out the window. "It's James," he said. "My middle name is James. Wyatt James Jacobs." He looked down at his feet and cleared his throat. "What can I say, I'm a cautious guy."

I nodded. That had always been clear to me.

"Sorry I didn't write much. I watched guys moon over letters and packages from women only out for themselves. Guys sent them their paychecks. Looked for promises from women they barely knew. I had to be sure."

A wave of relief flooded over me. "No, no. It's fine. I understand. You don't have to tell me more. I get it."

"I could tell that about you—that you take everything in," he said.

"Sometimes." I turned away, feeling my face get hot. I liked that he knew me, but it made me feel uneasy.

"A lot of guys were vulnerable over there. But I thought you were different . . . that you *are* different, and I wanted to see for myself. Plus, I was hoping that you might want to send me another care package. You know, cookies, pies, a gourmet meal."

"Well, Wyatt James, I think I've got the meal thing covered."

He laughed. "Yeah, well, how about socks—a couple pairs of those cushy double-soled jobs."

I laughed again. "You like to push it, don't you? Okay, I'll deal—two pairs for a mini bio."

"What do you want to know?" he asked.

"How did you become a bookbinder?"

"My father. He's my inspiration. He was a bookbinder, an artist, really. He did stunning work. I learned from a young age and have always known this is who I want to be—a man like my father, a printer and bookbinder."

"You're lucky. I still don't know who or what I want to be."

"You're a baker, right?"

I shrugged my shoulders. "Yeah. So what's with these books?" I ran my hand over across the lovely red and gilt embossed covers sitting on the corner of the table.

"I brought these to show you—books that I repaired along with 'before' photographs."

He explained that the first volume was a Civil War Era book, though not a first edition. On the title page, he showed me the date of 1870. The date on the verso, the back side of the title page, read 1862. The dates, he said, would have to match for it to be a first, and even then there might be other points—misprints in the first run but corrected in subsequent runs.

I flipped the page back and forth, repeating the word "verso" several times and admiring the marbled endpapers. "This is just beautiful," I said. "Amazing. The transformation from ruined to this."

He smiled shyly and went on to tell me what it took to repair a book: rebacking, replacing a spine and re-sewing the signatures—the groups of printed and folded pages that come together to become the text block. And he told how, when he has pricked his finger while sewing signatures, a drop of blood can be removed with one's own saliva.

I listened intently, admiring his passion.

"It's the enzymes," he went on. "The enzymes in your saliva that remove your own blood—no other," he said. Then he rambled on about headbands—that bit of decorative stitching at the ends of book spines. He did not mean those ornamental snippets of woven threads pasted to the spine of an already bound book, but a head-band that has been stitched as a functional part of a book, cleverly designed to protect the signatures when the volume is pulled from a shelf.

"But what about you?" he asked. "You seem a little ambivalent about being a baker."

"I guess I am at times." My voice drifted. I gazed out the window. "It's a family business, more or less foisted on me. My mother ran it for years, then one day, just left. Handed me the keys, and that was that. I never made a conscious decision of who I'd like to be when I grow up."

Wyatt's eyes widened, his mouth fell open. "Wow," he said. "All I know is that when I'd get a package, my buddies would ask if it was from 'the perfect baker.'"

"Nice," I grinned, "But I'm hardly perfect."

"Pretty close," he said. "Take this salad. It's outstanding—the pears and bacon and warmed dressing."

"Glad you like it. We can have some cookies for dessert." I dipped my fork into my salad. "So I take it your account about the kids running across the sand happened in Iraq? Part of the ruse?" I teased.

"I guess," he shrugged.

"There's more, isn't there?"

"There's always more on anything to do with Iraq." His voice was sarcastic, then flat.

I watched his mouth as he spoke, knowing the words he formed would be surreal.

"There were landmines in that strip of desert. Two little girls were killed that day. The boy lost a leg."

"I'm sorry."

He shrugged. "It happened again and again over there. Kids, women, their soldiers, our guys. . . ."

I imagined those beautiful dark-eyed children kicking up sand with their bare feet, the moon huge over the golden sand. Did they laugh and shriek wildly with their cookies in hand? I turned away. I couldn't tell him that I understood. That we had wandered into each other's darkness.

We still sit in each other's shadows out here in my mother's gloomy house.

"Are you hungry?" he asks. "Have you eaten anything today? I have dinner in the car." The lilt in his voice is hopeful.

"I guess we could eat," I mumble. "I'll set the table."

A few minutes later he comes back in with a cooler. "I brought some homemade ravioli, some with mushroom and the rest with crabmeat."

"From Caputo's in Carroll Gardens?"

"I didn't buy it. I've been practicing with that pasta maker you gave me."

"You made ravioli? Wow!"

"I guess we'll see if it's 'wow' or not."

We sit in the falling light, amidst the silverware clinking against the china plates, ice water tinkling in the glasses.

He says, "The temperature is thirty-three and falling. Maybe you better turn on the heat."

"I will," I say, "after dinner."

"I checked the forecast earlier. Snow's coming in this evening and on into the night."

I nod, quietly eating this too-thick pasta, though I have lied, saying, "No, no, it's perfect! Unctuous, toothsome, Yum-o!" We laugh, lampooning typical food writers. But tonight there will be no happy critique—like maybe you should have added a little more salt, or rolled the ravioli thinner, or what about chilling the dough for a full day?

He says, "I'll go into town and find a room. No sense driving back on icy roads."

"No, stay here," I say, giving the proper response. "I'll make up the bed in the guest room."

He nods. Smiles. "Thanks, but you don't have to. I'll do it."

"Just watch out for the mess in the hallway. I trashed my mother's room."

He raises his eyebrows. "Okay. Should I use the lampshade room?"

I laugh, remembering the first time we made love. We were in that room. Moonlit pillows and his beautiful face above me framed by the lampshade hanging over the bed. It was all I could do not to laugh at the illusion of Wyatt making love to me with a lampshade on his head. I wonder how we have become so broken. Not like a fractured arm where there is poetry in reconstruction, the set bone taken back by blood, by muscle. Or a book once tattered, transformed in the early morning light by a thick threaded needle, turning the twine downward, repairing with a careful weave of stitches. Brokenheartedness is a different creature. There are no reset remedies or stitches that can fill in these gangling wounds.

4

I wake in the morning to no other sounds but ice and wind rattling the windows. The rest of the house is quiet. I tiptoe to Wyatt's room. The door is ajar, his bed made. He must have woken early. I look around downstairs: no breakfast dishes or note saying goodbye. The Weather Channel forecasts a grim day of ice, snow, and probable power outages. I worry that he's driving back to Brooklyn is this mess. He doesn't answer when I call his cell.

Outside, the tree branches, the road, even the telephone wires are all covered in ice. "Wyatt," I holler, but my voice breaks against the sleet. I listen carefully, but I only hear the wind. There is no noise from a vehicle on the road. No one is coming up Sweet Milk Road. The fallen branches rattle and the wind whips against my thin sweater.

I should have been kinder last night, but he digs at me, pushes when I have told him time and again how much that bothers me. How am I supposed to know what I will do with this monstrosity of a house? I don't have answers for any of this and certainly none for Wyatt. I pivot on one foot, sliding on the ice, grabbing at the doorframe for balance. "Goddamn!" I mumble under my breath.

No use standing out here freezing, I think, but as I head in, I hear a motor in the distance. Up over the rise, the hood of a dark blue truck emerges, growing louder against the bluster and freezing snow. It slides and shimmies into my driveway, stopping just short of the porch. The door creaks open, and Wyatt cautiously steps out onto the thin ice, his arms loaded with bags.

"Thought I'd go for a spin," he laughs. "And get some groceries while I was at it. Looks like I'm at your mercy a while longer."

"That's fine," I say, pulling my sweater tighter around my body. "I'm just glad you're safe. I tried calling you, but got no answer."

"I didn't hear it . . . I'll check later." He drops the bags onto the kitchen counter. "Maybe you can put these away while I get the rest. Then I'll make breakfast."

I roll my eyes at his endless instructions on the mundane and more—when to put away eggs, where to hang my jacket, what I should read, who I should invite to lunch, when I should call or visit my father, or how to deal with him. I stow away the groceries, shoving the boxes and cans into the cupboards, then set the table, banging the flatware on the table. I make coffee, hoping a shot of caffeine will improve my mood.

"I got spinach and mushrooms," he says.

"I noticed." He brought home all my favorites. It's what he does—plies me with food when our relationship stumbles.

"How does an omelet sound?" he asks.

"Fine. I'll make toast and peel a couple of oranges to go with them." I resolve to be civil.

"Just like the old days," he says.

We sit together at the kitchen table; it all feels too familiar.

"Look, I'm sorry I'm in your way. I only meant to stop in for an hour—just to see how you were doing."

I wave my hand. "Why is it you think you have to fix everything, including me?"

He looks up at me, wearing that hounded expression, but says nothing.

"God, it never gets any easier between us," I mumble. "But I guess it's good you came. As usual, I didn't think about groceries. I would have been stuck here with nothing but gingersnaps and tea."

"You could have had ant-studded sugar cubes."

"Or I could make pine bark soup."

We both laugh and stare at the mess on the kitchen table.

I turn away and ask, "What do I owe you for the supplies?"

"Nothing. I don't mind. . . . "

"How much? No argument. Okay?"

He smirks. "Your eggs all right?"

"Great as always, Wyatt. What else would they be?" I hear the sarcasm fly off my tongue.

He smiles despite my tone and says, "I got up around six and looked around for something for breakfast. But you know. . . . The weather wasn't too bad then. While I was out, I took a look at that tree house you've talked about. It's in pretty rough shape."

"I know. I looked at it yesterday when I got here."

"It can be repaired. That is, if you're inclined."

"I don't know what I want, Wyatt. Okay?" My voice is caustic and I don't know why I am here. A part of me could fly up into that tree house and never return to ground. And another part that would run and run and keep on running, never looking back in the rearview again.

He flashes that crooked half-smile just as the lights begin to flicker. I wonder if it's apologetic or cluelessness.

"Better get some candles ready," he says.

"I know!" I glare at him. "You think I don't know if the electricity goes, it could be out for days? There are contingencies here for that: candles, oil lanterns upstairs, and bags and bags of ice in the big freezer in the basement."

My head is gone as he blathers on about how everything will green up with the snow melt. And that I should plant a garden with tomatoes, of all things.

"You should have a chicken coop. You could have dinners out here. Madame Marie's farm to table. Twilight dinners with the hens. I bet your Brooklyn customers would come to dine under the stars on a summer weekend."

"Christ, there you go again. I'll bite—the dinners might be interesting, but you know I hate tomatoes." How is it that we still speak like this—in the shorthand of lovers—as if nothing has changed? But that part of Wyatt, his ability to dream out loud, is as endearing as ever.

"Come on, Joss. I'm just looking on the bright side. Trying to to cheer you up a bit."

Wyatt looks down, shakes his head, and says, "Look, I'm trying here. Sorry, I'm telling you what to do again. Old habits. . . . But we've had some good times, too. Remember when we played on that softball team together, and you struck me out?"

I nodded, and chuckled.

"And remember how I got you back?"

"Oh, yeah! The big splat."

"You were a tiger with a high grip on that bat. You should have known it wasn't a red baseball. I never saw anyone wail a tomato like you did."

"You know, I used to grow tomatoes with Miss Euphrates."

"You did?"

"We started them on the windowsills in the winter."

I think back to that first week Miss Euphrates came to stay with me. I was just getting used to her voice, her strange name, and peculiar words, when she announced that we would have to start tomato seedlings—and soon!

"Miss Joss. We gotta get our tomatoes started. It's already halfway through January."

"I hate tomatoes," I reminded her. There are always too many of them, and my father insists I help pick them. It's hot, and the colanders are heavy out in those fields with the stink of rotten tomatoes.

"That can't be! I see you eating red sauce and pasta, dawta-girl."

I held my nose and said, "Tomatoes?"

She laughed. "That's right. Tomatoes! 'Josie Mo's Big Boys,' 'Daddy Jordon's Beefsteaks,' and 'Miss Carrie's Plums.'"

"How come they have names?"

"These seeds come from the same plants passed on and shared. All of us in Churchtown make up packets of seeds to share. We mark the names from who gave them way back. You see?"

I nodded but didn't understand.

"Naming a thing changes it. If you call some plant a weed, then it's a nuisance. With a name, everything becomes part of the known world." Her hands flew through the afternoon light.

I watched and listened and wondered about my names—Boy-o and Paulie-girl. And, of course, my real name, Joss Ellen. But which one was I? How would I ever know?

Miss Euphrates' voice was soft and worn like the pages of a favorite childhood book. "Names give a thing value and use," she said. "Now you take Queen Anne's Lace. That plant will take over a flower garden, but tomatoes—they just love Miss Queen Anne. She protects all that beautiful fruit from all kinds of insect predators."

As she spoke, she showed me how to swirl sheets of newspaper into a mortar and pestle like contraption that turned them into starter pots. We added a mixture of soil, peat moss, vermiculite, bone meal, and lime to the tiny pots, then poked a seed in and misted them. I gingerly set them on trays and carried them throughout the house, upstairs and down, in the sunlight of easterly and southern windows. Every day I checked for tiny sprouts and waited not-so-patiently for them to poke their sleepy heads up through the starting mixture.

"When are they going to sprout?" I asked. "It's been five days."

"You got to be patient, dawta-girl. God don't like being rushed."

Days later the first sprouts appeared from the trays in the warm kitchen. "Look!" I said. "A baby seedling! What do I do next?"

"You feel in the pots, gentle-like, to see if they need water. Too much water rots them, too little and the poor things shrivel. Just a few drops at a time." She handed me the watering can. "No chaka-chaka, now. That means 'don't be messy.'"

Every day I checked the plants in their rolled newspaper pots along the windowsills and poured the water in as carefully as I could. But still I spilled. Then wiped up the dribbles quickly. I didn't want to annoy Miss Euphrates.

"Good job, Miss Joss!"

"Where did you learn those words?"

"My patois?"

I nodded.

"When I was just a dawta, sometimes I lived with my madda. Folks call her Sista Bébé. Other times I lived with my auntie, madda's sister, Miss Dezzarae and her husband, Mr. Henry Moses in the Carolinas."

"How did you get here?" I asked. "Isn't New York a long way from the Carolinas?"

She laughed from her belly. "Yes, yes—long ways, but one day my madda, Sista Bébé, come around to take me back. She got herself a job working for Mr. Gerald and Miss Annika Van Vliet, right here in this house. She told me your grandma, Miss Annika, she come from Wisconsin. Lived on a dairy farm out there. She said that lady could sing and had a whole gaggle of women who come here every week to sing and play the piano—that same old piano that's out in the millhouse now."

I always wondered about my grandparents. My mother never talked much about them. She always said, *The past is gone and buried. Life's for the living.*

"Did you live here, too? With my grandparents?" I asked.

"No, no child. We lived with Henry Moses' brother Edwin out in Churchtown. I never left."

"So you still live with your mother and Mr. Edwin?"

She flashed her wide grin and said, "They all gone to heaven. But Edwin, he had a son my age by the name of Solomon-Joe Moses. When I got old enough I married Solomon-Joe."

"Did you know when you were a girl that you would marry him?"

"I did, child. He was my best friend when we was kids. And always been my best friend."

I wondered if I would meet a boy like that in my new school—a boy I could love forever—if that were even possible. My mother said that Daddy still loved her, but it didn't seem that way to me, or that she even loved him at all. I watched Miss Euphrates; her hands danced, and the lights in her eyes sparkled as she talked about her husband.

"So it was Mr. Solomon-Joe who taught you the patois?

"Solomon-Joe? That man be born and raised in Churchtown. Was mostly my auntie, Miss Dezzarae, who taught me. She lived all over the Caribbean when she was young."

"You didn't always live with your mother?"

"That's right, Miss Joss. Just like you."

I gaped at her, sinking into the kitchen chair as a little piece of me melted away. I didn't like that she knew about me and my mother, even if it was true. But she didn't see me sliding away. She just prattled on.

"I didn't always live with my madda. Miss Dezzarae taught me as much as any mother could have, how to clean and cook, how to care for myself, how to bake pies. I think you and me ought to bake a pie today."

"But, I don't know how to bake pies." And I didn't want to, either. She looked at me squarely, reading my disgruntled expression.

"I'm gonna teach you, just the same. Run upstairs and get yourself an apron."

I plodded up the stairs and opened the linen closet at the top of the stairs. I found only one large apron. I folded it, wrapping it twice around my waist, then tied it in the front the way my mother did in the bakery. It was the apron my father used to wear when he'd make big smiley-faced pancakes on Sunday mornings. We'd all sit at the kitchen table, and each eat one pancake the size of a dinner plate. They'd have indentations for eyes and snaggle-toothed smiles. Maybe if I called him, my father would come to the farm and make pancakes this weekend. I tiptoed into my mother's room, lifted the phone, listened for the dial tone, then called my father's shop.

"Ryckman Tailors."

"Is Mr. Ryckman there?"

"He's with a customer. Whom may I ask is calling?"

"Liam, it's me. Joss. Can you ask my dad if he's coming to make pancakes on Sunday?"

"Oh, Jossy-girl! You sound so grown up; I didn't recognize you."

I giggled at the flirtiness that rolled off his tongue.

"What are you chirping about, little birdy?"

"You make me laugh," I giggled.

"Well. Somebody's got to."

"Will you ask him? You, know, about coming this weekend?"

"Yeah. Sure. Sure."

But there was an edge in Liam's voice. It buzzed over the wires from Canaan to New York City and didn't stop, even as I slid the receiver back into its cradle and ran back downstairs.

"Everything all right, Miss Joss? Did I hear you talking to yourself upstairs?"

I nodded. "I do that sometimes."

We sat at the kitchen table, coring and peeling apples, then slicing them into a bowl, my reluctance fading as I counted the slices as they slid off my knife. Miss Euphrates added handfuls of sugar, pinches of allspice and nutmeg, lemon juice, and zest, and a generous tablespoon of cinnamon.

"Where did you live?" I asked. "You know, when you lived with Miss Dezzarae?"

She flashed me another wide smile and bobbed her head. "We was on the shores of South Carolina, just a ferry boat ride over to a tiny island—I was happiest on the island. We'd go over every Sunday. Mr. Henry and Miss Dezzarae had a vegetable stand there. They sold melons and sweet potatoes, okra, collards, and, of course, homemade pies: sweet potato pie, white potato pie, walnut raisin, strawberry meringue tarts, salvation pecan pie—that one gots coffee in it." She laughed and rolled back her eyes. "Divine!" she declared. "But my favorite is caramel plank porch pie. I make that one in a jelly-roll pan because everybody loves it so."

"I love caramel."

"Next time that's what we'll make. But today we got these pretty apples."

She showed me how to stir the fruit and spices together until it was syrupy and fragrant.

"Now we add a little flour and a little tapioca starch to the apples. That way, when the apples cook, their juices will thicken up. Go on and stir that in."

I used the big wooden spoon and stirred until everything was blended.

"Now we let the fruit set. The next part is the real trick." She took out King Arthur soft pastry flour, sugar, salt, and Calvados.

"First off, you got to have good soft flour. King Arthur is the best. Second, you have to measure. It's not like cooking. This is baking." She showed me how to sift the flour into a bowl and then measure out what we would need. To that, we added sugar and salt.

"Did Miss Dezzarae show you like this?"

"Oh, yes, dawta, just like this. Now you stir the dry ingredients altogether."

She handed me a wooden spoon, and I began to blend the textures.

"Did I ever tell you the story about Mister Henry and the whales?"

I shook my head.

"There was this one Sunday after a storm come through. It filled the channel between the mainland and the island with boatloads of sand, turned that bottle-green sea into a peninsula. What used to be a waterway now was a brand new beach. We had to walk over that new sand, strewn with stranded starfish and horseshoe crabs. There were lost buoys and garbage everywhere. I can tell you we did some high stepping that morning, carrying them baskets of produce and pies."

"How many pies?" I asked.

"Twenty . . . maybe more. It was First Communion Sunday. Lot of folks wanting pie after their picnic lunch." Her eyes sparkled. "We walked along that stretch of new sandy beach, stopping to rest and watch those little dawta-girls up ahead of us. All of them in their pretty white dresses, holding onto their rhinestone crowns, their tulle veils whipping in that wind. It was a sight. The mommas scolding their dawtas for getting sand on their dresses, grabbing their arms with a look that said, 'When we get home, my hand will show you what even Jiizus won't spare you from.'" Miss Euphrates waved her hands and laughed from her belly. "The dadas and the little bwoys all in their fresh haircuts and blue ties. They knew. They stayed back, made sure their ladies took the lead."

I watched her hands as she spoke. They moved in practiced patterns, carefully cutting the pale yellow pats of butter and fluffy white shortening into the flour mixture. To that she added sour cream and another splash of Calvados.

"All those children marched like little brides and grooms down the aisle and took their holy communion. After Mass, they ran out to for a picnic on the green while me and Miss Dezzarae sold pies. But you know what happened?" She looked at me wide-eyed.

I shook my head. "What happened?" I asked.

"In the middle of all that frivolity, Miss Hosanna Mayhew, from the other side of the island, come waltzing into town to tell us that whales been washed up onto the beach."

"Why did the whales do that?"

"Don't no one know, child. Some say crazy weather like that confuses them. We all went down there, not knowing what to do for those helpless giants."

Miss Euphrates shook her head, pressing the pie crust mixture into two balls. She flattened them into disks, then rolled them on their sides until they were even. "Can you wrap the dough in plastic wrap for me? Nice and tight."

I pulled out a sheet of plastic wrap and snugly covered the rounds of pie dough. "How's this?"

"Perfect. Pop 'em into the fridge, and we'll have a cup of tea while they cool."

"What happened to the whales?"

"Must have been a hundred of us began digging holes around those whales. We filled the holes with buckets of sea water to keep the whales cool, and so they wouldn't sunburn."

"Whales get sunburned?"

"Oh yes, child. They under the water most of the time. Not used to all that sunshine."

She wiped her hands on her apron, then pulled the cooled dough from the refrigerator and rolled it out on a floured board. When the dough formed an even round, she folded it over the rolling pin, then unfurled it over the pie plate.

"Now, Miss Joss, you go ahead and add the apples."

She helped me spread the apples evenly and then add the top disk of pie dough. I watched her hands, curling and pinching the crusts together into a running corkscrew shape. She cut in steam vents and cookie-cutter decorations from the crust scraps, then scattered them around the top.

"We going to brush a little cream over the top and sprinkle it with some sugar. Then into the fridge for half an hour before the oven."

"Did the whales live?" I asked.

"Most of them, baby girl, most of them. We stayed with them all night, waiting for the next high tide. Folks brought torches down to the beach. All those beautiful little girls in their white dresses and billowing veils, and the handsome boys just running and running, newly blessed and looking at the tragedy of Jah's helpless creatures in the sand. I sat on Mister Henry's lap, staring into the huge eye of one of those whales."

"Then what happened?" I imagined a whale's eye as big as a manhole cover, as bright as the moon.

"Well . . . Mr. Henry began singing old time songs in that melancholy tone. Telling that whale that he understood. Lord, that man could sing! Come on now, we gotta get that pie in the oven."

We drank more tea. Miss Euphrates hummed tunes I'd never heard before, explaining which ones Miss Dezzarae taught her and which ones were Mr. Henry's. I sat with my hands cupped around my chin trying to imagine what it was like when she was a little girl, singing to that whale, looking into his eye.

"Come on, Miss Joss. We better check on our pie." We peeked through the oven window at the crackly, bubbling crust. I caught the rich aroma of apples and spices.

"Another half hour or so," Miss Euphrates said. "Then we have to let it cool for an hour before we cut it."

It made me hungry, but then I thought of that giant fish stuck in the sand with nothing to eat. "I wish I had been there with you and that whale."

"I know you do, but you know what, those little girls and boys, they sang to the whales, just like Mr. Henry did, just like you would have."

"Did your whale get back into the ocean?"

"No, sweet baby. Not every one of Jah's creatures can be saved."

5

I stand at the kitchen sink, washing our breakfast dishes, Wyatt's and mine. Scraping off the egg yolk, scrubbing everything away. I wish that I could do that with those messy pieces of our lives—clean them off with dishwater, watch them swirl down the drain and be gone. But not everything can be cleaned or saved. I learned that long ago.

My phone rings, and I jump, startled.

"Joss Ryckman?" asks a crisp voice on the other end.

"Speaking."

"This is Officer Dowling at the Fifty-Second Precinct. We have your father, Paul Ryckman, in custody. Allegedly, he pulled a gun on his caretaker at his home."

"I'm sorry, can you repeat that? Did you say he pulled a gun?" My heart races. All I can think is, *God, here we go again.* Two years ago he pulled a gun on the building superintendent over a burned-out lightbulb that sat in the socket a few days longer than my father thought necessary. He went down the back staircase to take out the garbage and smashed his foot against a crate someone left on the landing. Of course, it wasn't his fault the light was out; someone else had to be blamed. So my father methodically went back to his apartment, grabbed a loaded pistol, and knocked on the super's door. In the end, we paid off the superintendent. No charges were filed. It seems this time there isn't going to be any wiggle room.

"Yes, that's right ma'am; he threatened his employee at gunpoint."

"Is anyone hurt?"

"Everyone is okay. But your father is in some serious trouble."

"Thank God that everyone's okay,"

"Can you hold just one minute?"

He clicks off before I have a chance to answer. I sit down because my legs are shaking. If my mother were here, she'd know how to handle this. But she isn't, and it's on my shoulders. I wonder what it will take this time. Or if my father can be saved from himself. Maybe he can plead old age, confusion—whatever will get him off with probation and community service.

"I'm back," Officer Dowling says. "There's more to this, Ms. Ryckman. Your father managed to get himself into a standoff with the officers involved. He seems incoherent and keeps asking for you. Can you tell me anything about him? Is he on medication? Does he have a psychiatric issue?"

"He's—uh—he's on blood pressure medication. That's all. He's a Vietnam vet—"

"Regardless—it's a criminal matter now. He'll be arraigned this afternoon and likely be committed to a psychiatric unit for up to thirty days."

"Where and when will that be?"

"Let's see—"

I wait, listening to papers shuffling on the other end, drumming my fingers while Wyatt looks on; the worry lines track along his face.

"Here it is—um—arraignment at three at the Bronx Criminal Court—the old court building at 15 East 161st."

I write down the address on the back of an envelope that is sitting on the kitchen counter. "I'll be there," I say. Though I didn't know how.

"Good enough."

I hang up and turn away, not wanting to answer any questions from Wyatt. He asks regardless.

"What's going on with your father, Joss? Can I help?"

"No. No. I can handle this. I need to get back to the city by three."

"How are you going to do that in this?" He waves toward the window.

"Christ, I don't know." I slam my phone on the counter. "What's the weather report?" I try to check it, but the connection is slow. "I'm going upstairs; maybe the signal is better up there."

He nods, clearing the table, filling the sink with hot soapy water.

Still no connection. I try my mother's room—nothing, Christ, how am I going to get back there? I sink on the bed, looking around at the mess I made. What I have done to my mother's room, her lovely things. She would be very disturbed by this.

I begin carefully folding the clothes I had tossed out of her dresser, rehanging slacks and dresses. I wonder what I should do with her clothes, her jewelry. My sister Naomi probably would like a lot of Mom's things. Maybe there are a few things I'll keep. Standing at the mirror, I hold up various garments to my frame. But my father's voice plays in my head: You look good in most anything, Paulie-girl, but better in what I make you.

"Joss," Wyatt whispers.

I jump, startled. "I didn't hear you come up the stairs."

"I know." He sits on the edge of my mother's bed. "Is there anything I can do?"

"Can you fly an airplane? Rent a helicopter?"

"I'm afraid that's what it will take to get out of here today. The roads are too icy, but I have an idea."

"Okay, I'll bite."

"Why not call your sister? Maybe Naomi can—"

"Not going to happen. I can't call her and ask her to do *anything* for my father."

"Fine. I'll leave you to your cleaning." He turns, averting his eyes, and slips out the door. His footsteps echo along the long, wide hallway until there is only threaded silence once again.

I wander from room to room, breathing everything in, trying to quell my jangled nerves. In what used to be my room, I gaze out the window over Sweet Milk Road to Edgefield where my first and best friend Fletcher used to live. I wonder who lives there now, what family eats in that tiny kitchen.

My mother and I were invited to a Saturday lunch at Fletcher's house shortly after we moved to the farm.

"Come on in," Mrs. Goodwin welcomed us in her thick southern accent. "Would you like a drink, Mrs. Ryckman?"

"Call me Lydah, but no thanks. Sorry, I don't know why, but I never asked you your first name."

"Why, I'm Reyanne Goodwin, married to that damn swamp-Yankee, Kenny," she said and laughed like tinkling glasses. "I had the unfortunate fate of taking a U-turn in life, falling for a northern creature. No offense, Lydah."

"None taken."

"You sure you wouldn't like a little drink? It's past noon." She laughed again and winked at my mother. "Goodness, where are my manners! Let me take your jackets. Have a seat."

We sat in the hard straight-back chairs while Fletcher's mother checked the oven. It was a cozy kitchen, all sunshine yellow and red checkerboard. Everything in the room matched in some way: the tablecloths and hot pads, canister, casseroles, dishtowels, colanders, and on and on.

I watched our mothers, their pasted-on smiles, their gestures that belied what they really thought and felt, my mother's clipped words in contrast to Mrs. Goodwin's long vowel sounds and colorful expressions.

"Fletcher!" she called. "Your little friend is here. I hope ya'll like fried chicken. I made greens and macaroni and cheese, too. A little Alabama cuisine. Joss tells me you're a baker, Lydah. I never was any good at baking."

"And I'm no good at cooking," my mother laughed.

"Oh, you're just saying that!" She flashed a smile at us, then turned the chicken pieces in the skillet, a cigarette between her fingers. "I bet you're the kind of woman who can do whatever she puts her mind to. Northern girls are like that."

I watched my mother eye Reyanne Goodwin with her high blond ponytail, her tight skirt, and pink sweater.

"I'm good at some things," my mother said. "But not cooking. I'm hoping Joss will learn that from Miss Euphrates. That woman can do it all."

"Well, yes, those people have to, now don't they?"

I had heard Mrs. Goodwin's bigoted comments on our drive to and from school, especially remarks about Miss Euphrates—a hardness and injustice repeated by Fletcher, and no matter how many times I asked him not to say those things, it never mattered to him. Even then, I understood it wasn't Fletcher's fault for repeating what he was taught.

My mother shifted in her chair, cleared her throat, and smiled. "Who taught you all your fine cooking skills, Reyanne? That chicken smells awfully good."

"My momma did. She was accomplished with the spatula and slotted spoon; that's for sure. She passed when I was real young, but not before she indoctrinated me." Reyanne lifted her glass, swirling the amber liquid and clinking ice. She sipped her drink. "At least this warms me. I'll never get used to this cold."

"It has been cold, even by Yankee standards," my mother laughed. "Can I set the table for you, Reyanne?"

"Why thank you! Everything's stacked right there on the counter. And yes, it's near tragic how cold it gets here."

"Layers, you have to dress in layers," my mother said.

"But then, don't you look fat with all those clothes on?"

My mother chortled. "It's either that or turn the heat way up."

"I can't win for trying. My Kenny wouldn't like that either."

"It's colder out here with so few houses," my mother said, as she set pretty china plates around the table. "The wind just whips through. I guess I'm used to it. I grew up on the farm. It was my parents' place and before that my grandfather's and on back."

"So ya'll are just dyed-in-the-wool Yankees!"

My mother chuckled, placing the sterling at each place setting. "This is a lovely pattern. A family heirloom?"

"My Momma's. I thought I'd break out the good things."

"Very gracious of you."

"Lydah, now when did your family first settle here?"

"Sometime in the late 1600s. Dutch sheep farmers and weavers. They grew flax and dammed the river, so they could rot the flax fibers and then weave them into cloth."

"And your husband's a tailor, right?"

"He is."

"So that early tradition continues."

"In a way. Do you work, Reyanne? Outside of being a home-maker?"

"Me? I always wanted to teach."

"Art or history, or . . . ?"

"Grade school, of course. Excuse me." She stood at the bottom of the staircase and yelled, "Fletcher! Lunch is ready. Come on down," then pulled out a bottle of bourbon from a low cabinet and poured another drink.

Fletcher clomped down the stairs, barely looking at me. He sat but was quiet—sullen through most of lunch as his mother prattled on and drank.

"Fletcher," I whispered while my mother and Reyanne Good-win chatted. "You want to come over tomorrow? I can show you my tree house."

"You got a tree house?"

I nodded. "My daddy built it."

"Can I, Ma? Go to Joss' house tomorrow?"

"Why not? But after church."

I remember walking home from that lunch with my mother, and her saying, "Honey doesn't stand a chance on those pouty lips." I asked what that meant, but she just laughed and called Reyanne, "a certain kind of a woman with those dew-drop eyes." I didn't understand what that meant either, but as I stand in the window now, looking out over the road, I don't think Reyanne Goodwin was any more damaged than we were.

I finish tidying up, then dust and vacuum all the rooms upstairs until it looks good enough for my mother.

"Hey, where are you?" I holler to Wyatt from the staircase.

"In the living room—reading."

"Another military book?" I ask.

"What else is there?"

"Right! I'm going to make some tea. You want some?"

"Sure."

When it's ready, I hand him the hot mug and sit with him. "I'm sorry. I cut you off. Not that I'm under any obligation to take your advice, other than to receive it with amusement."

"Well, this is a first. The apology, I mean. I know I have a way of pushing too hard."

I nod and smirk.

"But it seems like whatever is going on with your father is an emergency situation. Under those circumstances, maybe Naomi could help."

"She doesn't want anything to do with my father. She hasn't seen him in twenty years."

"But you could try. She might be willing."

"Look Wyatt," I said, my voice edgy and raised. "We're just not that close. And I know it was harder on her than me, losing Mom. I'd feel uncomfortable asking her to do that. I'm trying to maintain my humor here. But I have to say, this is not your business anymore. You know?"

"You're right, Joss. I'm sorry."

It was true. We were not very close, Naomi and I. She was twelve years older and my mother's favorite while I was my father's Boy-o. In our little quartet, each parent claimed one of us as their own. It left little room for a close sisterly relationship. And I guess I never tried to bridge that distance. She left home when she was seventeen, announcing at dinner one night that she was pregnant and going off to live with her boyfriend. I was only five and didn't understand.

My father had shot up from the table, screamed at Naomi, knocked a pitcher of water over, and slapped her hard across her cheek.

"You are no longer my daughter! You hear me?" His face was bright red, his mouth a thin red slash.

I had never seen him like that before. It confused me, and I was frightened. If Naomi was no longer his daughter, would that happen to me, too?

She was gone when I got up the next morning. My mother told me that her boyfriend had picked her up early, headed to California.

It wasn't until I was older that I found out that she stayed in California with her boyfriend for only a few months before she moved back to New York. She moved into one of the apartments above my mother's bakery and waited for the birth of her son.

6

I wake too early in the morning, a strange dream still playing in my head. In the narrative, my sister Naomi is an old woman who tells me she is going to have another baby. Another boy. I lie in my rumpled bedclothes while the peculiar dream evaporates and the demands of the day take hold. I pad to the bathroom and quietly shower. Wyatt is still sleeping, and I don't want to disturb him. Downstairs the coffee maker is ready to go. Wyatt must have gotten it ready before he went to bed. I write him a note and leave for the city. But before I go, I stand by the hall mirror, wrapping myself in one of my mother's beautiful scarves, and put on a pair of her crystal earrings. By ten o'clock, I arrive at the Bronx Psychiatric Hospital with a chocolate milkshake in hand and find my way to my father's room.

"Hey, Dad, how are you doing?"

"You got to get me home, Paulie-girl! They're doing terrible things to me."

He looks haggard, his hair is wild and uncombed, his eyes rheumy. "Remember we agreed? You have to call me by my name—not Paulie-girl, not Boy-o. Just Joss."

He ignores me as he struggles in his bed, restrained at his wrists. "Go down and start the van, Boy-o," he whispers.

"Not yet. Your doctors say you've got to stay awhile. You have to deal with your anger issues."

"Anger issues? What anger issues? Fly me outta here, Boy-o."
His eyes are instantly steely, but his voice is broken.

"To start with, haven't we had enough with the guns?"

"Goddamn, what *we*? As far as I remember, you've only fired a
gun once. I was just trying to teach you how to how to hit a target.
Everyone should know how to use a weapon."

I want to tell him that not everyone wants or needs to know
how to fire a gun, me included. But he will never understand that.
He always has to be right. . . .

When I was seven years old, we went to the farm for spring clean-
up earlier than usual. It was the first week of March and my school
had closed for extensive repairs. The boiler had gone down, and
the sprinkler system froze and burst, ruining ceilings and floors
throughout the building.

"We're going out to Red Mills, Paulie-girl. You're off school
for at least a week, so I decided to take some time off, too."

The next morning we headed out before dawn. We took the
same route we always did, up and down the rolling hills heading
north, the tunes humming on the radio, and me drifting in and out
of sleep. By seven, we made our usual stop at the West Taghkanic
Diner and had breakfast, eggs Benedict for Dad and pancakes for
me as my father flirted with all the waitresses.

I turned away, pretending not to notice. Where once my father
had seemed bigger than life and I was proud to be his Paulie-girl,
I was now embarrassed. I hated watching my father coo and fawn
over old women or young girls; it didn't matter which, as long as
they laughed and paid attention to him.

When we arrived at the farm an hour later, there were still a couple inches of snow on the ground. The sky was clear and bright blue, the temperatures warmer. It was a near-perfect sunny day in late winter.

We started right in, cleaning the kitchen and both bathrooms. We dusted, vacuumed, and made up the beds in my dad's room and mine.

"Come on, Paulie-girl. It's noon. Let's have lunch. Enough cleaning for today."

We sat at the kitchen table having soup and grilled cheese sandwiches.

"How come we're not cleaning the way we always do?" I asked.

"Because I've got a different plan for today. Come on, Boy-o! Let's get some fresh air."

I nodded and slipped my small hand into his, singing as we hiked to the dam. We stood close to the edge. I looked down at the stanners, a torrent of water striking the rocks, the spray in our faces. He held me back while I tried to wriggle away.

"I don't want you to slip," he said.

"I won't, Daddy. I never will."

He laughed.

"Do fish ever go over the falls?" I asked.

"Probably."

"What happens to them?"

"They just swim downstream."

I doubted that was true. I couldn't imagine any living thing hitting those boulders and surviving.

"Let's go on a little hike, Paulie-girl."

I nodded as we trudged on through the snow-covered cornfield, through the cornstalk stubble that had survived the winter. In the distance, we saw wild turkeys and crows pecking at whatever tidbits had weathered the winter.

"Just a little farther," he said, as we crossed the scarred field where a section of the barbed wire fence had been torn down. We turned and headed back toward the riverbank.

"What happened to the fence?" I asked.

"Oh, I took some of it down for a little project. It'll go back up in the spring."

I couldn't image why he did that. He had always made sure the fences were in good shape for winter; it helped to prevent drifting snow and kept the deer away from the shrubbery, or so he claimed.

"Do you see up ahead? Up in that tree on the edge of the river?" he asked.

"I see it, Daddy. Is that a tree house?"

"That's right. I built a tree house. Started it last November during deer season. We're here on this trip to finish building it. You and me, Boy-o."

"You built me a tree house, Daddy?"

"Well—yeah—sure, you can use it sometimes. Mostly I built it so I can watch over my cornfield."

"Oh," I said, trying to hide my disappointment, but I couldn't understand why a grown-up would want a tree house. Weren't tree houses for kids? Maybe it was a trick, and it was my tree house, after all.

We stood at the base of the supporting oak, looking up at the deck and the icy ladder leading to the door of the cabin.

"But won't it be hard to climb the ladder with all the snow?"

"Don't you worry! I got you."

I raised my arms and said, "Up, up, Daddy," and laughed. Even though I wasn't a little girl anymore—I was almost eight years old—I still liked to pretend. He hoisted me up to the fifth rung, and I scrambled up, simian-style, to the top. "I beat you, Daddy."

"Only because you tricked me, Boy-o!"

It was cold up there with openings where the windows and doors would go. There was a kitchenette with a place for a window over the sink, a cutout in the roof, and double-wide spaces that looked out over the cornfield. And on the other side of the cabin in the trees, there was an outside deck with a railing that hung out over the river.

"We're going to be closing everything in. Putting in windows and doors. But before we can do that, I need you to sweep out the snow and debris. You can do that, right? Just be careful out on that deck."

I nodded and began sweeping out the crusty snow and cobwebs, dried leaves, and acorns while my father measured and took notes.

"Right here, out over the cornfield," he said. "We'll have a big double window that opens on each side just like two doors, and here on the other side there's going to be a glass door that leads to the deck. Come on out here."

I was afraid and hesitated.

"Come on," he said, motioning me forward. "There's a railing all around, so it's safe."

I stood frozen to the floor.

"Get out here!" he barked. You're making a big deal over nothing."

I inched my way out onto the deck that hung out over the river. The roar of the water and the ringing in my head made me woozy.

He grabbed my arm and pulled me the rest of the way out onto the deck. "There, that's not so bad, is it?

He stared at me, and I didn't say anything.

"Is it?" he demanded.

"No, it's not bad, Daddy."

"Good girl. Now right here is a trap door." He lifted a small opening in the deck floor. Below we could see the river and all the rushing water.

"In the summer, we'll hang a rope ladder so you can jump off and swim in the river."

"But the water is so fast, Daddy. How will I be able to swim in the river?"

"There's not a thing to fret about, Paulie-girl. Your old man knows what he's doing. The river is deepest in this section. It will calm in the summertime. Just like a lazy pool."

It sounded good, but I wondered if that was true.

"Come on, let's go down and get this project going."

We went into town to the hardware store to pick up the windows and doors he had ordered, along with more lumber and nails.

"One of your jobs this week is to paint the cabinets. So why don't we pick out a color?"

"Any color?"

"Not pink, Boy-o. I know how you're always pushing for 'pink this' and 'pink that,'" he laughed. "We don't want it to look like a dollhouse, do we?"

I shook my head no, but a special place for me was what I wanted. In the end, we settled on butter-yellow for the cabinets with red knobs and mineral oil-finished pine for the counters.

In the morning, a couple of my father's friends came over and helped him. I stood at the bottom, watching as they jerry-rigged a block and tackle, then hauled up the lumber, windows, and doors through the wide window opening.

"That's a goddamn fancy crow blind, Paul," one of them hollered.

"What's a crow blind?" I asked.

"A place where your old man can hide and pick off crows with a shotgun."

"But he doesn't kill them," I said.

"Kid, your old man's a crack shot. Whatever he aims at is a goner for sure."

I didn't know what a "goner" was, but it didn't sound good. And I had seen him do that—stand out in the cornfield shooting at the crows. When I asked, my mother always said that he shot into the air to scare off the crows. But now I wasn't sure.

We spent the next three days up in the cabin, as it rocked gently back and forth in the wind. I painted all the cabinets in the small kitchenette behind a plastic screen to keep the sawdust out while my father sawed and nailed and measured, shimming the windows and doors in place. I moved on to the woodwork and plank walls, painting them shiny white and clean. Late in the afternoon on that third day, I painted the door a deep red color while my father painted the floor in green deck paint, working his way out the door and down the ladder.

"Now, Boy-o, we let the paint dry for a couple of days before we go back up and put on the finishing touches."

"What will we do for the next two days?" I asked.

"How about we have some fun?"

"Sure," I said. So far, not too much of our trip had included anything that was fun for me.

"But first we need to spiff up, Paulie-girl. Can't have this city tailor dressed down just because we're north of the city."

"But I didn't bring anything special."

"I got you covered. There's a garment bag hanging in your closet." He smiled and winked at me. "I'm going to take a shower and I'll meet you downstairs when you're ready."

I ran up the stairs two at a time and laid the bag across my bed. I held my breath but didn't look inside. I wanted to be clean and ready to try on whatever my father had made for me. As soon as I showered and toweled off, I ran back to my bedroom, unzipped the bag, and dressed as quickly as I could. The silky feel of the garments sliding over my head was brand new to me. I stretched the lacy tights over my legs and fastened the little black ankle boots, then ran to my parents' room to gaze into the mirror at a girl I didn't recognize.

"You ready, Paulie-girl?"

"I am," I said as I clicked my heels down the stairs. I could barely wait for my father's reaction.

He was standing on the landing, with a wide smiled painted across his face. "Look at you, Cinderella. You're stunning!"

And I felt like I was. He had made me a puffy black and white polka dot skirt with a lacy petticoat that peeked out from below the hem. And a white blouse with roll up sleeves. But the best part was the pink moiré vest.

"I can't believe you made me something pink, Daddy." I hugged him, smelling his cologne, feeling the roughness of his beard across my cheek.

"What about me?" he asked. "Don't I get a wolf whistle at least?"

"You always look good. I like your Windsor cap."

"Always go with a classic, Paulie-girl, though I guess I should call you Joss tonight."

"Why, Daddy?"

"Just look at yourself! You're all grown up."

We went out to dinner at a local family restaurant. It was nothing like the Floridian on Flatbush Avenue. There was no welcoming committee of comely waitresses; the other diners didn't smile or nod, or admire either of us. Instead, they stared with hard eyes or turned away with a smirk—except for a pair of old ladies with blue-gray hair and beaded clip-on earrings—they smiled and nodded, and one of them said, "Don't you look cute, honey!"

Someone else laughed and mumbled, "Flatlanders."

"What's a flatlander?" I asked as we slid into a green vinyl booth.

"A flatlander," my father answered in a voice too loud, "is a dashing dad and his beautiful daughter displaying their plumage and sophistication out here in the sticks."

A few people chuckled and smiled at me. But the rest of them sniggered and shook their heads. Somebody shouted out, "Where's the band? Cause I think there's gonna be a dance here tonight."

I was embarrassed and didn't like being the punch line of some gruff joke. "Should we leave, Daddy?"

"Hell, no. We got just as much right to be here as the rest of these jokers." He smiled and touched my cheek. "You look beautiful, Joss. Sit tall and be proud of yourself."

I laughed behind my hand and squared my shoulders, smoothing my skirt. I read the menu in my best-animated voice, this time laughing loudly with my father.

The owner's wife, with a dishtowel over her shoulder, pulled a pencil from behind her ear and scribbled our drink order while we looked over the menu. When our drinks arrived, my father's Dewars—they were all out of Glenfiddich—and my plain Coke, we clinked our glasses while our impatient waitress rolled her eyes.

"What'll it be?" she asked, with an edge to her voice.

"A fish fry for me and my beautiful daughter."

"Fish Fry, times two!" she yelled over her shoulder. "It'll be right out," she said, pivoting with her stockinged thighs swishing like sandpaper.

Our fish platters arrived ten minutes later. We stared at the soggy coleslaw, my father moving it around on his plate. He tucked a napkin inside the top of my shirt. "No sense ruining your new clothes," he said. "Dig in!"

I nodded, eating the French fries with my fingers and eyeing the thick-battered cod and jarred tartar sauce.

"At least the fries are good. Right, Joss?"

"They're crispy," I shrugged. But mostly they were soggy, just like the coleslaw. "I like them with the salt," I said, licking the brackish crystals from my lips.

"Me, too. With lots of salt. Kind of makes up for the quasi-fried fish," he whispered. Neither of us had eaten much of it.

I laughed. "Should we try the pie for dessert? The menu claims it's homemade."

"Why not! And a cup of what they euphemistically call coffee."

The pie was divine, the best pie I had ever had in my eight years. Apples with lots of cinnamon topped with caramel and walnuts. And a melt-in-your-mouth crisp, buttery crust.

"This is delicious, Daddy. You should have some."

"No, no. You enjoy!" He smiled, reaching over to pat my hand. "In the morning, I have another surprise for you."

"What is it?"

"I can't tell you. Then it wouldn't be a surprise."

"Come on, Daddy, tell me!"

He laughed and smirked and rolled his eyes. "You girls! You're all the same."

I didn't know what that meant or how all girls could be the same. When we got home, I looked at myself in the mirror, my curly hair springing out all over my head, my eyes wide-set, flint grey eyes in the yellow lamplight of my room. I lay in my bed playing itsy-bitsy spider along the shadows spilling over my bedroom walls.

I made phantom dogs and dusky rabbits by contorting my hands and fingers just like I learned in art class. My shadow creatures hopped and raced along my bedroom walls, chased by a granny goat and an elephant. They turned and raced, hiding and contorting while I laughed and whispered their silly names.

My father tapped at my door, asking, "Who are you talking to?"

"I'm just playing," I said.

"Lights out, Boy-o. We've got a lot to do in the morning."

I rolled over and turned off my light and then pulled out the sketch pad from beneath the mattress, along with the tiny flashlight I had hidden there. Inside the faded pages were stick figures and cityscapes, flying fish and diving birds I had drawn when I was six. Tucked between the pages were notes to my sister, who had left when I was five, and questions I wanted to ask my mother but knew she would never answer.

I whispered in the dark that no matter what my father said, I wasn't like other girls. I wasn't like anyone else I knew.

I woke up early the next morning to the sunlight washing through my room. I remembered what my father had said and ran downstairs in my scuffed fuzzy slippers, looking for my surprise. He was sitting at the kitchen table with a long cardboard tube on the table and curved triangular pieces of balsa wood.

"These are fins," he said.

"Like fish have?"

He laughed. "Kind of."

I wondered if he was making a cardboard fish, and if it would be like my shadow creatures.

"These are for a model rocket," he said.

"A rocket?"

"Yup! You and me, Boy-o, we're making a model rocket today." He cut the last fin with a utility knife and a straight edge while I stood there. "Then we're going to take it out into the field and launch it."

"You mean like into outer space?"

He laughed. "Not quite, Boy-o. But she'll fly a thousand feet high. You'll see." He grinned and laughed. "How about some breakfast? You can whip up eggs, can't you?"

I nodded, grabbing a bowl, and swirling eggs and milk into it. I buttered toast and spread jam while my father sanded and glued the fins to the rocket base.

"And how about some tea?" he added.

I put on the kettle and poured the eggs into an oiled pan and popped it into the oven. I swept up, watching over my shoulder while my father attached the clear plastic tubes where the launch wire would guide the rocket straight and true.

"Put the broom away, and come on over here. I'll show you how to get this baby ready for flight."

I stood in his shadow. He showed me how to fold the parachute and precisely pack it into the tube of the rocket. Then he shook out the folds and handed it to me. "Now you do it," he said.

I tucked and folded and tried to make the thing fit, but like always, he drummed his fingers and sighed in that stuttering exhale against the sharp whistle of the tea kettle.

He grabbed the bright nylon fabric from my clumsy hands. "Turn the kettle off," he snapped.

"Some days, Boy-o, I wonder if you're even my kid! You think you can manage to crumble up the fireproof sheets and pack them into the tube?"

I nodded but didn't look up at him. He'd said that before—about me not being his—and I had wondered if there was a whole other family somewhere missing me, looking for me. That I was their child. And that I would somehow fit into their world.

I stood quietly crumpling sheets of paper as my father had showed me. "What are these for?" I asked, keeping my voice even.

"So the whole assembly doesn't flame out." He looked at me, shaking his head, then refolded the parachute and inserted it at the top of the tube. "You think you can put the nose cone on? All you have to do is push it down into the opening."

I pushed back my chair and headed for the stairs.

"Where you going? You know I'm doing this for you."

"I have to use the bathroom."

But I stayed upstairs, organizing the bookshelves in my room, rearranging my closet. I carefully hung the puffy polka dot skirt and the pink moiré vest at the back of the clothes rack.

I wasn't Cinderella anymore.

The rest of the afternoon I spent coloring, and reading. I didn't return downstairs until I heard my father leave for the rest of the day.

The rocket sat in the middle of the kitchen table, painted in bright red with precise pinstripes along the fins. Beside it was a note saying that there was a tuna sandwich in the fridge for me, that he had errands to run and that the rocket launch was now postponed until the next morning He signed it with a smiley face—his de rigueur apology—and I smiled ruefully.

The following morning the sky was coppery blue, the color indigenous to late winter. We trekked out to the cornfield after breakfast, my father carrying the launch pad attached to a tripod.

"You want to help me connect the battery pack? That's the thing that ignites the rocket."

I looked at him, shuffling my feet in the snow. "Not this time, and besides, I won't do it right."

"Come on, Paulie-girl, you can do it. I promise I'll be patient."

His eyes were kinder, soft the way they were sometimes when he was happy.

I nodded.

"Good girl! It's pretty simple. We've got two small clamps and two igniter wires. One clamp for each wire. Make sure the clamps don't touch. Just like charging a car battery."

I didn't know anything about car batteries or clamps or their wires, but I nodded and smiled and connected the wires to the launch controller, just like my father showed me. It was easy.

"Okay, now we have to step back twenty feet, check the sky, and then we launch."

We looked for planes overhead, and jet trails, just to make sure we didn't scare some pilot up there in the clouds.

"We're clear," he said.

I could have lain in that snowy field and watched those white pencil lines move across the blue and copper morning for hours, tracing their movements into the dusk of day. I wondered how it felt to fly above the earth, to see the towns and roads and rivers. And I wondered, too, about the people on those planes. Maybe there were girls like me on board, or my secret family who would be proud of me regardless of my clumsiness. I stood in that moment under that peacock sky and knew then that my parents would never see me, would never know me.

"You ready?" my father hollered.

I nodded as the sun washed over me.

He inserted the safety key, and we counted down together.

"Five, four, three, two, one. Blast-off!"

We both pushed the button. The rocket hissed off the launch pad, screaming through the blue morning sky until neither of us could see it.

"Where is it? Where is it?"

"Keep watching, Paulie-girl."

We heard the secondary charge pop the nose cone and release the parachute, but we didn't see it floating down until ten seconds later.

"There it is, Daddy." I ran across the field, reaching up until the rocket was in my hands.

"So? Whaddya think?"

"We should build another rocket."

He laughed. "Next time we come out, we'll do that. Right now, we gotta check out the tree house."

I ran across the field scanning the sky, looking for more jet trails. I imagined rockets whizzing overhead whirling and spinning.

"Quit your daydreaming and come on up here." My father stood in the tree house doorway fifteen feet above my head.

I scrambled up the ladder and walked around the bright cabin, running my hands over the shiny counters. "It's so pretty up here."

My father opened the new double-wide windows. "This is why I built this tree house. Look at this view! I can see my tin scarecrow and the whole expanse of my cornfield."

"I like your scarecrow, Daddy." He'd cut it on a band saw, a tin figure that was more whimsical than frightening. And painted it in sharp colors with a silhouette of a black crow sitting on the tin man's hat.

"Get the hell off my man, you murderous crows," he yelled out the window. A half dozen of those fat jackals had lighted on the head, the shoulders, and the pointing finger of his wistful tin man.

"Why don't you like the crows?" I asked.

"Because they can pick a cornfield clean, pull the shoots right out of the ground. I've seen them hop from plant to plant hopscotch style, right down a row, pulling seedlings up by the roots."

"But don't you always have extra corn?"

"That's not the point. Bring my shotgun over," he said. "It's by the stove."

I hesitated, afraid of my father's guns.

"Come on, Boy-o. Bring it on over. Just don't touch the trigger."

"I don't want to, Daddy."

"Don't make me ask again, Joss."

His voice was frosty, and I knew not to push any harder. I gingerly carried the gun across the cabin and pushed it towards him. He grabbed it and wrapped his arm around me, pulling me onto his lap.

"No," I said. "I'm afraid."

"That's ridiculous!" he said with bark and spittle.

I nodded, not knowing what else I could do.

"Now here, I'll show you." He laid my finger around the trigger. "Don't squeeze your finger back just yet," he said. "Just let your hand relax."

I did what he told me.

"Now look down the sight. What do you see?"

"I don't know."

"Come on, Joss, look down the sight."

I didn't want to look. Instead I tried to count the seconds in my head. But I felt sick to my stomach, dizzy and confused, afraid of what was happening. Of what he would make me do.

"I see snow," I said. "Lots of snow."

"And . . . ?"

"Crows. I see three crows."

"Right, there you go. We're going to line up on one of them—the biggest one. Do you see it?" He moved the rifle ever so slightly. "Joss, do you see it?" The edge was back in his voice.

I nodded.

"Christ, don't nod. Don't move. Now we have to line up again."
He repositioned the rifle. "There, we're on target. Just push back
gently on the trigger."

"No. . . ." I whispered and tried to pull away, but he clamped
down on my hand and pushed my fingers until the shot fired
through the air, shoving us back slightly. I watched the crow sitting on my father's tin scarecrow pop up into the air, its feathers
scattered as it toppled backwards.

"Take that, you bastard crow," he laughed.

"You killed it, you killed it," I whispered.

"No, Joss, you did. You killed it."

"Cause you made me!" I yelled.

"What's the big deal? It's just one crow."

"You're a jerk, just like Mom says." I pulled away from his grip
and stood looking up at him. Daring a response.

"Don't you yell at me!" He raised his arm and slapped me hard
across the cheek. The sting took my breath away as quick tears
streamed down my face.

"Boys don't cry! Stop that goddamn crying!"

I screamed back, shocked at my own voice, "I'm not a boy,
Daddy! And I'm not going to wear those stupid clothes you make
anymore."

I saw the hurt look on his face and felt torn, not wanting to disappoint him, but not wanting to be the little boy I would never be.

"I'm right!" he yelled. "You'll see I'm right."

But he wasn't right at all, and his position has not wavered over
the years. He has a fierceness that aches through his bones and
spills out like an open hydrant. I wonder if it can ever be tethered.

I lay my hand over his bound one as he lies in his psych-ward hospital bed. He rolls his head across the pillow.

He asks, "Pops? Is that you? Is he in the other bed, Paulie-girl?"

My dad thinks his father is here, too. "He is," I say, but there is no one in the other bed. "But he's sleeping and he wants you to get some rest, too." My father settles down, thankfully submitting to this phantom authority. I feel momentarily relieved and think his Pops, too, must have been a lit fuse.

He looks at me, stares at me for the first time since I arrived. "What are you wearing, Joss? That scarf's not you."

"Enough, Dad."

"Shhhh! Shhhh! Don't wake him." He nods toward the empty bed. And then begins trying to thread an imaginary needle, carefully picking up something from the bed covers.

"What are you doing?"

"What? You've never seen me sew on buttons before?" He chuckles and shakes his head. "Loosen up my hands, will you?"

I untie his wrist restraints, and he smiles. "You're the only one I can count on."

I watch him twisting strands of invisible thread into a knot. His hands race, too fast to follow.

"What time is it?" he asks. "This suit has to be finished by nine." The ties from his loosened wrist restraints dance as he sweet-talks the needle with a thimble no one else can see. "I disappointed Lenny Ornstein once. Not going to let that happen again. Not good for business."

"Dad," I say. "Lenny says to wait till next week, when you're feeling better."

"Jeezus, did you see that?"

"That? I missed it. It went by too fast." He slashes at the light from the window, and I think his demons are flying out of his head.

He cannot control what he has left unmended. I stroke his forehead, but he pulls away.

"Pay attention!" he barks. "How can I finish if you don't watch out for me? I can't disappoint Lenny again."

The bitterness rises in my throat, but I tell him, "You won't, Dad. Lenny sent over this chocolate milkshake." I take the plastic cup from the bag and insert the straw. "He's not upset. It's all okay."

"Jeez, he didn't have to do that." My father's hands fall to the bed sheet, and I hold the straw to his mouth as he sucks in the icy chocolaty drink.

7

With one last swallow of my thick chocolate latte, I unlock the door to my father's apartment. The reek of garbage and dirty laundry choke the air. The place is in disarray: furniture shoved into corners, a chair overturned, clutter and broken glass everywhere—evidence of the struggle that ensued here. And I don't know whether to scream or cry as I sit in a now upright chair. But there is no time to feel sorry for my father or myself. There are rooms to straighten and bed sheets to change. I sort his dirty laundry, wondering why it's been left undone. What are his caretakers doing, if not this?

The busy work isn't enough to push back the sorrow and anger of forever picking up the pieces of my parents' lives. Or the emptiness of always being left behind. I dust and run the vacuum before I tackle the kitchen.

While I am cleaning out the refrigerator, I hear a timid knock at the door. I recognize the tapping; it's my father's neighbor Jeannette.

"Hello, Joss," she says. "I heard the vacuum running and I thought you might be here." She looks more delicate than when I last saw her, stooped and shorter. She holds onto a stack of mail, her hand shaking, and leans on the cane in her other hand.

"I'm so happy to see you, Jeanette. Come in, come in! Have a seat."

We sit by the window; the late morning light has that pale cast. "Is that Dad's mail?"

She smiles and nods. "How is he?"

Her voice is so tiny; I strain to hear her. "You were here during the incident?"

She nods, her white, wispy hair falling across her eyes. "Oh, yes. It was terrible. The police took him out in handcuffs. I heard that he threatened Miss Ortiz with a gun. Is that true?"

"I'm sorry to say, it is. He's at the Bronx Psychiatric Hospital for the next month. Maybe longer."

"Oh, dear."

"I know. I just came from there after seeing his doctors, but I don't think he realizes the seriousness of his situation. He's medicated right now. Apparently, he was belligerent yesterday."

"I'm so sorry. Is there anything I can do—go talk with him?"

"If I thought he'd listen to you, I'd bring you over right now."

"Well, maybe later on," she says. "When he's more settled. We always had a good rapport."

"I know you did. You and Dad take care of each other."

And they always had. He told me when my mother left him, it was Jeannette who sat with him in the evenings, listened to his despair, and comforted him in her quiet way. I always thought she was secretly in love with him. She never appeared to have anyone special in her life. I thought it was sad that he never really saw her. Jeanette and I have that in common. Both of us chasing after crazy love, mixed-up love, love that never accepts us just as we are.

I smile at her. "How are you these days?"

"I'm still here," she laughs. "I knit every day, though it's a challenge."

I watch her gnarled hands shake with Parkinson's and admire her perseverance.

"I do small chores and errands," she continues. Her voice is shaky. "But I seldom go out. It's just too much for me, now."

"I see you still manage to get the mail."

She chuckles and hands me a stack of letters and flyers. "It's like you said. Your father and I look out for each other. We're the oldsters here!" she sighs.

"Let me give you a key, so you can just come in whenever you want. You don't mind dropping off his mail, do you?"

"Of course not. It keeps me young," she laughs. "And don't bother about a key. I already have a set. And he has a set of mine, even my car keys."

"I didn't know you still drive."

"I don't, but in case the urge strikes, I still have a car. I'm not ready to give that up, too!"

"Good for you, Jeannette. How about some tea? I'm about to make myself a cup."

She smiles and nods, and we chat on about the young people in the building, the gossip, and how so much has changed. Before she leaves, I give her the produce and condiments from the refrigerator: apples, a bag of mixed greens, mustard, mayonnaise, and some fresh pasta and sauce.

By one o'clock that afternoon I make it to Madame Marie's. It's busy: people waiting in line at the bakery counter, the dining room and the bar filled with lunch patrons, and the baker restocking the case. I am happily lost in the bustle. I don an apron, wash my hands, and sidle up to Lynn, my day manager. "I'm in town seeing my father," I say in my cheeriest voice. "I thought I'd come over and give you a hand."

"Hey," she says. "Happy to see you."

"What can I do for you? Serve? Wait on customers? Bus?"

"Bakery customers! We're having a run on gingerbread tarts."

"Good. Glad they're going well." For the next hour, Lynn and I tag-team, filling bakery boxes and bread bags with cornmeal yeast rolls, lemon cheesecakes, iced macaroons, delicate petit fours, and all manner of baked goods. We restock the cases and run the register, all the while cleaning and wiping the glass counters.

When the rush subsides, we sit in the dining room for a quick lunch. "Everything looks great, Lynn. Looks like you've got a handle on things."

"Thanks. Course, you know how it is: the gossip, who's sleeping with who, prima donna cooks, the call outs—and then there's the real work of rushes and substitutions."

I hold my head in my hands. "Oh, Lord, I know how it is. Can I help you? I'm okay being the bad guy."

"I'm good for now," Lynn says. "How's it going out there at your farm? How's Wyatt?"

I turn away, wondering what to say about all the complications of my life. I don't welcome her questions, mostly because I don't have the answers; still I charge forward.

"I guess the big news is that Wyatt and I are no longer together."

She looks at me with buzzing horsefly eyes. "Really? What happened?"

I want to tell her life happened and that I have reasons that at some moments justify our breakup—his never-ending *suggestions*, his always pushing for what he wants, always wanting to be in charge in a seemingly sweet and quiet way. And then there are the moments when I doubt myself, when walking away from Wyatt feels like ripping out my own heart. Despite my confusion, I know

I don't want to be told what it is I want. Maybe walking away from him proves that I can, or maybe I'm just a kid stomping her feet. I laugh under my breath at my own ridiculousness.

Lynn stares at me, shifting in her chair. "What's so funny?" she asks.

"I'm just laughing at myself—we're all foolish sometimes."

"I don't know what that means. Sorry, I shouldn't have asked."

"It's okay. Like you say—gossip! I might just as well put it out there."

Lynn laughs. "That's one way."

"Don't get me wrong, Wyatt's a great guy, but he's too interfering. He needs to work on his issues, not mine. You know what I mean?"

"I guess. But that's what guys do. Either that or they don't give a shit."

"Right, all or nothing. Where are the guys in the middle?"

"Taken."

We both laugh.

But I wonder if I've gone too far, said too much. I smile at her and finish the dregs of my coffee. "Well," I say, "don't hesitate if you need something. A day off—whatever."

"I will. I hope you're doing okay. We heard about your father."

"Yeah, thanks. It is what it is."

She nods.

"I'm taking off now. I'll see you in a couple of days." I squeeze her shoulder as I leave to head for my car.

The roads are wet and slick in places; I have snow tires, so that helps. Still, I push to get back to Canaan before the roads freeze with black ice. Then, because of my wandering mind and ruminations over Wyatt, my father, and the house in Canaan, I take a wrong turn onto a secondary road that winds and curves around hills and corn stubble fields. The GPS directs me to another road, taking turn after turn until I am lost on a gravel road. I pull over to try to get my bearings. But I'm tired and close my eyes and remember being on trails in the past where I have lost my way, including a time when Fletcher and I got lost in the woods.

It was the Sunday after my mother and I had lunch at Fletcher's house with him and his mother. He came over later, knocked a few times on the back door, and then let himself in.

"Hello?" he called out. "Anyone home?"

Miss Euphrates was vacuuming, and I was upstairs. He kept calling until I eventually heard him.

I ran downstairs, calling out, "Fletcher, where are you?"

"Oh, hi!" He poked his head from the pantry doorway. "I got tired of waiting, so I was just looking around."

"Uh . . . what were you looking for?" There was confectionary sugar on his nose, so I knew he was into the powdered pecan cookies from the pantry.

"Nothing. Just killing time waiting for you."

"Do you want to listen to music in my room or play Monopoly?"

"Sure," he mumbled, turning to swallow the dry cookie. "Monopoly."

Fletcher was the race car, and I was the old shoe, just loping around the board, buying up railroads and landing in jail with nearly every loop. He snatched up Boardwalk and Park Place while I squatted on Baltic Avenue. Luck was not on my side and neither were the unconventional rule changes that Fletcher scattered into the mix like confetti. According to *his* edict, owners of certain properties—real estate that he held—could collect three hundred dollars for passing go, rather than the standard two hundred.

"You can't change the rules," I said.

"Sure you can. It's called creative gamesmanship. My father does it all the time."

Eventually, he got bored arguing with me, and I was just as happy to do something else.

"What about the tree house?" Fletcher asked. "Remember you said I could see the tree house."

"We have to climb a ladder to get inside. It might be kind of icy."

"So?"

"Hang on. I have to let Miss Euphrates know we're going out to play."

We ran out through the back fields, under an acid-wash blue sky, and down to the edge of the ice-covered river. We cautiously climbed up the ladder, hanging on as our feet slid over the icy round rungs. I was first because I knew how to get the door open even when it was frozen. My father kept a small screwdriver shimmed under the door just for such times. Inside, the cabin was bright in the midday sun.

"Wow, you got a woodstove," Fletcher said. "It's cold in here. Let's light it."

"We can't do that. I'll get in trouble."

"With who? Your nanny? She's not your mother."

"Yeah, but she can tell my mother, or worse, my father."

He stood in the center of the cabin, ginning and spinning until he stopped short. "Cool! There's a rifle here."

"Don't touch it, Fletcher. It's my father's."

But the rifle was already in his hands.

"Hand it back, Fletcher." I reached out and tried to take the gun from his hand, but he had a wide-eyed gleeful air.

He ran to the other side of the cabin. "You won't get it away from me," he cackled.

I stepped back. He scared me, and I didn't know what to do.

Fletcher started twirling the gun, flipping it around his back and over his shoulders and tapping the butt on the floor. "My father used to be part of the U.S. Army Drill Team. He's teaching me all the moves. Pretty cool, huh?"

"It is." I was surprised by his staccato, articulate movements. "But Fletcher, you have to put my father's rifle back. Please," I pleaded.

"Okay. Okay," he said. "But I know how to handle a gun. It's no big deal." He leaned the rifle in the corner where it had been and then sat at the table, pushing his chair back.

"Yeah, well, I don't like guns."

"That's because you don't understand them."

I shrugged. What was there to understand, other than they were dangerous?

He laughed and said, "Watch this." He pulled one leg up high, forcing his ankle around his neck and then did the same to his other leg and began rocking. "I'm a pretzel!" he said.

I laughed so hard that tears rolled down my cheeks. "Doesn't that hurt?"

"Nah!" He flexed his shoulder and untwined his legs, and then walked around the cabin, gazing out the windows. "I can see my street from here."

"Pretty cool, huh?"

"Come on. Let's go to my house and play in the woods out back."

"Okay," I said. "But first I have to tell Miss Euphrates where I'm going." I knew what she'd say: Have fun and be back by suppertime.

We trudged through the snow, across the road, and up the street to the back of his house. He ran inside and then came out with a ski pole for each of us and his backpack.

"We'll need the poles to get down there." He pointed below the backyard to the narrow ravine on the edge of a small tributary. "And I got snowshoes in my backpack for when we get into the deeper snow."

"You want to go down there?" I asked.

"Yup."

"But how? It's too steep."

"Watch and follow."

He began his descent, going from tree to tree, three at a time, then waiting for me. "If I can do it, so can you. Just be careful of the roots, so you don't fall and slide. I did that one day, and it hurt like crazy!"

"I bet."

When we got to the bottom of the ravine, we crossed the brook, our boots stomping through the slow moving water. Ahead was marshland with well-defined trails.

"Look over there," Fletcher pointed.

On the edge of the marsh were five white-tailed deer, four does and a buck. The does turned and watched us, their white tails high, while the buck groused under a gnarled apple tree. But he kept eating.

"He's eating fermented apples," Fletcher said. "It's like he's having a beer."

I laughed and stopped to watch them, not knowing that animals could get soused. And doubting Fletcher. The terrain was different from the farm, desolate and spare, not the lush deciduous woods and fields I had always known. It gave me a strange feeling, being dropped into this puzzling world with drunken deer.

"I've never been over here before," I said.

"Do you like it?"

"I don't know. It's kind of spooky."

He laughed. "You're safe, Joss. I know my way around these woods."

I nodded, but I didn't feel safe surrounded by twisted branches and grayed undergrowth. I had no idea where we were going. And no real faith in Fletcher's claims of expertise.

We walked a mile back to the tree line, into a dense pine grove. In places, the ground was spongy from the thick layer of needles beneath the windswept snow. There were birds everywhere, black-capped chickadees twittering and hopping from branch to branch, jays and cardinals, the rat-a-tat-tat of woodpeckers, and high in the branches we saw a red-tailed hawk, scanning for prey below.

We walked farther into the pine grove where it was darker and the snow deeper. Fewer birds perched in the trees. I listened to the creaking branches as we struggled to walk through the layers of snow.

"I think we need to put on our snowshoes." We sat on a fallen tree, and Fletcher showed me how to strap them over my boots.

"I'm sorry about yesterday," he said.

"What do you mean?"

"My mother. Sometimes she has too many drinks and acts like a jerk. That's what my father says: 'She acts like a jerk.'"

I shrugged my shoulders. "At least you have a mother and father every day."

"How come you don't?" His voice was quiet. Soft.

"Cause they fight all the time. Instead of fighting anymore, my mother left and took me with her. The stupid thing is that she has to be back to the city most days. That's where the bakery is."

"That doesn't make sense."

"Grown-ups never make sense." At least not in my family. I tried to understand why being here was better. Maybe it was for my mother, but I felt confused and scared most of the time. For me, the only good thing about living at Red Mills Farm was Miss Euphrates. And I worried that she might go away, too.

We tromped on top of the thick layers of snow, laughing and out of breath, looking for a spot to rest.

"Stop!" I said. "I think I hear something."

Neither of us moved. The quiet settled with only the sound of our breathing and a woodpecker in the distance.

"I don't hear a thing," Fletcher whispered.

I held a gloved finger to my lips.

We felt it before we saw it. A great gray owl with its dark ringed yellow eyes and nearly five-foot wingspan swooped past us. It landed thirty feet beyond, grabbed a small rodent, and then took to the air.

"Holy shit! That was an owl, right?"

I nodded, frozen to the path.

"That thing was huge."

I wondered what other creatures with yellow eyes were watching us. "Let's get going," I whispered.

"Aww. Are you scared, Joss?"

"No," I said and flashed Fletcher a look—the same kind of disapproving look my mother sometimes flashed at me. But my mouth was dry, my hands cold, and I was more fearful with every footstep.

We continued our trek through the creaking trees as the wind whistled through the high branches. Smaller gusts swirled across the forest floor. Dried leaves rustled, pine needles dropped, and we heard branches falling in the distance. We moved on, stepping over twisted fallen branches, each looking like the previous ones. I spun around, confused and disorientated. Every turn looked like the one we had just taken.

"Are we lost, Fletcher?"

"I think we were here a little while ago," he said. His voice was halting, hesitant.

"Which way should we go?" I asked. "This way, or that way?" I pointed towards a moss-covered downed tree that I didn't think we'd passed before. But I wasn't sure.

"We need to mark our way, break low branches and head toward the sun. If we come back to our broken branches, we'll know we're walking in circles."

I nodded but doubted that would help. There were broken low branches everywhere. The snow was littered with hundreds of twigs and fallen limbs. How would we know which were ours? I followed Fletcher, secretly wishing I'd never agreed to his plan.

"What time do you think it is?" I asked.

"Around two o'clock."

"We need to get out of here before it gets dark, before anything bad happens. . . ."

"What do you mean?"

"Jeez! Don't you know? There are coyotes around here, Fletcher!"

"You *are* scared, aren't you?"

"Quit being a jerk." But I imagined sallow-eyed wild dogs coming after us, tearing at our legs. Or being lost and having to spend the night in the woods. I started counting my footsteps, moving faster, listening to the strong beat of my own heart. How many chickadees would I see, and why were there no crows in this wood?

"I thought you knew your way around here?"

"Damn right, I do." His face was angry and sullen as we walked on in silence with nothing but tall pines ahead for as far as we could see. My heart raced. The sun ahead lowered on the horizon. We kept tromping onward. I began to consider going off on my own in a different direction.

"See, Joss?" Fletcher pointed. "It's lighter up ahead."

I breathed easier as we followed the sun through the grove and toward the light. We emerged onto an old field, studded with poplars and sumacs, edged with fieldstone walls. Noisy crows flew overhead.

"We must be getting close to a road or maybe some houses," Fletcher said.

"We should walk to the other side of this field," I said. "There's probably a road there."

We found our way to an old fire road on the other side of the field that led to macadam. The end of that road dropped us out onto Connor Road. We trudged up the hill to the top of Fletcher's street.

"Thanks for getting us out of there, Fletcher. I wouldn't have thought to follow the sun."

"We were never lost, Joss." He turned and waved. "See ya!" he said, as he ran over the last part of the hill and disappeared.

The sun was low in the sky. I ran the rest of the way home, past every crouched and ominous shadow. The wind, rattling dried grasses and stalking yellow-eyed watchers I was sure were lurking, ready to chase me. I wished Fletcher had walked me all the way to my door.

The kitchen was warm. I sat at the table, unlacing my boots, breathless but relieved to be safe and in the care of Miss Euphrates.

"Where's your little friend?" she asked.

"He had to go home."

"Did you have fun?"

"Yeah, Fletcher's pretty cool." And I had to admit he was. Fletcher did know how to get us back home. In spite of his antics, he was my friend. And I had the feeling that I could count on him, that he'd have my back.

She smiled at me. "There's hot cocoa on the back of the stove."

I smile, remembering how Miss Euphrates always nurtured me with food. Much the same way Wyatt does now. I wonder if he will be waiting for me at the farm. I back out and find my way to the rollercoaster macadam. Then pick my way along the slippery road, almost to my exit onto 295. I should have left the city earlier. Another half hour and I turn onto Sweet Milk Road and inch along, up the hill and into the driveway. The house is dark, except for the outside light. Wyatt's truck is gone. When I unlock the front door, the warmth and fragrance of cinnamon and yeast bread fill the house. On the counter is a pan of cinnamon rolls, still warm from the oven. The dishes are done, the floors swept.

But there is no note from Wyatt, no hint of when or if he'll be back.

8

Nearly a month passes before I hear from Wyatt. And in that time I struggle not to call him, not to "drop by" his shop with some lame excuse. But more unsettling is that I don't know why he hasn't called me. I gaze out of the window and wonder if he's finally given up on me.

Sunlight streams in as I clean up after breakfast. I watch a doe and two spotted skippers out in the fallow cornfield. The deer and wild turkeys still come to feed on the few errant shoots that pop through. It's been years since the rows of tasseled stalks reached for the sky. I dry the dishes and put them away in the pantry and then sit with the dregs of my coffee, thumbing through various cookbooks. I should at least bake something today. An idea from one recipe and a riff on another: a tart of poached pears in chestnut crème anglaise, topped with ganache in a walnut crust.

A concoction of butter, sugar, and toasted walnuts with a splash of vanilla and brandy chills in the refrigerator. Pear in pretty pink rosé poaches in the oven while I shape the walnut mixture into small tart tins and pop them into the oven to blind bake. As I close the oven door, I hear the mail truck drive up, stop, then move on. Today's delivery is mostly bills and advertisements, but this morning there are two letters in the stack. One is post-marked from Hudson, and the other is in Wyatt's florid handwriting on handsome watermarked paper. I run my fingers across the raised letters left by his fountain pen and lay both letters on the kitchen table.

The tart crusts are crisped and cooling. The finely ground roasted chestnuts steep in sugar, brandy, and vanilla. I pour eggs, cream, and more sugar into a saucepan, and I beat and whisk and whip, all the while wondering why Wyatt has written so formally. Is it an invitation of some sort? Or maybe a goodbye, a note of regret saying he'll always care.

My phone rings. Another call from my father. I hesitate, not wanting to answer. I breathe in, preparing myself for his perennial tirade.

"Hi Dad, how are you?"

"I'm okay, I guess. I just want to get out of here."

"Any idea of when that will be?"

"Well," he says, "it's hard teaching an old dog like me new tricks. But I have to do this."

"Glad you realize that." He's pleasant this morning. I hope this change will last. But I worry that his epiphanies will give way to his dark neediness and his all too often flash-fire anger.

"Plus," he says. "They got me on different medications. I don't like it, but maybe they help. How are things out there?"

"Okay. I'm just kind of wandering around."

"You miss your mother, don't you?"

"Yeah," I whisper. "I wish she were here today."

He babbles incoherently.

I only half-listen, thinking how my mother and I could have baked together today. That was our deepest connection. There is still so much of her that is a mystery to me. I miss her hands, her voice, her haphazard protection. I wish she had taken me for her own instead of leaving me to my father or my own devices. I wish I had listened better, understood more.

My father's voice cuts through, ". . . running back to Brooklyn every few days? Christ, we did that nonsense. It was hell. Me in the city all week at my shop. Your mother was trying to manage the farm and the bakery from Canaan and always in the car, running and running. Now you."

"I don't know. I just have to be here."

"I'm telling you, that farm, it's no good."

"Miss Euphrates always said that, too."

"That woman said things that weren't her goddamn business."

I want to tell him that she was all I had, but he'd never understand. And no good will come from adding to his burden.

I tell him, "I know."

"Yeah, that was your mother's doing. I should have never followed her out there. And speaking of that, Wyatt came to visit me."

"In the hospital?" I asked.

"I called him. Says he was out to see you. You gonna take him back?"

"I don't want to talk about that, Dad."

"Don't be like your mother," he says.

"Listen, I have to run. I'll stop by and see you on the weekend."

But I am like my mother in certain ways. It's what she gave me. It's irritating that he tells me how to be, who to be. I make tea and sit for a few minutes to calm myself. But my tarts won't wait, and this is the way I was taught to be. I mix the crème anglaise and chestnut puree together, streaming the mixture through the tamis until it shimmers. I pour the rich nutty mixture into the shells, add sliced pears, then finish the tarts with a drizzle of ganache before placing them in the refrigerator.

But I am not done deflecting. Upstairs I fill boxes with my mother's things, dust and vacuum the bedrooms, sweep the stairs, and throw the dirty laundry into the washer. The clamor fills the empty house, a tyranny well-known here.

When I am finished, with camera in hand, I head outside for a walk to clear my head. Out past the tree house to that hill with its copse of birches, I keep to the river's edge, tracing its path through the woodlot. The riverbank is alive with pale sprouts of ferns, flea-bane, and ramps, pushing their heads into the lime-green air. I snap frame after frame, hoping to capture a few good shots, then push on along the spongy moss trail, past the beaver dam, coming to the section where the barbed wire ends and the first wooden bridge takes over. It traverses the river, climbing in a high arc over the water. It has been repaired since I was last out here.

I climb the new steps up from the bank onto the slatted walk-way. At the highest point on the bridge, I am ten feet above the roaring water with a cool mist in my face. In the distance where the river widens into quiet, deep pools, I see her—a blue heron dipping her ballet legs through the rippling water, posing for me in our shared solitude. She holds her proud head high into the sun-light, breathing in the cool, clean air. She turns towards me, at the sound of my shoes clacking along the wooden walkway. I watch as she lowers her head, tucking her neck in with precision and grace, then taking flight through the soft May light. She takes my breath away as I watch her rise just above the treetops and disappear into the thicker forest ahead. As I turn to head back to the house, my cell phone jangles in my pocket.

A text from Wyatt. "Happy Birthday! Your first birthday at the farm! Enjoy!"

I smile. In my frenzy this morning, I forgot all about my birthday. Though it isn't the first birthday I've had at the farm. The first celebration out here was when I turned twelve. . . .

It was a beautiful May Sunday morning. My mother had surprised me, coming home the night before with a bakery box and wrapped gifts I pretended not to see.

"What are you doing up?" she laughed.

"I heard your car in the driveway, Mommy." I sat in her lap and wrapped my arms around her.

"Okay, okay," she said. "Give me a kiss and back up to bed."

I padded back upstairs, but I didn't sleep much, tossing and turning, listening to the train whistle, the church bells, and the distant rumble of water coursing over the dam. But mostly I was waiting for morning and my special day.

At daybreak, I heard the back door screen jangle against the frame. From my window, I watched my mother walk toward the water with a bottle of shampoo in her hand. She walked to the place along the riverbank where there was a gentle slope. She unpinned her long red hair and knelt at the water's edge, dipping and washing those tresses. I waited at my window until she came back up through the field, her hair wrapped turban-style in a towel. I had never seen her do this before and wondered why.

I lay back in bed and dozed off. Around nine o'clock, the smell of breakfast and dreams of smiley-faced pancakes woke me. I hoped that was what my mother was making. They were my favorite.

Before I went downstairs, I dialed my father's number, hoping this time he'd answer. His answering machine picked up. " . . . at the beep, leave a message."

"Daddy, it's me, Joss. Today's my birthday. I miss you." I hung up, happy and sure that he would call me today.

Barefooted and still in my pajamas, I wandered into the kitchen. My mother was sitting at the table with a young woman and a boy I had never seen before. The woman smiled at me.

"Is that you, Naomi?"

"That's right," my mother said. "Your sister Naomi and your nephew Haley are here to celebrate your special day."

"Naomi!" I buried my face in her neck. "I missed you so much."

"Me, too," she whispered. "Look at you, so grown up!"

I was mesmerized by her, her scent and beauty so much like our mother. I watched her and remembered she knew what our mother knew: all about colors and pretty things, and how to keep books and add sums in her head, and to categorize everything from soap powder to silver trays.

The boy sat in his chair, swinging his legs. He wore brightly colored striped socks that stuck out below his pant legs and Oxford tie-up shoes. He had dark bowl-cut hair and wide brown eyes.

He smiled at me, slid off his chair, and handed me a wrapped package. "Happy Birthday, Aunt Jossy. I brought you a present."

I stared at him, not knowing what to say or do.

"I saved you a place next to me," he said and tugged my hand. "Grandma's got pancakes for you."

"Who's 'Grandma?'" I asked.

My sister laughed. "Haley's my son, Joss."

I nodded but didn't understand. How could this little boy be her son?

Haley pointed to my mother. "You're silly, Aunt Jossy. She's my Grandma."

I sat next to him. My mother heaped a plate of pancakes in front of me.

"You want bacon and orange juice, Joss?" she asked.

I nodded.

"It's been a long time since I've seen you," Naomi said. "You're so big now! And today is your twelfth birthday."

I smiled. "I'm not eleven anymore."

"That's right. You're almost a teenager," Naomi laughed.

"Open your present, open your present!" Haley squealed. He handed me a heavy-ish oblong package.

"Okay." I pulled off the ribbons and began to rip the blue paper. "I wonder what it is," I said.

"It's the big box of crayons," Haley said before I had the paper off. "They're from me."

I laughed along with everyone else.

"Thank you, Haley. I like them a lot."

"My mom got you a paint set," he whispered.

"Haley!" Naomi cooed. "Now you've spoiled my surprise." She handed me a package and winked. "Go ahead. Open it up!"

Inside were pads of drawing paper and construction paper.

"I fooled you, Aunt Jossy. I fooled you!"

I laughed. "Yes, you did, Haley. You fooled me!"

"There's more breakfast goodies, everyone."

We ate scones with honey butter, fluffy scrambled eggs, and grilled polenta with blueberries. There was even hot chocolate with marshmallows for Haley and me.

"Now take your time," my mother said. "This morning is a birthday event. And I'm so happy we are all together. That we can be a family again."

I hoped that meant my father would be coming soon—that we would be a whole family, without fractures and missing pieces.

By eleven o'clock, we finished our extended breakfast with the promise of birthday cake later in the afternoon.

"Joss!" my mother said. "Are you going to stay in your pajamas all day?"

"Maybe I will, Mom!"

"Maybe you should run upstairs and see what's laid out on my bed. And then maybe you should take Haley out and show him the river and the tree house."

"He's just getting over a virus," Naomi said. "I think it's better for Haley to play inside today. Maybe you guys can color in your room, Joss."

"That sounds like a great idea." I ran upstairs and found the surprise for me in my mother's room: new jeans, a scrunchy, striped socks, sneakers, and a pink and lavender pullover. I went downstairs, modeling my new outfit.

"I got you some hair thingies," my mother said. "Hair bands, a couple bows, clips. Some hair products. Want to try them out?"

"Sure." I sat in a kitchen chair while my mother brushed and styled my hair, adding a little mousse and a touch of hairspray. "Even though your hair is curly, you can still change it up. Now run upstairs and look at yourself in the mirror."

"Come on, Haley," I said. "I'll show you my room." We clomped up the stairs in our striped socks and fancy shoes carrying the crayons and paper.

"Let's draw monsters," he said.

But not before I looked at my reflection in my mother's mirror. I wasn't Cinderella this time, but I looked more like a girl these days under my mother's wing. And that made me happy.

"Are you coming to color with me?" Haley asked.

We lay on my bedroom floor, sheets of paper spread like hopscotch squares, each of us hoarding our favorite colors: Radical Red and Razzamatazz, or Inchworm and Laser Lemon. I pulled out markers, glue, and glitter, too. Haley's creatures were medieval with pointy-toed shoes and frog heads. Or half boy and half bumblebee.

"Look at this one!" he said. "It's a codfish with a top hat and polka dot bow tie."

I laughed and showed him mine: red-haired aliens with antennae and huge almond-shaped eyes or fashion models dressed as old-school Sisters of Saint Joseph with long glittery hair flowing from beneath their headdresses.

We colored and squiggled, adding moonscape backgrounds to our collection, all the while telling each other stories. He told me that he played the piano and had since he was three years old. I told him the story of Miss Euphrates and how she was named after a river because of a talking mangar fish.

"Haley, Haley! Let's measure ourselves on the doorframe inside my closet."

"Cool."

"Yeah, we'll do it every year on our birthdays. When is yours?"

"Not until next March. I'll be eight then."

We marked the wall in pencil with our height, names, and the date. And then went on to drawing figures and monsters on the inside of my closet.

"I've got poster paints downstairs," I said. "I'll go get them. But don't tell anyone where we're using them."

Haley nodded and laughed.

But I knew I would get in trouble if my parents discovered our artwork.

When we finished, a sea of creatures with yellow eyes and green fangs guarded the entrance. Deeper inside were the delicate winged beings with ethereal smiles and bearded fiddle players with striped pantaloons.

"It's beautiful!" I said. "And all those colors!"

"Happy Birthday, Aunt Jossy!"

"This is the best present ever."

"Shhhh," I said. "Someone is coming up the stairs."

We quickly closed the closet door and threw ourselves into the artwork scattered across the floor.

"Hey kids," Naomi called. "What are you up to?" She came in and found us coloring and painting. "Wow! Look at these! You're artists."

"You want to bring a couple home?" I asked.

"How about that, Haley! Shall we bring a few home?"

He nodded and picked out three outrageous monsters.

"So, Joss, are you ready for cake and ice cream?"

We tumbled downstairs into the dining room, the ceiling filled with balloons, their curly ribbons hanging above the table. We sang and ate gooey, gooey cake, and I wished on my twelve candles that this day would never end.

9

On the evening of my thirty-third birthday, I sit on the front porch with a glass of madder red wine and a poached pear tart. It's been an unusually warm day in May and is even hotter tonight. The unopened letters lie in my lap. The one with a return address in Hudson must be from one of my mother's friends. I hold it up to the porch light and see that it's a card. Inside is a note:

Dear Miss Joss,

I was sad to hear about your mother's passing. She was a lovely woman, and I'm sure you miss her terribly. But we don't get to advise God on his plans for us. I am an old lady now, living in Hudson with my daughter and her husband, along with my grandbabies.

I don't get out too much anymore except for church and too many doctors' appointments. I would love to see you sometime if you have room in your busy life. I know all you young people have too much to do. No need to call ahead, just stop by if the spirit moves you.

I think of you from time to time and remember you fondly.

Miss Euphrates

I drop the card in my lap, and the note flutters to the floor. Miss Euphrates! How amazing to hear from her. She must be in her mid-eighties now. But in my mind's eye she is still that strong, vibrant woman from my childhood. I wonder now why I've never sought her out, never written to her.

I sit back, watching the stars, remembering Miss Euphrates—all her stories, her way with words, and her broad arms that kept me safe. She came out to the farm on the night of my twelfth birthday, just before everyone left.

That evening Haley's wide, wide eyes filled with light when he first met Miss Euphrates. He wiggled his hand around her long fingers. "Hello, Miss Euphrates," he said. "My name is Haley. Aunt Jossy told me how you were named after the river because of that magic fish."

She scooped him up and sat him in her lap. "You believe, don't you, Haley?"

"Course!" he squeaked.

"And your name is Haley? I bet you have a story there, too."

"Haley is my nickname. My real name is Nahaliel."

"Bwoy-boy, you mean like the Angel Nahaliel, the angel of the river? That's your name?"

He nodded.

"What else? Because I know there's more."

He told her that he played the piano, and showed her his monster drawings, and said that he was sure the birds had languages and that he was trying to understand the secrets of their songs.

"Let me see you play the piano, right here along this table," Miss Euphrates said.

His hands danced, tumbling forward and backward on an imaginary keyboard. He bobbed his head, tapped his feet, and scatted notes to some jazz piece.

Miss Euphrates snapped her fingers to the beat, calling out, "Yes, sir," and "Uh-huh," and "Bring me to church!"

When Haley finished, we all laughed and clapped.

"I wish we could stay longer," Naomi said. "But we have to go. Get your jacket on, Haley."

Miss Euphrates said goodbye, wrapping her arms around Haley. "I hope you come visit again real soon."

He smiled and said, "Bye, Aunt Jossy. I love you best."

In an instant, they were gone, the house empty and silent, except for the juddering of the wobbly balloons. Miss Euphrates and I sat in the dining room, each with a sliver of cake.

"I got you a little present, Miss Joss." She handed me a small package wrapped in white paper with a red and white bakery string bow. "You might need to grow into this gift, but I'm thinking you will."

Inside the paper was a spiral-bound book titled *Miss Euphrates' Pies*. There was a colorful illustration of a pie on the front and inside more pictures and pages of recipes. And stories, too.

"You wrote a book?"

"I guess I did," she said, laughing. "With a lot of help from my daughter."

"Is Salvation Pecan Pie in here?"

"Of course. Page 56."

I thumbed through the book, fascinated with all the pie names. And the pictures and drawings throughout. "Thank you, Miss Euphrates. I love it already."

"So did you have a nice birthday?"

"I did," I said. I told her about Haley and how I never knew about him until that day. About all the drawings we made. And how he tricked me. I even told her about the inside of my closet.

She laughed. "Good for you, dawta-girl! Everyone needs secret protectors. Inside your closet is as good a place as any."

"The only funny thing that happened was when my mother got up real early. She went down to the river. I watched her from my bedroom window, bending over and dunking her hair in river water. I never saw her do that before."

"Your Momma never told you about that?"

I shook my head.

"I know your mother since I was a dawta-girl like you."

I cupped my hands around my chin, listening to her voice and her words change the way they always did when she told a story.

"My madda, Sista Bébé, she work for your momma's people. Did the cleaning and cooking. My madda used to bring me here. I'd sit in the kitchen, peeling carrots, potatoes, whatever I could do to help."

"Did you used to play with my mother?"

"No, no, child-girl. Your momma's people didn't want their daughter taking up with no black child."

"That's stupid."

"You right! But now people are more educated, thank Jah and Jiizus. Like I was saying, long time ago, your momma, she lost her brother down there by the river. Didn't she ever tell you about her brother, your Uncle Morgan?"

I shook my head.

"There was a terrible accident. She was there when it happened. She saw too much. Sometimes when people see things like that, they blame themselves. My madda, she came to look after Miss

Lydah for a time. All that summer your momma would only bathe in the river."

"Why?"

"Because when people sometimes suffer, they do things to soothe themselves. Things other folks don't understand."

"I get that," I said. "Sometimes I like to count when I feel out of sorts."

"That's right. You understand now why your momma still goes down to the river every year on this date. It's the anniversary of her brother's death. Your Momma, she still trying to wash the red, red from her hair, her hands, her face."

I didn't know what that meant—washing the red from her hair, and I didn't want to ask. It was enough to know that for my mother my birthday was a complicated day.

"Miss Joss! Isn't that something! Same day you was born, you lost an uncle you never knew. And now the same day you found a nephew you didn't know you had."

I remember it being a cheery night, with a happy cake. But there is no happy cake on this birthday night. I sit in my front porch rocker, thinking that's what I should have made. I gulp the rest of the wine from my glass before I open Wyatt's letter. The envelope sits on my lap as I rock and watch the stars, counting them slowly with all the Mississippis in between that I can muster. I trace dot-to-dot shapes in the night sky with my finger and one eye closed. I tap out the rhythms of the dark until finally I pry open the envelope.

It's a birthday card with a letter inside. He explains that he's contracted some on-site work for a private library in Claverack, not far from the farm. His plan is to come out on the weekends, and he wonders, since I'll be in Brooklyn then, if he can stay at the farm. He says that my father called him and that he has visited Dad in the hospital a couple of times. And says that he is sorry and that he understands. He signs the note *Love, Wyatt. P.S. I hope you have a piece of lemon cake for your birthday. I know it's your favorite.*

It wasn't lemon cake that Miss Euphrates and I ate on my twelfth birthday. My mother made me an ooey-gooey chocolate cake. It's my father's favorite. She thought it was mine, too. Still, Miss Euphrates and I each had two pieces.

10

In the morning, I wake to a cold room. Thoughts of Miss Euphrates play in my sleep-addled head. And how I found and lost family on a birthday night a lifetime ago. My history repeats itself. Or maybe some revelations are gifts that spiral around in the guise of what is littered across the floor and left behind. Not that I'll ever know, but Miss Euphrates is more family than not.

I plod down the stairs, making coffee and eggs in the chilly kitchen. The temperature plunged during the night. Through the window, I see that a late frost has crept in, spreading its tentacles across the fields. All the soft-tissued plants, their capillaries frozen, have curled inward.

An errant thought whizzes through my brain: It's still too early to plant tomatoes. I laugh at myself, shower and dress quickly. Then I begin carrying boxes of my mother's things downstairs and out to the car. Some I will mail to my sister, others will be dropped off at the thrift store on my way to see Miss Euphrates. I pack up some tarts and print a few photos, then head out to Hudson, phoning her from the road to tell her I'm on my way.

By ten o'clock, I find Miss Euphrates' Allen Street address. At number 463, I park across from a pretty white clapboard with a handsome front porch. She is sitting outside waiting for me, her hair now gray, braided and pinned proudly on her head. But she is thinner than I remember, and her eyes seem darker, even from this distance. When I reach the top step, Miss Euphrates rises slowly and wraps me in her wide arms. In that moment, the world is gone. I dissolve in her warmth, the fragrance of her hair, her skin, and for the first time in as long as I can remember, I am home.

"My lost girl has come back," she says.

The singsong cadence of her words vibrates through me, though her voice is deeper, richer.

"Now stand back. Let me get a good look at you."

We both laugh as I twirl across the front porch. "Miss Joss! You look just like your mother."

"I do?"

"Why, sure you do, same hair and eyes, your voice, even the way you walk, dawta-girl. Just like your Momma. Now come on in the house. We'll have tea and whatever goodies you got in that bag."

The sparsely furnished living room with high ceilings and stretched canvas paintings from floor to ceiling, all of them frenzied allegorical Basquiat-like works. Street art. Miss Euphrates waves her arms through the room. "My son-in-law is a painter."

"It's breathtaking. The paintings, the whole room."

"He's fortunate," she says, motioning me to follow her into the kitchen. "Eli, he be a hard-working man. Late hours in his studio out back. Always promoting hisself." She fills the tea kettle and puts it on the burner, setting places at the red lacquer kitchen table. "I'm happy," she goes on, "helping Quinnie and the kids. I'm always here when the little ones get home from school."

"Just like you were for me."

"That's right, dawta-girl. Just the same." As she smiles, her black diamond eyes sparkle. "Now what you got in that bakery bag?"

She hands me a plate, and I arrange the tarts and cookies, along with some fresh fruit and cheese. We sit and fix our tea.

"This all looks so fancy. Must be from the 'Too Pretty to Eat Bakery.'"

"It's from my bakery in the city. Madame Marie's Patisserie, the bakery my father's aunt started where my mother worked."

"Well, well, you're a baker, too. Just like your Momma. How you doing with that? Her passing?"

"I don't know, Miss Euphrates. I don't know what I feel. We were never close. I didn't understand her. But I miss her."

"Uh. Families be that way, filled with people who never know each other. Still, you love them and miss them when they're gone."

"You think all families are that way?"

"Mine, yours, every one of them, Miss Joss."

"Then why can't I grieve?"

"Losing someone close, with some, there's a bubble around them until one day it breaks open."

"That must be it. I'm on autopilot."

"When you ready, that will change."

Maybe I'll be walking along Atlantic Avenue in Brooklyn and suddenly fall to the sidewalk, keening and pounding my fists on the cement. Or losing it with some difficult bakery patron. My grief breaking open for all to see.

Miss Euphrates squeezes my hand from across the table. "I see you brought pictures," she says.

"Just a few. The farm, the bakery, my Dad and Mom, and Wyatt."

"Tell, tell, who's Wyatt?" She thumbs through the stack of photos until she comes to pictures of him.

"He was a soldier in Iraq I met through letters. He came to New York after his discharge. But I had already won him over with all the cookies and cushy socks I sent while he was deployed."

Miss Euphrates laughs. "You was always so savvy, Miss Joss."

"I don't know about that."

"Well, I do. Older than your years, dawta-girl."

I watch Miss Euphrates hold up Wyatt's picture to the light. It's a photo of the two of us on the ferry from Portland, Maine to Peaks Island. We are laughing in the sunlight with the Atlantic spray on our faces, on our way to the wedding of a friend of Wyatt's.

"You two look so happy in this picture."

I nod. We were happy. But a photo is just a moment in time. Nothing more.

"He's one fine looking man. But I don't see no ring on your hand. You gonna marry him?"

"We're split up right now."

"How's that? Your face is all lights right now. You look like you're in love."

"I guess. It's not easy to turn it off."

"Why would you want to? You what, thirty-two now? Time to get married and have some babies."

"Thirty-three," I laughed. "You make it sound so simple."

"Isn't it? You fall in love. You eat, sleep, work, make love, and have babies. And accept your one imperfect man. He's never gonna be who you thought he was. He's gonna be better and worse, just like you."

"The problem is we want different things."

"What two people don't?"

"These are big things—Wyatt wants children and I don't see that for me. What kind of a mother would I be with all the crazy hours at the bakery?"

"That's your reason—work gonna keep you from being a momma? Because everybody's got that problem."

"I guess I'm afraid. I don't want to be like my mother. And so far, I am."

"Child, that is the beauty of being an adult. You choose who you'll be. You become your best self. Besides, I never met women who didn't have fears about being a momma."

Just then Miss Euphrates' phone rings. "Hello," she says, and then pauses. "That information's upstairs if you wait one moment." She presses the mute button and says, "I have to take this. Be right back down."

I drink my tea and look around the kitchen and out onto the back porch. There are starter tomato plants everywhere, on the windowsills: Pomodoros, heirlooms, San Marzanos, along with beefsteaks and cherry tomatoes. All lined up in trays with their paper labels, the same way she taught me when I first moved to Red Mills Farm.

I moved the trays of tomato plants as they got bigger. In a game of musical chairs, the trays went from the window sill to the top of the refrigerator or a bookcase, then back again. By April we moved them to the back porch, so they could become accustomed to the cooler temperatures. And by May, just after my birthday, they were ready to be planted.

That was when my father came back.

I was standing at the kitchen sink when a shiny, new, sporty red Toyota with pop-up headlights and a sunroof pulled into the driveway. I watched as my father got out, pulled luggage and boxes from the hatchback, and headed to the back door.

"Daddy!" I ran and threw my arms around him.

"Okay, okay." He pushed me away. "Grab some of these boxes." He nodded toward the back of his car.

"Are you moving in?"

"Your mother didn't tell you?"

"No."

"I'm surprised, you two being such pals now."

"What do you mean?"

"Just look at that outfit you're wearing."

"Mom gave it to me." I liked them when she brought them home, pink and white striped top and faded jeans with pink piping at the pockets. But now I stood in front of him, less than what he expected of me.

He smirked. "You've turned against me just like your mother and Naomi."

"I—"

"Forget it. There's nothing to explain."

I didn't understand what I had done wrong. Or why he was so angry with me. I carried boxes upstairs and offered to help put his things in the closet, his dresser, but he pushed me away.

"It's okay. I'll do it myself," he said, then kicked the door closed to his and my mother's room.

I stood in the hallway, staring at the family portraits that hung along the passageway. Their eyes watched, their papery fingers lifted and pointing. The sharp stink of tomato vines drifted through the open window. I counted those wretched souls in their gold frames, gagging on the pungent odor, rhymes running through my head. *Tinker, Tailor, Soldier, Sailor, Rich Man, Poor Man, Beggarman, Thief.*

"You look lost in thought," Miss Euphrates says.

"Oh, I didn't hear you come downstairs." I watch her; she looks different, her hair fallen a bit from its earlier height, her eyes dry and coal black.

"Your tomatoes look ready to go in the ground," I say. "As long as we don't have another frost like this morning."

"It's warmer here in town than out your way. Can I warm your tea?"

"You sit, Miss Euphrates. I'll do that."

"Now don't you start treating me like the old lady," she laughs.

"You're still beautiful and elegant."

She scoffs, "If only I felt that way. Always more doctors. Macular degeneration is on today's menu."

"I'm sorry to hear that." I feel like the kid arriving at the party just as it's about to break up.

"It's all right. Some folks burst out of this life like my Solomon-Joe did. His heart got too big for this world. Looks like Jah wants me to fade away, even with fancy new eye drops." She laughs. "They called them in over at the pharmacy."

"Can I pick them up for you?"

"You sure?"

I smile and nod.

"Now tell, you ever hear from that bandulu Fletcher?"

"Not ever." I think about him sometimes, how he and his family just disappeared. I wonder what became of him.

"I hear his momma drank herself to the grave. Poor woman. And that baddy bwoy, he been in and out of hospitals ever since."

I shake my head. "Do you know where he is?"

"My nephew works with his father in Albany. Last I heard Fletcher was in some group home over that way."

"I wish back then I had realized how fragile he was."

"You were just a child, Miss Joss. Besides, you was always good to him." She waved her hands in the air as if ushering in some shift in the universe. "You been thinking about all that happened back then?"

"I guess. With my mother's death, it's all come thundering back."

"Must be time to take it all out and make your peace."

I make more tea, we water the tomato plants, and we talk about the mundane that threads our lives to the present: where to find real olive oil, and how come no one makes those thin white cotton anklets anymore.

"Listen," I say. "I have a few errands to run. How about I pick up your prescription?"

"You sure?"

I smile and nod. I'll pick up some flowers, too. Something bright and cheerful.

We stand in the doorway. "How's your father?" she asks.

"About the same. He's in a hospital, too. An involuntary commitment. He waved a gun at his caregiver."

"Lord, when will it end? All these fools with guns."

11

On a July morning, two months after my father moved back in, my mother tacked an empty birdcage to the mill door and moved to the cottage on our property, while he was out shooting at the crows. Fletcher and I had watched from the tree house as she dragged boxes after bags from the big house into the cottage. She had said it was because my older sister Naomi was moving back home with her son Haley. That she needed help raising the boy right, given that he had no father. They would be here in a week and that it would be best if she, Naomi, and Haley stayed in the cottage while my father and I lived by ourselves in the big house. And that Miss Euphrates would come more often to help manage things.

As I drive from Brooklyn back to the farm, I remember what I thought about my mother's plan. I believed it would somehow end badly. She had a history of that. Not that she ever considered how all our lives could be so changed. She was too busy running and running to realize there were too many players, too much unsaid.

My cell phone buzzes. A message from my father. He's discovered texting and the satisfaction of a one-sided conversation. But he'll have to wait for an answer. The road beckons on this humid night.

I rise over the hill on Sweet Milk Road. The lights are on, and Wyatt's truck is in the driveway.

"Hey," I call out as I open the front door. "It's just me."

"Hey, just you. I didn't know you were coming out."

"Sorry. I forgot to tell you I'd be here. Lynn and I traded a few days."

He nods and smiles that crooked grin of his.

The house feels cool against the July heat. There's a welcome cross breeze floating in through the porch and the open windows. It's a relief to be out of the city.

"How's your Claverack Library project coming?" I ask.

"Come see."

Wyatt has transformed the annex from the living room into a book repair studio with book presses, a sewing frame, a small paper guillotine, gilding tools, and beautiful handmade marbled papers.

"I love these papers, Wyatt." They lie in stacks, waves of deep red with light olive and champagne cream. "What are they for?"

"I'm recasing, making whole new book covers, for a three-volume set. *The Fruits of America* by Charles Mason Hovey from 1853. Very rare to have all three volumes. And they were the first chromolithographs published in the United States." He shows me a few of the vibrant prints. The colors look alive.

"They're amazing."

"They are. It's a privilege just to see them. The boards for the covers will be wrapped in waxed marbled paper with caramel-colored leather spines and leather tips to the corners. I think it'll be a handsome combination."

"Sounds it. Don't let me interrupt your work."

"I was just finishing up for the day. About to make dinner. You hungry?"

"I could eat."

"It's nothing fancy. Leftover roasted chicken, salad, and a little white burgundy. Can I get you a glass?"

"Mmm," I nod.

We eat outside on the glider Wyatt bought, swinging back and forth like little kids, dangling our legs and laughing. The fields hum with clicking, chirping insects. We listen, breathing in the cooling twilight air, smiling at each other in the fading light. It seems so easy to slip into what we were. And maybe a little treacherous.

"This salad is delicious," I say. "The roasted beets and horseradish."

"I added orange zest to the recipe."

"Nice."

"I've been going out to the hospital to visit your father."

"Yes. You mentioned it in your letter." I stare at his dark eyes, but there is no reading them. "I was surprised. I never thought you two got along."

"I know, but he called me out of the blue. Asked me to stop by for a visit. I see him almost every week."

"That's kind of you," I say. No matter our differences, Wyatt has always been thoughtful.

"How long is he going to be there?"

"He plead guilty at his hearing to avoid jail, but the deal they struck was six months in a psych unit. Though he probably won't do more than four months."

Wyatt nods. We sit quietly watching the sun fade and the dusk rumble in from the woods. I feel the heat leave my body. My eyes are heavy. I nod off for a few minutes in the rocking glider.

"I think he's lonely," Wyatt says.

I startle at his voice. "What?" I ask.

"Your father. I think he's lonely. We talk. Military guys. Different wars but one sniper to another. It doesn't get better than that."

"Sniper? What do you mean?"

"You knew I was a sniper, Joss."

"Yeah, of course I knew you were. But my father? No, he wasn't a sniper. Where'd you get that idea?"

"Sorry, honey, but I got it straight from the horse's mouth."

I stare at him, shaking my head. "I would have known if that were true."

"Joss, people keep secrets all the time, especially former combat soldiers. That's why they explode—keeping all that stuff bottled up is no good."

I shake my head. How could I not know? And how is it that these two men who have framed my life are both snipers? "My father never talked about Vietnam," I say. "I knew not to ask."

"I get it, Joss. I'm so sorry. I thought you knew."

I nod. But my mind races. I think of all the crows he shot. They were little more than an object through a gunsight. They represented neither life nor death. It was what he had been trained to do, and perhaps he tried to make me understand this in his misguided way. The rest of the maybes, I push out of my head.

"Are you okay?" Wyatt asks.

"I don't know," I whisper.

He rises from the glider and bends to eye level. "I know this is hard stuff to hear, Joss." He strokes my hair.

"It's not so much the Vietnam part. I get that. Just like I understand what you did. It was courageous. But the fallout here. What he did here. It adds up to a dark sum."

"I know it does. We all pay, sometimes our families the most. And for years."

I nod, shaking my head.

"That's how it was, Joss. We learned skills and tapped into our rage, combining the two. We lived on adrenaline, always seeking the enemy—because there always was an adversary. And if there wasn't one, we looked until we found one."

"I remember your nightmares, Wyatt. You'd wake sweating and talking about water buffalo grazing in the saw grass, skeletal buildings filled with goats and donkeys."

"Yeah, near Fallujah—the hell we called 'Paradise Redux,' with heat mirages running like rivers through the dung piles and the stink of diesel. I remember, one day, watching a driver in a pick-up about six-hundred meters out. He had a red-striped khaffiyeh on his head. At first I thought he was okay—heading into the city with teenagers in the back, when a buddy yelled out, 'They're insurgents!' I ducked behind a berm, scoped the driver and called in my spotter. When I hit the driver, the truck flew through the air and flipped."

He sat down heavily, saying, "You push it back for a time. They were kids."

"But I'm glad you got some help, Wyatt. I know you worked to get better." My father never did, and we all paid, though Haley and Naomi endured more than the rest of us. When he heard that Naomi was moving to the farm, my father ranted, saying she was no longer his child, and Naomi's son, Haley, would never be a grandson to him.

And just like my mother promised, Naomi and Haley moved in on the following Saturday, with Fletcher and me watching from the tree house perch. Around ten o'clock that morning my sister's car turned into the driveway and curved around back to the cottage. Mommy stood on the porch, the screen door slapping in the breeze, waiting. When the car door creaked open, I saw his shoes, those same polished Oxford tie-ups with striped socks. Fletcher and I scatted down the ladder, through the field, hollering, "Haley! Come and play with us."

"I'm coming," he called back, running through the tall grass towards us. The three of us fell breathless beneath the butternut tree, with my sister Naomi following behind. She hugged me, brushing her soft hand against my cheek.

"Joss, you're even prettier than the last time I saw you," she said. "And so tall and strong. You'll watch out for Haley, won't you? I need to go help Mom."

I nodded. She kissed Haley and then me. And smiled at Fletcher.

The gap-toothed, frog-faced Fletcher flashed a grin at Haley and my sister. He shot up and shook her hand, saying in his imitation Alabama drawl, "It's a pleasure to meet you, Miss Naomi."

"Aren't you a clever boy," Naomi said. "A southern gentleman right under our old butternut tree."

Haley beamed back, putting his chubby hand in mine, telling Fletcher that I was his Aunt Jossy. Fletcher didn't understand how I could be an aunt. After all, weren't aunts old?

"I like the gristmill," Haley said, pointing to the reverse gabled structure looming on the edge of the river. "Can we go inside?"

"Joss's dad doesn't like us in there," Fletcher explained. "It's creepy in there."

"How would you know, Fletcher?" I asked. "You've never been inside."

"Because I just know. That mill was part of the Underground Railroad. Runaway slaves hid in the crawlspace. Once a nigger ran out too early." His voice faltered.

"You better not use *that* word in front of Miss Euphrates," I said.

"My momma says that everyone up here is just as bigoted as southerners. They just lie about it."

"Not everyone, Fletcher."

Fletcher smirked and rolled his eyes. "Haley," he said. "You want to know what happened?"

Haley nodded, his eyes wide, his hands cupped around his face.

"Those bounty hunters found that runaway slave and shot him in the back as he jumped over the fence down along the tree line."

The three of us turned, looking beyond the mill, past the river, through waves of grass. But there was no dark head thrown back in a runner's stride, no jaw that slacked as he fell from the sun, only distant crows that cawed and cawed in the background.

We watched my father, shotgun in hand, walk beyond the field, to the edge of the dammed river toward the tree house.

"Come on," I said. "Let's sneak into the millhouse."

"But what if your father catches us?" Fletcher asked.

"He's not the boss of me, and besides this was my mother's farm. Not his. We can play in the millhouse anytime we want."

We slinked around to the back of the reverse-gabled building. With its red clapboards, the millhouse rose three stories above the river, and sat on a stone foundation. I slid the wide, heavy door along the top rollers. The three of us tumbled inside. We stood breathless in the dark interior. Swirling dust motes rained down on us from the high transom windows. I felt the cold seep into my feet from the foundation and ran to the staircase landing. But Fletcher—that cold fixed him in place.

"Are you coming, Fletcher?"

He nodded, but his eyes were wild looking.

I was surprised that Fletcher was so scared. "Nothing bad is going to happen," I said.

"I know," he shot back.

Haley and I hammered up the steep stairs, two at a time to my father's office, with Fletcher hesitant on every step.

"It's cool up here," Haley said. "Come on and see."

My father's desk and swivel chair sat in the dusty light at one end of a room that ran the length of the building. His desk was surrounded by bundles of papers, sheet music, and flanked by gun cases—and in the rear corner, sat a piano. Fletcher spotted the gun case and opened its glass door.

"Fletcher!" I said. "Keep out of my father's guns. He'll know." My warning stung and his hand shot back.

Haley beelined to the piano stool and pulled himself up to the dusty keyboard. His small hands began softly, gracefully dancing over the keys, like raindrops trickling down the roof ridge, layer upon thin layer, until a waterfall of woven melodies tumbled over every post and beam. Fletcher leaned against the far wall, surrounded by each delicate measure, while I sat in the middle of the floor, hugging my knees, the dust elves prancing around my head.

"Not too loud," I warned. "We don't want my father to hear us."

"Oh, yeah. Sorry." Haley pulled his fingers off the keys.

"You're good," I said. "How long have you been playing?"

"I started when I was three, so four and a half years."

"I'm good, too," Fletcher said. "Wait till you hear me on the trombone. Plus I'm in the school band."

Just then, Haley spied the loft window and the narrow ladder that led to the six-foot-square window landing. Before I could warn him, he was on the third rung.

Fletcher whispered, "Quiet, you guys! I hear someone downstairs."

The three of us stood still, listening. We heard the treetops rustle, the crows cawing over the cornfield, the sound of our breath, but nothing else. There were no footsteps below or the squeal of the door sliding along its track.

"It's nothing," I said. "You must be imagining things, Fletcher."

Fletcher straightened and puffed out his chest. "My Momma knows how brave I am. I'm just like my daddy, and he's a Vietnam War hero."

I rolled my eyes and said, "Yeah, so is my dad. He fought in Vietnam, too."

Haley got to the window landing, nodding his small bowl-haircut head. "I can see your father way out in the cornfield."

We scurried up the ladder rungs to witness for ourselves, just in time to watch my father turn and point the shotgun right at us.

The first shot reverberated.

"Goddamn!" Fletcher hollered. "We gotta get outta here! He's shooting at us."

We scrambled down the rungs, hearing the second and third report of the shotgun. Then raced down the stairs to the stone floor.

"I could see the glint of the barrel," Fletcher whispered. "He was aiming at us."

"We need to sneak out of here," I said. "There's a side door, but we have to be real careful. It opens on the edge of the river."

But Haley stood still, fixed to the floor in a stream of sunlight. "He wasn't shooting at us," he said.

"Oh, yes he was!" Fletcher claimed.

"He was shooting at the crows," Haley said. "It was an optical illusion that he was shooting at us."

"Haley's right," I whispered. "My father always shoots at the crows. They sit on his scarecrow making fun of him. That always makes him mad." And lately he was angry with everyone and everything.

"Come on Haley, the door's over here."

But Haley stood in that brilliant light. "I can hear them, Aunt Jossy," he said.

"Who?" I asked.

"The crows. I can hear them cawing and calling."

"Come on!"

We scattered outside in the sunlight. They both retreated home, but I stayed outside on the swing, floating through the air.

I close my eyes, remembering that feeling of soaring into the sky and swinging back, low to the ground, trying to count how many cycles I've spun. We glide now, Wyatt and I, almost in the same place. And I feel sick to my stomach.

"Come on, baby," Wyatt says. "Let's go inside. You're shivering."

I am, but not from the cooler air. My mind races with the knowledge that my father was a sniper. Why was this a secret held from me until now? And did my mother know this about my father? She never spoke of his Vietnam days.

We grab the dishes, the wine bottle.

"I'll finish cleaning this up in the morning," he says.

We stretch out on the sofa in the living room, tossing my mother's *Heal with Prayer & a Dose of Gin* pillows to the floor.

He kisses my mouth, and I am at once lost and back where I belong.

"I still love you, Joss. I do."

"I know you do," I say and kiss him back.

He pulls me up and leads me upstairs to the lampshade room.

"No," I say. "My room."

We lie in the soft featherbed, his face, his hands all around me. And I think how foolish I am to toss away this beautiful man who loves me so. I am freed and connected in the same instance. Sailing on what is good and powerful.

12

On that Sunday morning, the day after Naomi and Haley came to live at Red Mills Farm, I woke to the sound of my father mowing the front and side yards. I turned over, pulling the sheet over my head, but couldn't get back to sleep. Finally, I gave up and went downstairs.

I poured cornflakes into a bowl, but there was no milk, or eggs either. I looked through the freezer and the pantry without success. There was always confusion over groceries, who would pick them up, what to get, when to go. Despite the fact that my mother ran a bakery, and my father was on the road often enough, neither one of them paid any attention to what was needed at home.

"What are you looking for, Joss?" my father asked.

"There's no milk or eggs for breakfast."

"We'll go in town and get a few things. Okay?"

I nodded and ran upstairs to change out of my pajamas and into jeans and a t-shirt.

"We'll take the van, instead of my car," he hollered to me.

"Okay, I'll be right down."

The horizon was thick with heavy air as we drove along the back roads. The farm ponds were choked with blue-green algae as heat waves shimmered off the pavement.

"It's going to be a hot one. We'll get lemons for iced tea and some ice cream for tonight. Maybe build a bonfire and make s'mores. You'd like that, wouldn't you?"

"Yeah, we haven't done that all summer." I looked at my father, happy to see him in a good mood.

We got to the store and cruised through the aisles, Dad tossing in baked beans, hot dogs, and beer, along with breakfast fare, and, of course, all the ingredients for s'mores. On the way home, he turned up the tunes on the radio. The music blared out the open windows.

When we were about halfway home, he pulled over, got out, and came around to my door.

"Shove over," he said. "You want to try driving?"

I must have looked at him in disbelief.

"Don't worry. I'll be right next to you. You'll do fine."

I don't know why I didn't protest. I had never driven a vehicle before. I guess I wanted to please him, make him proud of me. And he was in such a good mood that day, I didn't want to ruin it. I did what he asked: slid over and pushed hard on the key, as he showed me, then popped the van into gear. The engine rattled beneath my feet; I could feel the pull of it like a dog on a leash.

"Now let your foot off the brake."

I did, and the van rolled forward.

"Keep both hands on the wheel and aim towards the middle of the lane."

It was thrilling on that straight, smooth road. And it seemed surprisingly easy.

"You can go a little faster," he said. He showed me how to push the gas pedal, and we rolled faster, the tires spinning over the macadam, him smiling, the thrum of rock and roll filling the van.

I liked the feel of the steering wheel vibrating in my hands. But more than that, I liked making my dad happy.

"You can push the gas just a little more," he said.

I pushed a little harder, not realizing I had pressed down too hard. The van bucked and raced, lurching toward the one long wide curve in that road.

"Hit the brake!" my father yelled.

But I was confused and pressed the gas hard by accident. We raced ever faster.

"The other pedal, the other pedal!" he screamed.

He grabbed the wheel, but by then our trajectory had been cast. The van veered off the edge of the road. The wheels on my side of the van slipped into a ditch. I was terrified and confused as we tipped sideways. The sounds of creaking metal and canned goods slamming into the back of my seat roared in my ears. I hopelessly pounded my foot over and over against the brake pedal. But we had already stopped.

"Weepin' Jeezus, are you trying to kill us?" he yelled. He raised his arm and slapped me across my face.

The sting shocked me, but this time I didn't cry. I pushed my door open and dropped into the ditch, my father still screaming at me. I didn't look back, just scrambled up and over that embankment and walked home wet with sweat and anger. He was reckless, just like my mother said, always expecting too much from me. Always wanting me to be just like him. All the way home, I kept telling myself that it wasn't my fault. That he shouldn't have pushed me, and that's why we ended up in the ditch. And I promised myself that I would defy any punishment he tried to impose.

When I got home, I called Fletcher's mother. My father didn't like her much, and he surely wouldn't want to spend the evening with her. But that's just what he would have to do.

"Hey, Joss," she said. "How ya'll doing?"

"Fine, Mrs. Goodwin. My father asked me to call and invite you and Fletcher and Mr. Goodwin over for a cookout around six tonight. My mother and my sister Naomi will be there, too, along with my nephew, Haley."

"That sounds lovely. I heard you got family that moved in. Can't wait to meet them. Can I bring something? Macaroni salad?"

"Sure, that would be great."

After my phone call to Fletcher's Momma, I ran down the driveway and around the bend to the cottage. Through the screen door, I saw Mom, Naomi, and Haley sitting at breakfast.

"Come on in," my mother motioned. "You hungry? Want some scrambled eggs?"

"Sure." I said, the door clacking in the latch behind me.

"So what's happening today?" Naomi asked.

I sat at the kitchen booth, one of the original antique dark wood booths scavenged from the bakery. "That's why I came over. Dad is having a cookout tonight. Fletcher and his mother and father are coming. Can you come, too?"

"Can we?" Haley asked.

My mother looked at Naomi and shrugged her shoulders. "I guess," she said. "What time?"

"Six o'clock. Mrs. Goodwin's bringing macaroni salad."

"That and probably something to drink." She winked at Naomi, but I knew what she meant.

Haley grabbed my hand. "Come see my room, Aunt Jossy." He led me through the chintz-floral main room. It was wallpapered the last time I had seen it, but my mother had painted right over the paper, a soft peach color that glowed even in the daylight.

"Here's my room," Haley said.

It was a long narrow room that had once been a sunroom with three walls devoted to windows.

"Look at my new shades." Haley demonstrated the crisp black and white roman shades printed in musical notation. "And," he said, "my bed is bouncy." He jumped trampoline style from the floor onto the red quilt-covered mattress.

"Haley!" my sister called from the kitchen. "Are you jumping on that bed?"

"No, Mom."

We both laughed, flashing each other treacherous looks.

He showed me his Lionel train set, his tin windup robots. "Aunt Jossy, pull this lever and watch!"

We sat on the floor watching the Pennsylvania Flyer chug around the oval tracks, its green locomotive hauling a livestock car, a tanker, and a classic red caboose.

"Yeah, Mom and I built the base and set it all up."

I was mesmerized, watching the engine circle around and around. It whizzed by miniature people and telephone wires, and I held my breath, afraid it would crash, as the locomotive hit break-neck speeds on the curves. But nothing bad happened. It stopped at the railroad lights and the passenger station. This miniature world was safe, where reckless adults could not endanger plastic vehicles and synthetic children.

"Come here, Aunt Jossy. I almost forgot." Haley ran to his clothes wardrobe and opened the double doors. "See, I painted monsters in mine, too."

I laughed, pleased that we both had secret nighttime protectors.

"I like your room," I said, running my hand over the electric keyboard. "Is this your piano?"

"Yup," he said. "Put the headphones on and I'll play you part of Mozart's Piano Sonata No. 10."

We both donned headphones and Haley played the happy opening movement.

"You're so talented, Haley."

He laughed. "I have to learn the classics, even though they're not my favorites."

"What is your favorite?"

"Jazz! I love jazz."

"Really? So does my father. He belongs to a jazz ensemble. They play in the millhouse in the summer."

"What's he play?"

"Drums."

"Maybe he'll let me play with him sometime."

"Maybe," I said. I didn't want to tell Haley that my father wanted nothing to do with him, or Naomi. I didn't want him to be hurt by my father. I knew what that was like. Instead, I asked him if he wanted to decorate the backyard for our party.

"Sure, but how are we going to do that?"

"Come on. You'll see."

He grabbed a small spiral notebook and stuffed it into his pocket. "I keep this with me so I can write down musical ideas."

We ran out into the sunshine air and down the driveway. My father wasn't back yet, so we tumbled up the two flights of stairs to the attic and grabbed bags of party lights. By mid-afternoon, when my father pulled up in the van to the back porch, the tables and chairs were set up, the Chinese lanterns hung, and the tables were set with tablecloths and bouquets of garden flowers.

"What's going on here?" he asked.

"The cookout you promised," my mother said. "Did you forget?"

He glared at me, but I turned away, pretending not to care, even though my hands shook and my mouth went dry. I was confused and afraid of him, scared he might slap me again.

"You got place settings for eight. Who else is coming?"

"Fletcher and his parents—you invited them! I don't know what's going on with you, Paul, but we've been cooking all afternoon. Don't go changing your mind now."

Just before six o'clock, Naomi and my mother sent us inside to change. I dawdled, wasting time, until Mom finally insisted.

"Go on in and take a shower. Now! I bought you a new sundress you can wear, and a sweater for later when it gets cool."

Haley was already showered and dressed in new khaki shorts and a seersucker short-sleeved shirt, sitting on the porch rocker. "They're making us get all dressed up," he complained.

I rolled my eyes and nodded.

Shortly thereafter, Kenny and Reyanne Goodwin pulled up in Kenny's shiny red truck. They got out, Fletcher first with his hair slicked back, followed by his mother in a bright yellow dress. Mr. Goodwin looked like he always did: as if he had just crawled out from under a car.

"Welcome, Reyanne," my mother said, kissing her on the cheek. "So nice to see you. Are you having a good summer?"

"I am, but I have to say, I'm surprised at the humidity up here. Phew. Today's as bad as Alabama. A girl could use a drink in this weather."

"What can I get you, Reyanne, Kenny? We've got iced tea, beer, wine. And I made a pitcher of Kentucky punch. I remembered you like bourbon."

"Oh yeah, my girl likes her bourbon," Kenny said. He ran his hand down her back and grabbed her bottom.

She swatted him away like some pesky fly. "Cut it out, Kenny," she snapped.

"Now tell, what is Kentucky punch?" Reyanne asked.

"Bourbon, cherry liqueur, tea, lemon juice, and mint."

"That does sound refreshing."

Haley, Fletcher, and I sat on the long garden bench, lined up, cleaned up, and as bored as bowling balls on Easter Sunday.

"When are we going to eat?" Haley whispered.

I shrugged my shoulders, as a big tuxedo cat with large green eyes and a pink nose wicked in and out between my legs.

"Wow, what a huge cat," Fletcher said.

Haley grinned. "That's my cat, Mr. Big."

"He's so soft," I said, rubbing the top of his head and ears.

"Whose cat is that?" my father yelled.

"It's ours, Dad. Haley loves that cat," Naomi said.

"Lydah! You let her bring a cat? I hate cats. All they do is shit in the garden."

Haley and Fletcher laughed, but I didn't. I worried that he would make Haley give up his pet.

"I'll second that," Kenny said. "Not a big fan of cats, myself."

"You must be a man of reasonable sensibilities, Kenny."

Kenny laughed and slugged down a gulp of beer. "The only cat worth having is a barn cat; a dead cat's the next best thing."

"I got a cat story for you," my father said. "When I was a kid, my mother's cat had a litter of kittens. Of course, we'd never be able to find homes for all of them, so she told me to put the cats in a burlap bag and bring them down to the pond and drown them. I did just what she said, put the kittens and the mother cat into a sack, threw in some rocks and heaved that sack out in the middle of the pond. Man, she wailed my backside when she discovered I'd also drowned her precious momma cat."

Kenny laughed and slapped my father on the back.

"Aunt Jossy, is he going to drown Mr. Big?" Haley's eyes were as wide as silver dollars.

"No, don't worry. He won't. He's just saying stupid stuff to show off." Truthfully, I wasn't sure what he would do. But I was determined to protect that cat and Haley, too.

My father's voice lowered. "I remember telling my mother it upset me. The cats and all. I'll be damned if she didn't whack me again."

"Women!" Kenny said and nodded towards Reyanne.

"Yup, you just learn to keep close to the vest," my father smirked. "She was a beauty, too, my mother. Crazy, full of fool ideas. We had a barn out back, and she got it in her head that there were spirits out there. Said she heard sounds. Christ, it was only a lark stuck under the crawl space. But she wouldn't hear about any bird. She refused ever to go out in that barn again."

"You know, Paul, I thought you were gonna be one those arrogant types. But hell, you're as regular as rain. How'd you end up being some fancy New York City tailor?"

"My mother was mostly a farmwife out in Ohio, but to make ends meet, she did seamstress work at home. Somehow I ended up helping her. And the rest they say. . . ."

"Come on, everybody. Dinner's on the table." Naomi, Reyanne, and my mother set the last of the big platters on the table.

"After dinner, maybe you kids might like a snipe hunt," Kenny said.

"Right! A snipe hunt," my father laughed. "I don't think we've ever had one of those. I bet there are colonies of snipes on the farm."

"What's a snipe?" I asked.

"Well," Kenny said. "They're one of the wiliest creatures known to man. Smarter than any other critter. But they don't like the light of day. Not a lamplight or a candle, either. What they do like is singing. Especially little kids singing."

"That's true, that's true," my father said. "Now that I think about it, there was one time when me and some of the fellas went out after a concert in the millhouse. We thought we had heard an animal scratching at the door. Nobody paid much attention. But when we walked to our cars, we started humming and snapping our fingers to some jazz tune, and by God, we saw something—a couple of those snipes with their yellow-lantern eyes staring at us. I swear they were swaying to the music."

"A snipe will do that," Kenny said, nodding his head.

The three of us listened intently, looking for a sign from each other.

"You're kidding, right, Dad?" Fletcher asked.

"Now don't be such a skeptic, boy. My bet's that you'll find you a couple of them snipes tonight."

"What do snipes eat?" Haley asked.

"As a matter of fact, they eat cats," Kenny laughed.

"They do not," Reyanne said. "Don't you kids listen to any of this snipe talk. There's no such thing—"

"Reyanne! Now you be quiet. Have yourself another drink."

"I think I will, Kenny."

My father smirked. "Women! You can't live with them. You can't beat them."

"Oh, you can beat them all right," Kenny laughed. "That's why they make them big sunglasses. Isn't that right, honey?"

Reyanne shot him a look and poured herself another Kentucky punch.

"Course that's what she tells folks—that I popped her once or twice. But then again, my little Missus has a habit of falling down. Don't you, sweets?" His voice dripped like syrup.

I caught Fletcher's eye, but he turned away, his cheeks scarlet.

"Who's ready for dessert?" my mother asked. "We've got brownies and ice cream."

After dinner, my father and Kenny built a bonfire. We toasted marshmallows and made s'mores. And ran along the edge of the field with lit sparklers in our hands, competing with the fireflies and tracing our names into the chalkboard air. When the night rolled in deeper, my father brought us burlap bags and flashlights from the millhouse.

"For your snipe hunt," he said.

"I thought they didn't like light," Fletcher said.

"Here's what you kids got to do," Kenny said. "Walk out into the field using your flashlights so you can see where you're going. When you get halfway out, turn them off and stand there about ten minutes, then start singing. That's when they'll come out. Plus they like dancing, too. Let me show you how that's done."

He stepped away from the bonfire, pulled off his cap, and bowed to all of us. He tapped one foot and whistled a fast, fiery tune. His hips rocked; his shoulders hunched up around his neck as his wiry body step danced across the fading twilight.

We all clapped and sang a cappella like whiskey-throated birds. And cheered him on under the starry canvas.

"That's it!" he hollered. "You kids do that and you'll have all kinds of snipes partying out there in the field with you."

"But what do they look like?" Haley wanted to know.

"They're furry brown, about bigger than a skunk, but smaller than a fox, if you know what I mean?"

We didn't, but we nodded in unison, regardless.

"Now, when you see one, the trick to catching the thing is to stare it down. And a snipe is a sensitive creature. It don't like being looked at. But once you get the thing in your gaze, you stare right into its eyes. You can't blink or turn away, not even for a second. Eventually the snipe will turn, and that's when you pull one of them sacks right over its head."

"But why do we want to catch them?" Haley asked.

"I guarantee that you'll have a friend for life. Better than a cat, little man."

Haley nodded, his eyes as big as saucers.

"Okay, you guys," Fletcher said. "Let's go."

Our mothers slathered us with insect repellent, rolling their eyes at one another. "Be careful out there," they warned.

We nodded and headed out into the dewy field amidst the sawing crickets and buzzing mosquitoes. The full red moon of August was rising above the mountains.

"I think we better stick together," Haley said. His small voice quivered.

I held his hand. "Don't worry. Nothing bad is going to happen."

We continued slowly, stepping deliberately, the three of us in the dwindling shadows. We crisscrossed past the cornfield, over the barbed wire fence down to the river's edge and the tree house. Waist-deep sweet Timothy and gamma grass splashed our bare legs. A low fog had begun to hover over the landscape. We imagined crouching animals ready to pounce on us with their lantern-lit eyes.

Haley's grip on my hand tightened.

"I think we better start singing," Fletcher whispered.

"What song should we sing?" Haley asked.

"How about Miss Euphrates' rhyme about playing in the dark?" I suggested.

We put out our flashlights, huddled together, and chanted in singsong voices, watching for those football-shaped yellow eyes.

Girls and boys, come out and play
The moonlight shines as bright as day
Leave your supper, and leave your sleep
And come with your playfellows into the street
Up the ladder and down the wall,
A halfpenny roll will serve us all
You find milk and I'll find flour
And we'll have pudding in half-an hour

"We're supposed to dance, too," Haley said.

"Maybe we should walk farther out," I said.

We did both, listening to the trees bend in the light breeze as fog rolled in deeper. But there were still no lantern-eyed creatures in the dark.

We stopped singing, listening for tiny paws rustling in the grass. But the only sounds we heard were our parents laughing and chattering in the distance.

"I'm cold and wet," Haley said. "I want to go home."

"But we haven't seen any snipes yet," Fletcher said. "And if I don't come home with one, my father will rant from now till kingdom come."

"Come on, Fletcher. Haley's just a little kid. He needs to get warmed up."

"Fine. Bring him up in the tree house."

But Haley didn't want to climb twenty feet in the air on a ladder in the dark. And I didn't want him to get hurt. Or to be more scared than he was.

"We'll sneak into the side door of the millhouse. It will be warm in there," I said. "But we have to walk in the dark so my father won't see us."

We made our way across the field, keeping to the shadows, then slipped behind the millhouse and in through the narrow side door.

"It *is* warmer in here, Aunt Jossy."

"I'll get you a couple of blankets from upstairs," I said. "You'll be warm in no time." When I got back downstairs, Fletcher was walking around the room, aiming his flashlight into the corners and rafters above.

"Turn that off, Fletcher. My father will see."

"Jeez, I was just looking around, wondering if there was a shotgun in one of the rafters."

"What for?"

"So I can shoot one of those snipes when I see it."

"You can't shoot them," Haley said. "They're like pets."

"How do you know? You ever seen one?"

"No, but—"

"Well, I have. And they aren't so cute and furry."

"Quiet, you guys. I think I hear something outside."

We held our breath, listening, our eyes darting around the room. There were voices growing louder and nearing the millhouse.

"Quick, quick—hide under the stairwell," I said.

We squeezed our bodies into the tight space, pushed as far back as we could, and pulled the blankets over our heads and around our feet.

"I'm scared," Haley whispered. His small body was shivering.

"We'll be okay." I put my arm around him just as the large rolling door slid open.

"You kids in here?" My father's voice boomed.

My heart raced; everything in my body felt electric. But I tried to tell myself that even if I got caught it wouldn't matter. Somehow, I'd stand up to my father.

"I'll look upstairs," Kenny said. He clomped up the rickety stair treads, raining debris down on us.

"They're not up here."

My father looked around, shining one of the Chinese lanterns into the corners, and even into the stairwell, but he didn't see us behind our camouflage of blankets.

"You must have seen them shining their lights in from the outside, Paul. Nobody's in here."

They left, and we waited, still huddled together, listening for their voices to fade before we came out of hiding. I put away the blankets. We spilled out the side door and slithered along the edge of the river bank until we came to the bridge. We crossed the river and walked up to Sweet Milk Road about a half mile below our house—far from the millhouse. Then meandered home through the firefly light, all the windows on Sweet Milk Road colored in soft ochre.

Haley looked at me as we were walking down the driveway. His face was scrunched up, his eyes wide. "Why is your father so mean, Aunt Jossy?"

"I don't know."

"Men are just like that," Fletcher said. "If you're a guy, you have to be tough. That's what my father says."

I looked at Fletcher and felt sad for him. He didn't have it easy, and at least I had Miss Euphrates.

I think of Haley asking me that question in what seems a lifetime ago. It's true; the summer Haley knew my father, he was a sad, angry man who smelled of bitter sweat and tomatoes. Whatever tenderness he once had was ground out of him. It helps to remember that as I sit with him in the hospital dayroom.

"Thanks for bringing me a coffee," my father says. "It's a hell of a lot better than the mud they pass off here."

"Anytime, Dad."

"Both you and Wyatt always bring me a cup of joe." He looks out the window, babbling on, complaining. I barely listen but nod here and there to be polite.

"I've missed the whole summer," he says.

"It's been a hot one."

We talk about the weather because neither of us wants to go elsewhere. In truth, it has been a relief to have him here. Whatever acting out he does will be confronted. For once, it becomes his problem, and not mine.

"They tell me I'm going to be sprung in a couple of weeks."

"Yeah? So you'll be going home?"

He nods.

"Good for you. Your apartment is shipshape. I've been cleaning it once a month and Jeannette does a little dusting in between."

"Jeannette! She's a sweetie. She's always had a little mad love for me. She'll do anything for me."

"Oh, so what? You've known that?"

"Course."

"So have you ever—"

"God, no. She's not my type, but I play along, just to keep her happy. Not to say that it doesn't benefit me." He laughs.

I smile through my horror. Little has changed. He will be more careful for a while. But those of us who are useful to my sad, angry father, still standing in his tomato garden and shooting at the eternal crows, must choose to either rise or become his prey.

13

For most of the summer of my twelfth year, it was hard to stand up for myself. Hard not to be the object of my father's ire. But I had learned to be defiant. Instead of doing my garden chores, I would sit on the backyard swing, pumping my feet into the morning air and rising higher and higher.

"Paulie-girl! Boy-o! You better get off that swing and get your chores done!" my father yelled. The brim of his hat shaded his eyes, but his mouth was a slash of red. He loomed over me, wagging his finger in my face, the other hand on his square hip.

I jumped off the swing and stood frozen to the ground.

"Get the colander from that nigg—from Miss Euphrates, and pick the ripe tomatoes. And when you're done with that, go sweep out the millhouse. The fellas are coming over for an evening of jazz." He swiveled on his heels, then turned back with a scowl. "And wipe that hound-dog look off your face," he barked.

I glared at the back of his head as he walked away and wished the sun would melt him all over his putrid tomato plants. Or that some green tendril would grow oh so wicked and wise and bend its spiny arm round and round his haggard neck until it turned gray and broke. In the snap of a branch. Clonk. His head fallen off like one of his rotten, overripe tomatoes. Rolling and rotting beneath his Beefsteaks and Big Boys.

I would have stayed on that swing, pumping my legs higher and higher if I dared. But I got off and ran into the kitchen to help Miss Euphrates put up tomatoes. They were everywhere, tomatoes on the windowsills, along the stovetop. Some were red, split and oozing, with green, star-stemmed tops. Others were pale pink or limey green, all lined shoulder to shoulder ripening in whatever light was available: fireflies, lantern-eyed snipes still out there somewhere, and comets at eighty year intervals.

I hated canning-jar Augusts, afternoons in the kitchen, the ceiling dripping with condensation. Day by day, helping Miss Euphrates line the shelf-papered pantry with filled Ball Jars: rubber-ringed pickles, spicy watermelon rinds, peach marmalade, and green tomato mincemeat. And, of course, jarred stewed tomatoes peppered with bitterness for me. My father forced me to eat them even though he knew they made me gag.

I grabbed the colander, filled it with ripe tomatoes from the garden, and then came back in, plonking more tomatoes onto the drain board.

My mother popped through the doorway as I finished washing up. "What's wrong, Joss?" she asked. "You look so sad."

"I want you to come home, Mom."

She put her arms around me. "I know you do, but you need to be my big girl, my strong one. That's who you are—strong like your Daddy. Your sister needs me now."

"But—"

"No buts!" She kissed my forehead and grabbed a box of her things and disappeared through the doorway.

Miss Euphrates stood at the stove, her knotted hair tied back in a red scarf, dousing ripe tomatoes in pots of boiling water. She looked up at me and shook her head, never skipping a beat as she blanched more tomatoes.

"Come on, dawta-girl. Come sit."

We began peeling tomatoes, her practiced hands sliding the smooth tomato skins from the mushy pulp, me imitating as best I could. We filled pots with the crimson slime. It simmered with cloves, blades of mace, allspice, and dark brown sugar.

"Did you add the garlic?" she asked.

"Not yet." I chopped onions and fat cloves of garlic from the garden while Miss Euphrates added gingerroot, peppercorns, coarse salt, vinegar, and white wine. We waited until it cooked down to quicksand.

It was my job to strain the goop through cheesecloth and then into sterilized bottles. It seemed like too much work for just ketchup.

"This farm," she said, "it used to be a special place, but it changed generations back. Whatever kindness was here got stripped away."

"What do you mean?"

"Your people, the first ones who came to this land. They were kind folks, good to everyone, including the native families. They used to call this farm Mahican Trees."

"What's Mahican Trees?"

"These hills all have old-timey names and stories floating in the air and flying with these crows. They're the best storytellers, all those crows. They know nothing lives so long as lies and secrets."

I nodded, knowing Miss Euphrates had a story to tell.

"My little house, way out there past the river road, in the part of town they call Churchtown, got some stories, too. That's where most of the black folks live. Wildness comes to Churchtown." Miss Euphrates' eyes glowered at me. "Oh, I know that name some people call us. Niggers, right?" Her dark hand flew. The bowls filled. Seeds and red juice dripped from her fingers.

I could feel the heat flash across my face. She must have heard what my father had almost said.

"I never say that word and he shouldn't—"

"Hush, now."

We worked without words, the radio playing R&B, Luther Vandross. Miss Euphrates swayed in her chair until the softness returned to her face. She was beautiful, not a comeliness that those around me understood, but her allure was genuine, earthy, and mysterious.

We both jumped as my father came barreling through the door. "That garbage again!" He snapped off the radio and glared at me. "Boy-o, you better tell the truth. Were you in the Mill with that Fletcher kid and the other one again?"

I felt my heart race and my mouth went dry.

"*Other one?*" Miss Euphrates asked. Her voice had that high-pitched tone that made everyone stop whatever they were doing. "You mean your grandbaby, don't you?"

He didn't answer.

"No, Mr. Ryckman, Joss been here with me in the kitchen except for when I went out there." She squared her wide shoulders. "For canning jars," she said, nodding to the crate of jars in the sink.

"You make sure she stays out of there." He left, banging the door on his way out. I watched him walk out through what he claimed was his garden with its rows of plum tomatoes, Beefsteaks, and Big Boys. Most of it was started and planted by Miss Euphrates and me. My heart still raced as he disappeared into the cornfield.

"He's a jerk."

"He's still your father, Miss Joss, and you gotta be more respectful."

"Well, he should be nice to me."

"I know you are just a dawta-girl, and it's hard to understand. Some folks get mean when they sad. And your daddy, he's sad. Like I say, the kindness left this place generations back."

"Why?" I asked.

"The Mahican Tribes lived all around these parts when the white men first came. White people traded guns for land but then pushed for more. Robbed the Mahicans. Those white folks just took for themselves. But your people were different. The farmwife was a clothmaker. A spinner. She'd grow flax in the fields and harvest it and let it rot in the dammed-up river. Separate it, dry it in the sun, and then spin it into cloth. Color it up real pretty in pots of beets, dandelions, and hops. The Mahican women would come down to see all that brightly colored cloth laid to dry against the yellow mustard blossoms.

"The farmwife, she give those native women long pieces of flax cloth. Soon enough, they'd all be invited to supper. Course only the men could eat in the house. The women and children sat under the trees, drinking crowfoot milk from cows fed on buttercups. Sweet top milk, honey cakes, salt meat. Your people shared what they had.

"One summer day the women and children came early in the morning to sit under the trees. The farmwife was surprised to see them so early in the day and without their men. She brought out the crowfoot milk, the honey cakes. They cooked what they had. The children played. Those ladies all laughing and swirling in that brightly colored flax cloth. And while they were making a party and talking with their hands and eyes, their men were slaughtering all the other white folks in these parts with the guns they took in trade."

"They killed them all?" I asked.

"Yes, Miss Joss, they killed everyone. Just not your people."

My people. Back when I was twelve, I wanted to believe my people were different than the other Dutch empire builders who settled along the Hudson and its tributaries. Maybe they were. But time altered the flax spinner's trajectory. We Rykmans are descendants of brooders and planners, seekers of wealth and property. And I am as good at it as the rest of them, a business owner, a property owner at thirty-three.

I sit at the antique walnut kitchen table, running my hand over the dark crater in the center. It's not as rough as it used to be; treating it with lemon oil over the years has helped. Years ago, my father left the last of the garden tomatoes on the table when we packed up for the summer and headed back to the city. They sat there over the winter, rotting and eating away at the wood. The following summer, when my mother saw what had happened to her family heirloom she screamed at him, terrorizing all of us with her anger. When she was done blowing our eardrums through our heads, she was silent. She didn't speak to him for more than a week.

She was good at that—withdrawing, unwilling to give in, or give up. In the end, she won every argument. She was clear and straightforward, while I fret and worry about what to do with my life, what to do about Wyatt. He asks again if I want bacon and eggs. I ignore him, acting out the dance we both know too well, all the while thinking: *Why am I running from him again?*

He makes eggs regardless.

"Your breakfast okay?" he asks.

"They're a little runny." As soon as the words fall out of my mouth, I regret them. "Sorry," I say. "I don't know why I'm so out of sorts this morning."

"It's okay."

"No, it's not. I'm a jerk."

We sit without looking at each another. Neither of us wants to go over this impasse again. The trail is already too worn.

"Listen, I'm going to take off, head back to the city and get out of your hair."

"You don't have to, Wyatt."

"Yeah, I do. I don't want to fight with you, Joss."

I pour a cup of Wyatt's coffee and sit on the back porch, listening as he packs up his things and wishing I had not pushed him away once again.

He stands in the doorway. "I'll see you later."

"Sure. I have the same schedule next week. I was planning to bring Miss Euphrates over for Sunday dinner. If you're around. . . ."

"I've always wanted to meet her."

"Next Sunday's your day, then."

"I didn't say I'd be here, did I?"

I look up at him, surprised by the tone of his voice.

"You got a minute?" he asks. "I need to say a few things."

"Okay."

"What is it you want from me? You know I love you, but this? This leaving, then coming back together. I feel like you want me in your life, but then you push me away. One minute you're beguiling. The next, a cold fish. I'll grant you, I'm just a clueless guy, so just tell me what you want."

"I don't know what I want, Wyatt. And I know I'm unfair to you."

"At least we agree on that."

"All I can tell you is that I need time."

"All right, Joss, you got time. The other stuff that I put up with—I'm sick of it."

"I'm sorry, Wyatt. I'll do better."

He stands, his hip cocked, silent, watching the starched white curtains rustle in the breeze.

"Okay, so next week we'll have dinner with your Miss Euphrates." He kisses my cheek and leaves.

The sound of his truck navigating the washed-out section of the road fades, and I sit staring out the window. There's a haze across the fields as if it were a watercolor, hastily sketched and left to dry. I tried my hand at watercolors a few years back and soon learned you can't go back once the paint is laid down. You get what you get. Not like oils where you can fix your mistakes.

My coffee is cold, but I slug back the last swallow and retreat to the kitchen. There are dishes to be done, bed linens to be stripped and washed. The dust mop and vacuum stand at attention, waiting for their orders. I begin in the front gardens mulching, weeding, deadheading. When I have cleared away the dust and weeds, what remains is my jumbled mind, my uneven heart, and the minefield I continually plant around the perimeters of my life.

In the late afternoon, I head out to the cornfield gone fallow. The wild grasses and pokeweeds are waist high or deeper, filled with grasshoppers, crickets, and feeding fireflies. They are the symphony that charges the void. I haul my supplies: an easel, and my case of watercolors and brushes rummaged from the attic. And without expectation, I begin sketching the landscape.

Pane's gray and sap green wash against the white paper, while I watch a redtail hawk swoop across the August-bloom meadow in search of prey. He is a predator, like me, both of us pillagers. Scarlet and vermillion of the flowering prairie fire scatter across the field. The hawk seeks its kill. I breathe in. The raptor rises. I can hear its wings pulse against the green-gold sky, continuing the hunt.

All the while I paint, sheet after sheet. Feeble attempts. It is hard to relinquish the vision of perfection against my amateur results, but allowing just pure color against the white is a gift. Cerulean blue and cobalt, burnt sienna and raw umber, they fill the space between sunlight and nightfall.

And then I paint the dark.

Still in my blue cotton nightgown from the morning, I dance through the wet grass. Twirling and spinning, leaping fearlessly from shadow to shadow. It has been years since I waded through the night fields. It must have been to catch fireflies. We taught Haley all about those flying glow bugs, Fletcher and me.

Right after Haley moved to the farm, I convinced my mother and sister to let us show him how to catch those tiny floating lanterns. We went out as dusk was rolling in, each of us clutching an empty pickle jar with nail holes punched in their tops. We waited by a thicket of blackberry briars, sitting in the cool grass.

"Keep watching," I told Haley. "They'll be out soon."

"What do they look like?"

"You've never seen fireflies?" Fletcher asked.

Haley shook his head.

"That's right. I keep forgetting you're a city kid."

"He isn't anymore," I said.

"Look, look!" Haley said. "There's one and another one."

"The darker it gets, the more they come out."

We grabbed them in our cupped hands, transferring them to the jars now lined with grass and berries. We ran after them, screeching in the dark when they got away, racing through the dewy grass for more.

"What are we going to do with them?" Haley asked.

"We should let them go before we go inside," I said.

"Don't listen to her. I always put mine next to my bed."

We walked back toward the house as headlights flickered along the driveway. The cars rolled through the ruts and parked in front of the millhouse.

"What's going on?" Fletcher asked.

"My father's jazz group is playing tonight."

"Can we listen?" Haley asked with a squeal in his voice.

"You know we're not supposed to go in there," I said.

"Please, Aunt Jossy. You know I play jazz, too."

"You do?" Fletcher asked. "That's so cool."

We slithered into the millhouse, leaving our jars of fireflies outside. We whispered plans, our voices low and pinned to the floor.

"Hide in the shadows in case my father comes downstairs."

We listened to them above our heads, tromping across my father's upstairs office, moving chairs, hanging lanterns from the rafters.

One of the fellas yelled, "Hey, you got any more lamp oil?"

"Look in the closet."

"Gentlemen," another voice called out. "Come choose your poison: beer, scotch, a little whiskey in a jar?"

"Paul, what's with the birdcage hanging on the door?"

Someone shouted out, "Is it true? Your old lady flew the coop?"

"Fuck all of ya," my father answered.

Fletcher snickered out loud before he could cover his mouth, but the laughter upstairs camouflaged the sound.

One of the guys said, "She'll be back, Paul. You wait and see."

"Drink up, boys," he answered. "Time to play."

Otis Harrington struck the 'A' above middle C on the piano while Liam Michaels, my favorite and my father's apprentice, tuned his violin, finding the pure middle of the note, the place where God sings. That was what he always told me—that God sings on certain notes.

Martin Deitman on the stand-up bass, and Dave Posnick on the guitar, tuned up, too, pulling chords, listening for resonance and harmony. The others—Ray Correa, the clarinet player, Henry Moses from Churchtown on the cornet, with my father as drummer—all took their places, waiting for someone to shout out a tune and begin.

We hid downstairs, listening, ready to tap our feet, bob, and wobble.

"Why can't we go upstairs to watch?" Haley wanted to know.

"I told you this morning," Fletcher said. "Remember? Joss' dad doesn't like us in here."

"That's just dumb."

"Be quiet, you guys," I warned. "They'll hear us."

My father's voice boomed, "Let's start with 'Over the Rainbow.'" They began with Liam playing the violin intro, melancholy and haunting tones that could do a man's crying for him. The others came in, measure after measure. Waves of music drifted throughout the millhouse. And when they had finished that piece, off they spun into another tune, "Fleur De Lavande," an irreverent, foot-tapping jazz number that whirled around our heads.

"Come on, Joss! Let's sit on the stairs and spy on them," Fletcher said.

"Yeah! Let's!" agreed Haley.

Before I could object, they tiptoed over to the staircase and began crawling up on their hands and knees. I motioned for them to come back down, but they kept creeping to the top. I stood frozen, not knowing what to do. Someone called out "Bye, Bye Blackbird," followed by the nasal timbre of Clay Moses's cornet and the rasp of the drum brushes. Fletcher and Haley were just below the top stair tread, poking their heads up to watch, their feet wiggling to the beat.

I crept over and knelt on the bottom of the stairs, tossing loose gravel from the floor. Haley turned, and I motioned him to come down.

But Clay Moses saw him. "Who we got here?" he asked.

Haley jumped and said, "Can I play with you?"

I heard my heart pounding in my ears and stood rocking back and forth on my heels, not knowing whether to stay or run.

"Well!" Clay Moses said, "What do you play, little man? But more importantly, who are you?"

"Nahaliel Ryckman. That's my name, but everyone calls me Haley. And I've been playing the piano for a long time, now."

The guys chuckled. Liam winked at me and whispered, "Hey, there, Miss Jossy! What you doin sneaking around downstairs?"

"Well, well, well, you must be Paul's grandson."

My father mumbled something, but I couldn't hear him.

Just then, Fletcher popped up and said, "I play the trombone!"

"Fellas!" Clay said. "We got us a musical contingent right below our noses. Come on up here, boys. Let's see what you got. Otis, make some room on your piano bench for this youngster."

I heard a chair scuff along the floorboards on the other side of the room and knew it had to be my father.

He stood at the top of the stairs and said, "Come on up here, Joss. Join your buddies." His voice was flat.

I clomped up the stairs knowing there would be a price to pay when no one else was around and worrying what that would be.

"What you gonna play, little man?" Clay asked?

"*Rhapsody in Blue*," but just the first part." Haley sat straight-backed on the stool, his striped socks peeking out below his pant legs, his small fingers finding the first few tinkling notes followed by that iconic glissando.

The room quieted. I stole looks at my father's cronies, glancing from face to face, each set of eyes filled with wonder and excitement. All of them trained on Haley, even my father. He had softened, too. And I began to lose myself in the music. All of us stilled, waiting for the next passage, soft one moment so we'd have to hold our breath to hear, and the next, a passage so complex it would make our heads spin. Haley's hands flew up and down the keyboard as the frenetic composition electrified the room: the bluesy notes, the laid-back tempo changes, the shivering cadenzas. It rose and rose up and out of the high loft window, wild and magical, calling to the stars.

When he finished, my father shot to his feet, clapping and laughing. "Kid," he said, as he tousled Haley's bowl-cut hair, "You're a goddamn genius!"

14

It was a genius idea to bring Miss Euphrates out to the farm to meet Wyatt. At one o'clock they arrive, and I stand on the porch waiting, while Wyatt helps her up the steps.

"Miss Euphrates! You look cool and summery in your red and pink dress."

"The air is much better out here than in town." She fans herself, stops to catch her breath, and smiles at me.

"Yeah, but we have more bugs."

She laughs. "But I got this charmer on my arm. Maybe I won't let him go, Miss Joss." She winks at me and whispers for all of us to hear, "I wouldn't if I was you."

Wyatt laughs. "Maybe I'll take you up on that offer, Miss Euphrates. Both of us being charmers and all."

"Miss Joss, am I blushing yet?"

"Almost." I hold the front door open for her.

"Look at this. You got this place fixed up so nice. Fancy."

"This was my mother's sumptuous redo. It's grown on me. And it fits the house."

"Your momma, she always had an eye."

We walk through the living room, while Miss Euphrates runs her hand along the mahogany tables, the plush upholstery.

"My mother used to sit in this room with white paper spread over the floor and hem bridal gowns. It was something to see— her surrounded by all that chiffon and tulle. I've got pictures." We sit on the shell pink settee and leaf through my mother's bridal gown album.

"Miss Euphrates, Joss? Can I get you ladies something to drink? Iced tea, wine, seltzer?"

"See? A charmer, just like I was saying."

"Ladies! You're making me blush."

"I'd like a small glass of wine, with a little seltzer," Miss Euphrates says.

"That sounds refreshing. Make it two."

"Now you gonna make that with red wine? I like a little red wine."

"Will do," he says.

We page through the photo album, oohing over the beautiful dresses my mother created: sleek shantung halter gowns with endless slits to the top of the thigh, elegant necklines, or flirty bouffant skirts scattered with tiny hand-sewn winged creatures—birds, butterflies, and bees. I try to imagine the women who wore these iconic dresses.

"This is a wonderful tribute to your momma, Miss Joss. This book—don't it make you think about wearing your own special dress one of these days?"

"Are you going to start that again?"

"Child, don't let that man out in the kitchen get away. Ummum. He's delicious."

I laugh. "I guess he is."

"And he got a pretty face, too. A girl could look at a face like that for a long time."

"Miss Euphrates, you're a flirt."

"She is," Wyatt says, as he serves our drinks.

"Always was. I learned that from my madda. Sista Bébé, oooh, she could trifle with a man's heart. One time, when there was nothing in her pocketbook but an empty change purse and red, red lipstick, the landlord was after her. She made arrangements to stay with a cousin in Savannah. But we had to get there, Madda and me.

"She knew this old honky-tonk outside of town. We hitched and walked and got there by sundown. It was hot and I hungry, whining and complaining. She set me on a picnic table out back and said, 'You wait here, dawta. Madda be right back with a Coke.'

"I waited for hours. The sun was sinking behind the hills when she come out with a drink and a hot dog for me. 'I got us a ride, baby,' she say and led me to a beat-up Chevy. 'You got to hide in the back, lie down on the floor, and don't make no sound. I be right back out with that good ole boy.' She laughed in that tipsy way. 'He got a pocket full of money and mush for brains.'

"We drove from Gulfport, Mississippi to Savannah, Georgia stopping at every other open bar along the way. It took three days with Sista Bébé cooing in his ear the whole time."

"Did he ever know you were in the back?" Wyatt asks.

"Nope. I'd sneak in the back of whatever bar they were in, use the facility, and buy some greasy sandwich off the grill. That man never knew he was our bus ticket." She shakes her head, laughing. "My madda lived by the curves and wit God gave her. It wasn't always the best way, what she done. But it was human."

"That must have been hard for you."

"Sista Bébé was a certain kind of woman, and a lot of folks had a lot of things to say about her. People around here loves to talk."

"I know," I said.

"Course you do. All those stories about your daddy doing more than target practice years back."

I look at her dark eyes searching my face. It's hard to know what she means, or if it is gossip she is railing against or repeating. But what seems clear is that my father has his secrets, that discovering who he is might be like the dotted line on a treasure map. There is no secret cache. None of that is real. But the nightmare is. "How about I give you the tour?" I ask.

"That'd be nice. It's been a long time since I been in this house."

"While you ladies do that, I'm going to put the finishing touches on Sunday dinner."

"Something smells good," Miss Euphrates says.

"That's the red pepper sauce. It's a little sweet and a little spicy, too. Not too much spice."

"I like a little spice."

We walk around the house, touring the dining room, the annex turned bookbinding studio, before heading upstairs. At the top of the stairs, Miss Euphrates heads toward my old room.

"There's something I'm curious about." She opens the closet door, pulling on the overhead light. "They're gone," she says, her voice tinged with sorrow.

"You mean the closet monsters?"

We both peer inside the green-striped wallpapered closet.

"I loved them. I tell my grandbabies about those wild creatures. They painted beasts in their own closets."

"Really?" I laughed and imagined Miss Euphrates' grand-children slopping buckets of paint up the stairs, a trail into their rooms and closets. "Wait right here, Miss Euphrates," I said. "I think I know where there are some wild things." I grab a flashlight from the dresser and push back the few blouses hanging on the rod to reveal a small door to the eaves. Inside are bright scarlet monsters, dressed in electric lime green and robin's egg blue. They are still holding clubs and spears after twenty-two years, standing on their pointy heads, their red-violet, double jointed arms flailing against the sheathing of the house. Our scrawl print signatures yet remain, with heart shaped decorations and declarations of love and promises of forever.

"Oh my," she says. They still here." Her breathy voice is like magic in the dark.

"That they are." I smile and look deeper into the crawlspace. There are old toys and boxes of school papers, a baby blanket with worn, soft-frayed edges on a high rafter folded away like a memory. And deep in the back is a toy gun. I'd forgotten it was there. I push it back, not wanting Miss Euphrates to see it, not wanting anything to spoil this lovely day.

"Ladies," Wyatt calls from the bottom of the stairs. "Dinner is served."

Sunday dinner is outside under the Butternut tree on an old wooden table covered with a flowery tablecloth and decorated with a bunch of scrubbed clean red radishes shining through a clear glass vase.

"You two are so clever, she says. "Now what we got here? Deviled eggs and a pretty salad. The rest, I don't know."

"This is grilled polenta," I place a piece on her plate. "And that," I point. "That's catfish topped with fried and shredded sweet potato with a puddle of red pepper sauce."

"Miss Joss. You remembered, didn't you?"

"That catfish is your favorite? It's a little different than your recipe—Miss Euphrates makes the best fried catfish, Wyatt. Soaked in buttermilk and fried in cornmeal."

She laughs. "I remember that monster bullhead catfish you brought home."

I remember, too.

Fletcher, Haley, and I flew out on our rickety bicycles the morning after Haley's jazz debut in the Millhouse. Not wanting to encounter my father, we left early, each of us with knapsacks and fishing poles dangling from our backs. We pedaled past Fletcher's street off Sweet Milk Road, with its rustic houses and log homes tucked into the landscape that zigzagged along the river, rolling east where Sweet Milk becomes Connor Road. We screamed up and over the swayback hills, pumping our legs faster than our shadows that rippled across the pavement could catch us.

Up in the high field ahead, crews of carpenters were building Cape-style houses kitty corner along newly cut-in streets. We stopped and watched the cement mixers pop and roll along the dirt road like pachyderms. Then raced to the top of the next hill and coasted down the other side, our hearts pounding when some farmyard dog raced after us, snarling and biting at our ankles. We screeched and stretched our voices to hoarseness, cutting through the humid air, out-pedaling that growling monster.

We passed house after house, properties that rambled into sheds, barns, and haphazard outbuildings surrounded by acres devoted to squashes: hubbards, acorns, butternuts, and pumpkins. The stink of manure, of algae bloom on farm ponds, and of our sweat drove us until we came to the Mobile station with its low-slung brick façade just north of the lake. We parked our bikes; the kickstands wedged into the gravel turnaround and tumbled through the door.

Bo Davis or one of his brothers—they all looked alike in that plank and gnawed kind of way—came in from the garage. Mr. Davis leaned toward us, a rusted clock-faced gas pump in back of him. I imagined his face superimposed over the gas pump.

He eyed me, and I tried not to laugh. "What you all chuckles about, kid?" he asked.

I shrugged my shoulders.

"Don't waste my time. You want something or not?" He swaggered backward; his rag-dusted hands and oily fingernails drummed the countertop.

"Three Cokes," I said.

"Put yer money up."

We emptied our pockets onto the counter, the quarters clanking, our mouths like sandpaper, our hearts still racing. He handed us the sodas. We ran back out into the sunlight, slugging down that sharp, cool drink.

"Don't you kids leave them Coke cans around!" he hollered after us.

I ran the empties back inside, afraid not to.

Fletcher balanced on his bike, the swagger in him as if some of Bo Davis had rubbed off. "If that mutt chases us on our way home," he said, "I'm going to clock that bastard in the jaw!"

"How are you going to do that?" I asked.

"I'll lead going back, balance my legs on my handlebars. When he comes after me, I'll whack him in the jaw with the heel of my shoe. I seen my Daddy do that. Sent some lousy mutt to kingdom come." He snickered and strutted, upending that can of Coke, draining the last drop into his mouth.

Haley's eyes widened, "Your daddy killed a dog?"

"Well, duh!"

I didn't say anything, but the picture of Mr. Goodwin clocking some poor mutt played in my head. It wasn't much of a stretch imagining my father doing something equally cruel. I couldn't reconcile how our fathers had become such men.

At the lake, we bought bait and sandwiches and settled on the dock, threading worms onto fishhooks. I sat counting, tapping the air with my foot to the tune whirling in my head. Haley caught the beat with the bob of his head and giggled. We mouthed the words to En Vogue's "Hold On." We then dropped our lines into clear, smooth water, watching our bobbers for the slightest movement.

We fished earnestly, each with one eye on our lines while watching the pontoon boats skim the water like lazy swans. Floating, nodding on the surface, in no hurry to go anywhere. Queechy Lake had a monopoly on quirky, eccentric homemade pontoon boats—oil drums repurposed and attached to a deck with a folding chair lashed on, or a cabana of old bed sheets set on a couple of canoes. Some had potted plants on board, or charcoal grills and oil lamps for all day and night fishing, though mostly they were nighttime party boats with music and dancing and twinkling lights that glimmered on the moonlit water.

"Hey, you guys, look at that one!" I pointed out a boat configured to look like a giant rainbow trout. Fletcher and I laughed, but Haley looked worried.

"Are you going to be in trouble with your father?" he whispered.

"Probably."

"She's always in trouble," Fletcher said.

"Why?" Haley wanted to know. "What do you do to get into trouble?"

I shrugged my shoulders, watching the water, keeping my line still. We had already caught five perches. I had looked into their eyes, watching their gills rise and fall, before slipping them into my dark knapsack, pushing them down, proof of my cruelty.

We ate our sandwiches, tossing breadcrumbs into the water, and slid our feet into the lake, wiggling them back and forth to attract the curious and hungry perch. They darted in quickly, dicing at our toes, then raced away only to turn back again.

"I caught a bullhead here once," I said. "It had thick, black, long whiskers. But my father said it was a garbage fish. He ripped the hook from its mouth and heaved it way out into the lake." I wondered if that fat, old bullhead was watching, swimming below our choppy legs, his mouth still gaping to one side.

"Joss, do you think fish can talk in some language of their own?"

"I don't know, Haley." Secretly, I didn't want to know.

"I'm sure they do," he said with that telltale squeak in his voice. "Turtles, beavers, fish, the crows. All of them have ways of communicating."

I dropped my line in one more time, way out deep into the lake, baiting it with a little of the chicken salad from my sandwich. I watched the line, finishing the last of my lunch.

"Me and Haley are going back to the snack bar," Fletcher said. "You want another Coke?"

"Yeah, that'd be good."

I lay back on the dock, hooked my pole into a crevice there, and watched the clouds race across the lake. I counted them, trying to separate the wispy, fast moving cirrus clouds from the sloth-like stratus. But they moved too fast, and I knew I would have to go home soon and face my father.

"Hey kid," some stranger in a plaid shirt and cutoffs hollered. "You got something on your line."

I snapped back up and grabbed my pole from the crevice. Whatever was on my line was strong and a lot bigger than the perch we had been catching all morning.

Mr. Plaid Shirt stood in back saying, "Give him some slack."

I did what he said.

"Okay, now reel him in slowly, and then give just a little more back. It's a dance, don't you know? You and that fish. You got a net?"

I shook my head.

"I'll grab mine. Just keep on reeling that thing in nice and slow."

I did what he said, gently winding the reel, watching for him to come back. I waved when I saw him running toward the dock.

"You still got it?" he asked.

"Yup," I nodded.

"Steady, now." While I reeled it in, we watched its massive head come up just below the dock. The net man readied himself and scooped the bullhead up and out of the water. It thrashed and pulled, but its fight was over. We landed it onto the dock.

"Jeezus, look at the size of that mother," Mr. Plaid Shirt said. "Be careful of his whiskers. They can hurt."

Haley and Fletcher came running down the dock.

"What'd you catch?" Haley asked.

"A huge bullhead."

"It's a beauty, kid. Must be about twenty inches long. How about I clean it for you."

"Okay."

He got out his fish knife along with some newspapers. In one quick motion, he sliced the head off, then gutted the bullhead and wrapped it. He tossed the entrails into the lake, but not before I got a good look at that fish's mouth.

"Here now," he said, handing me the newspaper package. "Get this in your knapsack and on ice as soon as you can. That'll be a tasty dinner."

"Thanks, mister."

He tousled my head and walked back up the dock.

I stuffed the fish into my knapsack with the perch.

"Let's get going," I said.

We ran to our bikes and stitched our way back, roaring up and down those hills and curves with a half dozen crows calling and cawing while they followed us. Even when we stopped at the Mobile station, sliding our tires in the gravel turnaround and taking turns running to the bathroom, they waited, perched in the trees.

I was the last to use the bathroom. When I came out, Miss Euphrates was standing in the driveway, her grocery bag on the ground, her hands on her hips.

"What are you kids doing all the way out here? Your father been looking for you, girl."

They all stared at me, but I didn't say anything.

She sighed. "I worry about you, dawta-girl! Never met a child who could get herself into more difficulties. You best get home."

Eventually we made our way back to Red Mills Farm, the three of us dawdling, taking our time—sidetracked by a dirt road. We stopped to watch a farmer hay his field and saw a box turtle crossing the road. We stopped and picked it up.

"Look," Haley said. "His back looks like it has big square buttons on it." We laughed, then crossed the turtle to the other side so no oncoming car would crush it. The crows tagged us at every stop.

Haley pointed to my knapsack. "Was that the same fish that your father threw back? The one with the ripped mouth?"

I shrugged my shoulders like I didn't care and rode on.

15

I sit bolt upright in Wyatt's bed in Brooklyn, struggling to catch my breath.

"What's wrong, Joss?"

"I can't breathe."

Wyatt pulls me into his arms, circling me with his body. He strokes my forehead, my face, my arms. "It's all right. Just relax. It was just a dream."

"It was so real." I breathe in his soap-clean scent, the combed cotton, the softness of the rumpled sheets. My racing heart slows; the images in my head fade back across the windowpanes. But over the last weeks it has always been the same dream: some hollow-eyed shooter from my mother's secret story. Her running along the river's edge, with flowing wet hair to her ankles, and me in the river searching and searching. I sigh, knowing my mother was as lost to me when she was here as she is now.

"It was just a dream, baby. Nothing more," Wyatt coos. "Go back to sleep."

He turns over, and I hear his deep rhythmic breathing. I lie there awake until daybreak, though I must have dozed off at some point. When I wake, I hear Wyatt in the shower.

I holler to him, "The plumber is coming this morning to look at the café kitchen."

"Why? What's going on?" he shouts from the bathroom.

"We're getting backups."

"That's not good. Let me know if there's anything I can do."

"I will, but I have to run." I dress quickly, gulp down a couple of swallows of coffee, and get to the café barely on time. Joey Arpino, in his knitted cap, and his cousin, Ted, slide around the kitchen floor, banging on pipes in the walls and snaking drain lines from the basement out to the street.

"I hate to tell ya this, Ms. Ryckman," Joey says, pulling a pencil from behind his ear. "But you got major problems here."

It's as if this is some romantic comedy: The plumber delivering the bad news, the heroine fretting over an upcoming astronomical bill, and an opening like a proverb, *I hate to tell ya. . . .* I smirk. We nail down a price, and he says he can begin on Tuesday.

"Then Tuesday—right, Joey? I'm going to close down and furlough everyone for a week. That's a big deal. So I have to know you'll show when you say you will."

"Come on, you know me, Ms. Ryckman. I say I'll be here, then I'll be here."

He shows up Wednesday.

Knowing that my father will be coming home soon, I spend the first day of the furlough cleaning his apartment. I power through listening to tunes and drinking too much coffee. By mid-afternoon, I have the kitchen done, the cabinets cleaned out and washed, everything reorganized. The floor, the windows, the curtains— everything spotless.

In the bedroom, there are boxes and boxes of old letters. The romantic notion of my father as a letter writer paints a view of him that feels uncomfortable. It's at odds with the narrow window I allow him, the window that is more about darkness than light, but I sit on the floor opening the yellowed envelopes nonetheless. Most of them are from my mother, but quite a few are from old Army buddies. One name jumps out at me: Dale Pelletier, originally from Canaan, a guy who used to show up on the farm occasionally when I was a kid. He was why my father first visited Canaan. He was the guy who introduced my parents to each other.

It hits me. The dream. I wonder if Dale Pelletier knows about Morgan and the shooter in the high birch grove. I pull out all his letters and begin reading them. There is nothing direct in his letters, only a reference to an "incident," but that could be anything. He and my father were in Vietnam together. There must have been too many "incidents" to count. The majority of his awkward sentences are chatter about his wife, his job as a machinist, his sons.

I look him up on one of those people finder sites. His name appears, an address in Parma, Ohio, a suburb of Cleveland, but no phone number unless I want to pay. Which I do.

For the next three days, I call the number periodically throughout the day. But no one answers. Like most people, Dale Pelletier likely doesn't answer phone numbers he doesn't recognize.

At dinner that night I tell Wyatt the sordid story of how my mother's brother Morgan was killed in the mustard field. And that I'd never known about it until a few months before my mother's death.

"Amazing!" he says. "It's hard to keep the lid on a thing like that." He shakes his head and chews on the crusty bread.

I can see his mind spinning. "I know!" I say. "Nobody ever said anything, not even Miss Euphrates. When my mother finally told me, it was as if it was in passing—a comment on the weather or the price of gas. It must have been on her mind, but I don't think she ever intended to tell me. I'm not even sure Naomi knows."

"You could ask her. Maybe she can shed some light."

"It cuts a little too close to the bone with Naomi."

"Yeah. The subject of your father is touchy."

We wash the dishes, sending our doubts and questions down the drain. I try the Ohio telephone number again. Still no answer.

"Come on, Joss. Let's get out of here. Go for a walk. See what's happening at the bakery."

We tumble down the stairs and out into the evening sky. The sidewalk is hot; the heat of the day rises through our soles into our tired feet. We stop for ice cream, sliding the cool concoctions down our throats as we wait for the light in a queue of sweaty bodies. A little boy dangling from his mother's hip stares at my ice cream cone but turns away when I wink at him. I wonder what I might be missing without a toddler straddled to my side.

The light turns, and we bustle like ants to the opposite sidewalk and down another block to the red door to my bakery. I peer through the gold-lettered window. The sales area is draped in plastic. Once inside, we find the kitchen torn apart, too, and everything covered in heavy plastic or moved into the dining room. There is dust everywhere and a crater in the floor. We both stand above it and stare down into the basement.

"What a mess," I say, shaking my head. There are pipes cut away with bare ends hanging through the walls.

Wyatt walks around, running his hands through the dust and grime. "This is going to cost plenty!"

"Yup. I'm praying no overages. Joey's always been decent. Plus with the new dishwashing system, hopefully, he'll keep that in mind when he calculates the bill."

"Gotta kiss up to the plumber. So I hear."

"Nah. He's too short for me."

"Good to know," Wyatt laughs.

I sigh, locking the door behind us and thinking of the clean-up after Joey's done. With all hands on board, it will still take a few days.

"I can help, too," Wyatt says, "with getting this place back together."

I brush his face, his scratchy stubble. "You're too good."

We walk back to Wyatt's place, holding hands, watching the people bustle along Atlantic Avenue. Most everyone is in a hurry, though there are a few strollers like us. We nod to one another, acknowledging there is no urgency. No headlong rush.

"What would you think if I drove out to Parma, Ohio?"

Wyatt stops on the sidewalk and looks at me, his eyes dark and inscrutable. "You want to do that? You want to know definitively if your father was or wasn't the shooter?"

"I think so." I hear the waver in my voice.

"Then go. I'm all for excising ghosts that hold you back. But be prepared. Real answers can throw you. It's enough to live with yourself when you've survived combat and come home and raised some hell. It's a job to forgive it."

"I think I know."

"Yeah, you do."

Wyatt's words stay with me as I pack in the morning, tiptoeing into the tiny bedroom while he sleeps. I carry my bag down, stow it in the back of my car, thinking what it will be like to know the truth.

From his open bedroom window, Wyatt calls in a near whisper, "When you take a break, give a holler," mimicking a phone to his ear.

"I will. And I'll write—send you a beautiful postcard from downtown Parma." I laugh. "It's okay, Wyatt, you don't have to write back."

"Wise ass!" he hisses.

I blow him a kiss. "I should be there by dinner. I figure I'll show up at the Pelletier home a little after that."

"Be careful. Dress nice."

"Okay, Mom."

He laughs and watches me pull away from the curb.

It's still dark as I buckle my seat belt and wave goodbye. I watch him from my rearview mirror craning his head out the window, tracking my little car until I disappear into the traffic. He'll worry until he hears from me.

It's already sticky and hot. The Holland Tunnel is bumper to bumper with cars at breakneck speeds, rushing to get to work on time. I push through the first hour into Pennsylvania and I-80 West. The sun is coming up while crows scour the ribbons of macadam, calling and cawing. Redtails with their snowy breasts sit in the treetops. Just waiting. I watch for their shadows, their wingspans across the highway as they swoop for their prey. Oddly I admire their purpose, their ferocity.

After another half hour, I stop for coffee and a sweet roll, and I call Wyatt. "I'm out of the city, into PA."

"Okay. Be careful. Love you."

"I will. Love you, too." I hear the happy lilt at the tail of my voice. My little car tracks along the highway. The air smells good out here. And I think about my father. It propels everything in me—the thought of coming to some truth about him. Of being settled.

I turn up the radio; the tunes fill in all the spaces. I lower the window and remember driving through the night with my father ten years ago when I was twenty-three.

We were going to Canaan. He was antsy to get out, recovering from hip surgery. On that night, we drove up Second Avenue. It was past midnight; the night women were hawking their wares, the street boys looking to boil their blood. Lights flashed. Car horns and sirens filled the dark as we crossed the Triborough Bridge. From there to the Bronx River Parkway it was a straight shot onto the Taconic. The radio played classic rock, the volume low. My window was half open.

My father was sleeping, his head thrown back, his mouth slack, white hair blowing in the night wind, above his frayed collar. I turned up the volume and lowered both windows all the way.

He stirred. "Turn that radio down." Spit and bark rasped between his teeth with his maddening temper seeping through again. "And stop that wiggling, Paulie-girl. How can I cuff these pants with all your gyrations? They have to be right. You and I are going out."

I didn't tell him that he was still dreaming.

The city lights disappeared, the street people faded, and I drove onward, careening toward Canaan, gliding like a night zephyr against a light drizzle and the inky-black night. Headlights flashed through the rolling hills of the south-bound divide.

"Jeezus!" my father yelled.

His bellow startled me.

"What did you spill on this seat?"

"Your seat is wet, Dad?"

"Didn't I just say that?"

"You must have had an accident."

"Accident! Like hell. You spilled something and let me sit in it."

"Okay, okay," I said, barely hiding my frustration. "I'll pull over and see what I can do." I took the next exit and found an all-night grocery—they would have a bathroom where I could clean him up. I remember pulling the wheelchair out of the trunk and getting him settled with a blanket over his legs. I'd taken it over his strident objections.

"Christ, I don't need that goddamn thing."

"You're soaked, Dad. But we'll find something for you to change into at the grocery. No big deal."

"Easy for you to say. Where's my cane?" he asked.

"You don't need it. We've got the wheelchair."

"Give me my cane."

"Fine." I laid it across his lap and chastised myself for arguing with him. It was easier just to give him what he wanted.

We pushed through the automatic doors into a fluorescent world of pale green cabbages and canary-yellow squashes piled into bins at the store entrance. We wheeled along the aisles until I found sweatpants and the only underwear available—women's cotton panties. I held up the package.

"These are the only underwear they have that will fit you."

"What are those—pink? You gotta be kidding me." He jerked his head back.

"Dad, it's either these or Depends."

"Well, I'm not wearing no goddamn diaper."

"So these—right?" I laid the package on his lap. "Listen—you have to tell me next time you need to go. Help me out, okay?"

He didn't answer.

We checked out and then found the bathrooms down a corridor at the back of the store. I wheeled him into the handicapped stall of the ladies' room. "I'll keep this blanket on your lap while I pull off your wet clothes. Then you can wash yourself. Okay?"

He waved me off with his hand.

When he was done washing, I shimmied the pink panties up over his bottom. As I adjusted the waistband, his blanket fell to the floor. He looked down at himself and jerked his head back and smirked. "Oh, you love this! Dressing your father like a helpless girl. Your own father!"

Out of the corner of my eye, I caught the movement of his hand as he raised his cane above his head. His thin lips set hard. His eyes narrowed. But I stepped back just as he swung the thing through the air.

My heels spun across the floor, and I backed out through the doorway, watching his contorted face.

"Where are you going?" he barked. "Get back here."

I didn't answer.

His screaming followed me along the corridor. "Don't leave me, Joss!" His voice sounded hollow. The clack of my heels drowned out the rest. I left him, alone in the middle of the night in the ladies' room, wearing pink cotton panties.

Canned music, the chatter of twentysomethings stocking shelves, the whirl of floor scrubbers wobbled my legs. My thoughts rushed. My stomach churned as the whiz of the exit door pushed me out into the soggy night. It was pouring, but I couldn't stop myself, or will my feet to turn back.

Wet hair fell across my face as I fumbled for my keys. In the car, the engine gunned, the blower spewed cold air. I let it be. My fingers were cold, and I was numb as the tires splashed into the street. The wipers spun furiously against the windshield, though I couldn't see beyond ten feet. The lines in the road were faded, and I worried I was in the wrong lane. My hands gripped the steering wheel as I scanned for road markers. Still, the car staggered along the slippery road.

Headlights came towards me, and the other driver and I slowed as we passed one another. I breathed easier, momentarily reassured. The air was warmer now, the radio on. A soothing all-night voice talked me through the dark as rain pelted the roof. The wipers slowed, tracking their arc across the windshield.

I pushed away thoughts of my father alone in that bathroom miles back as I raced through the night. Onward, taking one turn after another, the road became rougher, now following the bend of a rutted lane. I heard a nearby river roaring through the trees. I had no idea where I was. But I knew I was lost. The radio voices were gone, replaced by a classical piece I didn't recognize. The rain let up again. I cracked the windows and sucked in the cool air. A soft rain was falling; the car whooshed through deep puddles. The night air rushed past me, taking with it music and beat. None of it stayed. I pulled off the road because there was nowhere else to go, no road beyond that point. I knew I would turn back; there was nothing else I could have done. But I laid my head back and closed my eyes, listening to the radio, to the sound of the running water and my father's voice in my head. I was wary of his recklessness.

Now I am wary of what will come next. What tragedies await my father's hands? I try to clear my mind, tell myself to be open and not to assume anything. The road calls me back, counting the barns and silos through Pennsylvania and into Ohio. Endless farmhouses and outbuildings whir past my little red Cooper as if they are moving and I am static. Hundreds of black and white cows move from milking stations back to the yellow-green pastures. The blues in the morning sky melt into the heat of the afternoon: aqua, to sky blue, electric ultramarine to indigo and cyan. I stop where I can and take pictures of the colors, the waves of heat coming off the pavement, and a selfie with a moustache of chocolate milkshake making me look like a kid on one last great adventure.

In the morning, I will have got on with it. But for now I am driving to Parma.

Around four in the afternoon, I cross the town line into Parma. My Mini Cooper weaves through the streets into downtown, with its classic brick storefronts dotted between new franchise-branded buildings. I find The Little Polish Diner on Ridge Road and order the Warsaw plate—homemade pierogis, stuffed cabbage, and a cup of chicken soup—enough to fortify me for the task ahead. On my way out, I poke my head into the kitchen and introduce myself to Sophy, the petite blonde responsible for the great food.

"Delicious!" I tell Sophy. "The pierogis were light and just perfect."

"I try," she says.

"You certainly succeed!" We both laugh and she tells me to come by again. I may have to get some to go and an ice pack. Wyatt would love them. A quick change in the restroom and I am ready to find Dale Pelletier.

I find my way to Whittington Drive, a 1950s neighborhood dotted with dormered, one and half story houses. The side yards festooned with strings of chili pepper and palm tree lights, the waft of barbecue drifts in the evening light, and kids squeal under the sprinkler hoses. I pull up to the Pelletier home, guided by my GPS. A young guy answers the door. He's tall, lanky, and long in the face with an even look to him. I hear a baby crying in the background, the distinct sound of a newborn.

"I'm looking for Dale Pelletier," I say, smiling, with my best hopeful look.

"You found him. What can I do for you?" His frame fills the doorway.

This couldn't be the Dale Pelletier from my father's letters. This guy is too young. "Oh," I say. "Maybe it's your father I'm looking for. He and my Dad served in Vietnam together."

"Who's your dad?"

"Paul Ryckman, from New York."

"Yeah, I remember Dad mentioning that name. In fact, your father came out here a few years back."

"He did? Do you know what for?"

"Come on in. Don't mind the mess. We have our hands full these days. Twins."

I smile and sit on the worn plaid sofa. There are piles of fresh-laundered onesies and tiny t-shirts. "How old are your babies?"

"Three weeks. Two little boys, Jake and Will."

"Congratulations! Wow, twins!"

"You have kids, Miss. . . ."

"Ryckman, same name as my father. Joss Ryckman. No children yet. Maybe someday." I am surprised by the wistfulness in my voice. "Like I was saying, I think I'm looking for your father."

"I'm sorry, but he passed away three years ago. Is there anything I can help you with?"

I look at this pleasant young guy and wonder how far I can go. Should I tell him all the gory details? I look at him, and there is something in his eyes that feels encouraging.

"It's kind of an involved story," I murmur.

He leans into me, staring, listening.

I clear my throat, swallowing back my uneasiness. "So," I say. "My father used to visit your dad in Canaan, New York, after they both returned from Vietnam. There was an incident in the summer of 1964. My uncle was shot and killed on our family property, and my father may have confided in your dad about that. I was hoping to meet him and see if he could shine any light on that event. Not that your dad was involved. I'm not suggesting that," I add.

Dale Pelletier nods. "Thanks for that," he says. "My dad was a medic, a gentle guy assigned to a combat unit. He'd never say so, but he was more of a pacifist than anything else. I don't think he'd hurt a fly."

I nod, relieved that Dale Pelletier knows I'm not here to make accusations.

He sinks into an easy chair, a broad smile across his face. "Canaan, New York! I haven't thought about that town in a long time. We used to go out there to visit my grandparents. We always had a blast out there. My grandparents had a farm a couple miles from some lake."

"Queechy Lake?"

"Yeah, yeah—that was it. With crazy-looking boats on it."

"Right," I chuckle. "The pontoon boats. They're hard to forget."

"So your uncle was killed, and you think my father may have known something about that. I don't get the connection."

I sigh and hold my head in my hands. "I'm trying to come to some peace about this. My father was a sniper, you know, when he was in Vietnam. As awful as this sounds, I'm trying to figure out if he was responsible for my uncle's death. Did your father leave any diaries, letters? Anything like that? I know he and my father corresponded."

"Nope, and he'd never have anything to do with something like that." There was an edge to his voice. He pulled back in his seat.

"I'm not suggesting he did."

"All I know is that when your father was here, my dad was real sick and they argued. I guess after that they had a falling out. I never knew what it was about. Maybe you should ask your father. He's still around, isn't he?" He paused and held my gaze. "The hard-edged guys always hang on the longest."

I nod, knowing he's right. "Yeah, he's still going strong. I'm sorry he upset your dad when he was so ill. I was hoping for corroboration before I have to go there with my father."

"Can't help you with that," Dale smirks.

I hear the sarcasm in his voice and look into his deadpan stare. I realize I have upset him, that he suspects I am accusing his father of some wrongdoing. "I'm not suggesting that your dad was involved in—"

"Are you the one who's been calling here?"

"Yeah, that would be me. Sorry." I look at my feet and feel myself shrinking into the floor, wishing I hadn't bothered this family with my troubles. "I better go," I say.

"Yeah, that's a good idea."

Dale Pelletier stands by the front door as I step out and turn to shake his hand. But the door latches with a thud and I stand in the dusk, my hand extended to the click of the deadbolt.

Back in my car, I drive around the streets, my window open to the cooler evening air. All I want to do is get out of this town. I look for the highway, the bypass to get around Cleveland and head east, away from this folly. But I miss the exit and wind up driving in a wide, long loop. I cannot seem to escape myself or this circular place.

I roll along the quiet streets and realize I can't drive anymore today. I find a room, a drive through, and a couple bottles of beer—they're lukewarm and bitter. I call Wyatt and tell him I struck out. I don't tell him how humiliated and foolish I feel.

"Some things you can't ever know, Joss. You just have to accept that."

"I know you're right. I don't know what I'd do with the information even if I had it."

"I hear you. Get some rest and come home in the morning,"

In the end, I traveled a thousand miles to find out that I didn't want to know. Maybe truth is overrated, and secrets are untold for reasons best known to their guardians.

16

I tell myself it won't matter that my father is being released from the hospital. That his behavior will not interfere in my life as it always has in the past.

Those are my fewer lucid moments.

One hot, humid day in August, his stay just shy of four months, I leave the bakery mid-shift to pick him up.

"Where you been?" he asks. "I've been waiting an hour." He stands in the lobby with bags and boxes piled in the corner.

"You've got a lot of stuff, Dad."

"Whaddaya expect? I been here forever."

"It must have seemed that way, Dad." I'm happy for him that he is getting out, but my vacation from perpetual drama is ending. "Are they going to see you as an outpatient?"

"You know it. Once they get their hooks into an old geezer like me, they don't let go."

"But you've come to appreciate some of your fellow 'inmates,' as you call them—yes?"

"Much as I hate to admit it, I'll miss them. Learned a couple-three things from some of 'em. A lot of guys there come back from Vietnam like me. You know, just messed up from living in the jungle, the heat, and the stink of mildew everywhere. One guy was a tunnel grunt. They sent him down so many times looking for boys to kill, he still wakes up screaming. Burrowed down at the foot of his bed. Another guy was a sniper like me. I think we had it easier. Not so up close and personal. Aim and pow—like a melon exploding."

I try to push the imagery from my mind. And the nagging question of his likely involvement in the death of Morgan Van Vliet.

He pulls a handkerchief from his pocket and wipes the sweat off his face. "Good to be sprung," he says.

Out in traffic, I am carried by a sea of honking taxis, quick accelerations, and mad-dash stops. I am glad for the noise and frenzy. I need to drop him off and get back to the bakery.

But he has other designs.

He makes me a list of groceries, wants his dry cleaning dropped off. "And go to the post office and pick up my mail."

"We never stopped delivery, Dad. Jeannette's been taking it in. There's a box in the closet. Most of it is junk. I've been taking care of the bills. I told you that."

"Fine. You told me." That sarcastic edge to his voice creeps in and fills every molecule of the space between us.

I do my best to ignore it. "Listen, I'll run your errands a little later. I left you some supper from the café, and some breakfast things, too. If I don't make it back tonight, I'll be here in the morning."

"What? You got no people at the bakery?"

I kiss his cheek. "I'll see you later, Dad."

But I didn't see him that night or the next. Instead, Wyatt takes care of him. Gets his groceries, fixes his printer, and handles the dry cleaning before meeting me for a quick supper at the café.

"He's difficult, that's for sure, Joss."

"But he seems to be more cooperative with you."

Wyatt smiles at me, sipping his coffee. "Maybe your father likes me better, or sees me as the son he never had."

"You mean, now that I've given up that role."

"Yeah, it's all your fault, Paulie-girl," he laughs and grins at me.

"I can fix the soup for you in a special way, now that you've insulted the cook."

"I'm not worried, Salmonella Sue! Lynn will protect me." He turns and waves to Lynn. She smiles and nods her head. "See, she's got my back."

"Speaking of Lynn, she and her husband approached me about buying the bakery."

He sets down his cup. "Are you considering that? I can't imagine you selling this place."

"I don't know. I've been doing this work since I was a teenager. It's not like I made a choice. It was expected."

"But you're so good at it."

I nod. "Thanks. At least it has real value, the name, the building. But I never had the opportunity to consider what I'd want to do, who I wanted to become. You know?"

"I guess that's true. I was lucky. I knew from a young age. But it's never too late, Joss."

"I just have to figure out what I want to be when I grow up."

"It seems like that's what this is all about—moving to Canaan, the farm. This might be the next step. Like my father always said, time will give you the answer."

"He's was probably right." I look around at the café and bar. They were my upgrades, with dire predictions from both my parents. But the café and bar added vigor to what had been a sleepy, neighborhood bakery. The place buzzes every day. If I could do all

of this, that ability could translate to whatever life presents. I have
to grab on for the ride, wait for the right vehicle to come into view.
And trust that I will recognize it.

We both finish our soup, with me dribbling broth down the
front of my white blouse.

"You need a bib, Joss."

"Miss Euphrates used to say that."

"She's very special. I can see why she means so much to you."

"She was the person who first taught me to cook, not my
mother."

"So you can blame Miss Euphrates."

"Exactly! The first pie I ever made by myself was under her
care."

That first pie was a blackerry pie, and I made it the day after I
brought Miss Euphrates that cleaned bullhead. The same day my
father banished me to my room for letting the boys into the millhouse. I watched from my upstairs window as my father pulled
up to the back porch in a rented U-Haul. A few of the jazz group
fellas followed. They cleared out the annex from the living room
and hauled in a baby grand piano wrapped in soft blankets like a
newborn.

I sat at the top of the stairs watching them.

My father's voice boomed. "One of my customers in the city
owns a music shop. We made a deal. That grandson of mine needs
a real piano."

The fellas set it in place, and the piano tuner started perfecting
each note.

"The little master will know if that piano is out of tune," my
father warned. "That kid's got an ear."

"Will do, Mr. Ryckman," the tuner answered.

"Miss Euphrates!" my father roared. "Tonight I want you to make a special dinner. I already put the extra leaves in the dining room table and hauled down the chairs. Everyone will be here. The whole family. Naomi, Lydah, Haley, and Joss. And you, too. Along with that Fletcher kid. If you need extra hands, Joss will come down and help. You hear that, Joss?" he hollered up at me.

"Yes, sir."

When I heard the U-Haul back out of the driveway, I crept down the stairs. "What should I do, Miss Euphrates?"

"First thing, go on out and pick a dozen ears of that sweet corn. We'll make a chowder. And some small ripe tomatoes for tomato tarts. Maybe ten. And another dozen green tomatoes, a big bunch of sweet basil, some fresh dill, chives, and a couple ripe melons. Oh, and some salad fixings: red lettuce, cucumbers, radishes, and green beans. We'll blanch them for the salad."

"Can I try making a blackberry pie?" I asked.

"Course you can. Get yourself about four cups' worth."

The green beans swung in the late afternoon heat as I scrambled through the rows simian style, swiping the finger-like beans from the mother plants. I filled wire baskets and colanders, then carried all of it into the kitchen, first washing each piece of produce, then lining the drain board with the colorful vegetables.

"You want to slice up those green tomatoes, about an eighth of an inch thick?"

I nodded.

"Lay the slices out on a cookie sheet lined with tea towels, top and bottom. They need to dry out for frying. And after that you can do your pie. You good making sweet pastry by yourself, dawta-girl?"

"I think so."

"I'll be making savory pastry dough with fresh chives and ground pepper for the tomato tarts. So you need help, you just call out."

I pulled the pans from the panty and lined them, just like Miss Euphrates said.

"You awfully quiet today, Miss Joss. You feeling all right?"

I shrugged my shoulders. I didn't want to talk to anyone. "I guess," I answered.

"Something troubling you?"

"My father's mad at me—you know, bringing the boys into the millhouse while the fellas were playing."

"I hear about that."

"I'm grounded for a week. It's not fair!"

"Fair or not fair, he's your father and you're obliged to respect his rules. Do you know what I mean by respect?"

I shook my head. "Not really."

"It means whether you like something or not, you do the right thing. You do what your mother and father ask of you. Even when you don't like it."

"What if your father asks you to lie? What then?"

"Has your daddy ever asked you to lie?"

"Well, no."

"You got nothing to worry about, now do you?"

We worked the rest of the afternoon, peeling and cutting vegetables for corn chowder, green salad, and fruit salad. Miss Euphrates made spicy buttermilk dressing for the fried green tomatoes, while I lined the dining room sideboard with tomato tarts and my blackberry pie.

Just before six, I set the table while Miss Euphrates dipped the green tomatoes in egg and breadcrumbs and then into the hot oil.

Fletcher was the first to arrive, in a white shirt and yellow bow-tie with his hair slicked back.

"Don't you dare say a thing, Joss! My momma made me wear this."

"Mister Fletcher, you look handsome," Miss Euphrates said.

He blushed and turned away. "You got the soup spoons in the wrong place, Joss." He changed them, placing each between the knife and teaspoon.

"How'd you know that?" I asked.

He rolled his eyes. "Duh—my mother!"

They arrived one by one, my father, my mother, and lastly Naomi and Haley.

"There he is!" my father's voice bellowed. "My grandson."

Haley smiled and then raced off into the living room with Fletcher.

"Joss," my father whispered, "looks like you did a nice job today. The table looks great. Your mother will be pleased, flowers and candles on the table." He squeezed my shoulder.

I nodded, still under the yoke of his punishment and not wanting to look at him.

"Drinks, anyone? That includes you, Miss Euphrates."

"Best to wait until I sit down." She dipped the perch and the bullhead filets into batter, then arranged them in the hot oil. "Miss Joss, you can begin bringing out the platters."

"Come sit, everyone," my father said. "Dinner's on."

We passed the platters as Miss Euphrates brought out the hot fried fish.

"Everything's wonderful," my mother said.

"We caught the fish," Haley announced. "All except the big one. Aunt Jossy got that one."

"It's delicious," my father said.

"I thought you said. . . ."

"Never mind what I said, Joss. Bullhead is just a type of catfish. Everyone likes catfish, right little man?"

"Who's the little man?" Haley asked.

"You are," my father answered. "Eat up because there is a special surprise for you after dinner."

"What is it, Grandpa?"

"That's right. I'm Grandpa, aren't I?" he chuckled. "And never mind what the surprise is. You have to wait."

When the fish platter came to me, I couldn't take any of the bullhead catfishes. Or even the fried perch.

"You feeling all right?" my mother asked.

"I'm not that hungry," I said. When I looked at that platter of filets, all I could see was the cut-off head of that fish with its one-sided gaping mouth.

"Miss Euphrates, you outdid yourself tonight."

"Couldn't have done it without Miss Joss. She's getting to be a good cook and a fine baker, too. She made tonight's dessert all by herself."

"I might have to steal her away for my bakery," my mother said.

Everyone laughed and oohed when dessert was served.

"Excellent crust," commented my mother. "Joss, you're going to have to teach me how you made this."

"Before we begin pie-making classes," my father said, "come on out to the living room and show Haley his surprise."

The room was dark. Dusk had crept into every corner.

"Let's get some light in here," my father said. "Haley, would you open the doors to the alcove?"

When he pushed back the tall doors to the alcove, light from the chandelier showered down on a shiny black lacquered baby grand piano. Haley stood there with his arms spread wide open against the doors.

"I didn't know you had a piano here," he said.

"We didn't," my father said. "This is yours, little man. I got it for you."

Haley wrapped his arms around my father's neck and buried his face into his shoulder.

"See, Mommy," Haley said. "I always knew Grandpa would like me."

Everyone smiled and clapped, including me. But I noticed from that day and for a long time afterward, my father stopped calling me Paulie-girl or Boy-o. He brought Haley with him everywhere he could, telling anyone who would listen that "the boy here, my grandson, is a musical prodigy." The two of them seemed delighted with one another. But I worried that Haley would see the hard-bitten side of my father way too soon. That my father would hurt Haley, too.

17

I stand in the bathroom, brushing my teeth and attempting to tame my unruly hair. I notice a few gray hairs along my temples. Henna rinse—that should cover and hopefully tame the intruders. They are wiry and wilder than the rest, calling for attention. It irritates me.

The phone rings. It's Wyatt, and I hesitate, trapping both of us in my dance of contradictions. I push him aside, but he never fails me in all the ways I fail him. I pick up the phone and he asks if I want to go the beach with him for a couple of days.

"I'll come to Canaan and get you. Don't be making any sandwiches or any of that. I'll take care of it."

"Where are we going?"

"Martha's Vineyard. I made arrangements with a former Army buddy. He has a place out there—a camp, pretty rustic. Are you game?"

"Why not, as long as I can arrange for someone to keep an eye on Dad while I'm gone. I've never been to the Vineyard."

"You'll like it. His place is a bit off the beaten track." His voice is high and light

It is all of that.

We drive from the Massachusetts Turnpike to 495, then south to Woods Hole at the southern tip of Cape Cod.

"Wake up, Sleepyhead. We're at the ferry dock. I got you a coffee."

I stretch and rouse, and sip the dark brew. "Thanks," I say. "I didn't realize we'd stopped."

"You were pretty gone. You must need a vacation." He strokes my face and rubs my shoulders.

We board the ferry and sit on the flush deck, watching the island grow larger on the horizon. I lie back on a deck chair, soaking in the rays, watching the gulls soar on the air currents like kids on rickety skateboards. One false move and they'll be blown off course.

"You better get out of the sun," Wyatt says. "You don't want to get too burned. I've got sunscreen in the car. Shall I get it?"

I stare at him, biting my lip, holding back my ire.

"Sorry! Sorry, Joss. There I go again. I really am trying. Please forgive me." His words are a jumble. "I know, I know, you've lived all these years without me directing your every move. Can we start over? Please?"

"Well, why not?" I smile and let all of it roll away. "It's beautiful out here, Wyatt. Thank you for this wonderful trip."

We get off in Vineyard Haven and wind our way west, up-island, along a narrow tree-lined road, eventually turning onto a lane that is little more than a cow path. We pass decrepit looking cottages and million dollar homes until we reach the rustic fixer-upper that is ours for the next few days.

"Hank says it can be a bit stuffy at night, but we'll see. He says we can use the screen porch as a bedroom. Pull the bed out there."

"That sounds romantic," I smile up at him and wrap my arms around him.

We walk through the cabin; the wood floors squeak and give under the scatter rugs strewn everywhere.

"Did you see the kitchen?" I ask. "The refrigerator must be fifty years old." I do my best to be upbeat, but the place is dirty and smells of mice.

"Hank's one of those cheap bastard kind of guys."

"Aren't you all cheap bastards?" I laugh.

"Not this trip, baby. I'm taking you out for breakfast and dinner. And getting takeout for lunch. No cooking allowed."

"Yes, sir."

"What, no salute?" he laughs.

I chuckle. "To tell you the truth, I don't want to cook in this kitchen; it's kind of disgusting. We should get some mousetraps; I see evidence of them all over the kitchen."

"I know," he says, his brow furrowed. "I don't want to eat here either. I brought some gear so we can cook out, but yeah, it's more than rustic. I guess I should have warned you. But we can't use traps. Hank's a Franciscan. He believes every creature is divine."

"I thought he served with you in Iraq?"

"He did. He was an Army Ranger. Could shoot a gnat from the sky at a thousand meters. But it got to him. He'd find ways to save the innocent, and consecrate the dead when he couldn't save them. I watched him wash bodies in the Euphrates, then cover them in white cotton. He'd recite prayers from the Qur'an."

"Wow. From the trigger to prayer." I paused, wondering how a man makes such a leap. "I'll adjust," I say. "The porch looks like the cleanest room. At least it doesn't smell as bad."

"Are you ready for the beach?"

"Sure." I grab my beach chair, an umbrella, and a book.

"Do you want your easel and paints?"

"You don't mind hauling all that?"

"This way I get to see your watercolors."

"Believe me, I'm less than fledgling."

"When my father began teaching me bookbinding, he'd find these worthless old books and set me loose. I made some pathetic repairs in the beginning."

"So why haven't you shown me any of those?"

"Oh, I've got that first book I repaired. I'll show you when we get back."

We walk down the cow path past another cottage and then onto a narrower path that leads up over the dunes to a view of the wild Atlantic. The beach is sparsely populated. On a sandy knoll we stop to survey the lay of the land. There is a farm in the distance and sheep grazing on the edge of the cliffs overlooking the ocean. We watch a thin melody of plovers and dowitchers dart over the water like swallows near a barn.

"This place is amazing," I say. "No casinos or hotels on the edge of paradise. No fast food joints or t-shirt shops."

"There's not much of that on the island. Some great clam shacks and a few t-shirt places scattered here and there. But no chain stores."

We trudge down the beach closer to the water, turning back to admire the clay cliffs that border the beach. Brick-red and gray striations intersected by bands of yellow ochre shimmer in the sunlight and the sea-salt air.

"They erode more and more each year," Wyatt says.

"They're beautiful."

"And protected, so no playing with the clay, little girl."

We park our chairs and umbrellas and stretch out in the sun, slathering sunblock on each other. We watch the waves gather, crash onto the beach, and rush back against the backdrop of the gulls and the wind. We smile at one another.

Wyatt falls asleep while I read. When I grow restless and bored with the pages, I set up my easel and attempt to paint what I see: the beach, the shimmer along the sand, the dunes and sky. Sheet after sheet of watercolor paper wetted and sketched in pencil before I add color and shadow, each a passing attempt until I finally turn to Wyatt. I watch the rise and fall of his chest. His hair blows in the brisk Atlantic wind. The sand sparkles on his skin, and I catch his relaxed muscles, his dreaming self, lying under the hot August sun. Wyatt translated on paper, sketched in sea water and pigment, lies on my easel. I have caught this beautiful man, and though my rendering is still amateurish, there is some mystery here. This one I'll keep.

In the evening, we drive to the westerly tip of the island, to Menemsha Beach to watch the sunset over the mainland.

Wyatt hands me a takeout menu from The Bite, one of the best-known clam shacks on the island. "What looks good to you?" he asks.

"It's all good. Surprise me."

He brings back fried oysters and quahog chowder for me. "What did you get?"

"Scallops and fried jalapeños. But I'm happy to share."

"Me, too."

We sit beneath the colors that move and deepen across the sky. The night air is cooler, and I pull the blanket up around my shoulders.

"Are you cold? Do you want to go?"

"I'm good with the blanket."

"So let me ask you, what are we doing? You know, the 'we' part?"

I have been waiting all day for this question, mulling it over, wondering if I have an answer. I tell him, "I don't know all of it, but I know we're friends. And that I love you in my own way."

"Friends?" he laughs sarcastically.

"It came out wrong, Wyatt."

He nods. "Well, at least we're that—friends, I mean. And whose way would you love me in, if not your own?" His voice is bitter, now.

"You get points for that one," I say.

"I need them," he scoffs.

I watch him funneling beach sand from hand to hand. "Don't you know, Wyatt? Your love is like a roaring river, lapping at my feet, and I am cold and wet already."

"What do you mean?"

"You push against me wanting more than I can give. You act like you're the only one who has felt the door close. I've been on the other side with you—wanting more when silence was your ally."

"You mean when I was dealing with the fallout from my time in Iraq?"

I nod and shrug. "But I waited it out, stepped back because that was what you needed."

He sighs, gazing out at the rolling waves.

"Maybe right now you're more in love with me, and I'm where I am," I say. "Why does ardor have to be equal? Most of the time it isn't. It's a dance."

"But you make me feel rejected, Joss. Like I'm not enough."

"Oh my God, Wyatt. You're the best. One in a zillion. I'm sorry that you have felt that way. I wish you didn't."

"But you did reject me, Joss. You said we were over. That you didn't love me anymore. How else am I supposed to feel?"

"I don't know—angry that I was that cruel to you?"

We watch the light fade with the roll of the waves, and neither of us speaks. I lean into Wyatt, wrapping my arms around him.

"Are you cold?" he asks.

"A little."

We finish our supper, stuffing the trash back into the takeout bag.

I take a deep breath. "Let me correct myself. I do love you. Even though I have been confused and sad most of this past year. Even though I have pushed you away time and again, I still want you, need you. I'm not saying my bewilderment, my inconsistency is done with—I just need time."

"Not to be arrogant here, but I get it—you need what you need. At the same time, I know that you love me. You wouldn't be here if you didn't."

I watch his face, his hands. He goes on, looking out to the dunes and cairns scattered like offerings to the gods. I wonder where he gets that faith, that constancy that marks him.

"Come on," he says. "Take my hand." He stands above me, the light all around him. "We need to play. I know it's your way, but you suffer things too much. Time for some fun."

I grab on. He pulls me up, and we trot along the beach, hand in hand, kicking up the sand, laughing like little kids. He stops short, picks me up and slings me over his shoulder.

"Fireman rescue!" he shouts and roars into the waves.

I screech through the salty spray, laughing, and begging, "Put me down."

"You sure? Are you really sure?" His voice is demonic.

"Yessss!"

"Into the drink you go!" He flings me through the air, into a crashing wave, then dives in after me to rescue me again, pulling me up and out of the surf.

"No more fireman! No more fireman," I holler, laughing and splashing water into his face.

"What will you give me to stop, huh? Tell me, tell me!"

"A chocolate-hazelnut Napoleon."

"Lies! Lies and briberies will get you nowhere. I ask you again, damsel—what will you give me?"

"A gold watch!"

"Into the drink again." Wyatt tosses me once more through the misty dusk.

I plummet down and down into the roily water, sand and salt in my mouth, my eyes. But I don't come up. I swim like a mongoose, like a sea turtle out into the bay where the water is cool and quieter. When I pop up through the surface to draw in the air, I see Wyatt, scanning for me, his face contorted into worry lines.

"I will give you a firefly in a jar," I shout. "And a snipe hunt on the river."

"What?" he hollers back. "Are you all right?"

"I will give you paper airplanes and mousetraps. I will give you broken books and abysmal watercolors. I will give you my sad and imperfect love tied up in knots. I will give you sobs and cries."

"I can't hear you," he shouts back.

I flip on my back, pushing through the water, floating and backstroking closer to shore.

He meets me just past the wave break. "Are you okay? I didn't mean—"

I wrap myself around him and kiss his mouth. I taste his lips, his breath, the salt and sweat that runs down his face.

We head back to the car, shivering, holding hands, and drive back to the cabin with the heat running full blast. I sweep the porch and wash the table and chairs. And light tall glass-encased novena candles in the windows. He starts a fire for roasted marshmallows. We sit on the porch playing gin rummy and drinking mojitos. The inky night rolls in, black and rich, the sky studded with starlight.

"Wait right here," he says. "I'll be right back."

I hear him wandering around in the dark. He talks to himself; his voice carries in the night against the dark and all the crickets. He is counting, not like I do in rhymes, but just numbers. I hear his feet swish through the wet grass and the bang of the screen as he tumbles through the door.

"Well," he says. "Are you ready?"

"For what?"

"The firefly report." He pulls up a chair and sits, his face close to mine. "When I was a boy," he whispers. "My father would go out every night, all summer long and look around counting the fireflies, noting how many times they flashed their tiny lights— double flashes and triple. All the particulars any kid would want to know. So I have my report ready."

I coo and laugh. "So, let's have it."

"Well, my dear Miss Joss, I counted fourteen fireflies in and around the cabin at approximately 10:45 p.m. There were three double flashers and one triple flasher. They mostly congregated out by some blackberry bushes, as is their wont. I wished them a good eve and they kindly returned the favor."

"Oh, that's lovely. What a sweet tradition." I watch his face, his large bony hands, and I think he should have a child, a little one with wide eyes who listens to every word, a little kid spellbound every night by the firefly report.

He smiles and asks, "Where are we going to sleep?"

"Out here in the clean night air."

We push the double bed onto the porch and lie on the cool sheets like children camping in the backyard on a too hot night.

"It's sad that the tree house is so damaged," I say. "Otherwise we could sleep out there on a summer night."

"Did you used to sleep out there when you were a kid?"

"Once. The three of us, Haley, Fletcher, and I, talked our mothers into letting us sleep up there just before the school year started. Course we needed an adult, and we talked my sister Naomi into chaperoning us."

Naomi had her hands full with the three of us as we came screaming through the fields of Joe-Pye weed, chrome yellow mullein, and goldenrod. It was a late Saturday afternoon. Haley, Fletcher, and I hopped the barbed wire fence, amid the pitched shrill of courting grasshoppers, and high-stepped through sweet Timothy and wild asters. I carried a bunch of blowzy zinnias to give to my sister while Fletcher clutched a can of baked beans, his contribution to our adventure.

"Let's sing a round," I said.

The boys began, their woolen voices carried the first line through, followed by my watery tones. Our tumbleweed voices floated over the bean field, drifted against the beetroot-colored hollyhocks, down to the loosestrife, where we spied a blue heron prancing at the edge of the river. I was convinced it was the same blue heron I had seen at the river's edge year after year.

We stopped momentarily and quieted, then whispered on through the coneflowers and late-blooming foxglove. At the base of the supporting tree, we climbed the wooden ladder up twenty feet into the branches and entered the cabin through the red-painted door.

"All right kids," Naomi said. "Change into your bathing suits, and then to the river with the three of you! Last one in has to peel the potatoes for supper."

We had all worn our swimming gear under our clothes, and in seconds we were out onto the deck, opening the trap door to the rope ladder that led to the pool of water below our dangling legs. Haley dove in first, followed by me. Fletcher was the last one in the water.

"Fletcher, you're the potato peeler!" we yelled in unison. He dove under, grabbing my legs as I pierced the deeper green, silent water. Spotted trout slithered below my thin legs, darting into crevices beneath the river rocks, while the blacknose dace and the golden shiners blithely swirled in the smaller eddies.

The three of us bobbed to the surface, taking turns diving from the rope ladder, while the beaver family just up-river stood on their haunches along their dam, watching us.

"Do you see them?" Haley asked. "Those beavers? I bet they are just like Homer and Marge Simpson. Homer's saying, "'Marge, don't discourage the boy! Weaseling out of things is important to learn. It's what separates us from the animals! Except the weasel.'"

We laughed, imagining those yellow-toothed swimmers with their beaver paws on their beaver hips, slapping their leathery tails, indignant at our antics. We continued to dive and swim, squealing through the trees at the river bend for the next hour. When we got too cold, we shivered up the rope ladder for thick towels and the tree house cabin warmth.

"Hurry, hurry," Naomi shouted above our shrieks. "You kids change into dry clothes before you get too cold."

I slid behind the privacy screen and changed back into my jeans and sweatshirt while the boys changed out on the deck. Once we were dry and combed, we sat at the table. Fletcher peeled potatoes, Haley diced onions, and I sliced tomatoes for a salad. Naomi lit the oil lantern over the table and the torches out on the deck.

Dinner was a raucous affair with Fletcher up to all his antics: wrapping his ankles around his neck and rocking in his chair, and making fart noises under his armpits.

"Fletcher," Naomi said, "you're the only boy I know whose digestive system runs under his arm! You must be a medical miracle!" We all laughed, but Fletcher looked crestfallen. Naomi tousled his hair. "I'm just teasing you, Fletcher."

"I know," he said, his face still flushed. "Got ya!"

"Yes you did, Fletcher!"

He blew spit bubbles when Naomi's back was turned. "My father plays that trick all the time," he whispered.

We all laughed.

"How did an Alabama boy like you end up in rural New York?" We all laughed, and Fletcher beamed. "My momma always says that she had the unfortunate luck of falling in love with a Yankee."

"Seriously, you must be part pretzel to be able to put your ankles around your neck like that."

"You should see him at school," I said. "He does it when Sister Michael Clare is writing on the board. Everyone starts laughing, and she whirls around with that number fifty-eight look, staring right at Fletcher. He sits there all innocent with his feet back on the floor. And Sister Michael Clare says, 'Which one of you brazen articles is disrupting my class?'"

"Fletcher, you are a devil," Naomi said.

"Oh, that's nothing, Miss Naomi! You should hear Sister Mike when I jump out the window!"

By the time the three of us cleaned up the supper dishes, heated the water on the potbelly stove, and washed, dried, and put everything away, the sun had escaped beyond the western hills. My sister made s'mores wrapped in aluminum foil and set them on the wood stove, while the three of us pulled on sweaters and jackets and warm wooly socks. The temperature had dropped. It would be a clear, cold night, and the air smelled of an early frost. We all sat outside on the deck, stargazing. The fields around us were a cacophony of crickets and other clicking, sawing life. We could hear the river flow over the beaver dam and some confused fish plop back through the water, daring to swallow a starbright. Acorns fell on the cabin roof and flew across the deck.

Haley lay back, pointing out the stars. "Do you see the Big Dipper? And above it the North Star?"

"Yeah, I see it!"

"Now draw a line from there to there and then to that third star." I watched his finger point to certain stars. "Do you see?" he asked. "The Dipper is part of the larger constellation, Ursa Major, the Big Bear."

"I see it!"

We played dot-to-dot with our pointing fingers, finding Cassiopeia, Hercules, and Aquila. Our imaginations took over, drawing phantasmagorical figures in the starry palette above our rumpled heads. We giggled, conspiring, imagining ourselves as creators of our small world while Fletcher sat behind us.

"Joss," Fletcher whispered in my ear, "am I still your best friend?"

"Course you are," I whispered back.

"Yeah, but you seem to like Haley more than me."

I think maybe Fletcher was right. It was hard not to be enchanted with Haley. But I wish I had understood back then how fragile Fletcher was. How fragile we all were. As I lie next to Wyatt while he sleeps, I realize we two are just as tenuous—that holding back, keeping Wyatt at bay, and pulling him back in invites disillusionment. I pull my nightgown back over my head and tuck in closer to my sleeping man, listening to the sounds of the night: singing crickets and the ocean in the distance. The smell of the salt air drifts in through the screens. I wonder as I drift toward sleep if selling the bakery would bring in enough money to buy a little slice of this island paradise.

18

Our summertime bliss ended too soon. On the too hot Wednesday after Labor Day, Mrs. Goodwin pulled up in her van and got out for a smoke. She leaned against the car in her too tight, black capri pants with a red wrap-and-tie strapless top that had a large bow in the back. And wobbled in her red spike-heeled sandals.

She caught me staring at her.

"You like?" she asked.

"Momma, we all know you're pretty," Fletcher said. "But we have to get going. We can't be late for the first day of school."

Haley, Fletcher, and I piled into Mrs. Goodwin's van for the trek to St. Mark's School. We were dressed in our new school uniforms, the boys in white short-sleeved shirts, blue chinos, and navy clip-on ties, and me in a new blue and green plaid jumper with a white blouse. We were fidgety, boxed in after a rowdy and footloose summer.

When we arrived, the schoolyard was filled with kids milling around in clusters. Girls played hopscotch and jump rope. The boys egged each other on, besting one against the other with rock throwing or burning rubber from their bicycles in the school parking lot. I joined a group of girls waiting for their turn to toss a pebble and hop the chalk drawn grid. Haley followed me.

Susan and Brianne and Tracy wanted to know who Haley was.

"He's my nephew, Haley. My older sister's son."

"Hi, Haley," they chanted. "What grade are you in?"

"I'm in fourth grade."

They looked from him to me, puzzled.

"He skipped two grades," I said.

"Oh, so you must be really smart," Brianne said.

Haley shrugged his shoulders. "I guess," he said.

They laughed. Then Brianne tossed her pebble onto the chalk grid. It landed on the seven square, the grid she had to skip. She hopped and jumped, and half circled around and began chanting. We all joined in, our singsong voices weaving through the chatter around us: *One crow for sorrow, Two crows mirth, Three crows a wedding, Four crow birth. Five crows for silver, Six crows gold, Seven crows a secret, Never to be told.*

When it was my turn, my stone landed on the two square. I jumped and sang: *Ibbity, bibbity, sibbity Sam. Ibbity, bibbity, whack!* When I got to the turnaround, Sister Mike came out and rang the bell.

"What's that for?" Haley asked.

"We have to line up for Mass."

We pocketed our lucky pebbles and queued up like wobbling bowling pins, not sure whether to topple and run or not. We had slipped out of line once last year and hid in the library, Fletcher and me, rejoining the throng of students as they filled the hallways. No one was the wiser.

Fletcher caught up to Haley and me as we marched into the church, sliding along the length of the pews to see who could make the best skin to wood squeals. The trick was to look away when one of the Sisters threw a withering look in our direction.

Father O'Neil said a short Mass for us unruly returning lambs of God. He prayed for our slightly soiled souls and for the blessings of vocation to shine on our golden heads.

"What's a vocation?" Haley whispered.

"That's when you decide if you want to be a priest or a nun."

"You can get good grades if you tell your teacher you got the calling," Fletcher said.

Sister Mike turned and glared at us, and we demonstrated our best innocent looks for Haley's benefit.

When Mass ended, we lined back up and marched across the street and into the school. Fletcher and I helped Haley find Sister Angelina's classroom.

"You'll like her. She came last year when I first started school here. She's nice."

"Okay, Aunt Jossy. I'll see you later."

"I think you should just call me Joss or Jossy, especially when we're at school."

He nodded and disappeared into a sea of new faces.

Fletcher's and my sixth-grade classroom was in another wing of the school. Our teacher was a lay teacher, Mrs. Hammond, and Fletcher and I hoped she would be less strict than the nuns.

Mrs. Hammond stood at her classroom doorway with a clipboard in her hand. She was tall and heavyset, with gray streaked hair in a tight chignon. She wore large red-framed glasses. When Mrs. Goodwin met her, she started calling her Sally Jesse Raphael and soon enough a version of the name stuck. Fat Sister Sally, as we called her, checked off our names and assigned us seats as we entered. Fletcher and I were now three rows apart.

"Good morning, class," she said.

"Good morning, Mrs. Hammond," we responded.

"You'll note that there are vocabulary words on the board and a list of this week's assignments." She smiled and pointed to the dry erase board. "The most important assignment is an autobiography. Who knows what 'autobiography' means?"

A sea of eager hands went up.

She looked around the room. "Fletcher?"

"Well, it's when you make up a story about yourself. Like, for instance, how I want to work toward becoming a priest."

Mrs. Hammond smiled, and other kids laughed. "Is that right?" she said. "I'm wondering, Fletcher, if you understand the difference between fiction and nonfiction. Does anyone else know the meaning of 'autobiography?'"

There were a few more answers, but eventually our new teacher explained: "Using two of our vocabulary words for this week, *validate* and *fictitious,* and in your best English composition, each of you is to write the story of your life. You must be accurate and *validate* the facts with family members, friends, and neighbors. Your account cannot be *fictitious.*

"While you're writing your autobiographies, I want you to think about what you would like to be when you grow up; think about what vocation you might want. But remember: God has a plan for all of us. Some of you will go on to college to become teachers or nurses, or police officers. Many of you will choose the vocation of marriage and raise families of your own. But a very select group of you will choose the vocation of a religious life."

I dropped my pencil so I could look back at Fletcher. He caught my eye and rolled his.

"Is there a problem, Miss Ryckman?"

"No, Mrs. Hammond."

"From my view, it looked otherwise. But given this is our first day, I'll give you the benefit of the doubt."

"Yes, ma'am." I suspected that it would be a *tedious* school year with Fat Sister Sally.

"Speaking of Miss Ryckman, her nephew, Nahaliel, will be joining our class for science and math. Nahaliel is young for our sixth grade but is advanced and needs to be challenged. So please make him feel welcome."

When Fletcher's mother picked us up after school, Fletcher and I sat glumly in the back while Haley chattered on about his teacher and new friends.

"And you know what?" Haley said. "My whole class went to the music room so I could play for them. I think they like me."

"Well, of course they like you, Haley," Mrs. Goodwin drawled. "Everyone likes you."

Fletcher's mother dropped us off, and Fletcher and I said goodbye.

But he called me an hour later, "Can I come over, Joss? I need to talk to you."

"Sure," I said.

"I'll meet you in the tree house."

I pulled on my jacket and ran out the door, slamming the screen behind me.

"Where are you going, Miss Joss?" Miss Euphrates stood in the doorway, her hands on her hips.

"Fletcher's coming over. We're going to play in the tree house."

"You be careful out there."

I waved and wallowed through the tall wet grass. I wondered what the urgency was, as I waited for Fletcher in the treetops.

He popped through the red-painted door, a scowl on his face.

"What's up, Fletcher?"

"Are you kidding? That Mrs. Hammond, that's what's up. And her stupid assignment. What kind of autobiography am I supposed to write? How me and my father try to keep my mother away from the booze? You know how she is."

I nodded. I had smelled it on her breath this morning when she picked us up for school. And I had seen Fletcher take care of her, protect her.

"Why would you have to write about that?"

"Because she said it had to be truthful."

"Fletcher, don't write about that. Just write about the good stuff."

"What good stuff?"

"That your mother makes great fried chicken, and how you know all about the woods. All the stuff your father has taught you."

"Okay, but what are you going to write about?"

I remember spin-doctoring the facts of my young life, just as Miss Euphrates had told me to do. I went home that day under the same gloom that Fletcher felt. I sat at the kitchen table with my head in my hands and explained the assignment to Miss Euphrates. She told me the difference between truth and privacy. That I didn't owe my soul to people who wouldn't cherish that honor.

I didn't understand all that she said, but I trusted her guidance when I was twelve years old. And I trust her now.

Miss Euphrates sits in my kitchen, her wild, wild hair as beautiful as ever.

"How about another piece of that cake," she says. "And a half cup more of that coffee to go with it."

"We're sort of back together, Wyatt and I."

"How's that, Miss Joss?"

"We went away for a few days to the beach. Lay in the sand and ate and made love."

"A little glue never hurts."

I laugh. "Yeah, I guess you're right. The strange thing is that I didn't use birth control, or even talk to Wyatt about it."

"And?"

"No surprises, but I guess I'm flirting with the possibility."

"Sounds like your head says one thing and your heart is saying something else."

"You think so?"

"What else could it be, Miss Joss?"

"I don't know. Am I crazy? Out of my mind?"

"Or maybe you're connecting to who you are. Maybe you're beginning to understand what your soul wants. You'll figure it out, Miss Joss. You always do. Does Wyatt know?"

"Not yet. I guess I have to tell him."

I stop by his shop later that week.

"Hey," I say, as the bell on his door jangles when I let myself in. "It's just me."

"Hey you! Nice of you to stop. Let me just finish this up."

I watch him hand stamp the last three gold foil words on the leather spine of a book. He heats the tools on a finishing stove, then presses the hot type into the foil laid across the book spine, putting his weight behind it to get a good clear impression. When he's finished, he rubs the lettering with a soft cloth to remove any excess and bring up the color.

"Done!" he says. "Want some tea?"

"Sure. I'll get the cups out."

"We'll have tea in my new rare book room."

He unlocks a door at the rear of the studio, and what I had assumed was a closet opens up to this airy, lightfilled room. There are floor-to-ceiling bookcases along the back wall, with more casework on the two facing walls set perpendicular, library style, jutting into the room. In the center is a sitting area with a small table, chairs, and a period loveseat with the light coming in from the west.

I wander among the stacks. Behind each illuminated glass door are brass nameplates on the shelves with the subject matter neatly

stamped in gold on charcoal paper: American 20th Century Litera-
ture, French Poetry, Ornithology, Slave Narratives, and on and on.
The books are pristine, repaired, cleaned; their covers are leather,
cloth covered, or papered boards with waxed finishes in aubergine,
cobalt, and rust-red, or deep green with gold and black lettered titles.

"It's stunning. The rooms, the casework, the books lined up
like soldiers in their dress uniforms. You've been busy."

"No rest for the wicked."

"I guess not."

"Come sit and have some tea with me. Plus, I have some
delicious scones I picked up from some joint down the street.
Madame Somebody-or-Other."

I laugh, joining him at the table, laying my package against the
sofa.

"What's in the package? A gift for me?"

"A tribute of sorts," I say.

"Can I open it?"

I hand him the package. He tears off the paper like a little kid
and pulls out my watercolor of him on the beach. "Wow. It's quite
good, isn't it?"

"Well, it's the least terrible of what I've done recently."

"I like the looseness of it—how it feels like a quick sketch. It
catches that day just as it was. Nice. I didn't know I was one of your
subjects."

"My best one." I fidget with my teacup, poking at the scone,
but not enjoying either. "I have something to tell you, Wyatt.
Something I should have done."

He sets his cup on the saucer and stares at me. "What is it?"
His voice is subdued.

I look at him, then turn away, stare at my feet, and run my hand
through my hair.

"Spit it out, Joss. God knows I've proven myself to you over and over. How bad can it be?"

"While we were at the beach last month, I didn't use any birth control. There. I said it."

"Are you—"

"No, no. Nothing happened. I'm sorry. I don't know why I behaved so irresponsibly. I—"

"Yeah, I know this subject is one of our hot button issues—me wanting kids and you being more than reluctant—but a sneak attack, Joss?"

"I know. It's a terrible betrayal."

"It's not exactly a betrayal. But if and when we do this—decide to have a kid, I want to be part of the decision-making process, barring a happy accident."

"Of course you do. I'm sorry, Wyatt."

"Does this mean that you've had a change of heart on the subject of babies?"

"I guess I'm moving in that direction."

He smiles broadly and sips his tea. "Well, this means that you and I will have to do some serious practicing."

"Okay," I laugh. "You're on."

We sit quietly in the sunlight finishing our tea, each of us lost in thought. I imagine Wyatt with a little boy of his own, showing him how to sew signatures or hand-letter book titles, or maybe just standing in the field at the farm, the two of them tossing a baseball one to the other.

19

The three of us sat in the back of Mrs. Goodwin's van, tossing a nerf ball back and forth, squealing, retrieving it from underneath the seat, each of us claiming digs on the next round as October slashed across the windshield. Sheets of rain tore down the colored leaves. Thick frost painted the morning landscape. The air had that acrid smell, a warning that winter was the next sharp left.

"Guess what, you guys?" Haley whispered.

"Yeah, what?" Fletcher asked.

"I'm not going to be in your class anymore for science and math."

"Why not?"

I could hear the lift in Fletcher's voice. Although he never said so, I knew he didn't like that Haley was in our class.

"Yup, I'm going to be in the seventh-grade class instead."

"That's great, Haley," I said.

He smiled and looked out the window the rest of our way to school.

We tromped into the classroom in our wet galoshes and yellow rain slickers. We hung the coats and lined up our boots at the bottom of the closet. To do less would incur Catholic wrath, a mixture of guilt and sin.

The bell rang, and we all hightailed to our seats as Sister Mike came through the door. Thursday mornings in Mrs. Hammond's sixth-grade class were devoted to Sister Mike's religious instruction. She was a classic Sister of St. Joseph, still dedicated to traditional garb; the white coif and black veil surrounded her puffy face. Her starched linen whimple covered her ample bosom. She was in charge of every student's eternal soul.

"Now girls," she said, "I want all of you to come forward and kneel on the floor in a nice even row. And face the class." She walked down the line of us, pressing the yardstick to the skirt of our uniforms, making sure that the length was no more than an inch above the floor.

"Most of you are fine for today. But you must realize that you are growing girls on your way to becoming proper ladies. Modesty is a grace. For the few who need a little re-hemming, I will send your mothers a note."

The boys lined up, too, with instructions about tucking in their shirts and straightening their miserable, wobbly ties.

Sister Mike began her lecture on the Holy Trinity, but my mind wandered. I was distracted. My parents had argued again late last night. Their shrill voices woke me. I tiptoed out of bed and lay on the floor, my ear to the kitchen below.

"What is it with you, Paul? You've got the boy you always wanted, and now you think you can just ignore your youngest. Oh, that's right, under my bad influence she's a girl, now. She still needs you, Paul. Be kind to her. Not like the bastard you are."

"Oh, and you're Saint Lydah? When the hell have you ever bothered with her?"

"I tried, but you took her away from me."

"Maybe I saw what you did with the first one. Look how she turned out."

"You're an ass."

"Better an ass than a—"

"Don't you dare!"

The back door slammed.

I lay on the floor a while longer, then tiptoed back under the covers, but sleep would not come.

Sister Mike's voice startled me.

"You boys in the back," she shouted. "Quiet!"

There was a quick knock on the door and then Father Rourke let himself in.

"Welcome, Father Rourke," we called out in unison.

"Good morning, boys and girls." He strode to the front of the room. "In celebration of the Holy Trinity, I want to bless each of you with the White Scapular of the Most Blessed Trinity."

"What do we say, class?"

We answered in unison, "Thank you, Father Rourke."

"Line up, children."

Father Rourke placed the ribboned necklace with its paper images at each end over our heads, blessing it and us with the magic of his hand.

"Now Sister Mike will tell you about the responsibilities of wearing your Scapular and the meaning of indulgences," he said.

"We are all sinners," Sister Mike said. "That is how God made us. After we die, but before we go to Heaven, you all know each of us must spend many days in Purgatory, atoning for our sins. Faithful Catholics like we all are in this room can reach the entrance to Heaven quicker by wearing your Scapular every day and saying the prayer printed on the back of the picture. Do you all want to get to Heaven sooner?"

"Yes, Sister Mike," we answered.

"Then you must be faithful wearers of your scapulars and pray every day."

Sister Mike and Father Rourke visited every class that day and the whole school wore their white scapulars with the pictures of God, the Father, Jesus Christ, and the white bird of the Holy Spirit.

Haley had his scapular on when he came to our room for science class late in the afternoon.

"What are you doing here?" Fletcher muttered.

Haley laughed, his hand over his mouth, then whispered, "I tricked you, Fletcher."

I smile now, sitting in Miss Euphrates' kitchen, remembering how much Haley liked his innocent tricks.

"Thank you for the apples," Miss Euphrates says. "Did you pick them yourself?"

"Wyatt and I did. And I brought you some more photos."

"Any pictures from back in the day—you and Haley and Fletcher? I always remember you kids and those birch bark canoes you used to make."

"My father has those pictures. I haven't seen them in years."

"How is your father?"

"He's home with new caretakers, though he seems to be a bit more independent since he was released from the hospital. And he has his friend Jeannette who lives in the same building. She looks in on him and they play scrabble every day."

"That's so good. You got to be happy about that. Does he still make those canoes?

"I don't think so, just paper airplanes." I laugh.

I tell my grandchildren about you kids and those little birch bark canoes. One of these days maybe you can show them how that's done."

"I'd love to," I say. "Your grandchildren could come out to the farm and launch them into the river."

"Here now, maybe you can draw out a pattern for those little canoes while I get the laundry out."

"Why don't I do that?"

"No, Miss Joss. I got to keep moving." She squeezes my shoulder. "Everything you'll need is in this drawer."

I sit at Miss Euphrates' kitchen table, sketching a toy canoe pattern onto heavy paper and cutting out the shapes. I smile and nod my head, remembering the three of us, Haley, Fletcher, and me, making those toy boats.

We had cut through the woods and the pricker bushes now turned lavender by a painterly God. It was a cold October day. The tall grass had gone from brick-pink to brown and then the knell of gray, like a bell tolling the coming changes. The bridge was out back then, so we crossed the river with our pant legs rolled up, our shoes tied together and slung over our shoulders. Inching and sliding over the slippery rocks, the water was thigh-deep in places. We screeched like banshees, our voices boomeranging through the river gorge, dressed in our orange hats. We watched the Canada geese flying in formation overhead, with a perennial straggler behind, honking like an impatient taxi driver.

"Do you hear that, Joss?" Haley asked, his voice a squeak. "Those echoes?"

I laughed. "Cool, isn't it!"

"It's a lonesome sound," he said.

"We should go back," Fletcher said, "before we drown!"

Haley stretched out his arm. "Hold onto my hand, Fletcher, then grab those branches up ahead."

We gripped the longer branches that arched out over the river, holding ourselves upright against the rushing water, fearful that we would not make it to the other shore. That some toothy predator lay just below the surface.

I wonder now what tender fish were in that river: wild browns and brook trout? I can almost taste them—the oil, the sweet layers, the crispy batter sliding down my throat.

We made it to the other side, chaining our arms together, creeping from rock to rock. From the shore, we climbed to the top of the hill, to the birch grove where thick white bark had fallen in curls. Perfect for hand-sewn canoes. River racers, we called them. We sat under the birches, and I pulled out scissors and thread hidden in my pockets. We transformed those bark curls into tiny canoes, cutting them out, then stitching them together, and taping a penny into each one for ballast the way my father had shown us.

We sat on the hill, tying off our final stitches and watching three hunters below tromp along the river's edge, heading for the open fields.

"We better let them know we're here," I said.

"Why?" Haley wanted to know.

"So they won't hear us in the brush and fire at us," Fletcher said.

We three stood up in our bright red and orange shirts.

"Hi," I called out. "We're up here playing."

"Okay," one of them called back. "We'll watch out for you."

Haley's eye's widened. "I don't like guns," he said.

Fletcher smirked and rolled his eyes. "You just don't understand guns."

"Come on, you guys," I said. "Let's launch them."

On that day nearly everything was in sync. We pushed our river racers into the water like hatchlings, watching all but three of them tip and capsize. But those survivors were made with perfect balance, their height proportional to their length. A breeze from the west pushed them onward, and eddies along the banks, far from the blacker pools, ran the wild water. We watched those tiny boats fly over the rapids from the beaver dam and settle upright, spinning in the clear pool below, before continuing their way to the savage white falls by the millhouse where they would surely be lost. We followed them as far as we could go, until the river's edge became sheer rock cliffs towering above the trees.

I wonder now if I can replicate that handiwork. I find needles and yarn in Miss Euphrates craft drawer and begin knotting the bright yellow yarn between the paper layers. My hands push the wide needle deep into the canoe ends, catching the loops to create the running edge. Neat and precise. They would be proud: Wyatt, my mother, my father, all those stitchers in my life.

"Well, look at these," Miss Euphrates says, holding a paper canoe in her hand, turning it, holding it to the light. "They're perfect, all that hand sewing as if you measured the spaces between each turn of the needle. My grandbabies are steeped in free form— like their daddy." She laughs and busies herself cleaning up the paper scraps and yarn ends, her hands flying. "We're likely to see some wild sewing from them."

I laugh. "I never learned that lesson. Everything I did had to be perfect."

"I remember that, Miss Joss. High expectations all around. Fine to do the best you can, but none of us were meant to be perfect."

But one of my little canoes was perfect that day.

We couldn't climb that steep face, and we couldn't cross the river, either. It was too wild and deep, so we ran all the way back, climbing up through the birch grove, looking for the barbed wire fence, looking for a narrow run in the river far below that could get us to the other side. But the fence was nowhere in sight. We had run in circles, prickers scratching our faces, our bare legs, too. We were confused and lost. We should have followed the river upstream, but we were disoriented and lost our way. Our perfect white canoes now gone. Our flawless stitches swept away: back-stitch, catch stitch, blanket stitch, and runnings.

20

Wyatt and I spend most weekends together at the farm, he with his stitches and signatures and gilded edges. I putter and do chores and paint watercolors of the falling leaves, the bones of the earth that November perennially reveals. At my urging, Wyatt posts "No Trespassing" signs around the perimeters of the farm. In the past, local hunters respected the limitations, but the last few years my mother complained bitterly about strangers tromping through her backyard without a wit or care.

"You want to help me get these signs up?" he asks. "We can check out the tree house while we're at it. Maybe figure out a plan for how to repair it."

"How about later, Wyatt. I'm in the middle of something here." The "something" is my attempt to make birch bark canoes for Miss Euphrates' grandchildren. They had all been sick with colds and sore throats and didn't make it out to Red Mills Farm, so I thought I would make them each a few for Christmas.

"Your dad told me about the hunters he used to allow on the farm."

"Yeah, there was a group he always let in during deer season."

"You going to do that? Because I thought I might like to join in. Maybe bring your father up for a couple of days."

"It's a fine tradition by me. Those guys always keep the bridges repaired, even rebuilding them when they have to. There's a list of names in the desk drawer."

I remember my father and me coming up from the city the day after Thanksgiving when I was nine.

"Paulie-girl, you and me, kid. We need a little male camaraderie."

By that time, he had a new van, with plush seats and electric windows. Gone were the rock tunes blaring out the windows; they were now replaced by Miles Davis and John Coltrane.

"Snap your fingers," he said. "Like this." He raised his arms over his head, letting go of the wheel. He moved his head and bit his lower lip, shaking his hips in that powder blue upholstery. Snapping, snapping his fingers to the roll of his shoulders.

"You see, Paulie-girl? You try it. It's a dance."

I raised my arms like he did and snap, snap, snapped my fingers.

"Now roll those hips, Boy-o. That's right. That's right. You got it."

We laughed and laughed, cruising down the highway in that airtight climate-controlled vehicle.

I was everything at that moment—a jazz diva, one of the guys. Perfect.

By the time we rolled into town, the hunters were already there. Pickup trucks from Massachusetts, Pennsylvania, and beyond parked along the side roads. They were cousins, Navy buddies, childhood friends, men sick of the diner, tired of the bar, the wife, and kids. Men needing men, the clarity of task and finished product. They talked about process and the near linear path of their accomplishments. They came to stay at camps and tromp through the woods and farmlands. They came to thin out the herds that would otherwise starve through the coming winter.

When we reached the farm, Big Paul set me at the kitchen counter on a high stool so I could peel potatoes and carrots.

"I'll do the onions," he said. "But these guys want beef. No goddamn turkey tetrazzini leftovers."

We made pot roast with roasted potatoes, turnip, carrots, and onions. Creamed peas, baked apples with maple syrup, and buttermilk biscuits, too. While the guys stoked the woodstove in the millhouse and set up the tables and chairs.

By five, once the hunters had come back to the house, showered, and dressed, we trooped out, clanging the porch door behind us, and headed to the mill house. The sky was rimmed in copper and gold with the indigo heavens rolling in. Lamp oil lanterns, garden torches, and strands of Christmas lights lit up the millhouse. As we walked through the field, we passed a rusted-out pickup with a gutted deer carcass, dragged from the woods. Those silent doe eyes stared at me. I turned away, listening to the music of Dad's jazz band as it wafted through the evening air. Counting the lights, the few evening stars shining in the pale sky, and a smattering of snow flurries shimmering in the light, I did my best to push back the image of that dead animal.

"Daddy, why do they have to kill the deer? They're so beautiful."

"They are beautiful. But there is an order to everything. There are things that are cruel. And we eat meat. That is how the world was made. Those deer had a happy life on this farm. Does that help?"

I nodded, but still the image of those empty eyes stayed with me.

Dinner was rowdy. Men drinking and smoking. Jokes that I should not have heard.

"Hey guys," my father said. "There's a young girl here."

"Right, sorry, Paul."

The warnings didn't help, and eventually my father walked me back to the house.

I remember thinking back then that I was missing out on all the fun. But I know better now. It's an easy answer when Wyatt asks me if I want to come to dinner at deer camp.

"No, thanks. I know what that's all about."

"True," he says. "It can get a little rough. Do you mind if we use the house? I'll make sure the guys behave themselves, don't trash the place."

"Sure. Just make them go outside if they smoke."

"Agreed." He picks up a birch bark canoe from the table, holding it up, examining the stitches. "Nice job. But what keeps it from absorbing water?"

"That's the last step. A coating of paraffin. Beeswax works, too."

"I don't know, Joss. Maybe you have the stuff to be a bookbinder."

I laugh. "You, too? My father would have loved it if I became a seamstress in his shop. But my mother nabbed me first. I'm working on finding my way for once."

"I know you are. I'm proud of you."

But it was challenging to know what or who to become, when my life has been all about replicating those around me. My mother and father, even Miss Euphrates. I remember Sister Mike modeling a life for us to imitate.

She stood in front of us as November bared the deciduous trees of their leaves. Those naked branches huddled together like skinny dippers caught sneaking back to the house. The grasses and pod plants rattled in the wind, and I was distracted, daydreaming and gazing out the window.

"Joss Ryckman, did you hear me?" Sister Mike asked.

I startled at the shrill in her voice. "I—"

"Catholic faith does not permit hesitation. Your attention is required inside this room, not out there watching birds that are not the Holy Spirit."

"Yes, Sister."

"We are obliged to be Catholic in order to be redeemed in Heaven."

She droned on, calling Fletcher and a few other students on the carpet whose attention wandered on an unbearable late Friday afternoon.

"You're lucky, young Mr. Goodwin, that I hold trombone players in such esteem."

For all of Fletcher's shenanigans, Sister Mike had a soft spot for him. Right after God, her next love was music. She gathered any child who knew the difference between a sharp and a flat into a makeshift band. For a school with no formal music program, Sister Mike's band produced converts in every classroom. Not only for the sheer joy of creating music, but also for the favor Sister Mike would bestow on their little Catholic heads. Sister Mike's wrath was legendary and any advantage a kid could master was greeted with enthusiasm.

The band practiced twice a week in the gymnasium, wheezing their way through polkas and anthems, with an occasional modern folk song tossed in for variety. Fletcher had more musical ability than most kids his age and was Sister Mike's favorite of the group.

Until Haley came along.

With Haley at the piano, Sister Mike pushed her students to reach higher, and easier popular tunes gave way to classics; two fourth graders joined with their brand new violins. The band was now a faith-based orchestra with occasional true pitch.

Just before the bell rang on that Friday afternoon in November, Sister Mike called the orchestra members in our class up to her desk. She handed out sheet music to each of them.

"Now practice twice each on Saturday and Sunday so that you've got it down cold. Play in tune, and remember this is a waltz. One, two, three. One, two, three." She danced in small circles, her wide skirts billowing.

I watched her glide across the floor, astonished at how effortlessly she moved. She must have been another person before the black habit and vows.

The bell rang, and we lined up at the door but broke into an open run to the waiting school buses and moms in family wagons and minivans.

The three of us piled into the waiting van.

When we were almost home, Mrs. Goodwin announced that she had to stop at the grocery store. "Just one little stop," she said. "To pick up a few things. I won't be long. Ya'll can wait in the car."

The three of us looked at each other, smirking and rolling our eyes. We knew she'd be gone for an hour or more. We watched her walk across the parking lot and through the sliding double doors.

"Come on, you guys," Fletcher said. "We can walk home from here. I'll leave her a note."

She might not notice we were gone. Fletcher's mother had left us more than once after we had wandered away from the car.

We slid open the van doors and ran to the end of the street. Cars whizzed past as we waited to cross the highway. We walked along the narrow ridge between the road and the embankment below, watching a freight train roll along the rails headed south.

"Let's go down and watch the trains," Fletcher said.

We slid down the ridge on wet leaves and mud, falling onto our bottoms until we hit the berm just above the tracks.

"This is cool," Haley squeaked.

We nodded like some three-headed creature as we waited for the whistle to blow as the locomotive crossed the road below.

I liked the sound of the cars clacking along the tracks and the short bursts of the whistle. It made me sleepy, even sitting in wet, muddy jeans in the November air. And made me wish I was lying in my bed. I listened for the train's whistle every night, followed by the church bells, the whispering trees—ritual lullabies of nightlife at the farm that soothed me when the shadows drew too close.

"Hey, you guys. Wait right here," Fletcher said.

"Where are you going?" I asked.

"Up to the store. I'll be right back."

I couldn't imagine what Fletcher was up to, but I knew it would be a prank.

When he slid back down to the berm fifteen minutes later, he had cans of spray paint sticking out of his oversized pockets.

"Let's be taggers," he laughed.

"What are taggers?" Haley wanted to know.

"You know, guys who do street art. They paint words and designs on buildings and buses. We can tag the railroad cars that are sitting in the yard."

"But won't we get in trouble?"

Fletcher laughed. "Only if we get caught."

We slid the rest of the way down off the cindery berm and flat ran across the rail yard. We hid below the rail office windows, poking our heads up to eye level. The offices were dark, the parking lot empty. We hightailed, crouching as we ran, across the lot to the standing rail cars.

"What should we paint?" I asked.

"Monsters!" Haley said. "Like the ones in our closets."

"Show me," Fletcher said.

Haley began on the body of a silver tanker, painting a purple comb-headed, three-legged chicken-man with beady yellow eyes and red feet.

"Wow. That thing must be three feet high," Fletcher said.

We painted until dusk, creatures with fins and wings. Three-eyed warriors wearing capes and boots, horned fiends with beguiling toothy smiles, and words: 'The Canaan Cool Kids' or 'Power' in purple and red, and cartoon captions in huge bubbles that said 'Eat Stinky Feet' and 'Rock On!'

"We better get going," I said.

"Why can't we stay a little longer?" Haley asked.

"We don't want to get caught."

The three of us walked the railroad tracks along Old Queechy Road until they veered north. We switched to kicking hockey-puck sized stones along the street and up the hill to Sweet Milk Road.

"Wham! It's yours, Haley," Fletcher said.

The rock slammed into Haley's foot. "Jeez, that hurt, Fletcher."

"Yeah, well, ever since you joined the school band we have to play all this classical stuff." There was a bitter edge to Fletcher's voice.

"I know," Haley said. "Just because I play piano, Sister Mike thinks we have to do classical pieces. They're not my favorite, either."

"They're not?"

"Nope. But teachers think the classics are the most important. They all think I'm going to be a pianist when I grow up. But I'm going to be a scientist."

"But you're so amazing on the piano!" I said.

"Music is a hobby for me. Everybody knows Einstein played the violin for fun." His small boy face turned to me and Fletcher. "His real work was being a physicist."

"So is that what you want to do? Be a physicist?" Fletcher asked.

"Maybe. It's you, Fletcher, who will be the great musician. I'll just be another scientist working on cancer or astronomy with a whole bunch of other people, while you're making a brand new kind of music."

"But I don't know how to play the piano and my momma says the piano is the root of all music."

"So I'll teach you how to play."

"You will?"

The two of them ran the rest of the way home, emperors in the kingdom of childhood on an autumn night. But I dawdled in the wan light, pulling the straggling leaves from low branches, shredding the last of the silk from milkweed pods that had dried and burst. It was Friday night, and my father would be waiting at the back door, sullen and angry. I didn't care that he worried. Or that he paced and called Mrs. Goodwin looking for me. I sucked in the dark raw air with the reek of wood smoke and vegetation gone to rot.

21

I wake to the sugary air, the tang of yeast bread rising and pungent cinnamon that daily breeze through the building. The new kid is in early—not that I recall his name. I used to know everyone's name, even the temporary holiday help. I shower and dress quickly, clomping down the back stairs to the bakery—late once again.

"Hey," I say. "How's it going, Teddy?" His embroidered name is on his chef coat.

"The breakfast pies are cooling, three trays of coffee muffins are in the oven, and dough for the cinnamon rolls is in the proofer. Rye is in the brick oven."

I look at the clock, and it's 4:15 a.m. Another hour and it will be sunrise. "You're ahead, Teddy."

"Yeah, Lynn said you've been sleeping in, so—"

"Really? She said that?"

"I—"

"Don't worry about it." I pull apples from the cooler and begin making filling for puff pastry turnovers—apple slices and cranberries sweet with honey and a balsamic reduction. By 5:30 a.m., we fill the bakery case and line the bread bins with righteous mammon—bags of crusty scented baguettes, rye, and sourdough.

During the mid-morning lull, while I hang wreaths with seed pods and cinnamon sticks in the windows, and string lights around the doorways, Lynn pops through the door.

"Oh, I love the wreaths," she says. "They look great."

"Never been a holiday season here without fabulous decorations." I hear the edge in my voice, but I don't care. "Oh, by the way, Lynn, There will be an extra crew on tonight, so I'll be going upstairs in a bit. They'll be in around eleven after the dining room closes."

"I wasn't told about—"

I smile. "That's because I just decided this morning. We need to get a jump on fruitcakes and plum puddings for the holidays. They have to age, after all, and I'm adding panforte this year."

"How many panfortes?" Lynn asks.

"Three hundred. Last year's figures warrant an increase."

"Are you sure?"

I motion for her to step into the office. "Grab a coffee for yourself and one for me if you don't mind—light, no sugar."

I wait at my desk, fuming, trying to calm myself. I will need just the right tone.

"Here's your coffee," Lynn says. She looks somber. "I just—"

"Before you begin, let me remind you . . . I have been working in this bakery since I was fourteen, and I managed the business by myself at twenty. I've got a few years under my belt, and yes, I tend to come down into the kitchen on my schedule. I'm useless before 4:00 a.m. Not that I need to explain this to you or anyone else."

"Okay. I get it Joss, I spoke out of turn, but you've included me in most of your business decisions."

"True enough, Lynn. I've collaborated with you over the last year or so, but when I encounter a temporary employee who describes my arrival as 'late,' I'm offended. And frankly, I'm pissed off. You stepped over the line, and I reacted."

"You're right. I'm sorry."

"Okay," I nod, staring at the spreadsheet on my screen. "Thanks for the coffee."

"On another subject, have you thought any more about my proposal? Buying Madame Marie's?"

"A little," I say, sipping my coffee. I watch her smirk, knowing that if I decline, she'll find another bakery to buy or do a start-up on her own. Once you get the bug, that's how it goes. But if I sell, then what do I do?

"And?" she asks.

I startle. Her voice drips with attitude. "I don't have an answer right now."

"But Joss, I don't get it. You're not here like you used to be, and you're living part-time upstate."

I look at her, not sure what to say. The bakery has been in my family for three generations. That alone gives me pause. And what would my father think? It was his sister who started the bakery. My other reasons, not that I can articulate all of them, are my own business. I've let her in, maybe too much, and she's impatient for a change. "I'll do this," I say. "Get an appraisal, and then we'll have a number to start with."

"Great." She beams back at me and is out the door.

I watch her walk out the door, knowing there's been a knife hiding behind her back for some time. Back at the numbers, making lists, crossing items off and adding new ones, I know I'm distracted, wanting to be in Canaan. It is only lately that I realize how much that year on the farm with Miss Euphrates has marked me. I rub my palm as if there is a score across my skin as broad as a handsbreadth that belies the injury below. I cannot rub it off; there

is no evidence of a wound—just the racing frenzy in my head. I
don't know if I'm in a foot race for some elusive prize, or running
away. I only know that I would rather be back in Canaan, baking
a few pies for a family holiday, or getting ready for Christmas with
Miss Euphrates.

We began in early November, Miss Euphrates and I, just like my
family did at the bakery. First the plum puddings—we chopped
the suet, rendering, straining, and cooling it. When it was cold,
Miss Euphrates showed me how to shred it like cabbage.

"Just like this," she said, pushing the rounds of cold fat in a swift
downward motion against a box grater. "Be careful not to cut your
knuckles." When I had filled the bowl, she added raisins, currants,
citron, and spices, while I washed my greasy hands.

"Now for the magic," she laughed and added a dose of cognac;
the scent of the sweet brandy filled the kitchen. "Now we cover
this and put it in the refrigerator. Every day we'll add a little more
cognac."

While we coddled the plum pudding mixture day by day, we
filled in with after-school cookie making: pfeffernusse, jam thumb-
prints, gingerbread people, and star-shaped cookies, buttery and
sweet. My favorites were the almond moon crescents. I couldn't
resist dipping a finger into that buttery almond batter.

"What'd I tell you about that, Joss Ryckman?" Miss Euphrates'
voiced boomed.

I twirled around to face her coal-black eyes burning into me.

"You go on now. Get yourself to the wash sink. And wipe
that batter off your face while you're at it. This here's a professional
kitchen." She shook her head, muttering under her breath. "You

want to taste something, we use a spoon here. A clean spoon for each taste. You got that?"

"Sorry," I nodded. Her willingness to indulge me flew out the window when I disregarded her rules. I knew this but had succumbed.

"You gonna put those cookies away, girl? They waiting on you."

I nodded, still hearing the disapproval in her voice. It lingered in me the way soap film sticks to a glass, tunneling down my throat into my belly, filling me with awkwardness and shame. I quietly arranged the cooled confections into containers, counting each one, writing their names and numbers on a sticky label. When the tubs and boxes were filled, I carried them to the freezer at the back of the pantry and stacked them on the frosted shelves.

"Did you save some cookies out for tea?" Miss Euphrates asked.

I swallowed hard. "I'm sorry, I forgot."

"No matter, dawta-girl. I got something tucked away. Come sit and stop your fretting."

The steamy cups of tea sat at the table, along with a plate of gingerbread squares slathered with butter and honey.

"I'm a gingerbread gal," she said, dunking a bit of cake into her tea."

I tried to follow suit, but the cake crumbled and sunk to the bottom of my teacup.

Miss Euphrates smiled and handed me a teaspoon. "Go on," she chuckled.

I scooped the soggy cake and slid it down my throat.

She laughed and clapped, then leaned into me and said, "I got a secret to tell you, Miss Joss. Can you keep secrets?"

I nodded, my mouth filled with honey and gingerbread. But the phone rang, her daughter on the other end talking about whatever loving mothers and daughters chat about: "did you hang out the wash?" or "how was school?"

Miss Euphrates never did tell me her secret, not that she was one for the hush-hush of gossip. I still wonder what she was going to say to me that day—probably some confidential about Santa Claus, or what she'd read on Haley's wish list. What could he have wanted? I push it all back, staring at the rows of graphs and numbers on my computer screen.

My phone rings.

"Hey!" Wyatt's cheerful voice calls through the airwaves. "Want to go to the movies tonight? Do the retro thing and see *Dial M for Murder?*"

"Sounds like fun, but I have to be back at the bakery by eleven. I'm running the 'retribution' shift."

"Retribution shift?"

"Yeah, Lynn pissed me off, so I'm an ass. You know what that's like."

He scoffs. "That, I do," and then chats on about some book, which theater, and what time to meet him. I half listen, still lost in thought about secrets and numbers.

"Don't be late," he says.

"I won't," I reply, but of course I am. I push through the doors of the cinema lobby a little after seven o'clock. Wyatt waves from the far end near the popcorn machine, tickets in his hand.

"Sorry, I'm late," I say.

He shrugs and rolls his eyes, then quick kisses me, and we scoot down the walkway and into the dark theater. The previews have already begun.

"I smuggled in sandwiches," I whisper. "And Coke."

"Of course you did!" Wyatt whispers. "It's your deviant nature."

He usually laughs when he says this, but not tonight. "I'm sorry I was late, Wyatt. I had customers."

"So did I." His voice is flat. "Alfred Hitchcock directed this," he says.

"I'd forgotten that," I answer sheepishly.

I hand him his sandwich and drink. We settle in just as the mawkish melody begins. Graphic credits flash across the big screen, opening to a kiss between Ray Milland and Grace Kelly. The liquor bottles, the antiques, all the lovely things of status in 1954 contradict the calculating Tony Wendice played by Milland.

I lean into Wyatt, as Grace Kelly in her red dress and red shoes kisses her lover, Robert Cummings. She is a fallen woman, and though I don't remember the story that well, I know she will pay a harrowing price. I wonder what my toll will be. In love, there always is a price and it may be high for as much as I push Wyatt back.

I breathe in his soap and aftershave. His silhouette in the dark movie theater imprints on me. Infatuation and attachment are the physical phenomena, and as much as I analyze what it is to love, it changes nothing. Grace Kelly, as Margot, never appears to struggle with this in the way I do, as she flickers in light and sound across the wide screen. The character she plays is thinly drawn. Still she has strength.

The audience holds its collective breath as Grace Kelly is about to stab Anthony Dawson, the would-be killer hired by Kelly's on-screen husband, with a pair of scissors. I lower my head. I never look at the gory parts in movies.

"I'll tell you when it's over," Wyatt whispers. He wraps his arm around me. I tuck into his chest, inhaling the smell of his sweat, feeling his large hands around me. It is a moment that slows my racing heart, softens my stiffened limbs, as the on-screen melo-drama continues. We sit together like this for the rest of the movie, waiting for the vengeful Tony Wendice to get his due. In the end, the wrongs are righted. Justice wins out. There are few murky ambiguities—a reflection of 1954. We stroll out of the theater into a chilly November night.

"Want to stop for a coffee or a drink?" Wyatt asks.

"Sure. How about Pete's Ale House? It's close."

We walk down Atlantic Avenue from the theater to the bar, the wind whipping our coats and catching the tips of our noses and cheeks. Wyatt holds the door for me, and the warmth and bustle of the tavern spill into the entryway. We sit at a table in the back and order drinks, something from the tap for Wyatt and a cappuccino for me.

"That was fun—the movie," I said. "I haven't seen it in years."

"I think I saw it once on a late night channel when I was a kid. It's much better on the big screen."

"Magical."

"It was. I like Hitchcock movies."

"Me, too, though his portrayal of women is shallow. I don't know if that's a reflection of him or the era."

"Maybe both," Wyatt says, as he gulps his beer. "I didn't tell you—I got a call yesterday from my sister. She invited us out for Thanksgiving back at the old homestead." He lowers his eyes, star-ing straight ahead.

I reach out and squeeze his hand. He is still mourning the loss of his father, even though it has been nearly two years. I met Wyatt's dad only a few times. I remember David Jacob as a curious looking man, with prominent ears and thinning hair. Wyatt got his sturdy build and good looks from his mother, but his esthetic is from his father. He was a sweet guy, though not a man who revealed his true feelings, always proper in his bowtie and vest. This habit began with his frequent forays to the Rare Book and Manuscript Library at the University of Illinois, eventually becoming his *de rigueur* attire on into retirement.

"It will be good to see some life back in the old place," he says.

Wyatt's sister Bailey bought out his half of their parent's estate about six months earlier and moved back to Savoy, just outside of Champaign-Urbana, Illinois.

"I've been thinking about that," I say. "How nice it would be to have holidays. I can't remember the last time we had a real family celebration."

Wyatt shakes his head. "Yeah, I guess owning a bakery trumps taking holidays off."

I hear the disappointment in his voice. "I'm glad you understand," I say. "I think you should go out to your sister's. I'm just sorry I won't be able to be with you."

He reaches over and gives my arm a squeeze. "We can be together for Christmas. How about I go out to Red Mills ahead of you, get things ready?"

I watch Wyatt's face, his eyes. He's always going to be like this, picking up the pieces, trying to create normalcy out of chaos. He deserves more from me than what I give him.

"I could close the bakery at four on Christmas Eve and be at the farm around seven. Then we would spend Christmas at the farm, which was what my mother did."

"Okay, that's what we'll do. But what about Thanksgiving? I hate the idea of you sitting alone above the bakery on Turkey Day."

"I'll spend it with my father. He'll probably be glad for the company."

"Yeah, but will you be?"

We finish our drinks and walk home, each of us catching our breath against the gyring wind along Atlantic Avenue. I dread spending another holiday with my father; him barking orders, demanding another beer, and always complaining. I wish I could be with Wyatt, but the bakery calls.

"Want to spend the night at my place?" Wyatt asks.

"I want to, but I have a crew coming in."

"That's right—your retribution shift."

"Which seems to have backfired," I say. We walk on; arms entwined. He drops me at the front door of the bakery, his mouth cold against mine before I dash inside. We wave to each other through the glass like little kids. He turns, tucking into his collar, and fades along the long dark avenue. I hear the remnants of his footsteps, and bolt the lock on the bakery door.

Upstairs, I wash and slip into clean clothes. A quick brush through my hair, and in a sideways glance at the mirror, I notice my eyes. They flash like my father's eyes—cold and distant—the softness that used to be there is gone.

22

I wasn't expecting much in the way of a warmhearted family holiday. That was not what we did. But when I get to my father's apartment, he opens the door for me with a big smile plastered across his face.

"Let me take your coat," he says. "How about a drink—you like wine, right?"

I nod, dumbfounded, handing him my jacket.

"I couldn't remember—red or white? I got a few of each."

"Red," I say, staring at him.

"What?" he smirks. "I'm making an effort. Jeannette says I need to try harder." He hands me a glass of red wine.

"It's a petite sirah," Jeannette calls from the kitchen. "I think you'll like it."

"Hi Jeannette, can I help?"

She sits at the kitchen table peeling potatoes. "That would be nice. How about peeling the squash?"

"If there's room in the oven, we can just pierce it and bake it like a big potato."

"Are you sure, Joss? I never did it that way." She looks up at me; the worry lines spread across her face.

"We do it all the time at the café. The flavor is richer."

She waves her hand. "Of course," she laughs. "You know what you're doing,"

"Some days," I laugh.

"Oh, come on—your father brags about you all the time."

"He does?"

"What's the matter?" my father asks. "You don't know I'm proud of you?"

I smile. "Course I know, Dad."

But it's too late, the magic breaks. Sourness creeps into his voice. He parks himself in his lounger and flicks on the TV to a football game, jacking up the volume.

"Jeannette, grab me a beer," he barks.

"That's all right, Jeannette," I say. "I'll get it. You want some more wine?"

"I shouldn't," she says. "With my medication . . . maybe just a little more." I pour more wine into her glass and bring my father his beer along with crackers and cheese.

"Be nice," I whisper in his ear. "You shouldn't be asking Jeannette to fetch for you. She's got Parkinson's. Remember?"

He rolls his eyes and half nods. I squeeze his hand and bring his empties back to the kitchen.

We sit, Jeannette and I, chatting softly in the kitchen, as the echo of my father's edginess fills the room. It is as if I am about to choke, waiting for his roar.

"Quiet!" my father barks. "Can't a man listen to the game in his own home?

"Paul!" Jeannette says in her sweetest voice, "Be polite."

"It's okay," I say, waltzing into the living room. I plug the head-phones into the TV and snap them over my father's ears. "There, now we all can enjoy the day."

Jeannette's eyes widen. "I can't believe you did that!"

"What's not to believe? Kowtowing to him only makes him worse." I look at her and wonder why she is here. I want to ask her why she doesn't run. Can't she see he's a bastard?

"He's not going to change, Joss," she whispers, shaking her head.

"True, but we can change how we deal with him. That's enough."

"My father was the same sort of man," Jeannette says. "And my mother was meek. She never so much as said 'boo' to him."

"Guys like your father, that's what they like—women they can keep under their thumb. Not that my mother was that sort. Which is why it didn't work—she had her opinions, her work."

"I wish I had learned to be more that way," Jeannette says.

While dinner cooks, we sip sherry and play Scrabble.

I come up with *ghazi* for eighteen points, which is an Arabic word for warrior, though Jeannette bests me with twenty-three points for *tazza,* an Italian word for a footed compote. She stuns me with *addax, codex,* and *hyrax.*

"What? Do you stay up nights studying the dictionary for 'x' words?" I ask.

"Still waters run deep and sometimes tricky."

"So you *do* have a dark side, Jeannette. And here I always thought you were goodness to the core."

She flashes me a wicked smile and says, "Maybe we should check the turkey. It must be about done."

"It smells awfully good," I say.

We check the bird, wiggling the drumsticks and decide that it's done. I make gravy; Jeannette sets the table. When the platters and steaming vegetables are on the table, I call my father to join us.

"What?" he says. "I can't hear you."

I motion for him to remove the headphones. He simpers and tosses the headphones over the back of his chair.

"And can you turn off the TV."

"Fine," he gripes, then smiles at me. "Hey Joss, I almost for-got—I got a surprise for you. He pulls a painted cardboard hatchet out from beside his chair.

I look up at the brown cardboard handle with paper feathers hanging from the end. There is a yellow floppy blade at the top.

"Remember how I used to chase you around the apartment with one of these?"

"Oh, Paul!" Jeannette scolds. "You must have terrorized her."

"He did," I whisper and wink. "But at the same time I loved it. Always as we were about to sit down to our evening Thanksgiving dinner."

My mother and sister would already be sitting at their places, waiting for Dad and me. I'd pretend nothing peculiar was about to happen. I'd walk the longest way around the dining room table, scuffing my feet along the floorboards, dragging my fingers along the chair rail.

"Joss, you're leaving fingerprints all over the walls," my mother would shrill.

She was always cranky and tired. She worked most holiday mornings. "Sorry, Mom," I'd reply.

It was then that my father would slip out of the bathroom, shirtless, with my mother's lipstick and eyeshadow smeared across his face.

"What are you doing with my make-up, Paul? You'll ruin it."

"You mean your war paint?" he'd laugh.

It was then that the chase began. Round and round the dining room table, me screaming, and my father chasing me with a paper ax.

He'd grab my arm and whack it into pieces—off with my hand, and then a cut from the elbow, with the final severing at my shoul-der. "It's mine now," he'd say.

I'd scream louder, laughing and running faster, losing bits of myself at every turn to my father's madness. When my mother had

had enough, she'd stand her ground against the blade, with my dad as Damocles, wavering destruction just above her head. They'd stare eye-to-eye until he backed out of the room, retreating to the bathroom only to emerge moments later in his starched white shirt with remnants of cold cream and lipstick smudges still on his face.

"Everything looks divine, Lydah," he'd say. "Let's have a blessing."

I'd still be giggling. He'd tap my foot with his and flash me a silly-stern look that made me laugh even harder. But then he'd begin the prayer he'd learned as a boy, and I'd be drawn to his voice: *Oh Gracious Light. Now as we come to the setting of the sun and our eyes behold the vesper light. . . .*

My head is a swirl of memories as I now sit across from my father, his paper hatchet fallen to the floor. "Dad, how about your prayer? Even though it's not evening. . . ."

"You have a prayer?" Jeannette asks.

He's quiet. We wait, watching his face, his hands.

He clears his throat and closes his eyes. The words come out in gasps. He stops, then begins again as a suitor, a warrior, a risen man.

I am thrown into the afternoon light with the washed gold that spills into the room. It spreads across my father's face and lifts his voice. He is young again, bright and fearless, but I am no child. I am the woman whose soul he pirated in exchange for demands I can never meet. I run my hand along my arm, feeling for those spidery scars—the ones with the red ridges and still purple vales—the marks no one ever sees but me.

Jeannette's warbly voice cuts through my haze. "Are you all right?" she asks.

"It's that bakery," my father snaps. "That damn bakery. Joss' mother was always the same—every holiday like a shipwreck survivor."

"I'm sorry, Dad. You're right. The place is a holiday killer."

"Good that you know. Let's just have a nice dinner."

We pass the platters and break out the warm rolls and butter. He'll want to sop up the gravy with a few.

"Thank you both for sharing this with me," Jeannette says. Her hands shake, navigating the fork to her mouth.

"You're practically family," Dad says, his voice husky.

"You're so sweet," she says.

"Jeezus, don't go getting all maudlin on me."

When we're finished, Dad and I wash the dishes and straighten the kitchen while Jeannette rests in the lounger.

"Do you have a lot to do to get ready for Christmas?" she calls from the living room.

"At the bakery, yes. The holidays make our year. It's always exhausting. The personal shopping isn't that much. Something for my sister and her husband, for Wyatt and Dad. This year I want to shop for Miss Euphrates and her family, too. That should be fun."

"Now, who is she, Miss Euphrates?"

"She was our housekeeper that year when I lived at the farm in Canaan. She taught me so much, including how to bake pies. I reconnected with her this past summer."

"Isn't that lovely!"

"Now, she knew how to get ready for Christmas like nobody I ever met. She was so well organized and made everything look so easy."

Miss Euphrates and I made pies and tarts two days before Christmas Eve: peach tarts with sour cherries and orange zest folded into sweet pastry crust with a measure of cornmeal. Those were my favorites. There were pies of mincemeat made from green tomatoes leftover from the end of the summer. There were always tomatoes. Rich berry pies made from blueberries, blackberries, and raspberries picked on the farm. We underbaked them just slightly and then popped them into the oven just before serving time.

On Christmas Eve day, Haley, my father, and I hiked into the woods to scout a Christmas tree. We pulled the toboggan over the thigh-deep snow, along with a bow saw and some rope. Haley and I plodded step by step, stopping to rest on the toboggan until my father prodded us along.

"Come on you kids, by the time we cut a tree and get it back to the house, Santy Claus will have come and gone."

"But the snow is so deep, we can barely walk through it."

"It builds character," my father retorted.

We rolled our eyes and slogged on.

In the darkest part of the forest, we found a handsome eastern white pine in a grove that my father planted years back. It had grown straight and true in the happy cold air, reaching over eight feet tall.

"This one will do. Right, little master?"

Haley smiled. "I didn't know you could cut Christmas trees from the woods."

"We can," I whispered. "Cause it's from our land."

By the time we returned to the house it was almost noon. Haley, Naomi, and I spent the next couple of hours decorating the tree with hundreds of white lights and ornaments that were in our family for generations: a pair of tiny black rubber boots, stamped with Goodyear on the soles, German glass bells, roly poly Santas, and miniature wooden nutcrackers.

When we finished decorating, I helped Miss Euphrates with the fish chowder and put the final touches on the dishes that I would later put in the oven.

"Miss Joss," she said. "You have a happy Christmas. I'll be seeing you in a couple days. I put something under the tree. Something for Haley, too. You know you my dawta-girl." She hugged me tightly and kissed my face and was out the door with the present I made for her tucked into her pocketbook, unbeknownst to her.

At school, we had made glass-fused spoon rests for our mothers in art class. Haley and I wrapped them in my room. But I wrote a different name on the tag: "To Miss Euphrates, From Joss."

"Don't tell my mother that I gave this to Miss Euphrates," I said.

"Okay, Aunt Jossy. It can be our secret."

I remember how delighted she was with that spoon rest, and how happy it made me to give it to her. As I head out to Canaan on a snowy Christmas Eve, I wonder if she still has it. But it doesn't matter. I bought her a new one this year, along with a scarf for her hair, some Ogilvie Sisters Soap, and a bracelet.

When I pull into the driveway on Sweet Milk Road, the house looks beautiful. There are candles in all the windows and spot-lighted wreaths on the front double doors. I can see the Christmas tree in the living room with its twinkling white lights and shiny glass ornaments.

"You're here!" Wyatt says. "Happy Christmas, Joss." He kisses me and grabs the bags out of my hands.

"Miss Euphrates always said that, 'Happy Christmas.' I can't wait to see her this week."

He smiles. "Me, too. But this is our night."

It is, and I am thankful for him, for this night, and for our somehow having found our way back together. As much as I try to deny him, he is a part of me.

"Did you bring goodies from the bakery—cookies, cakes, tarts?"

"Course. And I brought chocolate-hazelnut Napoleons, like I promised I would."

"I don't remember that."

I wave my hand and smile. "I'm hungry for real food. What are we having?"

"Something light—bouillabaisse and a warm spinach salad."

We sit in the living room after our supper, watching the tree, the lights so sparkly on this dark night. All those old ornaments. I wonder how many hands have hung them on pine branches and celebrated in the cold of December. I look at Wyatt and know that we are part of a long line of people from this land and this house who have loved each other in the dark.

"I have a gift I want to give you tonight, Joss." He hands me a small package. "It was my mother's," he says.

I hesitate.

"Go ahead. Open it."

Inside is a small Italian cameo. "It's lovely. Are you sure—"

"She'd love for you to have it. My sister has been saving it for me. For you." He closes the top button on my white blouse and pins it in the center. "There. Perfect. It looks beautiful on you."

I don't know what to say to him. This is how I need to live my life—in this simple quiet with this serene man.

"I have something for you, too. Nothing so elegant." I hand him the heavy square box.

He rips off the ribbons and paper and lifts the lid off the box. "Ice skates! Awesome!"

"Keep looking," I say.

Inside one of the skates is a small box wrapped in silver paper.

"Open your present before Santa takes it back."

He opens the small box and peeks inside. "Oh, wow—a pocket watch." He pulls it out, studying it, running his hand over the engraved case, opening the back. "It's a beauty, Joss."

"I found it in an antique shop and I thought you'd like it. Plus it will give you something to stare at when I make you wait."

"Thank you, love. I'll always think of you, even if I'm pacing or drumming my fingers."

"Do you like the ice skates? I thought we could go down to the river and the beaver pond tomorrow. It should be frozen with all the cold weather we've had. We used to skate there. Haley, Fletcher, and I. In fact, the three of us got skates on Christmas that winter we were together."

Haley and I were wild to get outside on the ice, tromping through that thigh-deep snow with our new skates slung over our shoulders, carrying shovels to clear the ice.

"You be careful out there," my father warned. "Stay clear of the thin ice."

We sat on the edge of the beaver pond, lacing the skates to our feet and wobbling out. Once we cleared the snow, we glided in the frigid air, our noses dripping, our cheeks bright red, our voices thin against the wind.

"Watch this," I said, as I awkwardly skated backward.

"Cool!" Haley sprinted and slid to a halt, ice crystals spraying from beneath his blades.

"Wow! You can skate!"

He laughed. "Mom and I skate every winter."

We stayed on the ice until our toes were nearly blue, then hiked back to the house in time for dinner.

"Fletcher called while you were out," my father said. "He and his parents are coming over around eight. He says he has presents for you and Haley. We got anything for him?"

"I bought him skates," Naomi said. "They'll all have fun over Christmas vacation."

They came over just as we were finishing dinner. But it was only Fletcher and his father.

"The missus is feeling under the weather," Kenny Goodwin explained. "But my boy here wanted to see his little friends."

"We're glad you came over," my mother said.

Haley, Fletcher, and I explored under the Christmas tree, showing off our gifts.

"I got you guys something," Fletcher said. He handed us each a package.

"Santa left you something here, Fletcher," Naomi said.

The three of us sat on the floor, ripping off colored paper and curly ribbons.

I opened my box, and inside were two pink toy guns, one a real-looking handgun, the other an assault-style rifle.

"Aren't they cool?" Fletcher squealed.

"Yeah. Cool," I said.

Haley's gift was a replica of mine, except his were black. He pulled them from the box, examining them, filling the chambers with the plastic bullets, then tucked the small gun into the belt of his pants.

I looked at him, bewildered. "You like it?" I asked.

"Yeah, they're kind of cool."

"I thought you were afraid of guns."

"This is just a toy, Aunt Jossy!"

"They got plastic bullets, too," Fletcher said. "We can play spies with them."

I nodded and smiled and handed Fletcher his gift.

When he opened the box, he looked at me the same way I had looked at him.

"Ice skates?" he asked.

"Yeah," I said. "Haley and I got skates, too. We walked to the river this afternoon and shoveled part of it off. We skated all around the beaver dam and up and down the river ice."

"Oh," he said. "Come on, Haley, let's go upstairs."

"No aiming at each other," my father warned. "Or anyone else."

They nodded and ran up the stairs, running from room to room, hiding out in the hallways and closets. I heard them shooting down the monsters in my closet and ghosts from the attic. They screeched and thundered along the long upstairs hallway.

"You don't want to play with them, Joss?" my mother asked.

"That's boy stuff."

My mother smiled at me. "Come and help me in the kitchen."

We made coffee and fixed a tray of desserts to bring into the dining room. I sat at the table with the grownups, drinking bitter coffee as if it were an everyday occurrence.

"You want some sugar in that?" Mr. Goodwin asked with a wink.

I nodded, adding first one teaspoon of sugar, then another, and a third to try to soothe the acrid taste in my mouth.

"Extra cream helps, too." He poured a little into my cup. "Stir that in and tell me what you think."

"Good," I said smiling, but it still tasted terrible. I drank it, dunking a gingerbread man in feet first the way Miss Euphrates did.

"Thatta girl!"

I still like gingerbread dunked in coffee. We sit by the fire, with coffee and cookies, Wyatt and I, then wander off to bed, snuggling under the down comforter with dreams of sugarplums in our heads.

I get up early in the morning while Wyatt still sleeps. I have presents to wrap and knitted stockings to hang—with our names sewn in yarn on each one: Miss Euphrates, Wyatt, Eli, Quinnie, Isabelle, Jackson, and me. I fill them the way my mother always did, with boxes of Crackerjacks, an apple, an orange, and mesh bags of foil wrapped chocolate coins. There are kitchen utensils for the adults and art supplies for the kids, and in each stocking I carefully place two tiny birch bark canoes, my river racers ready for springtime.

Later that morning, they trundle through the door smelling of cold and candy canes. The kids run to the tree but do not touch anything. Their grandmother gives them that look I know well.

"Let me give you the tour," Wyatt says. He escorts Eli, Quinnie, and their children around the house and, for his final show-and-tell, brings them upstairs to the closet in my old room and shows them all those painted monsters.

Miss Euphrates and I are in the kitchen putting the final finishes on our Christmas fare. We hear them squeal and laugh upstairs.

"Now what did your man give you for Christmas, dawta-girl?"

I show Miss Euphrates the cameo that belonged to his mother.

"Umm, hmm," she mumbles. "That is something special. A man don't give his momma's jewelry to just any girl. You know what I mean, Miss Joss?"

"I know."

"I can see you trying to wrap your head around all of that. No need. No need at all. Life just happens one day to the next."

After our Christmas lunch, we let the kids loose. They tear into their stockings. Miss Euphrates lines up all the river racers along the fireplace mantle. We pass out gifts. There are roller skates and scooters flying though the living room, and later we all skate hand in hand on the frozen beaver pond, while Miss Euphrates reclines on my mother's settee, her feet on a footstool. Before we go outside, we take pictures of her and chuckle as she mumbles and snores in her sleep.

They say their goodbyes with kisses and hugs and promises to come back for more skating and hot cocoa.

"They were so much fun," Wyatt says. "All that screeching and racing through the house."

"It's been a long time since this house has seen this much activity."

"You were wonderful with them, Joss. You made everyone feel so special."

"They are special. They're Miss Euphrates' grandchildren. They're like family to me."

"You're right."

"They loved the books you gave them."

"Did Miss Euphrates see the cameo I gave you? By the way, where is it?"

"She did," I say. "Oh, Jeeze, I left it upstairs. I didn't want anything to happen to it while I cooked. I'll be right back." I race up the stairs and pin it back onto my blouse, check my hair, and put on a little lip gloss.

Wyatt hollers up the stairs, "You liked all the craziness and the buzz of kids in the house, didn't you Joss?"

I roll my eyes. Subtlety is not his strong suit.

We sit mesmerized by the fire, sipping our coffee, listening to the wind pick up outside.

He gazes at the cameo pinned on my collar. "You understand what this means to me."

"I understand. Just give me some time and space. It scares me— all that you want. I had poor examples."

"Not today. This house was rich with love."

I don't say anything, but inside I am terrified. I'm so afraid I will make all the wrong moves, repeat all the same mistakes. That in the end I will run and run and keep running.

"You're going to be okay," Wyatt says. He squeezes my hand. "There's a storm coming in," Wyatt says. "We probably should stay another day."

I nod.

We watch the snow gather outside the windows. All the houses along Sweet Milk Road are tucked into the snowbanks, their lights glowing through the dark night. We are safe and warm on this Christmas night.

23

That year when I was twelve years old, it snowed and snowed from Christmas onward in Canaan against an egg-wash painted sky. I watched the winter sun, rimmed in watery gold from my bedroom window, and listened to my father below my bedroom floorboards. He was in the kitchen making breakfast. The aroma of coffee and fried potatoes drifted up the stairs, while I lay there tracing the arc of the rising sun in my window pane.

"Christ, Joss!" he yelled from the bottom of the stairs. "You better be up."

"I'm getting dressed." I hurriedly pulled on my corduroys and sweater and ran downstairs.

He loomed in the doorway. "Get your boots and coat on. I don't have all day."

We plowed through the snow on that Friday morning in the pale yellow light and pushed the creaking millhouse door open. Our breath trailed behind us, ghosts frozen in the frigid air.

"This is the damper," he said, showing me the handle on the stovepipe. "Leave it wide open when you first start the fire. Add the kindling, and then stack three or four smaller logs in like this." He shoved the cordwood into the firebox on top of the thin wood stakes, the butt ends clanking against the back of the stove. "Once the fire catches, you'll hear it begin to roar in about twenty minutes. That's when you close the damper halfway down." He showed me the correct position. "You be sure you do this. Otherwise, the stovepipe will get too hot and burn the place down. You got it?"

I nodded.

"Check the fire every couple of hours and add a couple logs. On a cold day like today, it'll draw fast and burn a lot of wood. I'm counting on you to get this place warmed up for our New Year's party."

"I'll help, Daddy."

"Okay. And don't be bringing Haley and that Fletcher kid in here. Make 'em wait outside." He looked at me, the red slash of his mouth hard in the morning air. "I'll be back late this afternoon. Your mother's going to cut my hair."

I nodded again.

"So what are you going to do next?"

"I–I'm going to wait," I stuttered, shuffling my feet back and forth, "and in about twenty minutes, make sure the fire has started, and then move the damper to the halfway point like you showed me."

"Good girl." He tousled my hair and left.

I waited in the millhouse, clapping my hands together and bouncing from foot to foot, trying to keep warm. I heard my father's car drive up the road, and then waited another ten minutes to turn the damper back before I ran across the frozen field to the warm kitchen.

The stovetop percolator sat red-hot on the burner. He had left the gas on again; the stink of burnt coffee hung thickly. I turned off the gas, scraped the dried egg yolk off his plate, and washed the breakfast dishes. I quick-mopped the kitchen floor, too, before Miss Euphrates arrived.

By nine o'clock, Haley and Fletcher spilled through the doorway, winter vagabonds, carefree icemen with skates slung over their shoulders.

"Hey, you guys. Wipe your feet. I just washed the floor."

"Jeez! You sound like my mother," Fletcher said.

I shot him a look, then snapped on my coat and boots.

"Bring your skates, Jossy," Haley said.

I grabbed them as we slithered out into the snowy world, sliding and screeching in that now bright yellow light. The wind blew and blew in spirals and curls along the swept landscape. Small birches bent, their brown curled leaves clinging to spidery branches, dark against all that raw white. Carcasses of milkweed pods swooned, Queens Ann's Lace skeletons weighted with snowy beards bowed.

"I brought the snowblock makers," Haley squealed. "Now we can build our castle."

"And inside," Fletcher said, "we'll make a storage area for snowballs—you know, in case we get attacked."

I nodded, turning away so he wouldn't see me laugh. I wondered if he was expecting hoarding bands of enemy kids striking from across the field.

"We can take turns as lookouts once we get the spy holes in," Fletcher said.

A half-dozen tin buckets waited in the snow with a thin layer of ice at the bottom of each bucket. This was Haley's brilliant innovation for windows.

"We'll have to carve openings. I brought a trowel from home."

"But we have to pry the ice out first," Haley said. "Can we bring the buckets in the millhouse? They could sit by the woodstove. . . ."

"Okay," I said. "But you guys have to wait outside. Otherwise I'll get in trouble."

We packed the sticky snow into plastic block forms, compressing, then loosening them with icing spatulas I had hijacked from the kitchen. We lifted the blocks one by one into place around the tromped-out footprint of our ice castle, mortaring them securely with more snow. I ran back and forth from the millhouse, carrying pails of ice windows and stopping to feed the fire.

By lunchtime, we could stack snow blocks no higher. The windows were installed. Haley polished their surfaces with icicles snapped off from the millhouse roof. And our bellies growled. We ran across the field, shrieking, our voices rolling like low thunder across the snowscape. We laughed, high-fived, and herded down the driveway, across Sweet Milk Road and down the hill to Fletcher's house.

"Mom!" Fletcher yelled. "You should see our snow fort!"

"Close the door!" she scolded. "You kids are letting the cold in."

We slid into the kitchen chairs, unlacing our boots, hanging our parkas on the backs of our chairs.

Mrs. Goodwin leaned against the kitchen counter, rubbing her arms clad in layers of cotton and wool. "You kids should know by now. I'm just an Alabama flower who had the unfortunate luck to fall for a Yankee."

Fletcher rolled his eyes. "You always say that, Ma!"

"Well, it's true, son. Now, I made ya'll kids a special lunch." She swirled the ice in her rocks glass and lit a cigarette. She set plates of thinly sliced meatloaf on spongy white bread in front of each of us. Then poured warmed tomato soup over the top like gravy.

"There!" she said. "An open-faced sandwich. Doesn't that look good."

We nodded in unison like baby birds sitting on a wire.

I had never eaten an open-faced sandwich before. I assumed it was some southern delicacy. Still I was alarmed by the look of the thing and the trajectory of getting a forkful into my mouth without slopping on the thick white napkins she insisted we tuck under our frost-nipped chins.

"Now Joss, don't be intimidated by new tastes." She laughed. She threw her head back and stumbled against the counter, slopping her drink onto the floor.

"Oh my," she said. "I should have stuck to martinis. But we only have sweet vermouth, and I like mine very dry. I bet your momma likes a dry martini, Joss?"

I nodded, not knowing what to say and wondering how something you drink could be very dry.

I watched Fletcher's face redden. "Mom, maybe you should take a little rest."

She waved her hand. "Don't you be making that same tired suggestion your swamp-Yankee father makes. You know how that upsets your Momma."

"Can I help you?" I asked.

"Why not! Grab yourself a butter knife and start slathering some bread slices." She nodded to the breadbox.

I buttered the bread slices like she wanted, not knowing why we needed them.

"That's right," she said, while Fletcher steered his mother up the stairs and into bed. Haley and I could hear their muffled voices as they argued.

When Fletcher came back downstairs, Haley and I were sitting at the table, quiet except for the clinking spoons.

"It's all right, Fletcher. We understand," I said.

"No it's not."

Haley gurgled in his milk, "Do y'all like yer lunch?"

I laughed, holding my hand over my mouth.

"Don't make fun of my mother, Haley."

"I wasn't making fun of her—"

"Yeah, right!" Fletcher slammed his spoon onto the table. "Everyone makes fun of her. She can't help it."

Haley looked up from his plate, wide-eyed. "Honest, Fletcher, I like the way she talks. I was just—"

"I have to check on her," he said, smirking at Haley and me. "When I come down, I want you guys out of here."

"Fletcher!" I pleaded. "Haley didn't mean—"

"Why are you always defending him, Joss? You used to be my friend."

"I'm still your friend."

Fletcher scraped his chair against the floor, grabbed our overflowing plates, and clanked them into the sink.

Haley and I pulled on our winter garb, let ourselves out, and trudged up the hill and back to Miss Euphrates' kitchen. We grabbed apples and tangerines and made quick peanut-butter sandwiches, then headed back out.

"I put our skates in the millhouse," I said, "so they'd be warm when we put them on."

"Let's make snowballs first. That will make Fletcher happy when he comes back. He'll be back, won't he?"

"Yeah, he'll get it through his head eventually."

"I didn't mean—"

"I know, Haley, but you have to be careful about whatever you say about Fletcher's mother."

He nodded. "I'll tell him I'm sorry."

We tracked through the snow, following the zigzag markings of a grouse, a rabbit, and the telltale signs of a red fox, his prints tracking right to our snow castle, shimmering in the early afternoon sun.

"Do you think the fox went inside?" Haley asked.

"He must have," I said. "Look right over here. There are more." We examined the markings on the inside corners.

Haley's eyes sparkled. "Maybe he's going to sleep here tonight!"

"Maybe!" I said.

We packed snowballs, tossing them between our hands, creating dense and deadly projectiles. We practiced lobbing them at the trees, listening for the watermelon like splat against the thick bark. We laughed roundly, our cheeks now red, our warm breath fluming in the cold, cold air. When we had made at least fifty frozen lobbers, we mounded them in the corners of our fort, hiding any trace of the mythical red fox. We now had pyramids of ammunition to protect us from our imaginary enemies. I knew it would please Fletcher.

"Haley, want to go skating?"

"Yeah!" he nodded, then ran to the millhouse. I followed, both of us slipping through the narrow door opening to grab our skates and feed the woodstove.

"Don't tell my father I let you in."

"I won't."

"We should bring Fletcher's skates, just in case he comes back."

We shoveled paths along the thickest river ice and cleared the beaver pond where the skating was always the best. We tossed the shovels onto the bank then swerved across the pond, traversing down along the frozen river. We traced the blue-white ice into curlicues and corkscrews. The crows flew above. Their shadow wings danced alongside our skate tracks. They cocked their heads, watching.

"The beavers must think there are monsters on the ice," Haley said. "Don't be scared, baby beaver; it's only me, the piano boy!" He tapped out a staccato rhythm with the toe of his skates. "Their blue-haired Momma says, 'Don't be afraid, baby.'"

"Yeah, and Homer the beaver says, 'D'oh! Don't have a cow, man!'"

"You know what else Homer says?" Fletcher jumped out from behind a tree and started pelting snowballs at Haley. "He says, 'I'm trying to be a sensitive father, you unwanted moron!'"

The first snowball hit Haley in the face. "That stings," he cried. The second and third landed on his upper torso. He fell onto the ice, trying to clear the snow from his face while snowballs rained down on him.

"What are you doing, Fletcher?" I yelled. "Stop it. You'll hurt him."

"He deserves to be hurt."

I ran up onto the field, clumsy in my ice skates, blocking Fletcher's throws.

"Get out of my way, Joss."

"Stop it!"

"No!" Fletcher yelled. "Not until he apologizes for insulting my mother."

"He wasn't making fun of her! He just likes her accent. Get that through your thick head."

Fletcher dropped his arms and stared at me. "You're lying," he said.

"Jeez, don't you get it? He's only seven. He doesn't have a mean bone in his body."

Fletcher turned and started walking back across the field.

"I didn't mean to hurt your feelings," Haley hollered across the ice.

"Where are you going?" I asked. "Come on and skate with us."

"Okay, okay," Fletcher said. "I have to get my skates."

"They're here," I said, lifting them. "Come on."

I watched Fletcher's sullen expression as we raced up and down the river, ringing around the beaver hut. I hoped he'd forget his anger soon.

"Let's play bumper cars," Haley yelled. He drifted over the ice, squatting, shifting his weight from side to side, coming up quickly on Fletcher and me, before veering off. "Only no real bumping!" he said.

"Why not?" Fletcher said "I want to know why not?"

"So no one gets hurt," Haley said.

Fletched shrugged and grimaced. "Fine!"

The three of us squatted, weaving back and forth, shrieking and laughing, chasing each other, spilling on our sides.

"Want to play tag like this?" Fletcher asked.

"Sure!"

We scurried along the frozen river and stood, pushing toe to ice when we needed more speed. We dropped into squats, extending a leg, trying to 'tag' whoever was nearest.

"I got you, Fletcher!" I hollered.

"Oh no, you didn't!" he spit back. He raced over the blue ice to the beaver pond, foot over foot, his skates slanted; his hips rolled and propelled him forward. "You can't catch me," he called over his shoulder.

But I did, scrambling out in front of him, tagging him. "Now you're it!"

He pivoted, pushed past me, and bee-lined for Haley. When he got in back of him, he shoved Haley forward. "You're it!" he yelled.

Haley struggled to keep his balance. He veered off toward the far bank onto the thinner ice. I heard it popping and cracking beneath his skates.

"Turn back, Haley," I yelled. "The ice is too thin there."

But his right foot broke through. His leg slipped into the rushing water.

"Fletcher, grab him!" I screamed as I raced to reach Haley.

"Stay back, Joss," Fletcher cried. "The ice is too thin to hold all of us." He lay across the partially frozen water, inched forward, and grabbed Haley by the back of his parka.

I lay in back of Fletcher on the thicker ice, ready to pull on his legs.

Fletcher locked his arms around Haley's waist and began shimmying backward.

"Do you want me to pull on your legs?" I asked.

"Yeah. Real easy, though."

The three of us edged backward off the fragile ice until we were sitting in a circle. Our faces red, our hearts pounding.

"I was so scared," Haley said. His hands shook; his lips trembled.

"It's okay. You're all right now," I said, "but we have to get you inside and out of those wet clothes."

"I'm sorry, Haley," Fletcher said. "I was just fooling around."

"I know," Haley said.

"Everything's going to be okay," Fletcher said.

I nodded. "You're safe, now, Haley."

We breathed easier as we tromped through the snow, then slid the wide millhouse door open and slipped inside.

"Take off your wet clothes. I'll get some clothes from upstairs," I said.

"I'll do it, Joss," Fletcher said. "It's all my fault."

We both looked at Haley shivering, his teeth chattering in front of the woodstove.

I filled the kettle while Fletcher ran upstairs.

"There's a sweater and sweatpants up there, too," I hollered. "Grab them okay?"

"Will do!"

I filled the mugs from the corner cupboard with hot water and cocoa. "Drink up, Haley. You need to drink as much as you can."

He nodded, slurping the hot cocoa and handing me his empty cup for more.

Fletcher helped him out of his wet clothes and into dry things. "I didn't mean to push you so hard."

Haley looked at him and smiled. "It's okay, Fletcher. I forgive you." But Haley trembled from cold and fear, his lips still blue-ish, and his fingernails, too.

"I *did* pull you out of the water, so that kind of makes up for it all."

Haley sat next to the woodstove, the color drained from his face, while I filled the firebox once again.

"Want to play cards?" I asked.

"Sure," Haley nodded. "Let's play Hearts."

"Are you in, Fletcher?' I asked.

"As long as I can deal."

I set the deck of cards on the table, and Fletcher expertly cut them. He split the pack and riffled them, cascading them together in a waterfall of cards. Each of us chose one card and set it face down in front of us while Fletcher dealt out the remainder.

"You lead out, Haley," I said.

We tossed the cards, collecting tricks while I kept score.

"I'm going to try to 'shoot the moon,'" Haley said.

"What's that?" Fletcher asked.

"You know, to win means getting the fewest points, right?"

We nodded our heads.

"Well 'shooting the moon' means taking all the points. But instead of a high score, I get twenty-six points off and you each get twenty-six added."

"No way!" Fletcher shrieked. "How can you even do that?"

"You have to get the right hand—lots of high cards and royalty."

We played hand after hand, without any sign of strategies or the moon.

"I'm sick of this," Fletcher said. "Let's do something else." He didn't wait for a reply. He scraped his chair on the scuffed wood floor and ran up the stairs. "I'm going to practice the piano."

We listened as Fletcher dragged the piano stool across the floor and began playing scales.

"He's not very good," Haley said, giggling behind his hand.

"I know," I whispered. "But at least he tries. Want to play something else?"

I re-hung Haley's still wet clothes nearer to the stove. We played Go Fish and Crazy Eights. And told silly stories, hair-brained jokes, and made bets neither of us could ever keep.

"I'm going to climb the Eiffel Tower in Paris!"

"How are you going to do that? You're so clumsy!"

"You'll see!"

"Oh yeah, well I'm going to write a book all in cartoons."

"Who's going to read a cartoon with just stick figures?"

We laughed and giggled and drank cups and cups of hot chocolate.

"Haley!" Fletcher yelled. "Why don't you come and give me a lesson."

"Sure!" Haley said, then turned and whispered, "He needs a lot of lessons."

He clomped up the stairs, and I listened to them review études and more scales until Haley gave in and showed Fletcher a few simple tunes he could mimic.

I heard my father's car ramble up the driveway and head towards the cottage. Could he hear us from there? Not very likely in the wind. I rinsed out the mugs and listened as Haley took over the keyboard. The playful notes began tinkling whimsically, softly building to that minor major seventh that Haley so loved. Like the sound of raindrops rolling from the ridgeline, gathering into waterfalls with the wind picking up. I tiptoed up the stairs, not wanting to interrupt him. The gold light from the transom windows flew into the room; the dust motes danced. Haley looked up and smiled. His hands fluttered along the keyboard. He was lost in the music.

When I got near the top step, I saw Fletcher pulling one of my father's rifles out of the gun cabinet. I motioned him to put it back.

But he waved me off, swung around, and aimed at Haley and then at me, saying, "Click, click, click," and laughed. "Haley! I'll show you what 'shooting the moon' is! Look through the window!" He aimed the rifle at the window, snorting and shouting, "Click, click, click! I got it, you guys. No more moon!"

We both gazed up at the transom window looking for the rising moon, faint as tissue paper.

"Do you see it, Jossy?"

"Just barely," I said, pointing to the lower window panes.

"Oh, yeah! There it is. I guess Fletcher didn't shoot it, after all," Haley whispered.

We watched the paper-thin Cold Moon of December peek into view in its trail across the firmament. I wondered about the mythical Man in the Moon shining down on us, as every moon-titled song ran through my head. We had poured over pictures, Haley and me—druzy lunar rocks of peridot and feldspar that sparkled off the page and disproved that green cheese theory. We'd planned our escape from Red Mills Farm on the next lunar rocket.

"Are you still going there first?" I asked.

"Of course I am," Haley laughed, staring into the darkening sky. "Just like Neil Armstrong."

"No way!" I said. I'm your aunt. I should—"

"Hey, you guys," Fletcher interrupted. "What's with the secret club?" He twirled the rifle in small circles against his shoulder and smirked.

Haley grinned. "I'm going to the moon!" he said.

"I'll send ya!" Fletcher laughed. "That's what my Daddy always says. Watch this—he taught me some new moves." The rifle twirled and spun and clanked against Fletcher's shoulder.

Haley clapped, ran to the piano, and began playing "The Stars and Stripes Forever."

Fletcher twirled on—the rifle at the back of his shoulder. "This one's the Rising Sun," he hollered above the music. He did three more intricate moves, naming each one as he did them: the Wrist Breaker, the Fireknife, and the Single Spool, tossing the rifle into the air and catching it from behind his back. When he was done, he thumped the rifle butt on the floor, then rolled the gun onto his shoulder, aiming up towards the transom window as if he was shooting the moon from the sky. "Click, click, click," he shouted and laughed.

"Fletcher!" I yelled. "Put my father's rifle back. Now!"

He swiveled and aimed at Haley, then at me, and back again at Haley, laughing and saying "Click, click, click."

I saw his finger balance against the trigger, pulling in slightly with each click.

"Fletcher!" I screamed. "Your finger!"

But it was too late. Fletcher's finger slipped, and the smell of sulfur and sawdust filled the air.

And in that moment the music was gone.

24

On a quiet Sunday morning just after Christmas in the year my mother died, my sister calls. Out of the blue, I hear her voice on the line.

"Joss, it's me, Naomi. How are you?"

"Naomi! Great to hear from you." I haven't seen her since our mother's funeral, and our phone calls are rare. I wonder if everything is all right.

"Hey," she says. "I'll be in the city tomorrow and I'm going to the Metropolitan Museum of Art to see the Paris Muse photography exhibit. Want to tag along?"

"Sure. Sounds like fun."

"Is ten good for you? We can meet in the lobby."

"I'll see you then."

I arrive, gliding across the sidewalk under a clear sky, the kind of brilliant blue atmosphere that barely holds your feet to the earth. It shines and crackles like sapphire. We meet outside, just as she's getting out of her taxi.

"Great timing," I say. "Wow, look at you. You're as beautiful as ever." Her blonde hair is streaked with a little gray; her hazel eyes are clear and lit with flecks of gold. There is lightness in her that I immediately recognize.

"Aren't you kind," she laughs. We hug each other for a long time.

"I didn't know you were interested in photography," I say.

"I guess it's a natural progression from graphic arts."

We find our way to the photography exhibits in two different galleries, our shoes clacking on the floors, the murmur of voices drifting in the high ceilings. A group of students enter the hall ahead of us, dressed in *de rigueur* grunge.

"Art majors," I say.

"I never looked like that when I finally made it to college!"

"I didn't go to college. I went straight to the bakery." As soon as the words slipped out, I regretted them.

"I'm sorry, Joss. I know you didn't have that opportunity. Sometimes I fool myself into believing you had it easier than you did."

I wave my hand, saying, "We each had challenges that shaped us."

"It's not too late. I'm always taking classes."

"Really? On what?"

"Right now a class on advanced computer illustration."

"You mean like Adobe Illustrator?"

"Exactly."

We enter the gallery to luminous albumen silver prints from glass negatives, daguerreotypes, and early direct positives on paper. I am drawn to the stark look of the perspective pieces depicting narrow alleyways with brick and stone walls on either side. Dilapidated buildings with flower boxes. It's easy to imagine some Parisienne tossing a bucket of wash water out the window to the alley below.

The photographs are mostly by Charles Marville but also include images from Alfred Stieglitz, Eugène Atget, and others. They depict Paris during the reign of Napoleon III, when the city was under transformation. Narrow streets were demolished to make way for grand avenues.

Naomi sits on a bench in the middle of the room, a sketch pad on her lap. I watch from behind as she lays in the figures leaning into one another, whispering, pointing to individual prints. She works quickly with no wasted motion.

"I like to draw crowd scenes," she says. "They can tell a story, and what's fun is to change the background completely."

I laugh. "So you get to play God."

"In a way, yeah."

We wander from gallery to gallery, my head spinning with the colors and images of people and events caught in a moment in time. They are like stories left to the viewers' imagination. I sit and pull out a sketchbook from my bag and lay down quick images, ideas for my ongoing adventures in watercolors.

"Look at you!" Naomi comments.

"Yeah," I say sheepishly. "I've been fooling around with watercolors lately."

"Awesome. I didn't know you were interested in fine art. But then again, why wouldn't you be? You've always been an artist in one way or another."

We sit in the gallery, each of us sketching the moving crowds, comparing viewpoints.

"I can take these people out of the museum and set them into a street scene, or a strolling park," I say.

"Exactly! Are you hungry, Joss?"

"Sure, I could eat a little something."

We pack up our bags and walk the brisk block to Caffe Grazie, the wind against us, and order a pot of tea as soon as we are seated.

"That was fun, Joss. And I got a lot of nice sketches."

"You're so fast. I enjoyed watching you. Any special plans for them?"

She smiles and says, "Something will come to me. Let me show you something else." She pulls a photo from her bag and hands it to me.

It's like a strip from one of those photo booths, only bigger. "Is this an ultrasound? It looks like my manager Lynn's prenatal pictures."

"That's right. Only it's mine."

"Yours? You mean—"

She nods and smiles. "Dave and I have been doing in vitro for a year and we have finally conceived."

"I had no idea. You look so good."

Her face lights up. I cannot remember the last time I saw her this happy, but I'm sure it was before Haley's accident. "So, in vitro?" I ask.

"Conception at seventeen is too easy." She laughs. "But at forty-five, not so much." Naomi looks around. "Where's our waitress? I'm starving."

"Of course you are," I chuckle. "Maybe we should order for three and share."

"Great idea."

We start with soup and goat cheese salad.

"When are you due?"

"The end of April. But given my advanced age, the docs are watching me carefully. I'll probably have a C-section."

"That's rough."

"I don't care. Whatever we have to do, it will be worth it. It's a boy, and from all the tests, it looks like he's a beautiful healthy kid."

The ultrasound images on the table catch the light, and all I can think of is Haley. That old sorrow sneaks in. I turn away so Naomi won't see. But she does.

"Hey, hey. I know. . . ."

"I'm so sorry, Naomi. I was such a stupid, defiant kid. If only I could take it all back. I know my burden is nothing compared to yours."

Naomi reaches over and holds my hand. "It's okay," she says. "You didn't do anything wrong, Jossy. Haley was wet and cold that day, and you took care of him. You always took care of him."

No one has called me that in years, and all I can do is nod and turn away.

"Come on, we're here to celebrate. Haley is finally getting the baby brother he always wanted. Oh my God, that kid used to harass me. 'Why can't I have a little brother? Why can't I have a little brother?'"

I laugh. "I can hear him saying that. Sometimes when the house is silent, I can hear his voice in my mind. It's still there—that little squeak in his voice."

"He loved the farm. And he's still here with us. Now let's eat. They're bringing our entrees."

We eat everything we order and have room for dessert, too. And say a long goodbye on the street with real promises to stay connected.

I hop into a yellow cab. I am cold and tired, not in the mood for the train. The taxi weaves through traffic, stopping short and lurching forward amid honking horns, steam rising from street vents, and women rushing back to work after lunch—their staccato boots click along the sidewalk, attempting to outrun time. But I am buffered in this foul-smelling vehicle with amulets hanging from the rearview mirror: a tooth on a rawhide string, beads, and charms that catch the light. I sit back and watch the sky change. There are hints of that spun gold light, and I am disembodied, counting and falling through all of that yellow, white-lipped by the laughing blue firmament just below. And I don't know why. It isn't until that evening I realize that today is the anniversary of Haley's death. My sister must have known, but she never said a word. She offered what she has found: a still image of hope that whirls just below her heart. But I can't stop thinking about Haley.

That night the gunshot had sounded across the farm, and they came running. First my father and mother. And then Naomi. Then the ambulance and the cops, and the priest. Fletcher telling everyone it was an accident. He cried and looked right through me as though I would be a shadow soon enough.

And I was.

I ran outside and vomited. They followed me, the police officers, my father, the priest.

"Did you see what happened?"

"Did he shoot on purpose?"

"Why did you let the boys in where they weren't supposed to be?"

I looked at them all, their mouths moving, their words falling out. But I couldn't answer.

The world had become swirling lights and radio blips. A voice said, "We've got a pulse." Another one barked, "Get an IV in him!" Men and women whizzed past me with Haley on a stretcher. They carried him into the ambulance and shut the doors behind themselves and shot out of the driveway and up the road.

I watched the swirling lights on the ambulance, their reflection in the dark sky until they disappeared. "Haley's going to be all right, isn't he?" I asked. A couple of the adults looked at me oddly, but no one said anything.

Naomi and my mother followed in the path of the ambulance, out of the driveway, racing up the road, their lights flashing, too.

"You wait here, Joss," my father said. "Miss Euphrates is coming to stay the night with you." He ran to his car and flew out of the driveway and up over the hill, following the caravan.

I stood in the snow, frozen flakes sticking to my eyelashes and eyebrows. I waited for Miss Euphrates to come and tell me Haley would be okay.

But she didn't.

And he wasn't.

My father came home in the morning. He came upstairs and sat on the edge of my bed and waited for me to wake.

"Hey, sleepyhead. Are you all right?"

I sat up quickly. Remembering. Knowing I was in trouble. "I know the boys weren't supposed to be in there, but Haley fell through the ice while we were skating and I was afraid he would get too cold, and . . . and . . . where is he?"

"Shhhh . . . shhhh . . . it's okay. I came to tell you about Haley." My father looked at his hands and cleared his throat, and then looked up at me. He stroked my hair and said, "Haley didn't make it. He died early this morning. He's in Heaven now."

"No, no, he isn't." I cried. "Haley can't go to Heaven yet. He's too little. I have to take care of him."

"I know," he said, as he pulled me into his chest. "But now I have to take care of you. Your mother and sister have gone back to Brooklyn. They'll come out for the funeral but then they are going to live in Brooklyn again."

"Why?"

"Because that's what they want to do. That means you'll have to go back to your old school and live with me. But not until I make all the arrangements. Okay?"

"Can Miss Euphrates come with us?"

"Her family is here, Joss. You wouldn't want her to be without her people, would you?"

I searched his eyes and listened to his words echo in my head. Their seemed like soap bubbles in the air. If I could pop them, they'd disappear.

"Do you understand, Joss?" His voice was soft, not the way he usually spoke.

I nodded and watched him walk down the stairs, staring at each step he took.

I stayed in my room all that day, sitting in my closet for hours surrounded by Haley's painted monsters. I didn't look at their eyes, but I knew they were watching me. Miss Euphrates brought me something to eat every few hours, never questioning my vigil in the closet.

In the afternoon, I found my mother's button box, emptying the buttons onto the closet floor. I separated them by color, counting them, stacking them, arranging them like a color wheel. I strung them on heavy thread into monochromatic necklaces and tacked them to the closet walls, a rainbow of buttons, saving out just enough to sew onto my stoplight quilt. Those red and yellow and green buttons were like a sea of twinkling stars scattered on what had been a happy yellow sky.

25

My mother came upstairs and sat on the edge of my bed, fingering the buttons I had sewn all over my stoplight quilt. She looked beautiful in her elegant slim black dress with her hair pulled back, wearing pearls and pale lipstick.

"I brought you something, Joss." She pulled my hair to the side and clasped a tiny string of pink pearls around my neck, then brushed my hair back like hers, pinning it with clips and a pale ribbon. "Come look," she said. She led me into what used to be her and my father's room so we could stand in front of the cheval mirror. The image looking back shocked me. We looked more alike than I could have imagined.

"You look beautiful," she said. "Haley would be proud to see you looking all grown up."

"But how can he see me?"

She pulled me into her arms. Then she gave me a white handkerchief edged with lace and showed me how to tuck it into the cuff of my new black dress. "You'll know right where it is when you need it."

The four of us, my mother, father, Naomi, and I, stepped out the back door to the car warming up in the driveway. I looked out over the torn landscape, tire tracks through the snow, debris picked up and flapping in that yellow air. Our snow castle had partially collapsed; its once-chiseled silhouette now sloped to the ground. But it was the smell of an acrid wind that drove me quickly into the back seat beside my sister Naomi.

We drove from Sweet Milk Road to Devanny Funeral Home. All along the way, every tree and telephone wire was encased in ice. The world sparkled with crystals; a gold hue hung in the air with ice-ghosts and angels swirling in a game of tag. I watched them, tried to follow their course. As we drove on, I would lose one but soon find another. I wondered if Haley had sent them to mark our way.

"Are you two warm enough?" my mother asked.

"We're fine, Mom," I said. "Right, Naomi?" But she was silent. No nod or wave of her hand. She just stared out the window.

When we arrived at the funeral home, a starched white Victorian with verandas and pillars, my father drove around to the back vestibule and let the three of us out.

"I'll park," he said. "Then I'll meet you inside and we'll go in as a family."

Haley lay in his coffin behind an array of snowy white roses, winter tulips, and white amaryllis. The thick, sweet fragrances sickened me. I turned to get a breath, afraid I would vomit again. My sister and mother kneeled, both crying uncontrollably. But I could not cry. Haley seemed like a plastic doll, so still and perfect.

My father helped Momma and Naomi up and guided them to their seats, as others arrived. I saw a sea of faces, powdered and somber, perfumed and clean-shaven, all dressed in mourning colors. The mothers and aunts and friends rushed at me. They held my hands and stroked my cheeks like a fallen sparrow.

Their eyes spoke: *Don't weep, our wee birdie. Don't cry, our angel left behind. It will be better in time. You'll see.* They cooed and preened around my dancing head. I didn't understand their quivering hands, their wide, wide eyes. The light was diffused; a strange yellow color twisted everything. The only face I could see clearly was Miss Euphrates. When I looked into her eyes, I knew none of this was right.

Father Rourke came to the funeral home and gave a benediction, and then the pallbearers, mostly my father's jazz ensemble, carried Haley to the waiting hearse. We followed in a black limousine. The sleet and ice had turned to a cold mist. We walked slowly up the stone walkway in back of Haley into the vestibule of St. Mark's where Father Rourke, the deacon, and the altar boys waited. They led us down the aisle, the pews filled with family, friends, and all the children and fluttering nuns from St. Mark's School. Fletcher and his mother and father were there, too, hidden behind dark overcoats and Mrs. Goodwin's wide-brimmed black hat.

Slowly we made our way to the altar and waited while Haley was pushed into place. The church was filled with risers of those same alabaster flowers, gleaming in the candles, gilt, and dark wood. There was a framed photograph of Haley on a small table next to his casket. That morning light filtered in from the stained glass windows and lit Haley's image. I watched his eyes stare back at me, and I wanted to tell him how much better he looked in that silver frame.

Above the knave, the children's choir sang "Ave Maria." Everyone stood, their bodies leaning into one another. When the choir finished, Father Rourke placed a white shroud over Haley's coffin and then he and the deacon began chanting the Solemn Mass:

In Nomine Patris, et Fílii, et Spíritus Sancti . . .

Naomi and my mother bowed their heads, tears running down their cheeks. I bowed my head, too, following along in the Latin Missal. But I was distracted by the light. Haley had always been fascinated by the glow coming through the stained glass. I wondered if Fletcher noticed, too.

I turned to look for him while Father Rourke chanted: *Jube, Domine, benedicere . . .*

When I spotted Fletcher with his slicked-back hair and dark suit, he glared at me. I didn't understand why.

When I quickly turned away I saw Haley, clomping down the stone aisle in his little boy shoes and striped socks, his small body shining in the light. He waved to me and skipped up to the coffin, then swished off the white shroud. He opened the lid, and where his body had been, now were eighty-eight glittering black and white keys.

He looked different, transformed in a way that would not withstand stillness; I wanted to run to him, tell him to slow down, to take his time and make this last. But his hands played frenetically; every fiber of his body filled with music.

Then Sister Mike ran up to the alter wearing one of Fletcher's mother's red dresses and a stiff paper wimple. Her mouth was outlined in bright red lipstick and her eyelids shaded in blue. She looked at me and said, "They're going to come, men in suits, to ask you questions." Then she nodded to Haley. He pounded the keys and the blare of cornets and Glenn Miller's "In the Mood" filled the yellow air.

Father Rourke started tapping his feet in his caramel-hued loafers peeking out from under his alb. He threw off his vestments, revealing a rust silk tie with dancing nuns against his blue Oxford shirt and gray chinos.

Sister Mike looked at me and said, "It's a sin to lie," and tossed a pebble from her pocket and began hopscotching across the tiled floor. As she jumped from square to square, she chanted: *"One-ery, two-ery, zigger-zoll zan. Holy bone, crack-a-bone, Yankee-doodle Dan. Harum, squarum, Virgin Marum. Sinctum, sanctum, twenty-one, done."*

"Not like that!" Father Rourke shouted. He grasped Sister Mike's hand, then threw her up into the air, to the top of the knave. Her paper wimple fluttered as she floated down. He caught her around her slender waist, spinning her, sliding her between his legs over the stone altar. They knew all the dance moves.

Haley's hands flew over the keyboard, his head bobbing to the beat as the parishioners chanted: *Kyrie eléison, Kyrie eléison, Christie eléison, Christie eléison . . .* Then the Glenn Miller piece ended. Father Rourke stood in front of the casket with his arms wide and his hands open.

"It is a sad day for all of us who knew Nahaliel," he said. His voice was somber and gray. It floated above our heads and through the dust motes that eddied in the air. "Haley, as we all called him, touched our lives profoundly in his brief time. But God has bidden Haley on this day to leave this world. He has been called back by God, the Father, our Creator, and blessed with the supernatural gifts of the Holy Spirit. We can take solace knowing that our Nahaliel has been escorted into Paradise by the Host of Heavenly Angels, led by his namesake, the Angel Nahaliel, the Angel of the Rivers."

As the priest spoke, Haley peeked out from behind, waving and smiling at the crowd. He made faces, stuck out his tongue, and shook his head as if to say, 'Not me! I'm not in Heaven!'

For a moment, I was puzzled. But then I realized Haley wasn't in Heaven, after all. I laughed behind my hand, but my mother saw and flashed me a look. I wanted to run and high-five him. It was his

best trick yet. All of this was a game, and Haley had fooled everyone—even me. I turned away and laughed even harder. Because I
knew this time Haley would be the one in trouble.

Father Rourke continued as if this was a real funeral. "As we
mourn in the days ahead, we each must call upon Jesus Christ, who
sacrificed his earthly life for us. In doing so, He showed us that
sorrow and sacrifice are supreme. As His apostles mourned, they
sought faith and grace bestowed on them by the Holy Spirit. These
are the spiritual ointments that we must seek to be at peace. We are
each soldiers of God."

When the altar boys began ringing the bells, Haley again sat at
the piano, this time playing ragtime tunes with that tension of the
major seventh. The notes floated down the aisle, each measure more
high-stepping foolishness than the previous one.

Father Rourke and Sister Mike stepped from the altar to offer
the four of us Communion in our pew. When they got to me,
Sister Mike replaced the Communion wafer with a dark chocolate
Peppermint Patty.

She winked at me and said, "Lip-smacking good," sputtering
gleefully through her red-red lips.

Haley swiveled in his seat, holding up handfuls of Peppermint
Patties and motioning the parishioners to dance their way to the
altar. Everyone rose from their pews and lined up, eager for that
minty-chocolaty goodness.

Suscipe, sancte, pater omnípotens ætérne Deus. . . .

I watched Fletcher take his turn at the altar, holding out his
cupped hands as Father Rourke placed the chocolate pasty in them.
Fletcher turned quickly, shoving the patty into his mouth, smearing
chocolate on his face and the collar of his white shirt. I tried not to
laugh but couldn't help myself. He scowled at me but turned away
when my mother scowled back.

None of that mattered anymore. He would understand once he realized this had all been a joke.

Dóminus vobiscum.

Et cum spiritu tuo . . .

Haley disappeared. I looked everywhere, craning my head this way and that, but he was gone. Father Rourke, now back in his alb and vestments, ushered the bearers carrying the casket past all those tear-streaked faces and into the saffron light. I was confused, as the wisps of a boy swarmed above my head. All the soldiers of God pressed forward, following Haley's casket into the snowy landscape, while I held back, not wanting to step out into the daylight, into that bitter wind.

26

The night after hearing my sister's news I awakened in my Brooklyn apartment from a recurring childhood dream, one that I haven't revisited in years. In my dream, Haley is living in the tree house and flying under the ice on the back of a button covered turtle while painted perch and that gape-mouthed bullhead follow him up and down the river bed. I lie in my rumpled bedclothes, wondering why I am having this dream again.

My phone startles me in the still-dark room.

"Joss?" a small voice asks. "Is that you?"

"Yes. Hello. Who's this?"

"I'm so sorry to wake you in the middle of the night. This is Jeannette."

I glance at my clock; it's 2:13 a.m. "Jeannette, is everything okay?"

"Well, not really. Your father took my car a few hours ago. He said he was going to the store, but he never came back."

"Did you call the police?"

"No, no. I didn't want to make any trouble for him. But you know, Joss, he's been talking about the farm, how much he'd like to visit again."

"He's been asking me, too, about going out there. Maybe that's where he's headed."

"Oh, dear. And we're supposed to get a snowstorm."

"I'll drive to Canaan. Hopefully, that's where he is. If he's not there, I'll call the police. Okay?"

"I'm not worried about the car. It's your father . . ."

"I know. One quick question—your car? It's a red Toyota—yes?"

"That's right. A 2005 red Toyota Camry."

I quickly dress and make a cup of tea for the road, and then I call Wyatt.

"I'm sorry to bother you at this hour—"

"It's okay," he says, but his voice is groggy. "What's up?"

"I'm wondering, did you hear from my father last night?"

"Nope. Why?"

"He took Jeannette's car a few hours ago. Said he was going to the store but hasn't returned. We guess he went to Canaan. He's been talking about seeing the place again."

"I can run out and see."

"That's all right, Wyatt. I'll go. You have your shop to open."

"Well, let me know when you find him, or if you need me. I'm here."

"I know you are. He could end up driving in a storm, so I'm just anxious to get underway."

I plow on, driving the route I think he'll take. As dangerous as it is on the Taconic in a snowstorm, my father wouldn't head to Canaan any other way. Once again, I remember how winter is always the enemy.

Winter was the enemy twenty-odd years ago. It raged, the bone-white jaw of it like a sorrowful animal, for two weeks after Haley's death. I remember standing watch each morning, like a captain of the guards, listening for him, looking for his silly drawings on the outside of my bedroom windows, characters etched into ice and condensation. Moon-faced dogs with loping ears or jack-o-lantern elves, their eyes in perpetual surprise.

Haley and I had spent countless hours in the company of Crayola and construction paper. We had advanced onto other surfaces as well: squiggles in books, stick figures in the stairwell, and an army of beasts on the walls inside my closet, where no one else would ever see them. Rebellion and graffiti had called to us early on.

But I knew he was there, outside my windows, leaving finger doodles. I had seen his bright face whisk across the glass pane just as I entered the room. Sometimes at night, I saw him looking in at me, his hands cupped around his face watching as I nodded off. I promised myself that in the morning I would catch him and drag his elf-like form back through the open window, over the sagging sills and forever hide him in my closet.

Every morning, Miss Euphrates poked her head into my bedroom and asked if I wanted to go to school that day. And every morning I shook my head beneath the vigilant covers.

"No, not today." Instead, I stayed inside, watching for him through the frosted windowpane, listening for his piano practice below my floorboards.

I dug out all the things he had left behind in my room and laid them across my yellow stoplight quilt. Secret notes. A metal windup frog. Special rocks we found by the river. And the single "U Can't Touch This" by MC Hammer. He loved that song. We'd mouth the words and dance, thinking we were all that. I put all of his things into a shoe box and hid it in the back of my closet. He'd like that. A treasure box filled with surprises. I imagined his small voice excitedly saying, "I remember this stuff!"

I stayed in my room, except for supper trays in the living room while we watched *Family Matters* or *The Fresh Prince of Bel-Air*. Steve Urkle and Will Smith filled in the corners. Their laughter left no urgent need for words. And Miss Euphrates said things like, "It's good to see you've got your appetite back" or "Would you like some pancakes? They're your favorite." I just nodded.

Pancakes were my favorite as a child and still are when I am stressed. I pull off at Route 82 and head to the West Taghkanic Diner. It was always one of my father's choice stops, and I'm hoping he'll be there.

It's not busy, but I look around carefully. No Big Paul there. I take a seat at the counter; the place looks the same as I remember: blue tile floors, blue swivel stools, and gleaming stainless everywhere. I order flapjacks with real Vermont syrup and whipped butter with a side of bacon.

"Coffee?" the waitress with 'Nan' on her name tag asks.

"Thanks," I say. "I'm looking for my elderly father. He may have stopped here. He's driving a red Camry, wears rimless trifocals. A bit of a snappy dresser. Vest, hat, the works. Have you seen anyone here like that?"

"Oh yeah, I seen him all right. He stiffed me on the check. Said he left his wallet in the car, and could he go out and get it so he could pay. Only he just took off."

"I'm so sorry. Let me pay his check. It's the least I can do."

"If I had gotten his plate number I would have reported him."

"I understand. Did you happen to see what direction he was headed?"

"I didn't, but he asked to use my cell before he left." Nan pulled her phone from her apron pocket. "Here's the number he called."

It was Jeanette's.

"Yeah," Nan replied, "he said he was going back to the city. That's all I know."

"Thanks. You've been a big help."

I call Jeannette, but there's no answer. After a last gulp of coffee, I pay the bills and leave a generous tip. But which way to go? Or should I simply call the police? It's not what I want to do. My contact with the local authorities cast a long shadow.

During that first week after Haley's death, two men in a black sedan parked in front of the house. They scuffed up the steps, and I heard Miss Euphrates let them in. Minutes later she was knocking on my door.

"Joss, some policemen come by to talk to you. You think you up for that?"

"Policemen?"

"Child, you not in any trouble. I called your daddy. He say it's okay to talk with them just so long as I'm with you."

"Why do they want to talk to me?"

"Because you were there, Joss. And Fletcher's momma and daddy won't let him talk to the police."

But I knew better.

The two men sat in the living room in the chairs next to the silent piano while Miss Euphrates and I sat on the sofa.

They smiled and nodded, introducing themselves. Detective Roberts had a large red nose and pink jowls like a bulldog, and the other one, Detective O'Neill, was short with wiry red hair and beady eyes like a fox.

"Did you see the incident?" Detective Roberts wanted to know.

I nodded, staring at my feet.

"Can you tell us about it?"

I nodded again. "We went in the millhouse, all three of us, me and Haley and Fletcher, to get warm. We had been playing all morning in our snow fort. And Daddy was having a party in the millhouse that night, and I had to keep feeding the woodstove so it would be warm enough. I wasn't supposed to let the boys come in with me, but it was cold."

"Why weren't the boys supposed to go inside?" Detective O'Neill asked.

"My father never liked us in there, not even me. I was allowed in there only when I had a chore to do."

"So you let the boys in there, even though you had been told not to?"

"Detective O'Neill, I think Miss Joss, she already say what happened."

"Yes, Mrs. . . . uh . . ."

"Mrs. Moses. Widow of the late Solomon Joe Moses. Maybe you heard of my husband? He was a long-time state senator around these parts. But most people just call me Miss Euphrates."

I watched as the fox and the Bulldog nodded, but there was no recognition in their eyes. If Haley were here, he'd start drumming out a beat, whispering, 'Can't touch this,' and then laugh.

"All right then, uh . . . Miss Euphrates. Now Joss," the bulldog-jowled cop interrupted. "The three of you were in the millhouse. What happened next?"

"Well, I was downstairs putting wood in the stove. Haley went upstairs where the old piano was and began playing." I pointed to the black lacquered piano next to the detectives. "That was his new piano that my father bought him."

"Yes, I hear he was a gifted musician. Must have taken after his grandfather."

I nodded.

"But what I want to know," the beady-eyed fox asked, "is why both your parents have left you on your own? Maybe you're the one who shot Haley? Isn't that what actually happened? My guess is that it's eating you up inside. Now's your chance to tell the truth."

"The child *is* telling the truth," Miss Euphrates protested.

The fox-faced detective glared at her. "Please!" he snapped. Mind your business."

I felt my stomach fall away; my legs went numb. I counted my breaths, the number of times the wind rattled the fireplace damper, the seconds that ticked away on the mantle clock, and I listened for the crows. In all of that I tried to find the beat, the tune, the squeak of Haley's voice, but he was gone. And I knew it was my fault. I was supposed to watch out for Haley. I was supposed to protect him.

"Why not just tell us what happened?" Detective Roberts quietly asked.

I stared at him. His eyes looked soft, caring. I took a deep breath, digging deep to feel the stilled breath of Haley with his bowl-cut hair and Oxford tie-ups. Maybe he wasn't gone. I had seen him, after all, playing jazz piano at his own funeral, and at night whisking past my bedroom window, his face so happy and bright.

"Joss?" Detective Roberts said. "We're asking because we need to know, and you're the only one who can help us. Can you do that?"

I nodded and found my voice, still counting, the lines on the hardwood floors, the pockmarks on the fox-faced cop.

I stared right through him. "When I finished loading the wood into the stove, I went upstairs. The gun case cabinet was open, and Fletcher had one of my father's rifles in his hand. He was twirling the gun around, showing us maneuvers he learned from his father who used to be in the U.S. Army Drill Team. Fletcher caught the gun on a coat hook, and when he pulled it out, the hook must have caught the trigger."

"That's a lie, Joss," O'Neill said. "We looked up there and there's no coat hook. We know you're the one who took the gun out. We know you're a defiant kid, a girl who does just what she wants to do despite being told otherwise. That's right, isn't it?"

I wanted to tell him it takes a liar to know one.

"Excuse me, detectives," Miss Euphrates said. "Ooh, nature calls! Now if you all could just hold off till I get back?"

"Sure, sure," they said. But they didn't. The fox-faced one kept telling me I was not talking straight, not telling the truth. Telling me that I aimed and fired on purpose. That I was jealous of Haley, jealous of my sister, Naomi. Angry. Defiant. A kid gone wrong.

When Miss Euphrates came back in the room, they stopped.

"Gentlemen, coffee? Just put a fresh pot on."

"Good idea," Roberts said.

"Let me bring that out. Now remember, no questions till we get done with our coffee." When Miss Euphrates returned after fussing with the cups and saucers and her little jokes, she sat and began to chatter, telling the story of Saleem and the giant mangar and how she shared her name with that great river in Iraq. She went on, telling the story of the Mahicans eating under the trees on this land and of the women dancing in beet-dyed flax cloth. The detectives smiled and nodded, not daring to interrupt her, though a pause in her storytelling came soon enough with a quick knock on the door followed by a stranger who let himself in.

A tall man strode into the living room, smelling of aftershave and hair tonic. "Detectives," he said, "allow me to give you my card—Dalton Obadiah Moses, Esquire—specializing in criminal law. I'm here to represent my client, twelve-year-old Joss Ryckman." He looked at me with deep, wide eyes that I recognized. "Joss, you don't have to answer any questions these police officers are asking you. And gentlemen, unless you are charging Miss Ryckman with a crime, it would seem that this tea party is over."

"How is it you're authorized to represent Joss?" O'Neill asked.

"Excellent question, detective! Given that my mother is this child's legal guardian when her parents are unavailable, everything is all legal and tidy." He pulled out a document, notarized and signed. O'Neill and Roberts both examined it, then rose, saying goodbye, and headed for the door.

"If you fellas have any more questions, feel free to call my office."

"Before you leave," Miss Euphrates said, "do you have children? Young children?"

They both nodded.

"Then you got no excuse for treating this grieving child so cruelly."

27

I turn onto Sweet Milk Road, rutted with ice and only a smattering of sand. I slow and slide up and down the hills. But, thankfully, up ahead I see Wyatt's truck along with the red Camry in the driveway. He's standing on the porch as I get out of my car.

"Glad to see you," he calls through the wind and falling snow. "I tried calling, but you know the cell service here."

"I'm glad you came, Wyatt. Though I should have known." I link my arms around his neck and kiss his cheek.

He hugs me hard, the way that always makes me feel everything will be all right.

"How's Dad?" I ask.

"He's okay. But how about some tea to warm up, first?"

We sit in the kitchen by the new pellet stove. "Feels good in here," I say. "I'm glad I let you talk me into this." We both laugh.

"You, hungry? I can make some breakfast."

"No thanks, I stopped at the West Taghkanic Diner. Thought Dad might be there. Where is he?"

"I need to talk to you about that."

I hold my breath, not wanting to imagine what trouble my father has created once again.

Wyatt pours hot water into the teapot and then slips in the infuser. "Jasmine okay?"

I nod my head, waiting.

He sets cups and saucers on the table. "Honey?"

"Yes, sweets." I laugh.

He sits, stretching his hands across the table. "You probably remember the client in Claverack I was working for during the summer. Restoring books and building bookcases."

"Of course I remember."

"Well, I actually was finished with that job in June, then spent a few weekends rebuilding the tree house."

"You rebuilt the tree house?"

"I did."

"But how? With that branch gone—"

"I poured footings and set posts. Then built a staircase and put in flower boxes under the windows."

"Flower boxes?"

"Yup, planted them with thunbergia, lobelia, potato vines. All those trailing flowers you like. I kept waiting for you to discover my surprise. But no, you couldn't go for a walk, even though I kept encouraging you," he laughs.

"That's right; you did keep suggesting that I walk more out back. I thought—"

"I know, I know. You thought I was butting in. But, I kept hauling out here every damn weekend to water your flowers."

"My God, I can't believe you did all that."

"What's not to believe, Joss? I want you to see what I know."

At that moment, I'm terrified of what he sees, the fool that I am. But I ask, "What is it you know?"

"That you bring a broken tree house, and I bring the tools."

We sit quietly. I watch Wyatt move through the ritual of tea, his fluid hands, pouring and stirring the right measure of honey into our teacups until it's blended. He pushes my cup to me.

I drink and remember Miss Euphrates' words: *You cannot direct what one heart gives. You can only accept the gift.* Or not.

I look at him, breathing him in. "Thank you," I say softly. "I can never repay your kindness. But I have things to give you, too" I say.

"Like what?"

"I give you briberies and lies. I give you chocolate-hazelnut napoleons and a gold watch."

He smiles, but looks at me oddly. "Briberies and lies?"

"You told me at the beach this summer that you wouldn't accept briberies and lies."

"I don't remember that, Joss."

"You threw me into the ocean and I swam out deeper and yelled out all the things I would give to you, only you didn't hear me, and I guess I didn't want you to. But I give you all those things—mousetraps and paper airplanes. I give you firefly light and tomato vines. I give you novena candles in the windows. I give you broken books and improved watercolors. I give you a reliquary for my heart."

"Shhhh. Shhhh. I know, I know," he says. "I want all of these things from you, but it will take years, and I suspect the list is longer." He rubs my shoulder and touches my face.

"It will take a long, long time." I whisper.

We sit together a while longer, finishing our tea. Wyatt washes the cups. I dry them and stack them in the cupboard.

"So, where is my father—upstairs sleeping? Does he know about the tree house?" I'm sure he was in on the plot the whole time.

"Yup. I think that's why he was hell-bent on getting there. He's in the tree house now."

"But—"

"Don't worry, Joss. It's safe. I built a stairway with a landing at the front door. Easy to get in and out. And there's a small woodstove, so he's cozy up there. I had to replace the old one. It had cracked."

"You thought of everything."

"That's my job, kid. I just didn't factor in your father's reaction. If I'd known, I would have brought him out myself."

"No one's ever been able to figure out Big Paul's next move."

"Maybe this is better. You and your father in the tree house together."

"I guess I'll go out to see him."

He smiles and kisses me, the way he used to kiss me in the beginning.

"I want you to know, Wyatt, I'm going to sell Madame Marie's to Lynn and her husband."

"I'm happy to hear that, Joss. So happy!"

I smile, watching his face, his hands. "That means living out here," I say.

"I'm a Midwestern boy who tracked you down to New York City. A few miles up the road is easy."

I linger, leaning into him, catching the scent of his body. "You know, Wyatt?" I whisper, "I woke up this morning before Jeannette called. I had that dream again. The one where I am convinced Haley is living in the tree house. That dream I first had after the police came. It's always going to be this way."

I saw him. I know I did. He was waving at me through the ice, calling me to meet him at the Mobile station out on Connor Road. I swung from the rope ladder from the tree house deck, calling and calling for him to come back, to wait for me. He stopped and shrugged his narrow shoulders, turned and was gone.

I watched the trail behind his little-boy socks and tie-up shoes bubble in spirals beneath the frozen river. He would beat me to the Mobile station, taking the river while I was confined to my bike and the road and all the barking, biting dogs surging around farmhouse bends. Black salacious-toothed mutts who would tear at my pant legs and tender ankles.

I trudged back to the millhouse, the wet, heavy snow pulling my bare feet deeper into drifts. My bike there, hidden in gilded straw, a scapular hanging like an amulet from the handlebars. As I climbed onto the seat, it fluttered with wings.

It was as if God had changed his mind about Haley, that he didn't yet need him in Heaven.

I pushed the frozen pedals; the creaking contraption rose into the nighttime sky, above the mill, above the tree house, and soared over Sweet Milk Road, turning east along the rickrack lane. The bike and I rose higher still, beyond the stars, each light now a butter cookie cut and laid on baking sheets in grandmotherly rows below my peddling feet. I couldn't see the river road or the edge of Haley's twirling body below the ice-topped water. The flying bicycle careened past rows of canister shelves. Jars of stewed tomatoes and floating wax beans flashed before my eyes. Husked ears of blackened corn filled the cargo trough of an elliptical track, a small boy's Lionel train in Purgatory. And then it was done.

I lay awake in my rumpled bedclothes, my stoplight quilt fallen to the floor. I sat bolt upright in bed because I knew where Haley had gone.

Miss Euphrates poked her head into my room and said, "Look who's up!"

I slid back under the warm covers.

She laughed. "I don't blame you, girl. It's below zero this morning, and I have to run errands. You be okay for an hour or so?"

I nodded beneath the covers.

"Miss Euphrates? Can I ask you something?"

"You know you can, dawta-girl." She sat on the edge of my bed and stroked my forehead.

"I see Haley. Dancing in the dust motes when the sun shines into my room. I try to catch him, but he disappears. Most of all, I see him in my windows at night, peering in at me. He's all smiles and laughing and calling me to come and play. It's like he doesn't know he's dead. It's so confusing. He just wants to play. Do you think that's okay?"

"It's all okay, Miss Joss. Haley's letting you know he's just fine. And you can be okay, too. You understand?"

"I guess so."

"You think about that while I'm gone. We can talk some more when I get back," she called from the doorway. I listened for her footsteps as they bit into the frozen snow. The green Chevy whined, coughed, then caught hold. I stood by the window watching her car back out of the driveway and then glide up over the hill and out of sight.

I grabbed wool socks, long underwear, and mittens. In the kitchen, I made a thermos of hot chocolate and sandwiches, too. And packed some star-shaped cookies left from Christmas. I stuffed everything into my backpack, along with dry matches and a toilet roll.

Tying my boots and zipping into my parka, I tromped out, across the field, past our now ruined snow castle, loaded like a pack animal in the dry silver-threaded air. Thigh-deep snow had blown into waves that would move no further as I made my trail to the tree house and the beaver-dammed river to wait for Haley.

The wooden tree fort ladder was crusted with ice and snow. When I got to the top rung, I had to chip my way through the ice clinging to that winter-abandoned door. I balanced in the wind, thinking that Haley must be going in through the window. The logic of that dream, the vision of Haley now living in this swaying cabin in the treetops, never faltered.

I think about Haley as I trek over the snowy field on this wintery morning, following the snowed-in footsteps left by Wyatt and my father. The crows in the trees announce my intrusion; the wind whips my scarf across my face. Still, there is something otherworldly about this place. As I climb Wyatt's staircase to the landing and the cabin door, I imagine Haley inside, but it is my father with a fedora balanced on his head seated in a comfy chair, drinking coffee.

"Look at you!" he says. "I was expecting Wyatt. When did you get here?"

"Hi, Dad. Happy to see you're in one piece. You gave me a scare, taking off, like you did, in Jeannette's car. I was worried about you."

"You know me better than that. I'm an excellent driver."

"You should call Jeannette to let her know you're okay."

"Wyatt already took care of that. Sit with your old man. Have a cup of coffee."

"I will," I say as I run my hand over the new counters and check out the tiny red enameled woodstove that pumps out shirt-sleeve atmospherics. I need time to compose myself, to say less and not more, to listen rather than lecture. His "borrowing" a car, driving one hundred plus miles north without a license— was one of his typical hair-brained stunts. But ranting won't do any good.

"Your fella did an excellent job rehabbing this place. Did you see the block and tackle on the side of the landing, for hauling up supplies—food, water, wood? A clever guy. He thought of everything. Got a dry sink, a commode behind a privacy screen, cupboards. Real 'Home Sweet Home.'"

I walk around the room. There is a small gas stove with a tiny oven, something you'd see in an RV. Cushioned chairs and a small table. In one corner is a curtained double bed with bolsters and pillows and a skylight above. "It is spectacular, isn't it? I can't believe Wyatt did this."

"What's not to believe? The guy loves you."

I nod and turn as quick tears fall.

"Come on now, Paulie-girl," he says, wrapping his arms around me, "tell me why you're crying?"

"When did you get so empathetic?"

"I'm trying, even though technically I may have stolen a car and driven, once again, without a valid license." He laughs and pours me a coffee. "Light with milk, right?"

I nod.

"Did you see the fishing deck? Room enough for a three-piece band, and a glass door, no less!"

"It's beautiful," I say. It has stopped snowing, and the air sparkles over the deck and the frozen river below. I can see the water running in places where the ice is thin.

"So tell me, Dad, what was the urgency in getting out here?"

"Too much time on my hands. Too much thinking, looking back. It's been painful for me, and there are things I need to make right."

"At two in the morning?"

"What can I say? I'm an impulsive guy. I haven't been here since you and I moved back to New York right after Haley."

"Yeah, right after Haley."

"I don't remember the last time I was in the tree house," he says. "You?"

"A couple weeks after Haley's funeral. I came out to look for him. I was convinced Haley was still alive, living out here."

"You always had quite the imagination."

"I still believe that, Dad. That he is out here. Whatever he was is out here."

"I couldn't say. All I know is that the dead don't ever stay dead."

I watch him shift in his chair and look away. He's still suffering old wounds and there isn't much I can do for him.

I tell him, "Well, at least it's warm out here. The last time I was in this cabin it was freezing."

I remember how barn-cold the treehouse cabin was that morning a couple weeks after Haley died.

The cabin had that stilled-air kind of cold. I stowed my supplies, hauled up kindling wood, then laid out my sleeping bag on the top bunk. From beneath the mattress fell beechnuts and acorns, hoarded there by invading squirrels.

I struggled to light the squat, potbellied stove. The wood was stubbornly wet. I had to fuel the spindly flame with scrounged paper and tend it for what seemed an hour. All the while, I planned all I would say to Haley when he came bouncing through the doorway, his cheeks ruddy, his voice a squeak in the winter air. When the fire began to rumble in the stovepipe, I dampened the flue and set a pot of snow to melt into wash water. We would have a feast when he got here.

I watched out the windows, pacing from one to the other, counting the pops and crackles in the woodstove, the chickadees in the branches, the crow calls, but there was no sign of Haley. He loved being out here in the fields and woods. I was sure I would spot him tromping across the snow, ready to climb inside to the warmth of the cabin. But while I was watching, I noticed a moving van roll up Sweet Milk Road and turn onto Edgefield. It stopped in front of Fletcher's house. I watched the men jump down from the cab and go inside. Not too long after, they came out carrying boxes, furniture, rolling racks of clothing.

I sat on the floor, not knowing whether to stay and wait for Haley or to run across the road to Fletcher's and beg him to stay.

I had kept my promise. Fletcher had to know that, didn't he?

I paced and counted. *One-ery, two-ery, Ziggeroll-zan.* Until I could take no more. I had to wait for Haley.

I lay in the top bunk. The world was quiet, except for the crackling in the stove and the tree house rocking in the January wind. Beech leaves still brittle and curled from November shimmered in the alabaster air and boards creaked the singsong rhythm of a child's verse. When I could take no more stillness, I swept the cobwebs and acorns away and washed down the counters. I was sure this was where Haley hid when he wasn't under the river with turtles and beavers. He had the supernatural powers of the Holy Ghost bestowed on his bowl-cut head. That was what Father Rourke said at his funeral Mass. But instead of waiting, swinging in the treetops, listening to riddles in my head, I decided to look for him.

I pulled on my winter garb, laces and buckles made foolishly difficult. And trundled through the field, still thigh deep in places, and headed for the beaver dam. The opaque sun was hidden by cloud cover. It wasn't bright enough to lure sleepy beavers out to slide on the crusted caps. I wondered if they, too, had rules numbered and printed in books. Would disregard become black marks on their eternal souls? Or maybe it was an easier life under the frozen river. Beaver jokes on winter evenings. Some beaver calling for his blue-haired wife, "Marge! Marge!" while she wailed and nagged. Did they have priests and detectives showing up to ask questions? Is this where Haley had gone? Slithering a happy life under that thick ice, under the Full Wolf Moon of January?

I listened to the ice sing as it froze in deeper and deeper layers, popping, crackling, and ringing like a tuning fork. I worried that Haley might get trapped in that expanding ice and have to wait for a thaw. "I'm here!" I shouted, hoping he would hear me. Over and over I hollered, "I'm here!" until my voice became a whisper, the words spinning in my head.

My head is spinning once again on this morning as I listen to the rumble-ticking of the woodstove, worrying about my father, wondering if he should go back to the hospital. He chatters above the din of the crows.

"A lot of guys at the hospital were Vietnam vets like me," he says. "All of us who survived have invisible wounds. That's what the counselor calls it, 'invisible wounds.'" He stares out the window, rocking back and forth on his heels. "It affected our families."

"I know, Dad. It's over."

"But I did things, Joss. Terrible things over there. Terrible things here."

I nod, but I don't know what to say to him. I am not used to seeing this side of him.

"I told her. Your mother. I eventually told her the truth. I had to . . ."

"Told her what?"

"You know—how it happened."

"Dad, how what happened?"

"Will ya listen!" he yells. "Christ, I'm trying to tell you." He paces the room, stopping in front of the glass deck door. "It happened up there," he says, pointing to the high hill, to the birch grove where Haley, Fletcher, and I sat sewing river racers all those years ago.

At that moment, I know what he is going to tell me. It all clicks in my head. I was right all along. I try to push it all back, but my stomach churns.

"I need some air, Dad. I'm feeling a little queasy." I slip through the glass door and stand out on the fishing deck in the cold, pushing my father away, remembering Haley. My stomach heaves and I stumble against the railing.

I had stumbled in the snow on that winter day years back, waiting for Haley. But I got up and then fell again into the deeper snow, my feet frozen, my belly growling. I wanted a sign, evidence. And when I saw it, blown open, a spiral bound pad, its pages flapping in the wind, I knew it was Haley's. His notepad lay on top of the snow as if some ghost-boy had set it there. I poked it into my pocket and looked for more clues. There were footprints beyond me. Footprints that I was certain were from a little boy in striped socks and Oxford tie-ups.

"You've come back," I whispered.

My reverie is interrupted. My father clomps out onto the deck and stands beside me at the railing. "You feeling any better?" he asks.

I shrug my shoulders.

"You know, don't you?"

"Goddamnit, of course I know. It makes me sick—what you did."

"You have to understand. I'd just come back from Vietnam—"

"Jeezus, I don't have to understand. You hear me. I don't have to do anything." I don't tell him I understand because of Wyatt, because of Wyatt's nightmares, and how he has suffered.

"Look, I'm trying to make this right."

"How on Earth would your telling me make this right? Burdening me with this terrible truth doesn't change anything, Dad." But he doesn't hear me. He rambles on.

"She was going to marry that Dietman boy. And I fell for her, that wild red hair of hers. I kept trying to woo her away."

"Well, obviously you did, Dad. Obviously in *your* way." I hear the anger in my voice and I don't care.

"Yeah. But what I did . . . that night Haley died, I had gone to the cottage. Your mother was going to cut my hair. And while she was cutting it, I told her how I had stood in that birch grove and fired at her brother. I only meant to scare him, but he moved, rested his weight on his other foot and the bullet . . ."

"You're saying it was an accident?"

"It was."

"I don't understand how anyone can aim a gun at someone, pull the trigger, and call it an accident."

"It's nuance, I know. I explained what happened when I confessed to your mother that night in the cottage."

"What did she say?"

"She didn't say anything. She raised her arm high over her head, holding onto those scissors. I could see her shadow on the wall. That's when we heard the shot from the millhouse. Both of us jumped. She dropped the scissors. We ran out the door, ran through the snow."

"Me, too. I ran through the snow, looking for him. Maybe I still am."

"You have to stop. It was never your fault. It was always mine."

I wave him away. "Enough! Just leave me alone."

He squeezes my arm.

I push him away. He leaves and I am left with my memories. It is easier to remember Haley than to accept what my father has done. I scan the snowbanks, imaging that little boy's footprints in the snow. I listen now for the crows, not wanting to see the birch grove, not wanting to imagine my father as a soldier turned murderer. There is no one to save me from this truth, not even Miss Euphrates.

On that day when I was twelve years old, when I was convinced I had found Haley's tracks, I ran through the snow, across the footprint field. I would need that shoe box from under the sink and a spatula, too. I lined the box with wax paper and raced back to the brittle snowbank to cut around the clearest footprint, lifting it like a fragile egg into the lined box.

When I got back, the door was banging in the wind, and inside a shiny blue-black crow was sitting on the windowsill. It looked at me, tilted its head, and cawed. I swung open the door to the fishing deck and slid the covered shoe box out to preserve Haley's imprint, all the while talking to the crow. It jumped to the floor, hopped out onto the deck, then stood on the box. It sat there looking in at me, cocking its head back and forth as if to tell me something.

I pulled out a sandwich and ripped off crusts of bread, tossing them onto the floor. The crow watched and stayed while I creaked open the door to scatter more breadcrumbs. It jumped off the box, pecking at the bread on the deck, and flew back into the cabin. We sat there, sharing the sandwich. When we were done, the crow sailed through the doorway, soaring over the river into the tall pines, past the high birch grove until I could no longer follow it.

Miss Euphrates found me in the tree house on that night as dusk rolled in. I was sitting at the table eating soup, playing pick-up sticks with an imaginary opponent. I heard footsteps on the ladder and stumbled to peer out the window, but I couldn't see out. Snow had colored in the lines of every pane like a careful second grader. "Haley!" I yelled. "You're here! You're here!" But it was Miss Euphrates who came through the door.

"Thank God, Joss!" She pulled me into her wool coat. "What are you doing here?"

I looked at her, confused that she didn't understand. "I'm waiting for Haley."

She brushed her large, warm hand across my cheek. "Let's get your things and head home."

"But I have to wait for him." My voice was fog-thick and far away.

Miss Euphrates took my hand. "Come on, baby girl. You can wait for him in the house. That's where he knows you'll be."

I hadn't thought of that. "But can I leave him some cookies for when he comes back?" She nodded, and I laid them on a tin plate. Star-shaped Haley Moonbeam cookies.

I had grabbed the shoe box from the fishing deck before we headed down the ladder. As we crossed the snowy landscape, I wondered if it was true what Father Rourke said, that sacrifice and sorrow were supreme. That grace and faith were the only healing ointments. I wondered if I could find any of that in time, before what was left of Haley melted from the wax paper edges.

My father stands at the door with a box in his hand. He raps on the glass and all I see is that box. All I see is what remains. A shoe box, a vessel for all we have lost.

"Paulie-girl, can I come out?" His voice is muffled through the glass, but I can hear his desperation.

I motion to him. "Come on, Dad."

We stand, leaning against the railing, watching the Stony Kill run wild below the blue ice.

"I brought paper airplanes," he says, then reaches into the clumsy box and tosses one after another into the air. They fly in curlicues, rising higher and higher like angels.

They are beautiful, and in that moment I am grateful for the smallness of them, for my foolishness, for his awful humanity. I pull one from the box and toss it out into the sparkling air. "Dad. There must be a hundred of them!"

"More than that!" he says. "I lost count while I was making them."

I try to reckon their numbers, tally each one, as counting songs swim through my head. *One-ery, two-ery, zigger-zoll zan. Holy bone, crack-a-bone, Yankee-doodle Dan* . . . The joyful sailplanes soar over the bitter wind. There cannot be one without the other. I watch as they skid along the ice, dropping their noses into that endless blue, and I want to tell him that I'm not sure it was an accident, the way Haley died. I wonder if Fletcher even knows. He was a child, after all. But what good would burdening my father do? In the end, we are all indicted in this tragic life. And each of us redeemed. We are angels on the Stony Kill—Haley, Fletcher, and I— gliding across that fragile ice.

One crow for sorrow, Two crows mirth . . . I have been my father's Paulie-girl, his Boy-o, stuck in that same stubbornness that has plagued him. *Three crows a wedding, Four crows birth* . . . We don't give up, my father and me. We stick to things. And I am my mother's daughter, too, running and returning, running and returning. But always returning. *Five crows silver, Six crows gold, Seven crows a secret, Never to be told* . . . I think I am finally done with wanting my life to be other than what it is. I am bound to this life, to my father, to my mother . . . and to Wyatt, too. The real stuff of who we are runs in rivers below our skin. We connect at our anger, our sorrow, our mixed-up love.

I watch as one paper airplane catches that egg-wash light. It soars higher and higher over the river, past the beaver dam, higher now, up and over the birch grove. It must be going out to the Mobile station way out on Connor Road. Although I think Haley will be there first. He is forever flying beneath the Stony Kill. *Harum, squarum, Virgin Marum. Sinctum, twenty-one, sanctum, done.*

"Look, look!" my father says. His voice has the squeak of a little kid. "I added a tiny bit of tinsel to draw the crows."

"Of course you did," I laugh. They chase those sailplanes, attracted to the glitter, swooping and spinning against the wind. They are magnificent birds, the crows. Survivors. I join in, tossing paper planes out over the river with my father, laughing, seeing whose goes the farthest. We race and squabble. And argue and love. That guardedness that has always been with me flies over the water on nothing but a folded piece of paper. As does the anguish of disappointing the mythical father I love.

I am softer by the river.

About the Author

Jeff Heimbach Photography

A SECRET WRITER FROM a pragmatic blue-collar neighborhood, Marie White Small brings her skills as a florist, waitress, antiquarian bookseller, bookbinder, cook, and pie baker to the page. She studied at the Center for the Book Arts in NYC and was the founder and moderator of a community literary critique group, North Gotham Fiction Writers, for ten years. Ms. Small is currently the writer-in-residence at a Vermont mountaintop writer's retreat. She has published short fiction in the anthology, *Southshire Pepper-Pot* (Lion's Mark Press, 2007). *Stony Kill* is her debut novel.

She and her family, along with two willful cats, live in Bennington, Vermont.